5/1

D0149496

FIELD GRAY

ALSO BY PHILIP KERR

FIELD GRAY

A BERNIE GUNTHER NOVEL

Philip Kerr

A MARIAN WOOD BOOK

Published by G. P. Putnam's Sons
a member of
Penguin Group (USA) Inc.
New York

A MARIAN WOOD BOOK
Published by G. P. Putnam's Sons
Publishers Since 1838
Published by the Penguin Group
Penguin Group (USA) Inc., 375 Hudson Street, New York, New York 10014,
USA • Penguin Group (Canada), 90 Eglinton Avenue East, Suite 700,
Toronto, Ontario M4P 2Y3, Canada (a division of Pearson Penguin
Canada Inc.) • Penguin Books Ltd, 80 Strand, London WC2R 0RL, England •
Penguin Ireland, 25 St Stephen's Green, Dublin 2, Ireland (a division of
Penguin Books Ltd) • Penguin Group (Australia), 250 Camberwell Road,
Camberwell, Victoria 3124, Australia (a division of Pearson Australia Group
Pty Ltd) • Penguin Books India Pvt Ltd, 11 Community Centre, Panchsheel Park,
New Delhi–110 017, India • Penguin Group (NZ), 67 Apollo Drive,
Rosedale, North Shore 0632, New Zealand (a division of Pearson
New Zealand Ltd) • Penguin Books (South Africa) (Pty) Ltd,
24 Sturdee Avenue, Rosebank, Johannesburg 2196, South Africa

Penguin Books Ltd, Registered Offices: 80 Strand, London WC2R 0RL, England

Library of Congress Cataloging-in-Publication Data

Kerr, Philip.
Field gray: a Bernie Gunther novel / Philip Kerr.
p.   cm.
"A Marian Wood book."
ISBN 978-0-399-15741-7
1. Gunther, Bernhard (Fictitious character)—Fiction.   2. Private
investigators—Fiction.   I. Title.
PR6061.E784F54   2011   2010045006
823'.914—dc22

Printed in the United States of America
1   3   5   7   9   10   8   6   4   2

BOOK DESIGN BY AMANDA DEWEY

This is a work of fiction. Names, characters, places, and incidents either
are the product of the author's imagination or are used fictitiously, and
any resemblance to actual persons, living or dead, businesses,
companies, events, or locales is entirely coincidental.

While the author has made every effort to provide accurate telephone numbers
and Internet addresses at the time of publication, neither the publisher nor the
author assumes any responsibility for errors, or for changes that occur after
publication. Further, the publisher does not have any control over and does not
assume any responsibility for author or third-party websites or their content.

"I don't like Ike."

—GRAHAM GREENE, *The Quiet American*

This book is for Allan Scott.

FIELD GRAY

CUBA, 1954

That Englishman with Ernestina," she said, looking down at the luxuriously appointed public room. "He reminds me of you, Señor Hausner."

Doña Marina knew me as well as anyone in Cuba, possibly better, since our acquaintance was founded on something stronger than mere friendship: Doña Marina owned the largest and best brothel in Havana.

The Englishman was tall and round-shouldered, with pale blue eyes and a lugubrious expression. He wore a blue linen short-sleeved shirt, gray cotton trousers, and well-polished black shoes. I had an idea I'd seen him before, in the Floridita Bar or perhaps the lobby of the National Hotel, but I was hardly looking at him. I was paying more attention to the new and near-naked *chica* who was sitting on the Englishman's lap and helping herself to puffs from the cigarette in his mouth while he amused himself by weighing her enormous breasts in his hands, like someone judging the ripeness of two grapefruits.

"In what way?" I asked, and quickly glanced at myself in the big mirror that hung on the wall, wondering if there really was some point of similarity between us other than our appreciation of Ernestina's breasts and the huge dark nipples that adorned them like mountainous limpets.

The face that stared back at me was heavier than the Englishman's, with a little more hair on top but similarly fiftyish and cross-hatched with living. Perhaps Doña Marina thought it was more than just living that was dry-etched on our two faces—the chiaroscuro of conscience and complicity perhaps, as if neither of us had done what ought to have been done or, worse, as if each of us lived with some guilty secret.

"You have the same eyes," said Doña Marina.

"Oh, you mean they're blue," I said, knowing that this probably wasn't what she meant at all.

"No, it's not that. It's just that you and Señor Greene look at people in a certain way. As if you're trying to look inside them. Like a spiritualist. Or perhaps like a policeman. You both have very searching eyes that seem to look straight through a person. It's really most intimidating."

It was hard to imagine Doña Marina being intimidated by anything or anyone. She was always as relaxed as an iguana on a sun-warmed rock.

"Señor Greene, eh?" I wasn't in the least bit surprised that Doña Marina had used his name. The Casa Marina was not the kind of place where you felt obliged to use a false one. You needed a reference just to get through the front door. "Perhaps he *is* a policeman. With feet as big as his, I wouldn't be at all surprised."

"He's a writer."

"What kind of a writer?"

"Novels. Westerns, I think. He told me he writes under the name of Buck Dexter."

"Never heard of him. Does he live in Cuba?"

"No, he lives in London. But he always visits us when he's in Havana."

"A traveler, eh?"

"Yes. Apparently he's on his way to Haiti this time." She smiled. "You don't see the likeness now?"

"No, not really," I said firmly, and was pleased when she seemed to change the subject.

"How was it with Omara today?"

I nodded. "Good."

"You like her, yes?"

"Very much."

"She's from Santiago," said Doña Marina, as if this explained everything. "All of my best girls come from Santiago. They're the most African-looking girls in Cuba. Men seem to like that."

"I know I do."

"I think it has something to do with the fact that unlike white women, black women have a pelvis that's almost as big as a man's. An anthropoid pelvis. And before you ask me how I know that, it's because I used to be a nurse."

I wasn't surprised to learn this. Doña Marina put a premium on sexual health and hygiene and the staff at her house on Malecón included two nurses who were trained to deal with everything from a dose of jelly to a massive heart attack. I'd heard it said that you had a better chance of surviving cardiac arrest at Casa Marina than you did at the University of Havana Medical School.

"Santiago's a real melting pot," she continued. "Jamaicans, Haitians, Dominicans, Bahamians—it's Cuba's most Caribbean city. And its most rebellious, of course. All of our revolutions start in Santiago. I think it's because all of the people who live there are related in one way or another."

She twisted a cigarette into a little amber holder and lit it with a handsome silver Tallboy.

"For example, did you know that Omara is related to the man who looks after your boat in Santiago?"

I was beginning to see that there was some purpose behind

Doña Marina's conversation, because it was not just Mr. Greene who was going to Haiti, it was me, too, only my trip was supposed to be a secret.

"No, I didn't." I glanced at my watch, but before I could make my excuses and leave, Doña Marina had ushered me into her private drawing room and was offering me a drink. And thinking that perhaps it was best that I listen to what she had to say, in view of her mentioning my boat, I replied that I'd take an *añejo*.

She fetched a bottle-aged rum and poured me a large one.

"Mr. Greene is also very fond of our Havana rum," she said.

"I think you'd better come to the point now," I said. "Don't you?"

And so she did.

Which is how it was that I came to have a girl in the passenger seat of my Chevy as, about a week later, I drove southwest along Cuba's central highway to Santiago, at the opposite end of the island. The irony of this experience did not escape me; in seeking to escape from being blackmailed by a secret policeman, I had managed to put myself in a position where a brothel madam who was much too clever to threaten me openly felt able to ask a favor that I hardly wanted to grant: to take a *chica* from another Havana *casa* with me on my "fishing trip" to Haiti. It was almost certain that Doña Marina knew Lieutenant Quevedo and knew he would have held a very dim view of my taking any kind of a boat trip; but I rather doubted she knew he had threatened to have me deported back to Germany, where I was wanted for murder, unless I agreed to spy on Meyer Lansky, the underworld boss, who was my employer. Either way, I had little choice but to accede to her request, although I could have felt a lot happier about my passenger. Melba Marrero was being sought by the police in connection with the murder of a police captain from the Ninth Precinct, and there were friends of Doña Marina who wanted Melba off the island of Cuba as quickly as possible.

Melba Marrero was in her early twenties, although she hardly liked anyone to know that. I suppose she wanted people to take her seriously and it's possible that this is why she had shot Captain Balart. But it's more likely that she had shot him because she was connected with Castro's communist rebels. She was coffee-colored with a fine gamine face, a belligerent chin, and a stormy-weather look in her dark eyes. Her hair was cut after the Italian fashion—short, layered locks with a few wispy curls combed forward across her face. She wore a plain white blouse, a pair of tight fawn trousers, a tan leather belt, and matching gloves. She looked like she was going riding on a horse that was probably looking forward to it.

"Why didn't you buy a convertible?" she asked when we were still a way short of Santa Clara, which was to be our first stop. "A convertible is better in Cuba."

"I don't like convertibles. People look at you more when you're driving a convertible. And I don't much like being looked at."

"So are you the shy type? Or are you just guilty about something?"

"Neither. Just private."

"Got a smoke?"

"There's a packet in the glove box."

She stabbed the lock on the lid with a finger and let it fall open in front of her.

"Old Gold. I don't like Old Gold."

"You don't like my car. You don't like my cigarettes. What do you like?"

"It doesn't matter."

I took a sideways glance at her. Her mouth always seemed to be on the edge of a snarl, an impression that was enhanced by the strong white teeth that filled it. Hard as I tried, I couldn't imagine anyone touching her without losing a finger. She sighed and, clasping her hands tightly, pushed them between her knees.

"So what's your story, Señor Hausner?"

"I don't have one."

She shrugged. "It's seven hundred miles to Santiago."

"Try reading a book." I knew she had one.

"Maybe I will." She opened her handbag and took out a pair of glasses and a book and started to read.

After a while, I managed to sneak a look at the title. She was reading *How the Steel Was Tempered,* by Nikolai Ostrovsky. I tried not to smile, but it was no good.

"Something funny?"

I nodded at the book on her lap. "I wouldn't have thought so."

"It's about someone who participated in the Russian Revolution."

"That's what I thought."

"So, what do you believe in?"

"Not much."

"That's not going to help anyone."

"As if that matters."

"Doesn't it?"

"In my book, the party of not much beats the party of brotherly love every time. The people and the proletariat don't need anyone's help. Certainly not yours or mine."

"I don't believe that."

"Oh, I'm sure. But it's funny, don't you think? Both of us running away to Haiti like this. You because you believe in something, and me because I believe in nothing at all."

"First it was not much you believed in. Now it's nothing at all. Marx and Engels were correct. The bourgeoisie does produce its own grave diggers."

I laughed.

"Well, we've established something," she said. "That you *are* running away."

"Yes. That's my story. If you're really interested, it's the same story as always. The Flying Dutchman. The Wandering Jew. There's been quite a bit of travel involved, one way or the other. I thought I was safe here in Cuba."

"No one is safe in Cuba," she said. "Not anymore."

"I *was* safe," I said, ignoring her. "Until I tried to play the hero. Only I forgot. I'm not the stuff of which heroes are made. Never was. Besides, the world doesn't want heroes. They're out of fashion, like last year's hemlines. What is now required are freedom fighters and informers. Well, I'm too old for the one and too scrupulous for the other."

"What happened?"

"Some obnoxious lieutenant of military intelligence wanted to make me his spy, only there was something about it I didn't like."

"Then you're doing the right thing," said Melba. "There's no disgrace in not wanting to be a police spy."

"You almost make it sound like I'm doing something noble. It isn't that way at all."

"What way is it?"

"I don't want to be the coin in anyone's pocket. I had enough of that during the war. I prefer to roll around on my own. But that's just part of the reason. Spying is dangerous. It's especially dangerous when there's a good chance of being caught. But I daresay you know that by now."

"What did Marina tell you about me?"

"All she needed to. I kind of stopped listening after she said that you shot a cop. That pretty much brings the curtain down on the movie. My movie, anyway."

"You speak like you don't approve."

"Cops are the same as anyone else," I said. "Some good and some bad. I was a cop like that myself once. A long time ago."

"I did it for the Revolution," she said.

"I didn't imagine you did it for a coconut."

"He was a bastard and he had it coming, and I did it for—"

"I know, you did it for the Revolution."

7

"Don't you think Cuba needs a revolution?"

"I won't deny that things could be better. But every revolution smokes well before it turns to ash. Yours will be like all the others that went before. I guarantee it."

Melba was shaking her pretty head, but warming to my subject, I kept on going: "Because when someone talks about building a better society, you can bet he's planning to use a couple of sticks of dynamite."

After that she remained silent and so did I.

We stopped for a while in Santa Clara. About 180 miles east of Havana, it was a picturesque, unremarkable little town with a central park faced by several old buildings and hotels. Melba went off by herself. I sat outside the Central Hotel and had lunch on my own, which suited me fine. When she reappeared, we set off again.

In the early evening we reached Camagüey, which was full of triangular houses and large earthenware jars filled with flowers. I didn't know why and it never occurred to me to ask. Parallel to the highway, a goods train moving in the opposite direction was loaded with timber cut from the region's many forests.

"We're stopping here," I announced.

"Surely it would be better to keep going."

"Can you drive?"

"No."

"Neither can I. Not anymore. I'm beat. It's another two hundred miles to Santiago, and if we don't stop soon we'll both wake up in the morgue."

Near a brewery—one of the few on the island—we passed a police car, which got me thinking again about Melba and the crime she had committed.

"If you shot a cop, then they must want you bad," I said.

"Very bad. They bombed the *casa* where I was working. Several other girls were killed or seriously injured."

"Which is why Doña Marina agreed to help get you out of Havana?" I nodded. "Yes, it makes sense now. When one *casa* gets bombed, it's bad for all of them. In which case it will be safer if we share a room. I'll say you're my wife. That way you won't have to show them your identity card."

"Look, Señor Hausner, I am grateful to you for taking me with you to Haiti. But there's one thing you should know. I only volunteered to play the part of a *chica* to get close to Captain Balart."

"I was wondering about that."

"I did it for the—"

"The Revolution. I know. Listen, Melba, your virtue, if there is anything left of it, it's safe with me. I told you. I'm tired. I could sleep on a bonfire. But I'll settle for a chair or a sofa and you can have the bed."

She nodded. "Thank you, señor."

"And stop calling me that. My name is Carlos. Call me that. I'm supposed to be your husband, remember?"

We checked into the Gran Hotel in the center of town and went up to the room. I crawled straight to bed, which is to say I slept on the floor. During the summer of 1941 some of the floors that I slept on in Russia were the most comfortable beds I ever had, only this wasn't as comfortable. Then again, I wasn't nearly as exhausted as I'd been back then. About two o'clock in the morning I awoke to find her wrapped in a sheet and kneeling beside me.

"What is it?" I sat up and groaned with pain.

"I'm so scared," she said.

"What are you scared about?"

"You know what they'll do to me if they find me?"

"The police?"

Her nodding turned into a shiver.

"So what do you want from me? A bedtime story? Listen, Melba. In the morning I'll drive you to Santiago and we'll get on my boat, and by tomorrow night you'll be safely off in Haiti, all right? But now I'm trying to sleep. Only the mattress is a little too soft for me. So if you don't mind."

"Strangely enough," she said, "I don't mind. The bed is quite comfortable. And there's room for two."

This was certainly true. The bed was as big as a small farm with one goat. I was pretty sure about the goat because of the way she took me by the hand and led me over to the bed. There was something erotic and alluring about that; or maybe it was just the fact that she left the sheet on the floor. It was a hot night, of course, but that didn't bother me. I do some of my best thinking when I'm as naked as she was. I tried to picture myself asleep in that bed, only it didn't work because by now I'd seen what she had displayed in the window and I was about ready to press my nose up against the glass and take a better look. It wasn't that she wanted me. I can never figure why a woman wants a man at all—not when women look the way they do. It was just that she was young and scared and lonely and wanted someone—anyone would have done, probably—to hold her and make her feel like the world cared about her. I get like that myself sometimes: You're born alone and you die alone, and the rest of the time you're on your own.

By the time we got to Santiago the next day, the dark orchid of her head had been resting on my shoulder almost a hundred miles. We were behaving like any young courting couple when one of them happens to be more than twice as old as the other, who also happens to be a murderer. Perhaps that's a little unfair. Melba wasn't the only one of us who'd pulled the trigger on someone. I had some experience of murder myself. Quite a lot of experience, as it happens, only I hardly wanted to tell her about that. I was trying to keep my thoughts on what lay ahead of us. Sometimes the future seems a little dark and frightening, but the past is even worse. My past most of all. But now it was the very present danger of the Santiago police I was worried about. They had a reputation for brutality that was probably well deserved and easily explained by the truth of Doña Marina's remark that all of Cuba's revolutions got started in Santiago. It was impossible to imagine much else that got started there. A start implied some activity, movement, or even work, and there wasn't much sign of any of these tiring nouns on the sleepy streets of Santiago. Ladders stood around idle and alone, wheelbarrows sat unattended, horses kicked their heels, boats bobbed in the harbor, and fishing nets lay drying in the sun. About the only people who appeared to be working were the cops, if you could call it work. Parked up in the shade of the city's pastel-colored buildings, they sat smoking cigarettes and waiting for things to cool down or warm up, depending on how you looked at it. Probably it was too hot and sunny for trouble. The sky was too blue and the cars were too shiny; the sea was too much like glass and the banana leaves were too glossy; the statues were too white and the shadows too short. Even the coconuts were wearing sunglasses.

After a couple of wrong turns I spotted the coaling station of Cincoreales that was a landmark for finding my way around the shantytown of boatyards, booms, quays, pontoons, dry docks, and slipways that serviced the flotilla of boats in Santiago Bay. I pointed the car down a steep, cobbled hill and along a narrow street. Heavy brackets for trams that were no longer running hung over our heads like the rigging of a schooner that had long ago sailed without it. I steered onto the sidewalk in front of an open set of double doors and peered down into a boatyard.

A bearded, weather-beaten man wearing shorts and sandals was maneuvering a boat that hung from an ancient-looking crane. I didn't mind when the boat clunked against the harbor wall and then hit the water like a bar of soap. But then, it wasn't my boat.

We got out of the Chevy. I fetched Melba's suitcase from the trunk and carried it into the yard, stepping carefully around or over tins of paint, buckets, lengths of rope and hose line, pieces of wood, old tires, and oil cans. The office in a little wooden hut at the back was no less of a shambles than the yard. Mendy wasn't about to win the Good Housekeeping Seal of Approval anytime soon, but he knew boats, and since I knew them hardly at all, this was just as well.

Once, a long time ago, Mendy had been white. But a lifetime on and by the sea had turned the part of his face that wasn't covered by a salt-and-pepper beard to the color and texture of an old baseball mitt. He belonged in a hammock on some pirate ship bound for Hispaniola, with a hornpipe in one hand and a bottle of rum in the other. He finished what he was doing and didn't seem to notice me until the crane was out of the way, and even then all he said was "Señor Hausner."

I nodded back at him. "Mendy."

He fetched a half-smoked cigar from the breast pocket of his grubby shirt and plugged it into a space between his beard and his mustache and spent the next few minutes while we talked patting himself down for a light.

"Mendy, this is Señorita Otero. She's coming on the boat with me. I told her it was just a crummy fishing boat—only she and her suitcase appear to be under the illusion that we're going sailing on the *Queen Mary*."

Mendy's eyes flicked between Melba and me as if he had been watching a game of table tennis. Then he smiled at her and said, "But the señorita is absolutely right, Señor Hausner. The first rule of going to sea is to be prepared for absolutely anything."

"Thank you," said Melba. "That's what I said."

Mendy looked at me and shook his head. "Clearly, you know nothing about women, señor," he said.

"About as much as I know about boats," I said.

Mendy chuckled. "For your sake, I hope it's a little more than that."

He led the way out of the boatyard and down to the L-shaped pontoon, where a wooden launch was moored. We stepped aboard and sat down. Mendy tugged a motor into life and then steered us out into the bay. Five minutes later, we were tying up alongside a thirty-five-foot wooden sportfishing boat.

La Guajaba was narrow, with a broad stern, a bridge, and three compartments. There were two Chrysler engines, each producing about ninety horsepower, giving the boat a top speed of about nine knots. And that was more or less everything I knew about her other than where I kept the brandy and the glasses. I'd won the boat in a game of backgammon from an American who owned the Bimini Bar on Obispo Street. With a full tank of fuel *La Guajaba* had a range of about five hundred miles, and it was less than half that to Port-au-Prince. I'd used the boat about three times in as many years, and what I didn't know about boats would have filled several nautical almanacs, possibly all of them. But I knew how to use a compass, and I figured all I needed to do was point the bow east and then, according to the Thor Heyerdahl principle of navigation, keep going until we hit something. I couldn't see how what we hit wouldn't be the island of Hispaniola; after all, there were thirty thousand square miles of it to aim at.

I handed Mendy a fistful of cash and my car keys and then climbed aboard. I'd thought about mentioning Omara and how it might have been better for me if he had kept his mouth shut, only there didn't seem to be much point. It would have risked incurring some of the brutal candor for which Cubans are justly famous, and doubtless he would have told me that I was just another gringo with too much money and unworthy of the boat I owned, which would have been true: If you make yourself like sugar, the ants will eat you.

As soon as we were under way, Melba went below and put on a two-piece swimsuit with a leopard-skin print that would have made a mackerel whistle. That's the nice thing about boats and warm weather. They bring out the best in people. Beneath the battlements of Morro Castle, which stands on the summit of a two-hundred-foot-high rock promontory, the harbor entrance is almost as wide. A long flight of crumbling steps, hewn out of the rock, leads up from the water's edge to the castle, and I almost made the boat try to climb them. Two hundred feet of open sea to aim at and I still managed to nearly put us on the rocks. So long as I was looking at Melba, it wasn't looking good for our chances of hitting Haiti.

"I wish you'd put some clothes on," I said.

"Don't you like my bikini?"

"I like it fine. But there's a good reason Columbus didn't take women with him on the *Santa María*. When they're wearing bikinis they affect the ship's steering. With you around, they'd probably have discovered Tasmania."

She lit a cigarette and ignored me, and I did my best to ignore her back. I checked the tachometer, the oil level, the ammeter, and the motor temperature. Then I glanced out of the wheelhouse window. Smith Key, a small island once held by the British, lay ahead of us. It was home to many of Santiago's fishing folk and pilots, and its red-tiled houses and small ruined chapel made it look very picturesque. But it wasn't much next to the scene in Melba's bikini pants.

The sea was calm until we reached the mouth of the harbor, where the water started to swell a bit. I pushed the throttle forward and held the boat on a steady east-southeast course until Santiago was no longer visible. Behind us the boat's wake unzipped a great white scar in the ocean that was hundreds of feet long. Melba sat in the fisherman's chair and squealed with excitement as our speed increased.

"Can you believe it?" said Melba. "I live on an island and I've never been on a boat before."

"I'll be glad when we're off this tub," I said, and fetched a bottle of rum from the chart drawer.

After about three or four hours it got dark and I could see the lights of the U.S. naval base at Guantánamo, twinkling on our port side. It was like staring at the ancient stars of some near galaxy that was at the same time a vision of the future in which American democracy ruled the world with a Colt in one hand and a stick of chewing gum in the other. Somewhere in the tropical darkness of that Yankee littoral thousands of men in white suits were engaged in the meaningless routines of their oceangoing, imperial service. In response to the cold imperative of new enemies and new victories they sat inside their floating, steel-gray cities of death, drinking Coca-Cola, smoking their Lucky Strikes, and preparing to free the rest of the world from its unreasonable desire to be different. Because Americans and not Germans were now the master race and Uncle Sam had replaced Hitler and Stalin as the face of the new empire.

Melba saw my lip curl and must have read my mind. "I hate them," she said.

"Who? The *yanquis*?"

"Who else? Our good neighbors have always wanted to make this island one of their United States. And but for them Batista could never have remained in power."

I couldn't argue with her. Especially now that we'd spent the night together. Especially now that I was planning to do the same again, just as soon as we were installed in a nice hotel. I'd heard that Le Refuge in the holiday resort of Kenscoff, six miles outside of Port-au-Prince, might be just the kind of place I was looking for. Kenscoff is four thousand feet above sea level and the climate there is fine all year round. Which is almost as long as I was planning to stay. Of course, Haiti had its problems, just like Cuba, but they weren't my problems. So what did I care? I had other things to worry about, such as what I was going to do when my Argentine passport expired. And now there was the small problem of taking a small boat safely through the Windward Passage. I probably shouldn't have been drinking, but even with *La Guajaba*'s running lights there was something about driving a boat across the sea in darkness that I found unnerving. And fearing that we might hit something—a reef, or a whale—I knew I wouldn't be able to relax until it was light again, by which time I hoped we would be halfway across the ocean to Hispaniola.

And then there was something more tangible to worry about. Another vessel was approaching quickly from the north. It was moving too fast to be a fishing boat, and the big searchlight picking us out of the darkness was too powerful for it to belong to anything but a U.S. Navy patrol boat.

"Who are they?" asked Melba.

"The American navy, I imagine."

Even above our twin Chrysler engines I heard Melba swallow. She still looked beautiful, only now she looked worried as well. She turned suddenly and stared at me with wide brown eyes.

"What are we going to do?"

"Nothing," I said. "That boat can probably outrun us and certainly outgun us. The best thing you can do is go below, climb into bed, and stay there. I'll handle things up here."

She shook her head. "I won't let them arrest me," she said. "They'd hand me over to the police and—"

"No one's going to arrest you," I said, touching her cheek in an effort to reassure her. "My guess is that they're just going to look us over. So do as I say and we'll be okay."

I throttled back and put the gearshift in neutral. When I came out of the wheelhouse, the blinding searchlight was in my face. I felt like a giant gorilla on a skyscraper with the patrol boat circling me at a distance. I went to the gently pitching stern, had another drink, and coolly awaited their pleasure.

A minute passed and then an officer wearing whites came to the starboard side of the gunboat with a bullhorn in his hand.

"We're looking for some sailors," he said, speaking to me in

Spanish. "They stole a boat from the harbor at Caimanera. A boat like this one."

I threw my hands up and shook my head. "There are no American sailors on this boat."

"Mind if we come aboard and take a look for ourselves?"

Minding very much, I told the American officer I didn't mind at all. There seemed to be little point in arguing. A sailor manning a fifty-caliber machine gun on the foredeck of the American boat had the best way of winning an argument I could think of. So I threw them a line, put out some fenders, and let them tie up alongside *La Guajaba*. The officer came aboard with one of his NCOs. There wasn't much you could say about either of them except that their shoes were black and they looked the way all men look when you take away most of their hair and their capacity for independent action. They were carrying sidearms, a couple of flashlights, and a vague smell of mint and tobacco, as if they'd just disposed of their gum and their cigarettes.

"Anyone else on board?"

"I have a lady friend in the forward cabin," I said. "She's asleep. On her own. The last American sailor we saw was Popeye."

The officer smiled a wry smile and bounced a little on the balls of his feet. "Mind if we take a look for ourselves?"

"I don't mind at all. But just let me see if my lady friend is dressed to receive visitors."

He nodded, and I went forward and below. The damp-smelling cabin had a closet, a little cabinet, and a double berth containing Melba with a blanket drawn up to her neck. Underneath she was still wearing the bikini, and I promised myself to drop anchor when the Amis were gone and help her take it off. There's nothing like sea air to give you an appetite.

"What's going on?" she asked fearfully. "What do they want?"

"Some American sailors stole a boat from Caimanera," I explained. "They're looking for them. I don't think there's anything really to worry about."

She rolled her eyes. "Caimanera. Yes, I can imagine what they were doing there, the pigs. Just about every hotel in Caimanera is a brothel. The *casas* even have patriotic American names, like the Roosevelt Hotel. The bastards."

I might have wondered how she knew this, but I was rather more concerned with satisfying their curiosity than the small matter of how they satisfied their sexual desires. "It's what Eisenhower calls the domino effect. When some guys lay one down they like to make a big show of it." I jabbed my thumb back at the cabin door. "Look, they're outside. They just want to check their men aren't hiding under the bed or anything. I said they could as soon as I checked you were decent."

"That's going to take a lot more time than might seem reasonable." She shrugged. "You'd better show them in anyway."

I went back up on deck and nodded them below.

They shuffled in through the cabin door, their faces pink with embarrassment when they saw Melba still in bed, and if I hadn't been enjoying that, I might not have noticed the NCO lay his eyes on her and then lay them on her again, only the second time wasn't for the obvious reason, that she belonged in a picture on a bulkhead above his hammock. These two had met before. I was sure of that and so was he, and when the Amis came back to the wheelhouse, the NCO drew his officer aside and said something quietly.

When their conversation became a little more urgent, I might have got involved but for the fact that the officer unbuttoned the holster of his sidearm, which prompted me to go to the stern and sit in the fisherman's chair. I think I even smiled at the man on the fifty-caliber, only the fisherman's chair looked and felt too much like an electric chair for my liking, so I moved again and sat down on the icebox, which had room for two thousand pounds of ice. I was trying to appear cool. If there had been any fish or any ice in the box, I might even have climbed in beside them. Instead, I took another bite from the bottle and did my best to keep a grip on the thin line holding my nerves. But it wasn't working. The Amis had a hook in my mouth, and I felt like jumping thirty feet into the air just to try and get it out.

When the officer came back to the stern he was carrying a Colt .45 automatic in his hand. It was cocked, too. It wasn't pointed at me yet. It was just there to help make a point: that there was no room on the boat for negotiation.

"I'm afraid I'm going to have to ask you both to accompany me back to Guantánamo, sir," he said politely, almost as if there wasn't a gun in his hand at all and like a true American.

I nodded slowly. "May I ask why?"

"It will all be explained when we get to Gitmo," he said.

"If you really think it's necessary."

He waved two sailors to come aboard my boat, and it was just as well he did, because both of them were between me and the machine gun when we heard a pistol shot from the forward compartment. I jumped up and then thought better of jumping any more.

"Watch him," yelled the officer, and went below to investigate, leaving me with two Colts pointed at my belly and the fifty-caliber pointed at my earlobe. I sat down again on the fisherman's chair, which creaked like a chain saw as I leaned all the way back and stared up at the stars. You didn't need to be Madame Blavatsky to see that they weren't looking good. Not for Melba. And probably not for me.

As things turned out, the stars weren't good for the American NCO either. He staggered up on deck looking like the ace of diamonds, or perhaps the ace of hearts. In the center of his white shirt was a small red stain that grew larger the longer you looked at it. For a moment he swayed drunkenly, and then dropped heavily onto his backside. In a way he looked the way I was feeling now.

"I'm shot," he said redundantly.

2

CUBA, 1954

It was several hours later. The shot sailor had been taken to a hospital in Guantánamo, Melba was cooling her high heels in a prison cell, and I had told my story, twice. I had two headaches, and only one of them was in my skull. There were three of us in a humid office in the building of the U.S. Navy masters-at-arms. Masters-at-arms were what the U.S. Navy called the sailors who specialized in law enforcement and correctional custody. Policemen in sailor suits. The three who'd been listening to my story didn't seem to like it any better the second time. They shifted their largish backsides on their inadequate chairs, picked tiny bits of thread and fluff from their immaculate white uniforms, and stared at their reflections in the toecaps of their shiny black shoes. It was like being interrogated by a union meeting of hospital porters.

The building was quiet except for the hum of the fluorescent lighting on the ceiling and the noise of a typewriter that was the size and color of the USS *Missouri*; and every time I answered a question and the Navy cop hit the keys on that thing, it was like the sound of someone—me probably—having his hair cut with a large pair of very sharp scissors.

Outside a small grilled window, the new day was coming up over the blue horizon like a trail of blood. This hardly augured well, since, not unreasonably, it was already clear that the Amis suspected me of a much closer acquaintance with Melba Marrero and her crimes—plural—than I'd admitted. Clearly, since I wasn't an American myself, and smelled strongly of rum, they found this relatively easy.

On a light blue Formica table covered with coffee-colored cigarette burns lay a number of files and a couple of guns wearing tags on their trigger guards as if they might have been for sale. One of them was the little Beretta pocket pistol Melba had used to shoot the petty officer, third class; and the other was a Colt automatic stolen from him several months earlier and used to murder Captain Balart outside the Hotel Ambos Mundos in Havana. Alongside the files and the pistols was my blue and gold Argentinean passport, and from time to time the Navy cop in charge of my interrogation would pick this up and leaf through the pages as if he couldn't quite believe that anyone could go through life being the citizen of a country that wasn't the United States. His name was Captain Mackay, and as well as his questions there was his breath to contend with. Every time he pushed his squashed, bespectacled face toward mine I was enveloped in the sour aura of his tooth decay, and after a while I started to feel like something chewed up but only half digested deep inside his Yankee bowels.

Mackay said with ill-disguised contempt, "This story of yours, that you never met her until a couple of days ago, it makes no sense. No sense at all. You say she was a *chica* you were involved with; that you asked her to come away on your boat for a few weeks, and that this accounts for the considerable sum of money you had with you."

"That's correct."

"And yet you say you know almost nothing about her."

"At my age, it's best not to ask too many questions when a pretty girl agrees to come away with you."

Mackay smiled thinly. He was about thirty, too young to find much sympathy for an older man's interest in younger women. There was a wedding band on his fat finger, and I imagined some wholesome girl with a permanent wave and a mixing bowl under her chubby arm waiting for him back home in some Erector Set government housing on a bleak naval base.

"Shall I tell you what I think? I think you were headed for the Dominican Republic to buy guns for the rebels. The boat, the money, the girl, it all adds up."

"Oh, I can see you like the addition, Captain. But I'm a respectable businessman. I'm quite well-off. I have a nice apartment in Havana. A job at a hotel casino. I'm hardly the type to work for the communists. And the girl? She's just a *chica*."

"Maybe. But she murdered a Cuban policeman. Very nearly murdered one of mine."

"Perhaps. But did you see me shoot anyone? I didn't even raise my voice. In my business, girls—girls like Melba—they're one of the fringe benefits. What they get up to in their spare time is—" I paused for a moment, searching for the best phrase in English. "Hardly my affair."

"It is when she shoots an American on your boat."

"I didn't even know she had a gun. If I'd known that, I would have thrown it over the side. And maybe her, too. And if I had any idea that she was suspected of murdering a policeman, I would never have invited Señorita Marrero to come away with me."

"Let me tell you something about your girlfriend, Mr. Hausner." Mackay stifled a belch, but not nearly enough for my comfort. He took off his glasses and breathed on them, and somehow they didn't crack. "Her real name is María Antonia Tapanes, and she was a prostitute at a *casa* in Caimanera, which is how she came to steal a sidearm belonging Petty Officer Marcus. That's why he recognized her when he saw her on your boat. We strongly suspect she was put up to the assassination of Captain Balart by the rebels. In fact, we're more or less sure of it."

"I find that very hard to believe. She never once mentioned politics to me. She seemed more interested in having a good time than in having a revolution."

The captain opened one of the files in front of him and pushed it toward me.

"It's more or less certain your little lady friend has been a communist and a rebel for quite a while now. You see, María Antonia Tapanes spent three months in the National Women's Prison at Guanajay for her part in the Easter Sunday conspiracy of April 1953. Then, in July of last year, her brother Juan Tapanes was killed in the assault on Moncada Barracks led by Fidel Castro. Killed or executed, it's not clear which. When María got out of prison and found her brother dead, she went to Caimanera and worked as a *chica* to get herself a weapon. That happens a lot. To be honest, quite a few of our men use their weapons as currency for buying sex. Then they just report the weapon stolen. Anyway, the next time the weapon turns up it's been used to kill Captain Balart. There were witnesses, too. A woman answering María Tapanes's description shot him in the face. And then in the back of the head as he lay on the ground. Maybe he had it coming. Who knows? Who cares? What I do know is that P.O. Marcus is lucky to be alive. If she'd used the Colt instead of that little Beretta, he'd be as dead as Captain Balart."

"Is he going to be all right?"

"He'll live."

"What will happen to her?"

"We'll have to hand her over to the police in Havana."

"I imagine that's what she was worried about in the first place. Why she shot the petty officer. She must have panicked. You know what they'll do to her, don't you?"

"That's not my concern."

"Maybe it should be. Maybe that's the problem you've got in Cuba. Maybe if you Americans paid a little more attention to the kind of people who are running this country—"

"Maybe you ought to be a little more concerned about what happens to you."

This was the other officer who spoke now. I hadn't been told his name. All I knew about him was that dandruff fell off the back of his head whenever he scratched it. All in all, he had rather a lot of dandruff. Even his eyelashes had tiny flakes of skin in them.

"Just suppose I'm not," I said. "Not anymore."

"Come again?" The man with the dandruff stopped scratching his head and inspected his fingernails before beaming a frown in my direction.

"We've been over this all night," I said. "You keep asking me the same questions and I keep giving you the same answers. I've told you my story. But you say you don't believe it. And that's fair enough. I can see the holes in it. You're bored with it. I'm bored with it. We're all bored with it, only I'm not about to cash my story in for another. What would be the point? If it sounded any better than the original, I'd have used it in the first place. So the fact now remains that I can't see any point in telling you another. And since I don't care to do that, then you'd be forgiven for thinking that I don't really care whether or not you believe me, because it seems to me there's nothing I can do that'll convince you. One way or another, you've already made up your minds. That's the way it is with cops. Believe me, I know, I used to be a cop myself. And since I no longer care whether or not you believe me, then it would be entirely fair for you to conclude that I don't seem to give a damn what happens to me. Well, maybe I do and maybe I don't, but that's for me to know and you to decide for yourselves, gentlemen."

The cop with the dandruff scratched some more, which made the room look like a snow scene in a little glass ball. He said, "You talk a lot, mister, for someone who doesn't say very much."

"True, but it helps to keep the brass knuckles off my face."

"I doubt that," said Captain Mackay. "I doubt that very much."

"I know. I'm not so pretty anymore. Only, that ought to make it easier for you to believe me. You've seen that girl. She was every sailor's hard-on. I was grateful. What's the expression you have in English? 'You don't look a gift horse in the mouth'? And if it comes to that, then neither should you, Captain. You've got nothing on me and plenty on her. You know she shot the petty officer. It's obvious. And it only starts to get complicated when you try to tie me in to some kind of rebel conspiracy. Me? I was looking forward to a nice vacation with lots of sex. I had plenty of money with me, because I was planning to buy myself a bigger boat, and there's no law against that. Like I already told you, I have a good job. At the National Hotel. I have a nice apartment on the Malecón, in Havana. I drive a newish Chevy. Now, why would I give all that up for Karl Marx and Fidel Castro? You tell me that Melba, or María, or whatever her name is, that she's a communist. I didn't know that. Maybe I should have asked her, only I prefer talking dirty when I'm in bed, not politics. She wants to go around shooting cops and American sailors, then I say she should go to jail."

"Not very gallant of you," said Captain Mackay.

"Gallant? What does it mean—'gallant'?"

"Chivalrous." The captain shrugged. "Gentlemanly."

"*Ah, cortés. Caballeroso.* Yes, I see." I shrugged back at him. "And how would that sound, I wonder. She was only trying to protect me? Give her a break, Captain, she's just a kid? The girl had a tough childhood? All right. If it makes any difference, you know, I really think the girl was scared. Like I already said, you know what will happen when you hand her over to the local law. If she's lucky, they'll let her keep her clothes on when they parade her around the police cells. And maybe they'll beat her with an ox-dick whip only every other day. But I doubt it."

"You don't sound too upset about it," said the cop with dandruff.

"I'll certainly pray for her. Maybe I'll even pay for a lawyer.

Experience informs me that paying is more useful than praying. The Lord and I don't get on the way we used to."

The captain sneered.

"I don't like you, Hausner. The next time I speak to the Lord, I'm just liable to congratulate him on his good taste. You've got a job at the National Hotel? Fuck you. I never liked that damned hotel either. You've got a nice apartment on Malecón? I hope a hurricane comes and wipes it out, you Argentine cocksucker. You don't care what happens to you? Neither do I, pal. To me you're just another South American greaseball with a smart mouth. You can't think of a better story? Then you're dumber than you look. You used to be a cop yourself? I don't want to know, you piece of shit. All I want to hear from you is an explanation for how it is that you were helping a murderer escape from this miserable fucking island you call home. Did someone ask you a favor? If they did, I want a name. Someone introduced you? I want a fucking name. You picked her off the sidewalk? Give me the name of the damned street, you asshole. It's talk or lock, pal. Talk or lock. We went fishing tonight and we caught you, Hausner. And I get to toss you in my ice locker unless you tell me everything I want to know. Talk or lock and I throw away the fucking key until I'm satisfied there's no information left in your lying body that you haven't puked onto the goddamn floor. The truth? I don't give a shit. You want to walk out of here? Give me some plain, straightforward facts."

I nodded. "Here's one for you. Penguins live almost exclusively in the Southern Hemisphere. Is that plain enough?"

I pushed the chair back on two legs, which was my first mistake, and smiled, which was my second. The Navy captain was surprisingly quick on his feet. One moment he was staring at me like I was a snake in a bassinet, the next he was yelling as if he'd hammered his own thumb, and before I could wipe the smile from my face, he'd done it for me, kicking the chair away and then grabbing the lapels of my jacket and lifting my head off the floor only so that he could punch it back down again.

The other two each caught one of his arms and tried to pull him off, but that left his legs free to stamp on my face like someone trying to put out a fire. Not that this hurt. He had a right as big as a medicine ball, and I wasn't feeling anything very much since it had connected with my chin. Humming like an electric eel, I lay there waiting for him to stop so that I could show him who was really in charge of the interrogation. By the time they got a ring in his pointy nose and hauled him off, I was just about ready for my next wisecrack. I might have made it, too, but for the blood that was pouring out of my nose.

When I was absolutely sure no one was about to knock me down again, I got off the floor and told myself that when they hit me again it would be because I had truly earned a beating and that it would have been worth it.

"Being a cop," I said, "is a lot like looking for something interesting to read in the newspaper. By the time you've found it, you can bet there's a lot that's rubbed off on your fingers. Before the war, the last war, I was a cop in Germany. An honest cop, too, although I guess that won't mean much to apes like you. Plainclothes. A detective. But when we invaded Poland and Russia they put us in gray uniforms. Not green, not black, not brown, *gray*. Field Gray, they called it. The thing about gray is you can roll around in the dirt all day and still look smart enough to return a general's salute. That's one reason we wore it. Another reason we wore gray was maybe so that we could do what we did and still think we had standards—so that we could manage to look ourselves in the eye when we got up in the morning. That was the theory. I know, stupid, wasn't it? But no Nazi was ever so stupid as to ask us to wear a white uniform. You know why? Because a white uniform is hard to keep clean, isn't it? I mean, I admire your courage wearing white. Because let's face it, gentlemen, white shows everything. Especially blood. And the way you conduct yourselves? That's a big disadvantage."

Instinctively, each man looked down at the blank canvas that was his immaculate white uniform, as if checking his zipper; and that was when I collected a nose full of blood in my fingers and let them have it, like Jackson Pollock. You could say I wanted to express my feelings rather than just illustrate them; and that my crude technique of flinging my own blood through the air at them was simply a means of arriving at a statement. Either way, they seemed to understand exactly what I was trying to say. And when they finished working me over and tossed me in a cell, I had the small satisfaction of knowing that, at last, I was truly modern. I don't know if their blood-spattered white uniforms were art or not. But I know what I like.

3

CUBA AND NEW YORK, 1954

The drunk tank at Gitmo was a large wooden hut located on the beach, but for anyone who wasn't drunk when he was locked up in there it was actually positioned somewhere between the first and second circles of hell. It was certainly hot enough.

I'd been imprisoned before. I'd been a Soviet POW and that was not so good. But Gitmo was almost as bad. The three things that made the drunk tank nearly unendurable were the mosquitoes and the drunks—and the fact that I was ten years older now. Being ten years older is always bad. The mosquitoes were worse—the naval base was not much more than a swamp—but they were not as bad as the drunks. You can stand being locked up almost anywhere so long as you manage to establish some sort of a routine. But there was no routine at Gitmo, unless you could count the routine that was the regular dusk-to-dawn turnover of loudly intoxicated American sailors. Nearly all of them arrived in their underwear. Some were violent; some wanted to make friends with me; some tried to kick me around the cell; some wanted to sing; some wanted to cry; some wanted to batter the walls down with their skulls; nearly all of them were incontinent or threw up, and sometimes they threw up on me.

In the beginning I had the quaint idea that I was locked up there because there was nowhere else to lock me up; but after a couple of weeks, I started to believe that there was some other purpose to my being kept there. I tried speaking to the guards and on several occasions asked them by what jurisdiction I was being held there, but it was no good. The guards just treated me like every other prisoner, which would have been fine if every other prisoner hadn't been covered in beer and blood and vomit. Most of the time these other prisoners were released in the late afternoon, by which time they'd slept it off, and for a few hours at least I managed to forget the humidity and the hundred-degree heat and the stink of human feces and to get some sleep—only to be awakened for "chow" or by someone washing out the tank with a fire hose or, worst of all, by a banana rat, if rats these truly were: At thirty inches long and weighing as many pounds, these rats were rodent stars who belonged in a Nazi propaganda movie or a Robert Browning poem.

At the beginning of the third week, a petty officer from the masters-at-arms office fetched me from the tank, accompanied me to a bathroom where I could shower and shave, and returned my own clothes.

"You're being transferred today," he told me. "To Castle Williams."

"Where's that?"

"New York City."

"New York City? Why?"

He shrugged. "Search me."

"What kind of place is it, this Castle Williams?"

"A U.S. military prison. Looks like you're the Army's meat now, not the Navy's."

He gave me a cigarette, probably just to shut me up, and it worked. There was a filter on it that was supposed to save my throat, and I guess it did at that, since I spent as much time looking at the cigarette as I did actually smoking it. I'd smoked most of my life. For a while I'd been more or less addicted to tobacco, but it was hard to see anyone becoming addicted to something quite so tasteless as a filter cigarette. It was like eating a hot dog after fifty years of bratwurst.

The petty officer took me to another hut with a bed, a chair, and a table and locked me in. There was even an open window. The window had bars on it, but I didn't mind that, and for a while I stood on the chair and breathed some fresher air than I was used to and looked at the ocean. It was a deep shade of blue. But I was feeling bluer. A U.S. military prison in New York felt a lot more serious than the drunk tank in Gitmo. And it wasn't very long before I had formed the opinion that the Navy must have spoken about me to the police in Havana; and that the police had been in contact with Lieutenant Quevedo of Cuban military intelligence—the SIM; and that the SIM lieutenant had told the Americans my real name and background. If I was lucky, I might get to tell someone in the FBI everything I knew about Meyer Lansky and the mob in Havana and save myself a trip back to Germany and, very likely, a trial for murder. The Federal Republic of Germany had abolished the death penalty for murder in 1949, but I couldn't answer for the Americans. The Amis had hanged four Nazi war criminals in Landsberg as recently as 1951. Then again, maybe they would deport me back to Vienna, where I'd been framed for the murders of two women. That was an even more uncomfortable prospect. The Austrians, being Austrians, retained the death penalty for murder.

The following day I was handcuffed and taken to an airfield, where I boarded a Douglas C-54 Skymaster with various military personnel returning home to their wives and families, and we flew north for about seven hours before we landed at Mitchell Air Force Base in Nassau County, New York. There I was handed over into the custody of the U.S. Army military police. On the main airport building was a board detailing the major units that were assigned to Mitchell AFB and a sign that read "Welcome to the United States." It didn't feel as if I was. Air Force handcuffs were exchanged for no-less-uncomfortable Army ones and I was shut inside a paddy wagon like a stray dog with a bad case of fleas. The wagon was windowless, but I could tell we were driving west. Having landed on America's northeast coast, there was nowhere else for our solitary wagon train to go but west. One of the MPs was carrying a shotgun in case we ran into Red Indians or outlaws. It seemed like a wise precaution. After all, there was always the possibility that Meyer Lansky might be worried about the jam I was in; maybe even worried enough to do something about it. Lansky was thoughtful like that. He was the kind of man who always looked after his employees, one way or the other. Like all gambling men, Lansky preferred a sure thing. And there's nothing as sure as a bullet in the head.

Ninety minutes later, the doors of the wagon opened in front of a semicircular fortress that appeared to be built on an island. The fortress was made of sandstone bricks and was about forty feet high with three stories. It was old and rather ugly and looked as if it belonged properly in old Berlin, somewhere other than New York anyway, an impression that was reinforced by the view of lower Manhattan's much taller buildings. These stood gleaming on the opposite shore of a large expanse of water and resembled nothing so much as the walls of some modern Troy. This was my first sight of New York City, and like Tarzan I wasn't as impressed as maybe I ought to have been. Then again, I was still wearing handcuffs.

The MPs herded me up to an arched doorway, unlocked my handcuffs, and delivered me into the custody of a black Army sergeant who fitted me with a new set of cuffs and, tugging them, led the way into a keyhole-shaped courtyard where at least a hundred men wearing green fatigues were milling aimlessly around. A crooked brick tower higher than the castellated walls backed onto a series of concrete balconies where armed military warders watched us from behind a wide pane of wired glass. The courtyard was open to the air, but it smelled of cigarettes, freshly cut timber, and the unwashed bodies of convicted American soldiers who regarded my arrival with a mixture of curiosity and disdain.

It was warmer than Russia and there were no pictures of Stalin and Lenin to admire, but for a moment I felt I was back at Camp Eleven in Voronezh. That New York City was just a mile away seemed almost unthinkable, yet I could almost hear the sizzle of hamburgers and french fries and immediately I started to feel hungry. Back in Camp Eleven we were always hungry, each day and all day; some men in prison play cards, some try to keep fit, but in Voronezh our main pastime was waiting to be fed. Not that we were ever fed with food: water soup *kasha* and *chleb*—a dark, moist, breadlike stuff that tasted of fuel oil—was what we ate. These men in Castle Williams looked better off than that. They still had the look of resistance and escape in their eyes. No *pleni* in a Soviet labor camp ever looked like that. Just to look at an MVD guard with that amount of insolence would have been to risk a beating or worse; and no one ever thought of trying to escape: There was nowhere to escape to.

The sergeant led the way into the crooked tower and up a spiral steel staircase to the second level of the fortress.

"We're gonna give you a cell all to yourself," he said. "Given that you're not going to be with us for very long."

"Oh? Where am I going?"

"Best you is in solitary," he said, ignoring my question. "Best for you, best for the men. New shit and old shit don't mix well in this shit hole. Especially when the new shit smells different. I don't want to know what you are, you maggot, but you ain't Army. So you is quarantined while you're our guest. Like you had yellow fucking fever one day and dysentery the next. You hear me?"

"Yes, sir."

He opened a steel door and nodded me inside.

"Would you mind telling me what this place is?"

"Castle Williams is a disciplinary barracks for the First United States Army. Named after the commandant of the U.S. Corps of Engineers who built it."

"And the island? We are on an island, aren't we?"

"Governors Island, in Upper New York Bay. So don't you get any foolish ideas about trying to escape, new shit."

"I wouldn't dream of it, sir."

"You don't just smell different, new shit. You sound different, too. Where you from?"

"It doesn't matter," I said. "A long way from here and a long time ago. That's where I'm from. And I won't be getting any visitors. At least no one I want to see."

"No family, huh?"

"Family? I can't even spell it."

"Then it's lucky for you we gave you a view of the city. In case you get lonely."

I went to the window and looked across the bay. Behind me the door banged loudly shut like a cannon going off. I let out a sigh. New York was huge, so huge it made me feel small; so small it would have required a large microscope just to see me.

4

NEW YORK, 1954

Castle Williams was a military barracks until 1865, when it became a detention facility for Confederate POWs, which to me made it seem like a home from home. Then, in 1903, the castle was fitted up as a model prison for the U.S. military. In 1916, they even wired it for electricity and installed central heating. All of this I was told by one of the guards, who were the only men who ever spoke to me. Only it certainly wasn't a model prison anymore. Crumbling and overcrowded, the castle frequently stank of human excrement when the plumbing went wrong, which was all the time. It seemed that the drainage was poor, the result of the castle being built on landfill brought to the island from Manhattan. Of course, I assumed this landfill was just rock; back in Russia landfill often meant something very different.

The view from my window was the best thing about Castle Williams. Sometimes I could see yachts sailing up and down the bay like so much seagoing geometry; but for the most part it was just loud waste cargo boats sounding their foghorns that I saw, and the relentless, growing city. I had very little else to do but stare out of that window. You do a lot of staring in prison. You stare at the walls. You stare at the floor. You stare at the ceiling. You stare at the air. A nice view felt like a little bit of a luxury. When prisoners kill themselves, or each other, it's usually because they're short of something to do.

I gave killing myself quite a bit of thought, because a city view will only keep you going for so long. I figured out how to do it, too. I might not have had a belt or any shoelaces, but most convicts manage to hang themselves perfectly well with a cotton shirt. Almost all of the prisoners I knew who killed themselves—in Russia it was about one a week—hanged themselves using a shirt. After this, however, I decided to keep a closer eye on myself in case I did something foolish, and from time to time I would try to engage myself in conversation. But this wasn't so easy. For one thing, I didn't like Bernhard Gunther very much. He was cynical and world-weary and hardly had a good word to say about any-one, least of all himself. He'd had a pretty tough war one way or the other, and done quite a few things of which he wasn't proud. Lots of people feel that way, of course, but it had been no picnic for him since then either; it didn't seem to matter where he spread life's tartan rug, there was always a turd on the grass.

"I bet you had a difficult childhood, too," I said. "Is that why you became a cop? To get even with your father? You've never been very good with authority figures, have you? It strikes me that you'd have been a lot better off if you'd just stayed put in Havana and gone to work for Lieutenant Quevedo. Come to think of it, you'd have been a lot better off if you'd never been a cop at all. Trying to do the right thing has never really worked for you, Gunther, has it? You should have been a criminal like most of the others. That way you'd have been on the winning side a little more often."

"Hey, I thought you were supposed to be talking me out of killing myself. If I want someone to make me despair, I could do it myself."

"All right, all right. Look, this place isn't so bad. Three meals a day, a room with a view, and all the peace and quiet a man of your age could ever wish for. They even wash the dinner plates. Remember those rusty cans you had to eat from in Russia? And the bread thief you helped murder? Don't say that you've forgotten him. Or all the other dead comrades they had to stack like firewood because the ground was too cold and hard to bury them? And maybe you've forgotten how the Blues used to get us shoveling lime in the wind. The way it used to make your nose bleed all day. Why, this place is the Hotel Adlon next to Camp Eleven."

"You talked me out of it. Maybe I won't kill myself. I just wish I knew what was happening."

After all that talking I was as quiet as Hegel for a spell; maybe it was for several days, weeks probably, I don't know. I hadn't been marking time on the wall the way you were supposed to, with six marks followed by a seventh through their middle. They stopped making those calendars after the man in the iron mask complained about all the graffiti on the wall of his cell. Besides, the quickest way to do the time is to pretend it's not there. People pretend a lot when they're in jail. And just when you've managed to persuade yourself that there's something almost normal about being locked up like an animal, two strange men wearing suits and hats walk in and tell you that you're being deported to Germany: One of them puts the cuffs on you and before you know it you're on your way to the airport again.

The suits were good. The creases in their pants were almost perfect, like the bow of a big gray ship. The hats were nicely shaped and the shoes brightly polished, like their fingernails. They didn't smoke—at least not on the job—and they smelled lightly of cologne. One of them had a little gold watch chain on which he kept the key to my handcuffs. The other wore a signet ring that gleamed like a cold white burgundy. They were smooth, efficient, and probably quite tough. They had good, white teeth of the kind that reminded me I probably needed to see a dentist. And they didn't like me. Not in the least. In fact, they hated me. I knew this because when they looked my way they grimaced or snarled silently or gritted their teeth and gave every sign of wanting to bite me. For much of the journey to the airport there were just the white teeth to contend with; and then, after about thirty minutes, when it seemed they could no longer restrain themselves, they started to bark.

"Fucking Nazi," said one.

I said nothing.

"What's the matter, you Nazi bastard? Lost your tongue?"

I shook my head. "German," I said. "But never a Nazi."

"No difference," said the other. "Not in my book."

"Besides," said the first one. "You were SS. And that makes you worse than a Nazi murderer. That makes you someone who enjoyed it."

I couldn't argue with him about that. What would have been the point? They'd already made up their minds about me: John Wilkes Booth would have received a more sympathetic hearing than I was likely to get from these two. But after weeks of solitary, I had an itch to talk a little:

"What are you? FBI?"

The first man nodded. "That's right."

"A lot of SS were cops just like you," I said. "I was a detective when the war started. I didn't have much choice in the matter."

"I'm nothing like you, pal," said the second agent. "Nothing. You hear me?" He poked me on the shoulder with his forefinger for good measure, and it felt like someone drilling for oil. "You remember that when you fly home to your mass-murdering pals. No American ever killed any Jews, mister."

"What about the Rosenbergs?" I said.

"A Nazi with a sense of humor. How about that, Bill?"

"He's going to need that when he gets back to Germany, Mitch."

"The Rosenbergs. That's very funny. It's just a pity we can't fry you, Gunther, the way we fried those two."

38

"They had lawyers and a fair trial. And I happen to know that the judge and the prosecutor were Jews themselves. Just for your information, kraut."

"That is reassuring," I said. "However, I might feel more reassured if I'd ever seen a lawyer myself. I believe it's not uncommon for someone in this country to have to appear before a court when there's a move to have him deported. Especially when it seems possible I might be facing a trial in Germany. I had the strange idea that civil liberties actually meant something in America."

"Extradition was never meant for scum like you, Gunther," said the fed called Bill.

"Besides," said Mitch, "you were never legally here. So you can't be legally extradited. As far as the American courts are concerned, you don't even exist."

"Then it was all a bad dream, is that it?"

Bill put a stick of gum in his mouth and started to chew. "That's it. You imagined the whole thing, kraut. It never happened. And neither did this."

I ought to have been ready to sign for it. Their faces had been sending me telegrams ever since we'd got in the paddy wagon. I suppose they were just waiting for a chance to make the delivery, and when it came, in the belly, hard, right up to his elbow, I was still hearing the bell ringing in my ears ten minutes later when we stopped, the doors opened, and they clotheslined me out onto the runway. It was a real professional blow. I was up the steps and onto the plane before I could draw enough breath to wish them both good-bye.

I got a good view of the Statue of Liberty as we took off. I had the peculiar idea that the lady in the toga was giving the Hitler salute. At the very least, I figured the book under her left arm was missing a few important pages.

GERMANY, 1954

I'd been in Landsberg before, but only as a visitor. Before the war, lots of people visited Landsberg Prison to see cell number seven, where Adolf Hitler was imprisoned in 1923 following the failed Beer Hall Putsch, and where he had written *Mein Kampf*; but I certainly wasn't one of those. I never liked biographies very much. My own previous visit had occurred in 1949 when, as a private detective working for a client in Munich, I'd gone there to interview an SS officer and convicted war criminal by the name of Fritz Gebauer.

The Americans ran the prison and there were more convicted Nazi war criminals locked up there than anywhere else in Europe. Two or three hundred had been executed on the prison gallows between 1946 and 1951, and since then, a great many more had been released, but the place still housed some of the biggest mass murderers in history. Of these, I was well acquainted with several, although I avoided most of them during the times when we prisoners were allowed freely to associate. There were even a few Japanese prisoners from the Shanghai war crimes trial, but we had little or no contact with them.

The castle was from 1910 and, unlike the rest of the historic old town, was west of the River Lech: Four white brick-built blocks were arranged in a cross shape at the center of which was a tower from which location our steel-helmeted iron-faced guards could swing their white batons like Fred Astaire and watch us.

I remembered once receiving a postcard of Hitler's cell and I had the impression that my own was not dissimilar: There was a narrow iron bedstead with a small nightstand, a bedside light, a table, and a chair; and there was a big double window with more bars on the outside than on a lion tamer's cage. I had a cell facing southwest, and that meant I had the sun in my cell during the afternoon and evening and a pleasant view of Spöttingen Cemetery, where several of the men hanged at WCPN1—which was what the Americans called it—were now interred. This made a nice change from my view of New York Bay and Lower Manhattan. The dead make quieter neighbors than waste-cargo barges.

The food was good, although not recognizably German. And I didn't much like the clothes we were obliged to wear. Gray and purple stripes never suited me very well; and the little white hat lacked the all-important wide snap brim I'd always preferred and made me look like an organ-grinder's monkey.

Soon after my arrival I had a visit from the Roman Catholic chaplain, Father Morgenweis: Herr Dr. Glawik, who was a lawyer appointed by the Bavarian Ministry of Justice; and a man from the Association for the Welfare of German Prisoners whose name I don't recall. Most Bavarians, and quite a few Germans, too, regarded all of the inmates at WCPN1 as political prisoners. The U.S. Army saw things differently, of course, and it wasn't very long before I was also visited by two American lawyers from Nuremberg. With their strongly accented German and their bullshit bonhomie, these two were patient and very, very persistent; and it was only a relief in part that they seemed hardly interested in the two Vienna murders— which had nothing to do with me—and not at all interested in the killings of two Israeli assassins at Garmisch-Partenkirchen, of which

I was undeniably guilty, albeit in self-defense. What they *were* interested in was my wartime service with the RSHA—which was the security office created by the mergers of the SD (the security service of the SS), the Gestapo, and Kripo in 1939.

Several times a week we would meet in an interview room on the ground floor near the main entrance of the castle. They always brought me coffee and cigarettes, a little chocolate, and sometimes a Munich newspaper. Neither man was older than forty, and the younger of the two was the senior officer. His name was Jerry Silverman, and before coming to Germany he'd been a New York lawyer. He was hugely tall and wore a green gabardine military jacket with pink khaki trousers; there were several ribbons on his breast, but instead of the metal bars most American officers wore on their shoulders to indicate their rank, Silverman and his sergeant had a cloth patch sewn on their sleeves that identified them both as members of the OCCWC—the Office of the Chief Counsel for War Crimes. The fact was, they were wearing uniforms but they didn't belong to the U.S. military; they were Pentagon bureaucrats, prosecutors from the American Department of Defense. Only in America could they have given lawyers a uniform.

The other, older man was Sergeant Jonathan Earp. He was a head shorter than Captain Silverman and had—he told me, in an idle moment when I asked him—graduated from Harvard Law School prior to his joining the OCCWC.

Both men had one or two German parents, which was why they spoke the language so fluently, although Earp was the more fluent of the two; but Silverman was cleverer.

They came armed with several briefcases that were full of files, but they hardly ever referred to these; each man seemed to carry a whole filing cabinet in his head. They did, however, take copious notes: Silverman had small, very neat, distinguished handwriting that looked as though it might have been written by Völundr, the ruler of the elves.

At first I assumed they were interested in the workings of the RSHA and my knowledge of Department VI, which was the office of Foreign Intelligence; but it seemed they knew almost as much about that as I did. Perhaps more. And only gradually did it become clear that they suspected me of something far more serious than a couple of local murders.

"You see," explained Silverman, "there are some aspects of your story that just don't add up."

"I get a lot of that," I said.

"You say you were a Kommissar in Kripo until—?"

"Until Kripo became part of the RSHA in September 1939."

"But you say you were never a party member."

I shook my head.

"Wasn't that unusual?"

"Not at all. Ernst Gennat was the deputy chief of Kripo in Berlin until August 1939, and he was to my certain knowledge never a Nazi Party member."

"What happened to him?"

"He died. Of natural causes. There were others, too. Heinrich Muller, the Gestapo chief. He never joined the party either."

"Then again," said Silverman, "maybe he didn't need to. He was, as you say, head of the Gestapo."

"There are others I could mention, but you have to remember that the Nazis were hypocrites. Sometimes it suited them to be able to use people who were outside the party system."

"So you admit you allowed yourself to be used," said Earp.

"I'm alive, aren't I?" I shrugged. "I guess that speaks for itself."

"The question is how much you allowed yourself to be used," said Silverman.

"It's been bothering me, too," I said.

He was clever, but he couldn't ever have played poker; his face was much too expressive. When he thought I was lying, his mouth hung open and he shifted his lower jaw around like a cow chewing tobacco; and when he was satisfied with an answer, he looked away or made a sad sound like he was disappointed.

"Maybe you'd like to get something off your chest," said Earp.

"Seriously," I said. "You don't want me."

"That's for us to decide, Herr Gunther."

"Maybe you could beat it out of me, like your friends in the Navy and the FBI."

"It seems like everyone wants to hit you," said Earp.

"I'm just wondering when you two are going to figure that it's your turn."

"We're not like that in the Chief Counsel's Office." Silverman sounded so smooth I almost believed him.

"Well, why didn't you say so before? Now I feel completely reassured."

"Most of the people in here have talked to us because they wanted to talk," said Earp.

"And the rest?"

"Sometimes it's hard to say nothing when all your friends have ratted on you," said Silverman.

"That's okay, then. I don't have any friends. And very definitely none in this place. So anyone who rats on me is probably a bigger rat himself."

Silverman stood up and took off his jacket. "Mind if I open a window?" he said.

The politeness was instinctive and he started to open it anyway. Not that I could ever have jumped out; the window was barred, just like the one in my cell. Silverman stood there looking out with his arms folded thoughtfully, and for a moment I remembered a newspaper photograph of Hitler, in a similar attitude, on a visit to Landsberg after he'd become Reich Chancellor. After a moment or two he said,

"Did you ever meet a man called Otto Ohlendorf? He was

a Gruppenführer—a general—in the Reich Main Security Office."
Silverman came back to the table and sat down.

"Yes. I met him a couple of times. He was head of Department
Three, I think. Domestic Intelligence."

"And what was your impression of him?"

"Intense. A dedicated Nazi."

"He was also head of an SS task group that operated in the
southern Ukraine and the Crimea," said Silverman. "That same task
group murdered ninety thousand people before Ohlendorf returned
to his desk in Berlin. As you say, he was a dedicated Nazi. But when
the British captured him, in 1945, he sang like a canary. For them
and for us. Actually, we couldn't shut him up. No one could figure
it. There was no duress, no deal, no offer of immunity. It seems he
just wanted to talk about it. Maybe you should think about doing
that. Get it off your chest, as he did. Ohlendorf sat in that very chair
you're sitting in now and talked his damn head off for forty-two
days in succession. He was very matter-of-fact about it, too. You
might even say normal. He didn't cry or offer an apology, but I guess
there must have been something in his soul that just bothered him."

"Some of the guys here quite liked him," said Earp. "Up until
the moment when we hanged him."

I shook my head. "With all due respect, you're not selling this
idea of unburdening myself very well if the only reward is the one
in heaven. And I thought Americans were supposed to be good
salesmen."

"Ohlendorf was one of Heydrich's protégés, too," said
Silverman.

"Meaning you think I was?"

"You said yourself it was Heydrich who brought you back to
Kripo in 1938. I don't know what else that makes you, Gunther."

"He needed a proper homicide detective. Not some Nazi with
an anti-Semitic ax to grind. When I came back to Kripo, I had the

unusual idea that I might actually be able to stop someone from murdering young girls."

"But afterward—"

"You mean after I solved the case?"

"—you continued working for Kripo. At General Heydrich's request."

"I really didn't have much choice in the matter. Heydrich was a hard man to disappoint."

"But what did he want from you?"

"Heydrich was a cold murdering bastard, but he was also a pragmatist. Sometimes he preferred honesty to unswerving loyalty. For one or two people such as myself, it wasn't so important that they stick to the official party line as that they should do a good job. Especially if those people, like me, had no interest in climbing the SS ladder."

"Oddly enough, that's exactly how Otto Ohlendorf described his own relationship with Heydrich," said Earp. "Jost, too. Heinz Jost? You remember him? He was the man Heydrich appointed to take over from your friend Walter Stahlecker in charge of Task Group A, when he was killed by Estonian partisans."

"Walter Stahlecker wasn't ever my friend. Whatever gave you that idea?"

"He was your business partner's brother, wasn't he? When you and he were running a private investigation business in Berlin in 1937."

"Since when has one brother been responsible for another's actions? Bruno Stahlecker couldn't have been more different from his brother Walter. He wasn't even a Nazi."

"But you met Walter Stahlecker, surely."

"He came to Bruno's funeral. In 1938."

"On any other occasions?"

"Probably. I don't remember when, exactly."

"Do you think it was before or after he organized the murder of two hundred and fifty thousand Jews?"

"Well, it wasn't afterward. And by the way, he was Franz Stahlecker, never Walter. Bruno never called him Walter. But to come back to Heinz Jost for a moment. The man who took over Task Group A when Franz Stahlecker was killed. Would this be the same Heinz Jost who was sentenced to life imprisonment and then paroled from this place a couple of years ago? Is that the man to whom you're referring?"

"We just prosecute them," said Silverman. "It's up to the U.S. high commissioner for Germany who's released and when."

"And then last month," I said. "I hear it was Willy Siebert's turn to walk out of here. Now, correct me if I'm wrong, but wasn't he Otto Ohlendorf's deputy? When those ninety thousand Jews got killed? Ninety thousand, and you people just let him walk out of here. It sounds to me that McCloy wants his head examined."

"James Conant is high commissioner now," said Earp.

"Either way, it beats me why you boys bother," I said. "Less than ten years served for ninety thousand murders? It hardly seems worth it. My math isn't great, but I think that works out to about a day of time served for every twenty-five murders. I killed some people during the war, it's true. But by the tally handed down to the likes of Jost and Siebert and that other fellow—Erwin Schulz, in January—hell, I should have been paroled the same day I was arrested."

"That gives us a number to aim at, anyway," murmured Earp.

"To say nothing of the SS men who are still here," I said, ignoring him. "You can't seriously believe that I deserve to be in the same prison as the likes of Martin Sandberger and Walter Blume."

"Let's talk about that," said Silverman. "Let's talk about Walter Blume. Now, him you must know, because like you he was a policeman and worked for your old boss, Arthur Nebe, in Task

Group B. Blume was in charge of a special unit, a Sonderkommando, under Nebe's orders, before Nebe was relieved by Erich Naumann in November 1941."

"I met him."

"No doubt you and he have had a lot to reminisce about since you came here and were able to renew your acquaintance."

"I've seen him, of course. Since I've been in here. But we haven't spoken. Nor are we likely to."

"And why's that?"

"I thought it was free association. Do I have to explain who I choose to speak to and who I don't?"

"There's nothing free in here," said Earp. "Come on, Gunther. Do you think you're better than Blume? Is that it?"

"You seem to know a lot of the answers already," I said. "Why don't you tell me?"

"I don't understand," said Earp. "Why would you speak to a man like Waldemar Klingelhöfer in here and not Blume? Klingelhöfer was also in Task Group B. One's just as bad as the other, surely."

"All in all," said Silverman, "it must seem like old times for you, Gunther. Meeting all your old pals. Adolf Ott, Eugen Steimle, Blume, Klingelhöfer."

"Come on," insisted Earp. "Why speak to him and none of the others?"

"Is it because none of the other prisoners will speak to him because he betrayed a fellow SS officer?" asked Silverman. "Or because he appears to regret what he did as head of the Moscow killing commando?"

"Before taking charge of that commando," said Earp, "your friend Klingelhöfer did what you claim to have done. He headed up an antipartisan hunt. In Minsk, wasn't it? Where you were?"

"Was that just shooting Jews, the same as Klingelhöfer?"

"Maybe you'll let me answer one of your questions at a time," I said.

"There's no rush," said Silverman. "We've got plenty of time. Take it from the beginning, why don't you? You say you were ordered to join a Reserve Police Battalion, number three one six, in the summer of 1941, as part of Operation Barbarossa."

"That's correct."

"So how come you didn't go to Pretzsch in the spring?" asked Earp. "To the police academy there for training and assignment. By all accounts, nearly everyone who was going to Russia was at Pretzsch. Gestapo, Kripo, Waffen-SS, SD, the whole RSHA."

"Heydrich, Himmler, and several thousand officers," said Silverman. "According to previous accounts we've heard, it was common knowledge after that what was going to happen when you all got to Russia. But you say you weren't at Pretzsch, which is why the whole business of killing Jews was such an unpleasant surprise for you. So why weren't you at Pretzsch?"

"What did you get? A sick note?"

"I was still in France," I said. "On a special mission from Heydrich."

"That was convenient, wasn't it? So let me get this straight: When you joined Battalion Three One Six, on the Polish–Russian border in June 1941, it's really your impression that your job would involve nothing more than hunting down partisans and NKVD, right?"

"Yes. But even before I got to Vilnius I'd begun to hear stories of local pogroms against the Jews because the Jews in the NKVD were busy murdering all of their prisoners instead of releasing them. It was all very confused. You've no idea how confused. Frankly, I didn't believe these stories at first. There were plenty of stories like that in the Great War, and most of them turned out to be false." I shrugged. "In this particular case, however, even the worst, most far-fetched stories were nearly all true."

"Exactly what were your orders?"

"That our job was a security one. To keep order behind the lines of our advancing army."

"And you did that how?" asked Silverman. "By murdering people?"

"You know, being a detective in the police battalion, I paid a lot of attention to my so-called comrades. And it turned out that a lot of these murdering bastards in the Task Groups were lawyers, too. Just like you guys. Blume, Sandberger, Ohlendorf, Schulz. I expect there were others, but I can't remember their names. I used to wonder why it was that so many lawyers took part in these killings. What do you think?"

"We ask the questions, Gunther."

"Spoken like a true lawyer, Mr. Earp. By the way, how come I don't have one here? With all due respect, gentlemen, this interrogation is hardly consistent with the rules of German justice; or, I imagine, the rules of American justice, either. Doesn't every American have a Fifth Amendment right not to be a witness against himself?"

"This interrogation is a necessary step in determining if you should be tried or released," said Silverman.

"This is what we German cops used to call an Eskimo's fishing trip," I said. "You just drop a line through a hole in the ice and hope that you catch something."

"In the absence of any clear evidence and documentation," continued Silverman, "sometimes the only way to gain knowledge of a crime is by questioning a suspect such as yourself. That's usually been our experience with war crimes cases."

"Bullshit. We both know you're sitting on a ton of documentation. What about all those papers you recovered from Gestapo headquarters that are now in the Berlin Document Center?"

"Actually, it's two tons of documentation," said Silverman. "Between eight and nine million documents, to be precise. And eight or nine represents our total staff at the OCC. With the Einsatzgruppen trial we got lucky: We found the actual reports that were written by the Task Group leaders. Twelve binders containing a gold mine of information. As a result, we didn't even need a prosecution witness against them. All the same, it took us four months to put the case together. Four months. With you it might take longer. Do you really want to wait here for another four months while we work out if you have a case to answer?"

"So go and check those Task Group leader reports," I said. "They'll clear me for sure. Because I wasn't one of them, I've told you. I got an exeat back to Berlin, courtesy of Arthur Nebe. Out of the task area. He's bound to have mentioned it in his report."

"That's where your problem lies, Gunther," explained Silverman. "With your old friend Arthur Nebe. You see, the reports for Task Groups A, C, and D were very detailed."

"Otto Ohlendorf's were a model of accuracy," said Earp. "You might say he was a typical fucking lawyer in that respect."

Silverman was shaking his head. "But there are no original reports written by Arthur Nebe from Task Group B. In fact, there are no reports from Task Group B until a new commander is appointed, in November 1941. We think that's why Walter Blume took over from Nebe. Because Nebe was falling down on the job. For whatever reason, he wasn't killing nearly as many Jews as the other three groups. Why was that, do you think?"

Arthur Nebe. It had been a while since I'd really thought about the man who'd saved my life and, perhaps, my soul, and whom I'd repaid so unkindly: Effectively, I'd murdered Nebe in Vienna during the winter of 1947–1948, when he'd been working for General Gehlen's organization of old comrades, but I hardly wanted to tell the two Amis anything about that. Gehlen's organization had been sponsored by the CIA, or whatever they called it back then, and possibly still was.

"Nebe was two different men," I said. "Perhaps several more than just two. In 1933, Nebe believed that the Nazis were the only alternative to the communists and that they would bring order to Germany. By 1938, probably earlier, he'd realized his mistake and was plotting with others in the Wehrmacht and the police to overthrow Hitler. There's a propaganda ministry photograph of Nebe with Himmler, Heydrich, and Muller that shows the four of them planning the investigation of a bomb attempt on Hitler's life. That was November 1939. And Nebe was part of that very same conspiracy. I know that because I was part of it, too. However, Nebe quickly changed his mind after the defeat of France and Britain in 1940. Lots of people changed their minds about Hitler after the miracle of France. Even I changed my mind about him. For a few months, anyway. We both changed our minds again when Hitler attacked Russia. Nobody thought that was a good idea. And yet Arthur did what he was told. He'd plot away and do what he was told even if that meant murdering Jews in Minsk and Smolensk. Doing what you were told was always the best kind of cover if you were simultaneously planning a coup d'état against the Nazis. I think that's why he seems like such an ambiguous figure. I think that's why, as you said, he was falling down on the job as commander of Task Group B. Because his heart was never in it. Above all, Nebe was a survivor."

"Like you."

"To some extent, yes, that's true. Thanks to him."

"Tell us about that."

"I already did."

"Not in any great detail."

"What do you want me to do? Draw you a picture?"

"Really, we want as many details as possible," said Earl.

"When someone is lying," said Silverman, "it's nearly always the case that they start to contradict themselves in matters of detail. You should know that from being a policeman yourself. When they start to contradict themselves on the small things, you can bet they're lying about the big things, too."

I nodded.

"So," he said. "Let's go back to Goloby, where you murdered the members of an NKVD squad."

"The ones you claim had murdered all of the inmates at the NKVD prison in Lutsk," said Earp. "According to the Soviets, that was just German propaganda, put out to help persuade your own men that the summary execution of all Jews and Bolsheviks was justified."

"You'll be telling me next that it was the German army who murdered all those Poles in the Katyn Forest."

"Maybe it was."

"Not according to your own congressional investigation."

"You're well-informed."

I shrugged. "In Cuba, I got all the American newspapers. In an attempt to improve my English. Nineteen fifty-two, wasn't it? The investigation. When the Malden Committee recommended that the Soviets should answer a case at the International Court of Justice in the Hague? Look, it's a story I've been interested in for a long time. We both know the NKVD killed as many as we did. So why not admit it? The commies are the enemy now. Or is that just American propaganda?"

I fetched a packet of cigarettes from the pocket of my prison jacket and lit one slowly. I was tired of answering questions, but I knew I was going to have to open the door of my mind's darkest cellar and wake up some very unpleasant memories. Even in a room with bars on the window, Operation Barbarossa felt like a very long way away. Outside it was a bright and sunny June day, and although it had been a very similarly warm June day when the Wehrmacht invaded the Soviet Union, that wasn't the way I remembered it. When I recalled names like Goloby, Lutsk, Bialystock, and Minsk, I thought of infernal heat and the sights, sounds, and smells of a hell on earth; but most of all I remembered a clean-shaven young man aged about twenty standing in a cobbled town square with a crowbar in his hand, his thick boots an inch deep in the blood of about thirty other men who lay dead or dying at his feet. I remembered the shocked laughter of some of the German soldiers who were watching this bestial display; I remembered the sound of an accordion playing a spirited tune as another, older man with a long beard walked silently, almost calmly toward the fellow with the crowbar and was immediately struck on the head like some ghastly Hindu sacrifice; I remembered the noise the old man made as he fell to the ground and the way his legs jerked stiffly, like a puppet's, until the crowbar hit him again.

I jerked my thumb at the window. "All right," I said. "I'll tell you everything. But do you mind if I put my face in the sun for a moment? It helps to remind me that I'm still alive."

"Unlike millions of others," Earp said pointedly. "Go ahead. We're in no hurry."

I went to the window and looked out. By the main gate a small crowd of people had gathered to wait for someone. Either that or they were looking for the window of cell number seven, which seemed a little less likely.

"Is someone being released today?" I asked.

Silverman came over to the window. "Yes," he said. "Erich Mielke."

"Mielke?" I shook my head. "You're mistaken. Mielke's not in here. He couldn't be."

Even as I spoke, a smaller door in the main gate opened and a short, stocky, gray-haired man of about sixty stepped out and was cheered by the waiting well-wishers.

"That's not Mielke," I said.

"I think you mean Erhard Milch, sir," Earp told Silverman. "The Luftwaffe field marshal? It's him who's being released today."

"So that's who it is," I said. "For a moment there I thought it was a real war criminal."

"Milch is—was—a war criminal," insisted Silverman. "He was director of air armaments under Albert Speer."

"And what was criminal about building planes?" I asked.

"You must have built quite a few planes yourself, if the state of Berlin in 1945 was anything to go by."

"We didn't use slave labor to do it," said Silverman.

I watched as Erhard Milch accepted a bunch of flowers from a pretty girl, bowed politely to her, and was then driven off in a smart new Mercedes to begin the rest of his life.

"What was the sentence for that, then?"

"Life imprisonment," said Silverman.

"Life imprisonment, eh? Some people have all the luck."

"Commuted to fifteen years."

"There's something wrong with your high commissioner's math, I think," I said. "Who else is getting out of here?"

I took a puff on my tasteless cigarette, flicked the butt out of the window, and watched it spiral to the ground trailing smoke like one of Milch's invincible Luftwaffe planes.

"You were going to tell us about Minsk," said Silverman.

MINSK, 1941

On the morning of July 7, 1941, I commanded a firing squad that executed thirty Russian POWs. At the time, I didn't feel bad about this because they were all NKVD and, less than twelve hours before, they themselves had murdered two or three thousand prisoners at the NKVD prison in Lutsk. They also murdered some German POWs who were with them, which was a miserable sight. I suppose you could say they had every right to do so, given that we had invaded their country. You could also say that our executing them in retaliation had considerably less justification, and you'd probably be correct on both counts. Well, we did it, but not because of the "commissar order" or the "Barbarossa decree," which were nothing more than a shooting license from German field headquarters. We did it because we felt—I felt—they had it coming and they would certainly have shot us in similar circumstances. So we shot them in groups of four. We didn't make them dig their own graves or anything like that. I didn't care for that sort of thing. It smacked of sadism. So we shot them and left them where they fell. Later on, when I was a *pleni* in a Russian labor camp, I sometimes wished I'd shot many more than just thirty, but that's a different story.

I didn't feel bad about it until the next day when my men and I came across a former colleague from the Police Praesidium at the Alex, in Berlin. A fellow named Becker, who was in another police battalion. I found him shooting civilians in a village somewhere west of Minsk. There were about a hundred bodies in a ditch, and it seemed to me that Becker and his men had been drinking. Even then I didn't get it. I kept on looking for explanations for what was essentially inexplicable and certainly inexcusable. And it was only when I realized that some of the people Becker and his men were about to shoot were old women that I said something.

"What the hell do you think you're doing?" I asked him.

"Obeying my orders," he said.

"What? To kill old women?"

"They're Jews," he said, as if that was all the explanation that was needed. "I've been ordered to kill as many Jews as I can, and that's what I'm doing."

"Whose orders? Who's your field commander and where is he?"

"Major Weis." Becker pointed at a long wooden building behind a white picket fence about thirty yards down the road. "He's in there. Having his lunch."

I walked toward the building, and Becker called after me: "Don't think I want to do this. But orders are orders, yes?"

As I reached the hut, I heard another volley of shots. One of the doors was open and an SS major was sitting on a chair with his tunic off. In one hand he held a half-eaten loaf of bread and in the other a bottle of wine and a cigarette. He heard me out with a look of weary amusement on his face.

"Look, none of this is my idea," he said. "It's a waste of time and ammunition, if you ask me. But I do what I'm told, right? That's how an army works. A superior officer gives me an order and I obey. Chapter closed." He pointed at a field telephone that was on the floor. "Take it up with headquarters if you like. They'll just tell you what they told me. To get on with it." He shook his head. "You're not the only one who thinks this is madness, Captain."

"You mean you've already asked for the orders to be confirmed?"

"Of course I have. Field HQ told me to take it up with Division HQ."

"And what did they say?"

Major Weis shook his head. "Questioning an order with Division? Are you mad? I won't stay a major for very long if I do that. They'll have my pips and my balls, and not necessarily in that order." He laughed. "But be my guest. Go on, call them. Just make sure you leave my name out of it."

Outside there was another volley of shots. I picked up the field telephone and cranked the handle furiously. Thirty seconds later, I was arguing with someone at Division HQ. The major got up and put his ear to the other side of the telephone. When I started to swear, he grinned and walked away.

"You've upset them now," he said.

I slammed the phone down and stood there trembling with anger.

"I'm to report to Division, in Minsk," I said. "Immediately."

"Told you." He handed me his bottle, and I took a swig of what turned out to be not wine but vodka. "They'll have your rank, for sure. I hope you think it was worth it. From what I hear, this"—he pointed at the door—"this is just the smoke at the end of the gun. Someone else is pulling the trigger. That's what you have to hold on to, my friend. Try to remember what Goethe said. He said the greatest happiness for us Germans is to understand what we can understand and then, having done so, to do what we're fucking told."

I went outside and told the men I'd brought with me in a Panzer wagon and a Puma armored car that we were going into Minsk, to make a report on the morning's antipartisan action. As we drove along I was in a melancholy frame of mind, but this was only partly to do the fate of a few hundred innocent Jews. Mostly I was concerned for the reputation of Germans and the Germany army. Where would this end? I asked myself. I certainly never conceived that thousands of Jews were already being slaughtered in a similar fashion.

Minsk was easy to find. All you had to do was drive down a long straight road—quite a good road, even by German standards—and follow the gray plume of smoke on the horizon. The Luftwaffe had bombed the city a few days before and destroyed most of the city center. Even so, all of the German vehicles moving along the road kept their distance from one another in case of a Russian air attack. Otherwise, the Red Army was gone and Wehrmacht intelligence indicated that the population of three hundred thousand would have left the city, too, but for the fact that our bombing of the road east out of Minsk—to Mogilev and Moscow—had forced as many as eighty thousand to turn back to the city, or at least what remained of it. Not that this looked like a particularly good idea either. Most of the wooden houses on the outskirts were still ablaze while, nearer the center, piles of rubble backed onto hollowed-out office and apartment buildings. I'd never seen a city so thoroughly destroyed as Minsk. This made it all the more surprising that the Uprava, the City Council, and Communist Party HQ had survived the bombing almost unscathed. The locals called it the Big House, which was something of an understatement: Nine or ten stories high and built of white concrete, the Uprava resembled a series of gigantic filing cabinets containing the details of every citizen in Minsk. In front of the building was an enormous bronze statue of Lenin, who viewed the large number of German cars and trucks with an understandable look of anxiety and concern, as well he might have done, given that the building was now the headquarters of Reichskommissariat Ostland—a German-created administrative area that stretched from the Byelorussian capital to the Baltic Sea.

Pushing a heavy wooden door that was so tall it might still have been growing in a forest, I entered a cheap, marble-clad hall that belonged in a Métro station and approached a locomotive-sized central desk where several German soldiers and SS were attempting to impose some kind of administrative order on the ant colony of dusty gray men who were pouring in and out of the place. Catching the eye of one SS officer behind the desk, I asked for the SS divisional commander's office and was directed to the second floor and advised to take the stairs, as the elevator was not working.

At the top of the first flight of stairs was a bronze head of Stalin, and at the top of the second there was a bronze head of Felix Dzerzhinsky. Operation Barbarossa looked like it was going to be bad news for Russian sculptors, just like everyone else. The floor was covered with broken glass, and there was a line of bullet holes on the gray wall that led all the way along a wide corridor to a couple of open facing doors, through which more SS officers were passing to and fro in a haze of cigarette smoke. One of these was my unit's commanding officer, SS-Standartenführer Mundt, who was one of those men who look like they came out of their mother's womb wearing a uniform. Seeing me, he raised an eyebrow and then a hand as he casually acknowledged my salute.

"The murder squad," he said. "Did you catch them?"

"Yes, Herr Oberst."

"Good work. What did you do with them?"

"We shot them, sir." I handed over a handful of Red identification documents I'd taken from the Russians before their executions.

Mundt started to look through the documents like an immigration officer searching for something suspicious. "Including the women?"

"Yes, sir."

"Pity. In future, all female partisans and NKVD are to be hanged in the town square, as an example to the others. Heydrich's orders. Understand?"

"Yes, Herr Oberst."

Mundt wasn't much older than me. When the war broke out he'd been a police colonel with the Hamburg Schutzpolizei. He was clever, only his was the wrong kind of cleverness for Kripo: To be a decent detective you have to understand people, and to understand people you have to be one of them yourself. Mundt wasn't like people. He wasn't even a person. I supposed that was why he had a pet dachshund with him—so that it might make him seem a little more human. But I knew better. He was a cold, pompous bastard. Whenever he spoke he sounded like he thought he was reciting Rilke, and I wanted to yawn or laugh or kick his teeth in. Which is how it must have looked.

"You disagree, Hauptmann?"

"I don't much care to hang women," I said.

He looked down his fine nose and smiled. "Perhaps you'd prefer to do something else with them?"

"That must be someone else you're thinking of, sir. What I mean is, I don't much like waging war on women. I'm the conventional type. The Geneva Convention, in case you were wondering."

Mundt pretended to look puzzled. "It's a strange way of observing the Geneva Convention you have," he said. "To shoot thirty prisoners."

I glanced around the office, which was a good size for just one desk. It would have been a good size for a sawmill. In the corner of the room was a fitted cupboard with its own little sink, where another man was washing his half-naked torso. In the opposite corner was a safe. An SS sergeant was listening to it like it was a radio and trying, without success, to persuade the thing to open. On top of the desk was a trio of different-colored telephones that might have been left there by three wise men from the East; behind the desk was another SS officer in a chair; and behind the officer was a large wall map of Minsk. On the floor lay a Russian soldier, and if this had ever been his office it wasn't anymore; the bullet hole behind his left ear and the blood on the linoleum seemed to indicate he would soon be relocated to a much smaller and more permanent earthly space.

"Besides, Captain Gunther," added Mundt, "it may have escaped you but the Russians never signed the Geneva Convention."

"Then I guess it's fine to shoot them all, sir."

The officer behind the desk stood up. "Did you say Captain Gunther?"

He was a Standartenführer, too, a colonel, the same as Mundt, which meant that as he came around the desk and placed himself in front of me I was obliged to come to attention again. He had been spawned in the same Aryan pond as Mundt and was no less arrogant.

"Yes, sir."

"Are you the Captain Gunther who telephoned to question my orders to shoot those Jews on the road to Minsk this morning?"

"Yes, sir. That was me. You must be Colonel Blume."

"What the devil do you mean by questioning an order?" he shouted. "You're an SS officer, pledged to the Führer. That order was issued to ensure security in the rear for our combat forces. Those Jews set their houses on fire after having been ordered to make them available as billets for our troops. I can't think of a better reason for a reprisal action than the burning of those houses."

"I didn't see any burning houses in that area, sir. And Sturmbannführer Weis was under the impression that those old women were being shot only because they were Jews."

"And if they were? The Jews of Soviet Russia are the intellectual bearers of the Bolshevik ideology, which makes them our natural enemy. No matter how old they are. Killing Jews is an act of war. Even they seem to understand that, if you don't. I repeat: Those orders must be carried out for the safety of all army areas. If every soldier only carried out an order after having considered the niceties of whether or not it agreed with his own conscience, then pretty soon there would be no discipline and no army. Are you mad? Are you a coward? Are you ill? Or perhaps you actually like the Jews?"

"I don't care who or what they are," I said. "I didn't come to Russia to shoot old women."

"Listen to yourself, Captain," said Blume. "What kind of an officer are you? You're supposed to set an example to your men. I've a good mind to take you to the ghetto just to see if this is some kind of an act—if you really are this squeamish about killing Jews."

Mundt had started to laugh. "Blume," he said.

"I can promise you this, Captain," said Colonel Blume. "You won't be a captain anymore if you can't manage it. You'll be the lowest private in the SS. Do you hear?"

"Blume," said Mundt. "Look at these." He handed Blume the papers of the NKVD I'd executed at Goloby. "Look."

Blume glanced at the documents as Mundt opened them for him. Mundt said: "Sarra Kagan. Solomon Geller. Josef Zalmonowitz. Julius Polonski. These are all Jewish names. Vinokurova. Kieper." He grinned some more, enjoying my growing discomfort. "I worked on the Jew desk in Hamburg, so I know something about these yid bastards. Joshua Pronicheva. Fanya Glekh. Aaron Levin. David Schepetovka. Saul Katz. Stefan Marx. Vladya Polichov. These are all yids he shot this morning. So much for your fucking scruples, Gunther. You picked a Jewish NKVD squad to execute. You just shot thirty kikes whether you like it or not."

Blume opened another identification document at random. And then another. "Misha Blyatman. Hersh Gebelev. Moishe Ruditzer. Nahum Yoffe. Chaim Serebriansky. Zyama Rosenblatt." He was laughing now, too. "You're right. How do you like that? Israel Weinstein. Ivan Lifshitz. It sounds to me like you hit the jackpot, Gunther. So far you've managed to kill more Jews in this campaign than I have. Maybe I should recommend you for a decoration. Or at the very least a promotion."

Mundt read out some more names just to rub it in. "You

should feel proud of yourself." Then he clapped me on the shoulder. "Come, now. Surely you can see the funny side of this."

"And if you can't, then that only makes it all the more funny," said Blume.

"What's funny?" said a voice.

We all looked around to see Arthur Nebe, the general in charge of Task Group B, standing in the doorway. Everyone came to attention, including me. As Nebe came into the office and walked up to the wall map, with hardly a look at me, Blume attempted an explanation:

"I'm afraid this officer was exhibiting a degree of scrupulousness with regard to the killing of Jews that turns out to have been somewhat misplaced, Herr General. It seems he already shot thirty NKVD this morning—apparently unaware that they were all Jews."

"It was the nice distinction between the two we found amusing," added Mundt.

"Not everyone is cut out for this kind of work," murmured Nebe, still studying the map. "I heard that Paul Blobel's in a Lublin hospital after a special action in the Ukraine. A complete nervous breakdown. And perhaps you don't remember what was said by Reichsführer Himmler at Pretzsch. Any repugnance felt at killing Jews is a cause for congratulation, since it affirms that we are a civilized people. So I really don't see what's funny about any of this. In future, I'll thank you to deal more sensitively with any man who expresses his inability to kill Jews. Is that clear?"

"Yes, sir."

Nebe touched a red square on the top right-hand corner of the map. "And this is—what?"

"Drozdy, sir," said Blume. "Three kilometers north of here. we've established a rather primitive prisoner-of-war camp there on the banks of the Svislock River. All of them men. Jews and non-Jews."

"How many in total?"

"About forty thousand."

"Separated?"

"Yes, sir." Blume joined Nebe in front of the map. "POWS in one half and Jews in the other."

"And the ghetto?"

"South of the Drozdy camp in the northwest of the city. It's the old Jewish quarter of Minsk." He put his finger on the map. "Here. From the Svislock River, west on Nemiga Street, north along the edge of the Jewish cemetery, and back east toward the Svislock. This is the main street here, Republikanskaya, and where it meets Nemiga, that will be the main gate."

"What kind of buildings are these?" asked Nebe.

"One- or two-story wooden houses behind cheap wooden fences. Even as we speak, sir, the whole ghetto is being surrounded with barbed wire and watchtowers."

"Locked at night?"

"Of course."

"I want monthly actions to reduce the number of Byelorussian Jews there in order to accommodate the Jews they're sending us from Hamburg."

"Yes, Herr General."

"You can start reducing the numbers now in the Drozdy camp. Make the selection voluntary. Ask those with university degrees and professional qualifications to come forward. Deprive them all of food and water to encourage volunteers. Those Jews you can keep for now. The rest you can liquidate immediately."

"Yes, Herr General."

"Himmler is coming here in a couple of weeks' time, so he'll want to see that we're making progress. Understand?"

"Yes, Herr General."

Nebe turned and finally looked at me. "You. Captain Gunther. Come with me."

I followed Nebe into the adjacent office, where four junior SS officers were reading files taken from an open filing cabinet.

"You lot," said Nebe. "Fuck off. And close the door behind you. And tell those lazy bastards next door to get rid of that body before it starts stinking the place out in this heat."

There were two desks in this office, overlooked by a set of French windows and a poor portrait of Stalin in a gray uniform with a red stripe down the side of his trouser leg, looking rather less Caucasian and more Oriental than was usual.

Nebe fetched a bottle of schnapps and glasses from one of the desk drawers and poured two large ones. He took his own drink without a word, like a man who was tired of seeing things straight, and poured himself another while I was still sniffing and tensing my liver.

MINSK, 1941

I hadn't seen Nebe in more than a year. He looked older and more worn than I remembered. His previously gray hair was now the same silver color as his War Merit Cross, while his eyes were as narrow as his pillbox slit of a mouth. Only his long nose and prominent ears seemed much the same.

"It's good to see you again, Bernie."

"Arthur."

"A whole lifetime spent arresting criminals, and now I've become a criminal myself." He chuckled wearily. "What do you think of that?"

"You could put a stop to it."

"What can I do? I'm just a cog in Heydrich's machine of death. The machine's in gear, too. I couldn't stop it even if I wanted to."

"You used to think you could make a difference."

"That was then. Hitler has the whip hand since the fall of France. There's no one who dares to oppose him now. Things will have to go badly in Russia for us before that can happen again. Which they will, of course. I'm certain of it. But not yet. People like you and me will have to bide our time."

"And until then, Arthur? What about these people?"

"You mean the yids?"

I nodded.

He tossed back his second drink and then shrugged.

"You really don't give a damn, do you?"

Nebe laughed a wry sort of laugh. "I've got quite a lot on my mind, Bernie," he said. "Himmler's coming here next month. What do you expect me to do? Sit him down somewhere quiet and explain that this is all very wrong? Explain that Jews are people, too? Tell the Emperor Charles the Fifth and the Diet of Worms, 'Here I stand, I can do no other'? Be reasonable, Bernie."

"Reasonable?"

"These men—Himmler, Heydrich, Muller—they're fanatics. You can't reason with fanatics." He shook his head. "I'm already under suspicion after the Elser plot."

"If you don't, you're no better than they are."

"I've got to be careful, Bernie. I'm only safe as long as I'm doing exactly what I'm told. And I've got to be safe if there's ever going to be another opportunity for us to get rid of Hitler." He poured his third drink in as many minutes. "Surely you of all people can understand that."

"All I know is that you're planning mass murder in this town."

"So go ahead and arrest me, Kommissar. Christ, I wish you would. Right now I'd love to see the inside of a police cell back at the Alex instead of this ghastly frontier town." He put down his glass and held out his wrists. "Here. Put the cuffs on. And get me out of here if you can. No? I thought not. You're as helpless as I am." He picked up his glass, drank it, and started another cigarette. "Exactly what did you tell those two bastards, anyway? Blume and Mundt?"

"Me? I said I didn't come to Russia to kill old women. Even if they were Jews."

"Unwise, Bernie. Unwise. Mundt is very highly thought of in Berlin. He's been a party member since 1926. That's even longer than me. Which counts for something with Hitler. You ought not to say such things again. At least not to the likes of Mundt. He could make life very awkward for you. You have no idea what some of these SS are capable of."

"I'm beginning to have a clear idea."

"Look, Bernie, there are others here in Byelorussia and in Germany who think the same way as me and you. Who are ready to move against Hitler when the time is right. We'll have need of men like you. Until then, it might be best if you were to keep your trap shut."

"Keep my trap shut and shoot some Jews, is that it?"

"Why not? Because you can take my word for it, shooting the Jews is just the beginning. After all, it's hardly the most efficient method of killing thousands of people. You wouldn't believe the pressure I'm under to come up with some other means of killing Jews."

"Why don't you just blow them all up?" I said. "Take all of the Jews in Byelorussia, assemble them in a field with a couple of thousand tons of TNT under their feet, and put a match to it. That should solve your problem very nicely."

"I wonder," said Nebe thoughtfully, "if that might work."

I shook my head in despair and, at last, downed the schnapps.

"I'd like to be able to count on you, Bernie. After all we've been through. In Berlin. There's no one in this godforsaken country I can really trust, you know. Certainly none of these other officers."

"I'm not even sure I can trust myself, Arthur. Not now that I've seen what I've seen. Not now that I know what I know."

Nebe refilled our glasses. "Hmm. That's what I suspected, you mad bastard." He grinned, bitterly. "You're just about capable of doing it, aren't you? Shooting your mouth off about the Jews when Himmler comes here to Minsk next month. Something like that. What am I to do with you?"

"I can be shot. Like some old Jew."

"If that was all there was to it," said Nebe, "then perhaps I'd make it happen. But you're being very naïve, just like always.

No German officer of RSHA gets shot without the Gestapo getting involved. Especially not a man with your background. Who was close to Heydrich. Who was close to me. They would want to interrogate you. To ask you questions that don't have a yes-or-no answer. And I can't afford that you might tell them something about me. About my past. About our past."

I was shaking my head, but I knew he was probably right.

Nebe grinned and started biting his fingernails, which I noticed were bitten right down to the quick.

"I wish I could stop doing this," he said. "My mother used to dip my fingers in cat shit to try to prevent me from doing it. Doesn't seem to have worked, does it?"

"You've still got shit on your fingers, Arthur."

"But I can see now it was me who was being naïve. About you. I need you out of Minsk before you open that stupid trap of yours when I'm not around to prevent it, and get yourself arrested. And possibly me, too. You're too old for frontline duty. They wouldn't take you. So that's out." He sighed. "I can see it's going to have to be intelligence. There's precious little of that to go around in this war, so you should fit in. Of course, they'll think you're a spy, so this will have to be a temporary attachment. Until I can think of something to get you safely back to Berlin, where you can't do any harm."

"Don't do me any favors," I said. "I'll take my chances."

"But I won't. That's rather the point I've been making." He pointed at my drink. "Come on. Get that down and cheer up. And stop worrying about a few Jews. People have been killing Jews since the Emperor Claudius ordered them expelled from Rome. What does Luther say? That next to the devil there is no more bitter, more poisonous, more vehement enemy than a real Jew. And let's not forget the Kaiser, Wilhelm the Second, who said that a Jew cannot be a true patriot—that he is something different, like a bad insect. Even Benjamin Franklin thought that Jews were vampires." Nebe shook his head and grinned. "No, Bernie. You'd better pick another reason to hate the Nazis. There are any number of reasons. But not the Jews. Not the Jews. Maybe if there are enough pogroms in Europe they'll get their fucking homeland, like that British idiot Balfour promised, and then they'll leave the rest of us in peace."

I drank the schnapps. What else was I going to do with it? People say all kinds of crazy things when they've had a drink—me included. They talk about God and the saints and hearing voices and seeing the devil; they shout about killing Franzis and Tommies, and they sing Christmas carols on a summer's day. Their wives don't understand them and their mothers never loved them. They'll say black is white, up is down, and hot is cold. No one ever expects a drink to help you make sense. Arthur Nebe had taken several drinks, but he wasn't drunk. Even so, what he said sounded crazier than any drunk I'd ever heard and ever hope to hear again.

I stayed at Lenin House for two or three weeks, sharing a seventh-floor billet with Waldemar Klingelhöfer, who was an SS-Obersturmbannführer—a colonel—in overall charge of the anti-partisan hunts in the Minsk area.

Minsk was one place where German propaganda did not exaggerate the strength of local partisans, who took advantage of the huge thick forests called *pushcha* that characterized the area. Most of these fighters were young Red Army soldiers, but quite a few were Jews who'd fled from pogroms to the comparative safety of the forest. What did they have to lose? Not that the Jews were always welcomed with open arms: Some of the Byelorussians were no less anti-Semitic than Germans, and more than half of these refugee Jews were murdered by the Popovs.

Klingelhöfer spoke fluent Russian—he'd been born in Moscow—but he knew nothing about police work or hunting partisans. Real partisans. I gave him some advice on how to recruit some informers.

Not that my advice to Klingelhöfer really mattered, because at the end of July Nebe ordered him to Smolensk to obtain furs for German army winter clothing, and I was ordered to Baranowicze, about one hundred fifty kilometers southwest of Minsk, to await transport back to Berlin.

Formerly a Polish city until the Soviets occupied it at the beginning of the war, Baranowicze was a small, prosperous town of about thirty thousand people, more than a third of whom were Jews. In its center was a long, wide, suburban-looking tree-lined street with two-story shops and houses, which the occupying German army had renamed Kaiser Wilhelm Strasse. There was an Orthodox cathedral recently built in the neoclassical style, and a ghetto—six buildings on the outskirts of the city—where more than twelve thousand Jews were now confined, at least those Jews who had not escaped into the Pripet Marshes. Two whole regiments of the SS Cavalry Brigade commanded by Sturmbannführer Bruno Magill were searching the thirty-eight-thousand-acre marshland, killing every Jew they could find. This left the city quiet—so quiet that for a couple of days, until a seat became available on a Ju 52 back to Tegel Airfield in Berlin, I was able to sleep in a proper bed in what formerly had been Girsh Bregman's Leather Goods and Shoe Store.

I tried not to consider the sudden fate that had overtaken Girsh Bregman and his family, whose framed photographs were still on top of an upright Rheinberg Söhne in the little parlor behind the shop; but it was only too easy to think of them enduring the close privations of the ghetto, or perhaps fleeing their persecutors, who included not just the SS but also the Polish police, former Polish army soldiers, and even some local Ukrainian clergy who were keen to bless these "pacifications." Of course, it was possible that the Bregmans were already pacified, which is to say that they were dead. That's about as pacified as you could get in the summer of 1941. Most of all, I just hoped they were alive. Only, it was the kind of hope that looked like a canary in a mine full of gas. I wouldn't have minded a little gas myself. Just enough to sleep for about a hundred years and then wake up from the nightmare that was my life.

GERMANY, 1954

"At least you did wake up," said Silverman. "Unlike six million others."

"You're a funny guy. Are you always so quick with math, or is it just that one number you like?"

"I don't like anything about it, Gunther," said Silverman.

"Neither do I. And please don't ever make the mistake of thinking I do."

"It's not me that makes mistakes, Gunther. It's you."

"You're right. I should have made sure I was born somewhere other than Germany in 1896. That way maybe I could have ended up on the winning side. Twice. How does it feel, boys? To sit in judgment on someone else's mistakes? Pretty good, I imagine. The way you two act, anyone might think you Americans really do believe that you're better than anyone else."

"Not everyone else," snarled Earp. "Just you and your Nazi pals."

"You can keep telling yourself that, if you like. But we both know it's not true. Or is it that occupying the moral high ground is more than an aspiration for you Amis? Perhaps it's also a constitutional necessity. Only, I suspect that underneath all that sanctimony you're just like us Germans. You really do believe that might is right."

"At this moment," said Silverman, "all that really matters is what we believe about you."

"He tells a good story." Earl was speaking to Silverman. "A regular Jakob Grimm, this guy. All it lacked was the 'once upon a time' and the 'happily ever after.' We should get him some heated iron shoes and make him dance around the room in them like Snow White's stepmother until he's straight with us."

"You're quite correct," said Silverman. "And you know? Only a German could have thought of a punishment like that."

"Didn't you say you had German parents?" I said. "Just a mother you're sure about, I presume."

"Neither of us feels very proud of our German background," said Earp. "Thanks to people like you."

For a while the three of us were silent. Then Silverman said:

"There was a Gunther we heard about in that town you mentioned. Baranowicze. He was an SS-Sturmbannführer with one of the small killing units belonging to Arthur Nebe's Task Group B. A Sonderkommando. He organized one of the early gassings. Everyone in a mental hospital at Mogilev was killed. That wouldn't be you, would it?"

"No," I said. But seeing that they were hardly likely to be satisfied with a straight denial, I lifted my finger to indicate that I was trying to remember something. And then I did. "I think there was an SS-Sturmbannführer called Günther Rausch. Attached to Task Group B in the summer of 1941. It must be him you're thinking of. I never gassed anyone. Not even the fleas in my bed."

"But it was you who suggested to Arthur Nebe the idea of mass killings using explosives, wasn't it? You admitted as much yourself."

"That was a joke."

"Not a very funny joke."

"When it comes to blowing people up, I don't think anyone has ever managed that more efficiently than America," I said. "How many did you blow up in Hiroshima? And Nagasaki? A couple of hundred thousand and still counting. That's what I've read. Germany might have started the process of mechanized mass killing, but you Americans certainly perfected it."

"Did you ever visit the Criminal Technology Institute in Berlin?"

"Yes," I said. "I often went there in the course of my duty as a detective. For forensic tests and results."

"Did you ever meet a chemist called Albert Wildmann?"

"Yes. I met him. Many times."

"And Hans Schmidt? Also from the same institute?"

"I think so. What are you driving at?"

"Isn't it the case that you returned from Minsk to Berlin at the behest of Arthur Nebe, not to join the German War Crimes Bureau, as you told us, but to meet with Wildmann and Schmidt in pursuit of your explosives idea?"

I was shaking my head, but Silverman wasn't paying attention, and I was gaining a new respect for him as an interrogator.

"And that, having discussed the idea in detail, you yourself returned to Smolensk with Wildmann and Schmidt in September 1941?"

"No. That's not true. Like I said, I think you must be confusing me with Günther Rausch."

"Isn't it the case that you brought with you a large quantity of dynamite? And used it to rig a Russian pillbox with explosives? And that you then herded into it almost a hundred people from a mental asylum in Minsk? And that you then detonated the explosives? Isn't that what happened?"

"No. That's not true. I had nothing to do with that."

"According to the reports we've read, the heads and limbs of the dead were strewn across a quarter-mile radius. SS men were collecting body parts from the trees for days afterward."

I shook my head. "When I made that remark to Nebe . . . about blowing up Jews in a field. Look, I had no idea he would actually try something like that. It was sarcasm. Hardly a genuine suggestion." I shrugged. "Then again, I don't know why I'm surprised, given everything else that happened."

"We've always thought it was Arthur Nebe himself who came up with the idea of the gas vans," said Silverman. "So maybe that was another of your jokes, too. Tell me, did you ever visit an address in Berlin—number four Tiergartenstrasse?"

"I was a cop. I visited a lot of addresses I don't remember."

"This one was special."

"The Berlin Gas Works was somewhere else, if that's what you're implying."

"Tiergartenstrasse number four was a confiscated Jewish villa," said Silverman. "An office from where Germany's euthanasia program for the handicapped was planned and administered."

"Then I'm sure I was never there."

"Maybe you heard about what was happening there and mentioned it in passing to Nebe. As a little thank-you for getting you out of Minsk."

"In case you've forgotten," I said, "Nebe was head of Kripo and, before that, a general in the Gestapo. It's quite likely he knew Wildmann and Schmidt for the same reason I did. And I daresay he would have known all about this place in Tiergartenstrasse as well. But I never did."

"Your relationship with Waldemar Klingelhöfer," said Silverman. "You were quite helpful to him. With advice."

"Yes. I tried to be."

"Were you helpful in any other ways?"

I shook my head.

"Did you accompany him to Moscow, for example?"

"No, I've never been in Moscow."

"And yet you speak Russian almost as well as he does."

"That was later, when I learned. In the labor camp, mostly."

"So between September 28 and October 26, 1941, you say you were not with Klingelhöfer's Vorkommando Moscow, but in Berlin?"

"Yes."

"And that you had nothing to do with the murders of five hundred and seventy-two Jews during that time?"

"Nothing to do with it, no."

"Several of them were Jewish mink ranchers who failed to provide the prescribed quota of furs for Klingelhöfer."

"Never shot a Jewish mink rancher, Gunther?"

"Or blown one up in a pillbox?"

"No."

The two lawyers were quiet for a moment, as if they'd run out of questions. The silence didn't last long.

"So," said Silverman. "You're not in Moscow, you're back on the plane to Berlin. A Junkers 52, you said. Any witnesses?"

I thought for a moment. "Fellow named Schulz. Erwin Schulz."

"Go on."

"He was SS, too. A Sturmbannführer, I think. But before, he'd been a cop in Berlin. And then an instructor at the police academy in Bremen. After that, something in the Gestapo, maybe in Bremen, too. I don't remember. But we hadn't seen each other in more than ten years when we both got on that plane out of Baranowicze.

"He was a few years younger than me, I think. Not much. I think he'd been in the army during the last months of the Great War. And then the Freikorps while he was at university, in Berlin. Law, I think. Tallish, fair-haired, with a mustache a bit like Hitler's, and quite tanned. Not that he looked well when he was on that plane. There were huge bags under his eyes that were more like bruises, almost as if someone had punched him.

"Well, we recognized each other, and after a few moments we started talking. I offered him a cigarette and I noticed the hand that took it was shaking like a leaf. His leg wouldn't stay still either. Like it had Saint Vitus' dance. He was a nervous wreck. Gradually, it became clear that he was returning to Berlin for much the same reason I was. Because he'd put in for a transfer.

"Schulz said that his unit had been operating in a place called Zhitomir. That's just a shit hole between Kiev and Brest. No one in his right mind would want to go to Zhitomir. Which is probably why the SS brass in the person of General Jeckeln had established its Ukrainian HQ there. Jeckeln was never in his right mind, as far as I could see. Anyway, Schulz said that Jeckeln had told him that all of the Jews in Zhitomir were to be shot immediately. Schulz wasn't bothered about the men. But he had more than a few qualms about the women and the children. Fuck that, he said. But no one was listening. Orders were orders and he should just shut up and get on with it. Well, it seemed that there were a lot of Jews in Zhitomir. Christ only knows why that should be the case. After all, it's not like the Popovs ever made them feel welcome there. The tsar hated them, too, and they had pogroms in Zhitomir in 1905 and in 1919. I mean, you would think they'd have got the message and cleared off somewhere else. But no. Not a bit of it. There were three synagogues in Zhitomir, and when the SS showed up, there were thirty thousand of them just waiting around for something to happen. Which it did.

"According to Schulz, the first day the SS got there they hanged the mayor, or perhaps it was the local judge, who was a Jew, and several others. Then they shot four hundred right away for one reason or another. Marched them out of town to a pit, had them lie down like sardines, one on top of the other, and shot them in layers. Well, Schulz thought that would be it. He'd done his bit and that was enough. I mean, four hundred, he thought. But no, he said, they kept on coming. Day after day. And four hundred Jews soon became fourteen thousand.

"Then Schulz was told that they would have to do the women and children as well and for him that was the last straw. Fuck this, he thought, I don't care if Almighty God has ordered this, I'm not killing women and kids. So he wrote to the personnel officer at RSHA HQ. To a General Bruno Streckenbach. And put in for a transfer. Which was why he was on that plane with me.

"They were pretty pissed off with him, apparently. Especially his CO, Otto Rasch. He accused Schulz of being weak and letting the side down. He asked Schulz where was his sense of duty and all that crap. Not that Schulz said he was surprised about this. He said that Rasch was one of those bastards who liked to make sure that everyone, officers included, had to pull the trigger on at least one Jew. So that we were all equally guilty, I suppose. Only he had another word for it: one of those compound words that Himmler used at Pretzsch. *Blood part,* I think it was.

"Anyway, Schulz didn't know what fate awaited him back in Berlin. He was nervous and apprehensive, to say the least. I suppose he was hoping his behavior would be overlooked and he'd get the okay to resume his police work in Hamburg, or Bremen. 'I'm not cut out for this kind of thing,' he said. 'Don't get me wrong, he said, 'I care nothing for the Jews, but no one should be asked to do this kind of work. No one. They should find some other means of doing it,' he said. That's what he told me, anyway."

"So," said Earp. "Are you telling us your alibi is another convicted war criminal?"

"Schulz was convicted? I didn't know that."

"Gave himself up in 1945," said Earp. "He was convicted in October 1947 of crimes against humanity and sentenced to twenty years. That was commuted to fifteen years in 1951."

"You mean he's here, in Landsberg? Well, then he can confirm our conversation on the flight back to Berlin. That I told him what I already told you. How I was sent back for refusing to kill Jews."

"He was paroled last January," said Earp. "Too bad, Gunther."

"I don't think he'd have made such a great character witness for you, anyway," said Silverman. "He was a brigadier general in the SS when he gave himself up."

"The reason Bruno Streckenbach went easy on Schulz is obvious," said Earp. "Because he participated in the murders of fifteen thousand Jews before he sickened of the work. Probably Streckenbach figured Schulz had done more than his fair share of killing."

"And I guess that must be why you let him go, too," I said.

"I told you," said Silverman. "That was down to the high commissioner. And the recommendations of the Parole and Clemency Board for War Criminals."

I shook my head. I was tired. They'd been nipping at my heels the whole day like a pair of nine-to-five bloodhounds. I felt like I was trapped up a tree with nowhere left to run.

"Have you considered the possibility that I could be telling the truth? But even if I wasn't, I might be tempted to put my hands up just to get you two off my back. The way you hand out paroles around here, I'd have to be Hideki Tojo to get more than six months."

"We like things to be neat," said Silverman.

"And you have got more loose ends than an old maid's sewing basket," added Earp. "So that when we leave this job, we can be sure that we gave it our best shot."

"Pride in the job, huh? I can understand that."

"So," said Silverman. "We're going to look into your story. Comb it through for nits."

"That still won't make me a louse."

"You were SS," said Silverman. "I'm a Jew. And you'll always be a louse in my book, Gunther."

GERMANY, 1954

It was easy to forget that we were in Germany. There was a U.S. flag in the main hall and the kitchens—which were seemingly always in action—served plain home-cooking on the understanding that home was six thousand kilometers to the west. Most of the voices we heard were American, too: loud, manly voices that told you to do something or not to do something—in English. And we did it quickly, too, or we received a prod from a nightstick or a kick up the backside. Nobody complained. Nobody would have listened, except perhaps Father Morgenweiss. The guards were MPs, deliberately selected for their enormous size. It was hard to see how Germany could ever have expected to win a war against this more obvious-looking master race. They walked the landings and corridors of Landsberg Prison like gunfighters from the OK Corral, or perhaps boxers entering the ring. With each other they had an easy way about them: They were all big, well-brushed smiles and booming laughs, shouting jokes and baseball scores. For us, the inmates, however, there were only stone faces and belligerent attitudes. Fuck you, they seemed to say; you might have your own federal government, but we're the real masters in this pariah country.

I had a cell for two to myself. It wasn't because I was special or because I hadn't yet been charged with anything, but because WCPN1 was half empty. Every week, it seemed, someone else was released. But immediately after the war Landsberg had been full of prisoners. The Amis had even incarcerated Jewish displaced persons there, from the concentration camps of nearby Kaufering, alongside prominent Nazis and war criminals; but forcing those same ragged, threadbare Jews to wear SS uniforms had, perhaps, demonstrated a want of sensitivity on the part of the Americans that almost bordered on the comic. Not that the Amis were capable of seeing the funny side of anything very much.

The Jewish DPs were long gone from Landsberg now, to Israel, Great Britain, and America, but the gallows was still there, and from time to time the guards tested it just to make sure everything was working smoothly. They were thoughtful like that. No one really believed the German federal government was planning to bring back the death penalty; then again, no one really believed the Amis gave a damn what the federal government thought about anything. They certainly didn't give a damn about scaring the prisoners, because at the same time that they tested the gallows they rehearsed the whole ghastly procedure of an execution with a volunteer prisoner taking the place of a condemned man. These monthly rehearsals took place on a Friday, because it was an old Landsberg tradition that Friday was a hanging day. A team of eight MPs solemnly marched the condemned man into the central courtyard and up the steps to the roof where the gallows was, and there they slipped a hood over the man's head and a noose around his neck; the prison director even read out a death sentence while the rest of them stood at attention and pretended—probably wished—it was the real thing. Or so I was told. It might reasonably be asked why anyone, least of all a German officer, would volunteer for such a duty; but as with everything else in Germany, the Amis got exactly what they wanted by offering the volunteer extra cigarettes, chocolate, and a glass of schnapps. And it was always the same prisoner who volunteered to step onto the gallows: Waldemar Klingelhöfer. Perhaps the Amis were unwise to do this, given that he'd already tried to open a vein in his wrist with a large safety pin; then again, it's no good looking for a whole flock when you've only got one sheep.

It wasn't guilt about killing Jews that made Klingelhöfer try to kill himself and volunteer for a practice execution; it was his guilt over the betrayal of another SS officer, Erich Naumann. Naumann had written a letter to Klingelhöfer instructing him what to tell his interrogators and reminding him that there were no reports for the activities of Task Group B, which he himself had commanded after Nebe; but this advice also revealed the true depth of Naumann's own criminality in Minsk and Smolensk. Klingelhöfer, who was deeply conflicted about the collapse of the German Reich, handed Naumann's letter to the Amis, who produced it at the Einsatz-gruppen trial in 1948 and used it as prima facie evidence against him. The letter helped convict Naumann and send him to the gallows in June 1951.

The consequence of all this was that none of the other prisoners spoke to Klingelhöfer. No one except me. And probably no one would have spoken to me either but for the fact that I was the only one currently being interrogated by the Americans. This made some of my former comrades very nervous indeed, and one day two of them followed me out of the common room where we ate, played cards, and listened to the radio, and into the courtyard.

"Hauptmann Gunther. We would like a word with you, please."

Ernst Biberstein and Walter Haensch were both senior SS officers and, regarding themselves not as criminals but as POWs, persisted in the use of military ranks. Biberstein, a Standarten-führer, equivalent to a full colonel, did most of the talking, while the younger Haensch—only a lieutenant colonel—did most of the agreeing.

"It's several years since I myself was interrogated by the Amis," said Biberstein. "I think it must be almost seven years ago now. No doubt these things are different from the way they used to be. We live in rather more hopeful, even enlightened circumstances than we did back then."

"The Americans no longer seem to be driven by the same sense of moral superiority and desire for retribution," added Haensch redundantly.

"Nevertheless," continued Biberstein, "it's important to be careful what one tells them. During an interrogation they sometimes have an easygoing way about them and can appear to be one's friends when in fact they're anything but that. I'm not sure if you ever met our late lamented comrade Otto Ohlendorf, but for a long time he made himself very useful to the Amis, volunteering information without restraint in the misguided expectation that he might curry favor with them and, as a result, secure his freedom. Too late, however, he realized his mistake and, having given evidence against General Kaltenbrunner at Nuremberg and effectively sent him to his death, he discovered that he had managed to talk his way onto the gallows."

Biberstein had a thoughtful-looking face, with a broad forehead and a skeptical cast to his mouth. There was something of the serious clown about him—an authority figure and white-faced straight man whose sour, rising diphthongs and way of speaking at someone instead of to them reminded me that before joining the SS and the SD, Biberstein had been a Lutheran minister in some northern peasant town where they didn't seem to mind that their pastor was a long-standing Nazi Party member. Probably they hadn't minded, either, that he led a murder commando in Russia before being promoted and asked to take charge of the Gestapo in southern Poland. A lot of Lutherans had seen Hitler as Luther's true heir. Maybe he was. I didn't think I'd have liked Luther any more than I ever liked Hitler. Or Biberstein.

"I wouldn't like you to make the same mistake as Otto," said Biberstein. "So I'd like to give you some advice. If you can't remember something, then really you should just say so. No matter how feeble that might seem or how culpable it might make you look. When you're in any doubt at all, remind the Amis that this all happened almost fifteen years ago and that you really can't remember."

"Speaking for myself," said Haensch, "I have always maintained that any prisoner has the right to silence. This is a legal principle known and respected throughout the civilized world. And especially in the United States of America. I was a lawyer in Hirschfelde prior to joining the RSHA, and you can take it from me that there is no court in the Western world that can force a man to give evidence against himself."

"They managed to convict you, didn't they?" I said.

"I was convicted in error," insisted the bespectacled Haensch, who had a lawyer's slimy face to match his lawyer's slimy manner and even slimier patter. "Heydrich did not order me to Russia until March 1942, by which time Task Group C had more or less completed its work. Quite simply, there were no Jews left to kill. However, all of this is beside the point. As Biberstein says, this happened almost fifteen years ago. And one cannot be asked to remember things that happened then."

He took off his glasses, cleaned them, and added exasperatedly, "Besides, it was war. We were fighting for our very survival as a race. Things happen in war that one regrets in peacetime. That's natural. But the Amis weren't exactly saints in wartime themselves. Ask Peiper. Ask Dietrich. They'll tell you. It wasn't just the SS who shot prisoners, it was the Amis as well. To say nothing of the systematic mistreatment of the Malmédy prisoners of war that has occurred in this and other prisons."

Haensch twitched nervously. His were the kind of chinless, weak features that gave war criminals and mass murderers a bad name. Not that the Amis looked on Haensch with any more disgust than anyone else. That particular distinction was reserved for Sepp Dietrich, Jochen Peiper, and the perpetrators of the so-called Malmédy Massacre.

"Just remember this," said Biberstein. "That we're not without friends on the outside. You certainly should not feel that you are alone. Dr. Rudolf Aschenauer has represented hundreds of old comrades, including Walter Funk, our former economics minister. He is a most ingenious attorney-at-law. As well as being a former party member, he is also a devout Roman Catholic. I'm not sure what your religious affiliations are, Hauptmann Gunther, but it cannot be denied that in this part of the country, the Catholics have the louder voice. The Catholic bishop of Munich, Johannes Neuhäusler, and the cardinal of Cologne, Joseph Frings, are active lobbyists on our behalf. But so is the evangelical bishop of Bavaria, Hans Meiser. In other words, it might be in your interests to find your Christian faith again, since both churches support the Committee for Church Aid for Prisoners."

"I myself have had the personal support of the evangelical bishop of Württemberg, Theo Wurm," said Haensch. "As has our comrade, Martin Sandberger. And you needn't worry about paying for a defense. The committee will take care of all your legal team's expenses. The committee even has the backing of a few sympathetic U.S. senators and congressmen."

"Quite so," said Biberstein. "These are men who have been most vocal in their opposition to Jewish-inspired ideas of vengeance." He turned for a moment and waved his hand dismissively at Landsberg's brick walls. "Which is all this is, of course. Keeping us here, against all the rules of international law."

"The important thing is that we all stick together," said Haensch. "The last thing we want now is any unnecessary speculation as to what some of us did or did not do. Do you see? That would only complicate matters."

"In other words, it would be desirable, Hauptmann Gunther, if your statements to the Amis concerned only yourself."

"Now I get it," I said. "And here I was thinking it was really my welfare you were concerned about."

"Oh, but it is," said Haensch. "My dear fellow, it is."

"You've got a big pile of potatoes in the office of the Parole and Clemency Board," I said. "And you don't want anyone like me knocking it over."

"Naturally, we want to get out of here," said Haensch. "Some of us have families."

"It's not just in our interest that we're released soon," said Biberstein. "It's in Germany's interest that we draw a line in front of what happened and then move on. Only then, when the last prisoner of war has been released from here and in Russia, can we Germans plan for the future."

"Not just German interest," added Haensch. "It's in American and British interest, too, that good relations are fostered with a fully sovereign German government, so that the real ideological enemy can be effectively opposed."

"Don't you think we've killed enough Russians?" I asked. "Stalin's dead. The Korean War is over."

"No one is talking about killing anyone," insisted Biberstein. "But we're still at war with the communists, whether you like it or not. A cold war, it's true, but a war nonetheless. Look, I don't know what you did during the war and I don't want to know. None of us do. No one in here talks about anything that happened back then. The important thing is to remember that every man in this prison is agreed on one thing: that none of us is or was criminally responsible for his acts or those of his men because we were all of us following orders. Whatever our personal feelings or misgivings about the odious work we were tasked with, it was a Führer order and it was impossible to disobey. As long as we all stick to that story, it's certain we can all of us be out of this place before the decade is out."

"And hopefully, well before that," added Haensch.

I nodded, which was misleading, because it made me look as if I cared what happened to any of them. I nodded because I didn't want any trouble, and just because they were convicts was no reason they couldn't give me any. The Amis wouldn't have minded that at all. Unlike the Parole and Clemency Board, most of the MPs in Landsberg were of the opinion that we all deserved to hang; and possibly they were right. But most of the reason I nodded was that I was tired of not being liked by anyone, including myself. That's okay when you can go and put that feeling under several milliliters of alcohol, but the bars in prison are never open, especially when you need a drink the way I needed one now. Life in most prisons would be improved by the ration of a daily tot of liquor, like the British Royal Navy. That's not a penal theory with which Jeremy Bentham would have agreed, but you can take it to the bank.

Most of all, I could have used a drink at night just before I went to bed. Perhaps it was having to talk about and relive the summer of 1941, but while I was in Landsberg, sleep provided little respite from the cares of the world. Often I would awake in the unfocused gloom of my cell and find myself soaked in sweat, having dreamed an awful dream. And more often than not it was the same dream. Of earth shifting strangely beneath my feet, turned not by any unseen animal but by some darker, subterranean elemental force. And as I watched closely, I saw the black ground as it shifted again and the blank-eyed head and spiderlike hands of some murdered Lazarus, self-rising from its own corpse gases, appeared on the mysterious surface. Thin and white like a clay pipe, the naked creature lifted its behind, its chest, and, last of all, its skull, moving backward and unnaturally, the way a collapsed puppet might arrange its various limbs until, at last, it appeared to be kneeling in front of a cloud of smoke, which cleared suddenly as it was sucked into the muzzle of the pistol in my steady hand.

GERMANY, 1954

I t's one of life's little jokes that whenever you think things can hardly get any worse they usually do.

I must have fallen asleep again, and for a moment I thought it was just another bad dream. I felt several pairs of hands upon me, turning me over onto my stomach and ripping the pajama jacket off my back; and then I was simultaneously hooded and handcuffed. As the manacles pinched my wrists painfully I cried out, and for this sound I received a punch on the head.

"Quiet," murmured a voice—an American voice. "Or you'll get another."

The hands, which wore rubber gloves, hauled me onto my feet. Someone dragged down my pajama trousers and I was dragged and then marched out of my cell, along the landing, and down the stairs. We went outside briefly and crossed the yard. Doors opened and slammed behind us, and after that I quickly lost track of where I was beyond the obvious fact that I was still within the walls of Landsberg. I felt a hand push down on top of my hooded head.

"Sit down," said a voice.

I sat, and that would have been fine except that there was no chair and I heard several loud guffaws as I lay sprawled in pain on the stone-flagged floor.

"Did you think of that one all by yourself?" I said. "Or did you get the idea from a movie?"

"I told you to shut up." Someone kicked me in the small of my back, not so hard as to cause any damage but enough to shut me up. "Speak when spoken to."

More hands picked me up again and dumped me onto a chair, and this time it was there.

Then I heard lots of footsteps leaving the room and a door closing but not being locked, and I might have supposed myself alone but for the fact that I could smell the smoke from a cigarette. I would have asked for one myself if I thought I could have smoked it with a hood over my head. There was that and the chance I might get kicked or punched again. So I stayed quiet, telling myself that despite their threats this was the opposite of what they wanted. Unless you're going to put a man on a gallows trapdoor and hang him, you hood him for only one reason: to help soften him up and make him talk. The only thing was, I couldn't imagine what they wanted me to say that I hadn't already told them.

Ten minutes passed. Maybe longer. But probably less. Time starts to expand when they take your light away. I closed my eyes. That way it was me in control and not them. Even if they took the hood off now I wouldn't see anything. I took a deep breath and let it out as steadily as I could, trying to get ahold of my fear. Telling myself I'd been in tighter spots. That after the mud of Amiens in 1918 this was easy. There weren't even any shells bursting over- head. I was still wearing four limbs and my balls. A hood was nothing. They wanted me not to see anything, then that was fine with me. I'd lived through black and sightless days before; they don't come much blacker than Amiens. The black day of the Ger- man army, Ludendorff called it, and not without justification. What else do you call it when you're facing a force of four hundred fifty tanks and thirteen divisions of Anzacs? With more arriving all the time.

I heard a match and caught the smoke of another cigarette. A chain-smoker, perhaps? Or someone else? I took a deep breath and tried to get ahold of some smoke in my own lungs. American tobacco, that much was clear from the sweet smell. Probably they put sugar in it the way they put sugar in almost everything—in coffee, in liquor, on fresh fruit. Maybe they put sugar on their wives, too, and if the men were anything to go by, they probably needed a little sweetening.

Not long after my arrival at Landsberg, Hermann Priess, the former commander of the offending SS troop at Malmédy, during the Battle of the Bulge, had told me about this kind of rough treatment at the hands of the Americans. Before their trial for the murder of ninety U.S. servicemen, Priess, Peiper, and seventy-four other men had been hooded and beaten and forced to sign confessions. The whole incident had caused quite a stink at the International Court of Justice and in the U.S. Senate. Since I hadn't yet been beaten, it was perhaps a little too early to say that the American military was incapable of learning a lesson in human rights, but underneath my hood, I wasn't holding my breath.

"Congratulations, Gunther. That's the longest anyone wearing a hood in here has ever kept his mouth shut."

The man was speaking German, quite good German, too, but I was sure it wasn't Silverman or Earp. For the moment I kept my mouth shut. And what was there to say? That's the thing about being interrogated: You always know that eventually someone is going to ask you a question.

"I've been reading over the case notes," said the voice. "Your case notes. The ones made by Silverman and Earp. By the way, they won't be joining us for the rest of your questioning. They don't approve of the way we do things."

All the time he was speaking, I was tensed for the blow I felt sure was coming. One of the other prisoners told me the Amis had beaten him for a whole hour in Schwabisch Hall in an effort to get him to incriminate Jochen Peiper.

"Relax, Gunther. No one is going to hit you. So long as you cooperate, you'll be just fine. The hood's for my protection. Outside of this place it might be awkward for both of us if you ever recognized me. You see, I work for the Central Intelligence Agency."

"And what about your friend? The other man in here? Does he work for the CIA as well?"

"You've got good ears, Gunther, I'll say that for you," said the other Ami. "Maybe that's why you've lived so long." His German was good, too. "Yes, I'm also with the CIA."

"Congratulations. That must make you both very proud."

"No, no. Congratulations to you, Gunther. Silverman and Earp have cleared you of any criminal wrongdoing." This was the first voice speaking now. "They're satisfied that you didn't murder anyone. At least not by the inflated standard of everyone else who's in here." He laughed. "I know. That's not saying much. But there it is. As far as Uncle Sam is concerned, you're not a war criminal."

"Well, that's a relief," I said. "If it wasn't for these handcuffs, I might punch the air."

"They said you had a smart mouth. And they're not wrong. They're just a little naïve, perhaps. About you, I mean."

"Over the years," said the other man, "you've caused us quite a few problems. Do you know that?"

"I'm pleased to hear it."

"In Garmisch-Partenkirchen. In Vienna. As a matter of fact, you and I have met before. In the military hospital at the Stiftskaserne?"

"You didn't speak German then," I said.

"Actually, I did. But it suited me to let you and that American army officer, Roy Shields, think otherwise."

"I remember you. Like it was yesterday."

"Sure you do."

"And let's not forget our mutual friend, Jonathan Jacobs."

"How is he? Dead, I hope."

"No. But he's still adamant you tried to kill him. Apparently, he found a box full of anopheles mosquitoes in the backseat of his Buick. Fortunately for him, they were all dead of cold."

"Pity."

"German winters can be brutal."

"Not brutal enough, it would seem," I said. "Almost ten years after the war, and you're still here."

"It's a different kind of war now."

"We're all on the same side."

"Sure," I said. "I know that. But if this is how you treat your friends, I'm beginning to see why the Russians went over to the other side."

"It wouldn't be sensible to get smart with us, Gunther. Not in your position. We don't like wise guys."

"I always thought that being wise was a useful part of intelligence."

"Doing what you're told when you're told is of greater value in our work."

"You disappoint me."

"That's of no real consequence beside the fact that you don't disappoint us."

"I can feel that. I can't feel my hands, but I can feel that. But I should warn you. I might be wearing a hood, but I've seen your cards. You want something from me. And since it can't be my body, it must be because you think I possess some information that's important to you. And believe me, it won't sound the same if you've just kicked my teeth in."

"There are other things we can do to loosen your tongue, besides kicking your teeth in."

"Sure. And I can do fiction as well as nonfiction. You won't even see the join. Look, the war is over now. I'm more than willing to tell you whatever you want to know. But you'll find I respond a lot better to sugar bread than to the whip. So how about you take off these hand irons and find me some clothes? You've made your point."

The two CIA agents were silent for a minute. I imagined one nodding at the other, who was probably shaking his head and mouthing a very clear "No" like a couple of gossipy old women. Then one of them laughed.

"Did you see this guy bring a case full of samples in here?"

"A regular Fuller Brush man, isn't he?"

"Red Skelton with a bag over his head. Still trying to make a sale."

"Not buying, huh?" I said. "Too bad. Maybe I ought to speak to the man of the house."

"I don't think a bag over his head was enough."

"It's not too late for a noose. Maybe we should just hand him over to the Ivans and have done with it."

"Aw, look, he's stopped talking now."

"Did we get your attention, Red?"

"You don't want brushes," I said. "Okay. So why don't you tell me what you do want?"

"When we're ready, Gunther, and not before."

"My friend here could tear a phone book in half, but he prefers this as a demonstration of our power over you. It's a lot less effort, and more than just seeing the power of the spirit, you can feel it, too. We wouldn't want you walking out of here and telling all your Nazi friends how soft we are."

"We worked it out. People were more afraid of the Ivans than they were of us."

"So you decided to be more like them," I said. "To play just as rough as they do. Sure, I get it."

"That's right, Gunther. Which brings us back to brushes. Or rather, one particular brush."

"A name you mentioned to Silverman and Earl. Erich Mielke."

"I remember. What about him?"

"They formed the distinct impression that you knew him."

"We've met. So what?"

"You must have known him quite well."

"How did you figure that out?"

"You were looking out of a window at Erhard Milch when he was being released from the front gate. How far is that?"

"Sixty, seventy feet. You must have good eyesight, Gunther."

"For reading I wear glasses," I said.

"You can have them. When you sign your confession."

"What confession?"

"The one you're going to sign, Gunther."

"I thought you said that Silverman and Earp had cleared me."

"They did. This is our Ohio Casualty policy. It adds fidelity and surety to whatever you tell us about Erich Mielke."

"That means we own your ass, Gunther."

"What's in this confession?"

"Does it matter?"

He had a point. They could say anything they wanted and I'd have to like it. "All right. I'll sign it."

"You took that in your stride."

"I used to be a tall man in a circus. Besides, I've been walking around for a while now and I'm tired. I just want to go home and give my long legs a rest."

"How about you give us a different act? Like Mr. Memory."

"You haven't yet told me why you're so interested in him," I said. "Which means I don't know what to leave in or to leave out."

"All of it," said the other. "We want all of it. Every detail. We'll get to why later."

"You want the whole of Leviticus? Or just Mielke?"

"Let's go back to the beginning."

"Genesis, then. Sure. Darkness was upon the face of Berlin. For me, at any rate. And Walter Ulbricht said let there be some communist thugs; and Adolf Hitler said let there be some Nazi thugs, too. And Chancellor Brüning said let the cops try to keep these two sides apart. And God said why don't you give the cops something a little easier than that to do? Because the evening and the morning were just one thing after another. Trouble. And the name of the river was the Spree and we were fishing bodies out of it every day. One day a communist and the next day a Nazi. And some men looked at that and said that it was good. As long as they're killing each other, then that's fine, isn't it? Me, I believed in the Republic and in the rule of law. But a lot of cops were Nazis and were not ashamed. From that moment on, you might say, Berlin and Germany were finished and all the host of them." I sighed. "I forget. Didn't you know? That's our national pastime in Germany."

"So remember."

"Give me a minute here. This is twenty-three years ago we're talking about now. You just don't cough that up like a fur ball."

"Nineteen thirty-one."

"An unlucky year for Germany. There were, let's see, how many? Four million unemployed in Germany? And a banking crisis. Austrian Kreditanstalt had collapsed, what, yes, a couple of weeks before. I remember now. That was May eleventh. We were staring ruin in the face. Which is all the Nazis were waiting for, I suppose. To take advantage of that. Yes, things were bad. But not for Mielke. His luck was about to take a turn for the better. Got your notebooks handy?"

"Like I was your girl Friday."

GERMANY, 1931

I t was a Saturday, May 23. I know that because it was my birthday. You tend to remember your birthday when you have to spend it in Tegel Prison, interviewing one of the men convicted in the Eden Dance Palace trial. An SA storm trooper by the name of Konrad Stief. He was just a kid, really, not much more than twenty-two, with a couple of convictions for petty theft, and he'd joined the SA the previous spring. For the last years of the Weimar Republic, his was a fairly typical Berlin story: On November 22, 1930, Stief and three other chums from SA Storm 33 had gone to a dance hall. Nothing wrong with that except that they weren't going there to do the Lindy Hop; and instead of ties and neatly combed hair, they took some pistols because the Eden Dance Palace was frequented by a communist hiking club. Surprisingly, communist hiking clubs used to do what everyone else did in dance halls: they danced, but not that night. Anyway, when the Nazis arrived they went straight upstairs and opened fire. Several of the happy wanderers were hit and two of them seriously wounded. Like I say, it was a typical Berlin story, and probably I wouldn't have remembered many of these details except for the fact that the Eden Dance Palace case at

Berlin's Central Criminal Court in Old Moabit was hardly a typical trial. You see, the defense attorney, a fellow named Hans Litten, called Hitler to the stand and cross-examined him about his true relationship with the SA and its violent methods; and Hitler, who was trying to sell himself as Herr Law and Order, didn't much care for that, or for Herr Litten, who happened to be a Jew. Anyway, the four of them were convicted, Stief was sentenced to two and a half years in Tegel, and, the very next day, I drove over there to see if he could shed any light on a different case. It was something to do with the murder of an SA man. The gun Stief had used in the Eden Dance Palace was used to murder another SA man. And my question was this: Had the SA man been murdered by communists because he was in the SA? Or, as was beginning to seem more likely, had he been murdered by the Nazis because he was really a communist sent to spy on Storm 33?

"Finally, I got a name out of Stief, and a Storm tavern in the old town that was frequented by Storm 33. Reisig's tavern, in Hebbel Street, in the western district of Charlottenburg. Which wasn't so very far from the Eden Dance Palace. So when I left Tegel I decided to drop in there and take a look. But as soon as I arrived outside I saw a group of SA men piling into a truck. They were armed and clearly bent on some murderous mission. There was no time to phone headquarters, and thinking that I might for once prevent a homicide instead of merely investigating one, I followed.

"If this sounds brave or foolhardy, it wasn't. In those days, a lot of cops used to carry a Bergmann MP18 in the trunk of the car instead of a pistol. The Bergmann was a nine-mil submachine gun and perfect for sweeping crap off the streets. So I followed the gang all the way to Felseneck Colony in Reinickendorf-East, a Communist Party stronghold. Felseneck Colony was just a series of allotments for Reds who wanted to grow their own food; and what with money being so tight, a lot of them needed those vegetables just to live. Some of the Reds actually lived there. They had their own guards, who were supposed to keep a lookout for Nazis, only they hadn't been doing their job. They'd run away or been tipped off, or maybe they were in on the attack, who knows?

"But when I got there, the Nazis were just about to lay down a beating on a young man of about twenty. I didn't get a good look at him immediately—there were too many storm troopers on him, like dogs. They probably figured to beat the crap out of the boy and then take him somewhere else and put a bullet in his head before dumping his body. I swept the air over their heads with the Bergmann, marched them back to their truck, and told them to beat it because there were too many of them to arrest. Then, in case they decided to come back, I told the boy to get in my car and said I'd drop him somewhere—somewhere safer than where we were, anyway. He thanked me and asked me if I could take him to Bülowplatz, and that was the first time I got a good look at Erich Mielke. In my car, on the way to Berlin.

"He was about twenty-four years old, five feet, six inches tall, muscular, with lots of wavy hair, and a Berliner—from Wedding, I think. He was also a lifelong communist, like his father, who was a carpenter or wheelwright. And he had two younger sisters and a brother who were also in the Communist Party. Or so he told me.

"So it's true what they say," I said to him. "That madness runs in families."

He grinned. Mielke still had a sense of humor in those days. That was before the Russians got hold of him. About Marx and Engels and Lenin they never did have a sense of humor.

"There's nothing mad about it," he said. "The KPD's the largest Communist Party in the world outside the Soviet Union. You're not a Nazi, that much is obvious. I suppose you're SPD."

"That's true."

"I thought so. A social fascist. You hate us more than you hate the Nazis."

"You're right, of course. The only reason I helped you back

there was because I want you to die of shame when you have to tell your lefty pals that it was a cop that supports the SPD who took your pot off the stove. Better still, I want you to go and hang yourself like Judas Iscariot for the betrayal of the movement brought about by a Red being indebted to a Republican."

"Who says I'm even going to tell them?"

"I guess you're right. What's another lie on top of all the other lies told by the KPD?" I shook my head. "It's a low, dishonest decade that's ahead of us, make no mistake."

"Don't think I'm not grateful, polyp," said Mielke. "Because I am. Those bastards would have cut my throat for sure. They wanted to kill me because I'm a reporter for *The Red Flag*. I was doing a story about the workers' community at Felseneck Colony."

"Yeah, yeah. Brotherly love and all that crap."

"Don't you believe in brotherly love, polyp?"

"People don't give a damn about brotherly love. They just want someone to love who loves them back. Everything else is bullshit. Most folk would give the keys to the door of workers' paradise for a chance at being loved for themselves, not because they're German, or working-class, or Aryan, or the proletariat. Nobody really believes in the euphoric dream that's built on this book or that historic vision; they believe in a kind word, a kiss from a pretty girl, a ring on a finger, a happy smile. That's what people—the individuals who make up a people—that's what they want to believe."

"Sentimental rubbish," jeered Mielke.

"Probably," I said.

"That's the problem with all you democrats. You talk such unutterable nonsense. Well, there's no time for that kind of claptrap. You'll be giving that speech in the cemetery if you and your class don't wake up soon. Hitler and the Nazis don't care for your individuals. All they care about is power."

"And things will be different when we're all taking orders from Stalin in some degenerate workers' state."

"You sound just like Trotsky," said Mielke.

"Is he a Social Democrat, too?"

"He's a fascist," said Mielke.

"Meaning he's not a true communist."

"Exactly."

Our route back into the center of Berlin took us along Bismarck Strasse. At a tram stop just short of the Tiergarten, Mielke spun around in his seat and said, "That was Elisabeth."

I slowed the car to a halt and Mielke waved over a handsome-looking brunette. As she leaned in the window of the car I caught a distinct whiff of sweat, but I didn't hold that against her on a hot day. I was feeling kind of warm myself.

"What are you doing here?" asked Mielke.

"I was fitting a dress for a client who's an actress at the Schiller Theater."

"That's a job I'd like," I said.

The brunette shot me a smile. "I'm a seamstress."

"Elisabeth, this is Kommissar Gunther, from the Alex."

"Are you in any trouble, Erich?"

"I might have been, but for the Kommissar's enormous bravery. He chased off some Nazis who were planning to give me a kicking."

"Can I give you a lift somewhere?" I asked the brunette, changing the subject.

"Well, you could drop me anywhere near Alexanderplatz," she said.

She climbed into the backseat of the car and we set off east again, along Berliner Strasse, across the canal and through the park. At first I jealously supposed that the brunette was involved with Mielke, and she was, although not in the way I had supposed; it seemed that she had been a close friend of Mielke's late mother, Lydia, who also had been a seamstress, and after her death, the brunette had tried to help Mielke's widowed father to bring up his four children. Consequently Erich Mielke seemed to regard Elisabeth more like a big sister, which suited me just fine. That year I was keen on handsome brunettes, and there and then I resolved to try to see her again, if possible.

Ten minutes later we were approaching Bülowplatz, which was Erich Mielke's preferred destination, being the location of the KPD headquarters in Berlin. Occupying a whole corner of one of the most heavily policed squares in Europe, Karl Liebknecht House was a noisy indication of what all buildings might look like if the lefties ever got into power, each of its five stories decorated with more red flags than a dangerous beach and several bromide slogans in large white capital letters. If architecture is frozen music, then this was a partly thawed Lotte Lenya telling us we must die and not to ask why.

Mielke slid down in the passenger seat as we entered the square. He said, "Drop me around the corner, on Linien Strasse. In case anyone sees me getting out of your car and thinks I'm a spy."

"Relax," I said. "I'm in plain clothes."

He laughed. "You think that will save you when the Revolution comes?"

"No, but it might save you this afternoon."

"Fair enough, Kommissar. If I sound ungrateful, it's because I'm not used to getting a square deal from a Berlin bull. Pork Cheeks is the kind of polyp I'm used to."

"Pork Cheeks?"

"That swine Anlauf."

I nodded. Captain Paul Anlauf was—among the communists at least—the most hated cop in Berlin.

I pulled up on Weyding Strasse and waited for Mielke to get out.

"Thanks. Again. I won't forget it, polyp."

"Keep out of trouble, yeah?"

"You, too."

Then he kissed the brunette on the cheek and was gone. I lit a cigarette and watched him walk back onto Bülowplatz and vanish into a crowd of men.

"Don't mind him," said the brunette. "He's really not so bad."

"I don't mind him as much as he seems to mind me," I said.

"Well," she said. "I'm grateful for the lift. This is fine for me here."

She was wearing a bright print percale dress with a heart-shaped button waistline, a lacy collar, and cute puff sleeves. The print was a riot of red and white fruit and flowers on a solid black background. She looked like a market garden at midnight. On her head was a little white trilby with a red silk ribbon, as if the hat were a cake and it was someone's birthday. Mine perhaps. Which, of course, it was. The smell of sweat on her body was honest and more provocative to me than some expensive, cloying scent. Underneath the midnight garden was a real woman with skin on every part of her body, and organs and glands and all the other things about women I knew I liked but had almost forgotten. Because it was the kind of day when girls like Elisabeth were wearing summer dresses again, and I remembered just what a long winter it had been in Berlin, sleeping in that cave with just my dreams for company.

"Come for a drink," I said.

She looked tempted, but only for a moment. "I'd like to, but— I should really be getting back to work."

"Come on. It's a warm day and I need a beer. There's nothing like spending a couple of hours in the cement to give a man a thirst. Especially when it's his birthday. You wouldn't want me to drink alone on my birthday, would you?"

"No. If it really is your birthday."

"If I show my identity card, will you come?"

"All right."

So I did. And she came. Immediately next to the police station on Bülowplatz there was a bar called the Braustübl, and, leaving my car where it was, we went in there.

The place was full of communists, of course, but I wasn't thinking about them, or about Erich Mielke, although for a while Elisabeth kept on talking about him as if I were interested, which I wasn't. But I liked watching her red lips open and close to show off her white teeth. I was especially taken with the sound of her laughter, as she seemed to like my jokes, and that was really all that mattered because when we parted she agreed to see me again.

When she'd gone I bought some cigarettes, and heading back to my car I caught the eye of one of the uniformed cops on the square and stopped to chat with him in the sunshine. Bauer, that was his name, Sergeant Adolf Bauer. Our chat was the usual splash on the wall: the trial of Charlie Urban for a murder at the Mercedes Theater, Brüning's emergency decrees, Hitler's evidence at the court in Moabit. Bauer was a good bull, and all the time we were speaking I noticed how he had his eye on a car that was parked in front of Karl Liebknecht House, as if he recognized it or the man waiting patiently in the driver's seat. Then we were both watching three other men come out of the Braustübl and get into the car with this other fellow. And one of the men was Erich Mielke.

"Hullo," said Bauer. "There goes trouble."

"I know the kid," I said. "The one with the quiff. But I don't know the others."

"The one driving is Max Thunert," said Bauer. "He's a low-ranking KPD thug. One of the others was Heinz Neumann. He's in the Reichstag, although he doesn't limit causing trouble to when he's there. I didn't recognize the other fellow."

"I was just in that bar," I said. "And I didn't see any of them."

"There's a private room upstairs that they use," said Bauer. "It's my opinion that they keep some weapons there. Just in case we decide to search Karl Liebknecht House. Also, if the SA mounts a demo here they won't be expecting anything from the top floor of that bar."

"Have you told the Hussar?"

The Hussar was a uniformed sergeant called Max Willig, who was frequently about Bülowplatz and almost as unpopular as Captain Anlauf.

"I've told him."

"Didn't he believe you?"

"He did. But Judge Bode didn't when we went to get a warrant. Said we need more evidence than an itch on the end of my nose."

"Think they're planning something?"

"They're always planning something. They're communists, aren't they? Criminals, most of them."

"I don't like criminals who break the law," I said.

"What other kind are there?"

"The kind that make the law. It's the Hindenburgs and Schleichers of this world who are doing more to screw the Republic than the commies and the Nazis put together."

"You got that right, my friend."

I might never have heard the name of Erich Mielke again but for two things. One was that I saw a lot more of Elisabeth and, now and again, she'd say that she'd seen him or one of his sisters. And then there were the events of August 9, 1931. There's not a policeman from Weimar Berlin who doesn't remember August 9, 1931. The way Americans remember the *Maine*.

12

GERMANY, 1931

To say the least, it had been a difficult summer. In spite of some new laws that made political violence a capital crime, Nazis were killing communists at the rate of almost two to one. After the March elections, in which the Nazis got more than three times as many votes as the KPD, the communists became increasingly violent, probably out of desperation. Then, in early August, there was a call for an election in the Prussian Parliament. Most likely this was something to do with the world economic crisis. After all, this was 1931 and we were in the middle of the Great Depression. Almost half the banks had failed in America, and in Germany we were still trying to pay for the war with almost six million men out of work. And you can blame the French with their Carthaginian peace for a lot of that.

Prussian elections were always a barometer for the rest of Germany and usually bad-tempered affairs. For that you can blame the Prussian character. *Jedem das Seine* is a Prussian's motto. Literally it means "To each his own," but more figuratively it means everyone gets what he deserves. Which is why they put it on the gates at the Buchenwald concentration camp. And probably why, given the peculiar character of the Prussian Parliament, we got what we deserved when, on the ninth of August, the results were announced and it turned out that not enough people had voted to force an election at a national level. With no quorum for a vote, tempers all over Berlin got even worse. But especially on Bülowplatz outside Karl Liebknecht House. Figuring that some sort of dirty deal had been done between the Nazis and the Prussian administration, thousands of communists gathered there. Possibly, they were correct about a deal. But things turned ugly when the riot police showed up and started cracking Red heads like eggs. Berlin cops were always good at making omelettes.

Probably the rain didn't help, either. It had been warm and dry for several weeks, but that day it rained heavily and Berlin cops never did care to get wet. Something to do with all that leather on the shako helmets they wore. There was a cover you were supposed to put on it when the weather was bad, but no one ever remembered them, which meant you had to spend ages cleaning and polishing the shako afterward. If there was one thing guaranteed to piss off a Berlin bull, it was getting his hat wet.

I guess the Reds decided they'd had enough. Then again, they were always shouting about police dictatorship, even when the police were behaving with exemplary fairness. The local police had been threatened before, but this was different. The talk was about killing policemen. About eight o'clock that evening, shots were fired and a full-scale gun battle between police and the KPD kicked off in a big way—the biggest we'd seen since the 1919 uprising.

News started to come in to Police Headquarters on Berlin Alexanderplatz at around nine o'clock that several officers, including two police captains, had been shot and killed. We were already investigating the June murder of another cop. I'd helped to carry his coffin. By the time I and some other detectives reached Bülowplatz most of the crowds had left, but the gunfight was still very much in progress. The communists were on the rooftops of several buildings, and cops with searchlights were returning fire while, at the same time, they were searching apartment houses in the area for weapons and suspects. A hundred people were arrested, maybe more, while the battle continued. This meant that we couldn't get near the bodies, and for several hours we traded shots with the Reds; one time a rifle bullet clipped off a piece of brickwork just above my head and, more in anger than the hope of hitting anything, I let fly with the Bergmann until the magazine was empty. It was one in the morning before we got to the stricken police officers who were lying in the doorway of the Babylon Movie Theater, by which time one communist had been shot dead and seventeen others wounded.

Of the three policemen in the doorway, two were dead. The third, Sergeant Willig, "the Hussar," was seriously wounded. He'd been shot in the stomach and in the arm, and his blue-gray tunic was purple with blood, not all of it his own.

"We were set up," he gasped as we sat with him and waited for the ambulance. "They weren't on the rooftops, the ones who got us. The bastards were hiding in a doorway and shot us from behind as we walked past."

The officer in charge, Detective Police Counselor Reinhold Heller, told Willig to save his breath, but the sergeant was the kind who couldn't do anything until he'd made his report.

"There were two of them. Handguns. Automatics. Shot my pistol at them. A full clip. Couldn't say if I hit either of them or not. Young they were. Tearaways. Twenty or so. Laughed when they saw the two captains hit the ground. Then they went into the theater." He tried a smile. "Must have been Garbo fans. Never much liked her myself."

The ambulance men arrived with a stretcher and carried him away, leaving us with the two bodies.

"Gunther?" said Heller. "Go and speak to the theater manager. Find out if anyone saw something more than just the movie."

Heller was a Jew, but I didn't have a problem with that. Not like some. Heller was Bernard Weiss, the Kripo head's golden boy, which would have been fine but for the fact that Weiss was also a Jew. I thought Heller was good police, and that was all that mattered as far as I was concerned. Of course, the Nazis thought differently.

The movie was *Mata Hari,* with Garbo in the title role and Ramón Novarro as the young Russian officer who falls in love with her. I hadn't seen it myself, but the movie was doing well in Berlin. Garbo gets shot by the treacherous French, and with a plot like that, it could hardly fail with Germans. The theater manager was waiting in the lobby. He was swarthy and worried-looking, with a mustache like a midget's eyebrow, and to that extent, at least, rather resembled Ramón Novarro. But it was probably just as well the blonde from the box office didn't look like Garbo, at least not like the Garbo on the lobby card; her hair was frightful-looking, like Struwwelpeter.

Everything around us was red. Red carpet, red walls, red ceiling, red chairs, and red curtains on the auditorium doors. Given the politics of the area, it all seemed appropriate. The blonde was tearful, the manager merely nervous. He kept adjusting his cuff links as he explained, loudly, as if he were a character in a play, what he'd seen and heard:

"Mata Hari had just finished seducing the Russian general, Shubin," he said, "when we heard the first shots. That would have been at about ten past eight."

"How many shots?"

"A volley," he said. "Six or seven. Small arms. Pistols. I was in the war, see? I know the difference between a pistol shot and a rifle shot. I stuck my head through the box-office door and saw Fräulein Wiegand here on the floor. At first I thought there had been a robbery. That she'd been held up. But then there was a second volley and several of the bullets hit the cash window. Two men ran through the lobby and into the auditorium without paying. And since they were both holding pistols, I wasn't about to insist that they buy tickets. I can't say that I got a very good look at them, because I was scared. Then there were more shots, outside. Rifle shots, I think, and people started running in here to take cover. By now the projectionist had stopped the movie and switched on the lights. And the people in the auditorium were going through the exit door, onto Hirtenstrasse. It was plain from the noise and the crowd that the movie wasn't going to continue, and before one of your colleagues came in here to tell me to stay inside, almost everyone had left the auditorium through the back door. Including the two men with guns." He left his cuff links alone for a moment and rubbed his brow furiously. "They're dead, aren't they? Those two police officers."

I nodded. "Mmm hmm."

"That's bad. That's too bad."

"How about you, Fräulein?" I said. "The two with guns. Did you get a good look at them?"

She shook her head and pressed a sodden handkerchief to her red nose.

"It's been a great shock to Fräulein Wiegand," said the manager.

"It's been a great shock to us all, sir."

I went into the auditorium and walked down the center aisle toward the exit. I pushed open the door and was on a small red staircase. I tap-danced my way down to another door and then out onto Hirtenstrasse just as an underground train passed beneath my feet, shaking the whole area as if it hadn't been shaken up enough already. It was dark and there wasn't much to see in the yellow gaslight: a few discarded red flags, a couple of protest placards, and maybe a murder weapon if I looked hard enough. With so many cops around, it didn't seem likely that the killers would have risked holding on to their guns for very long.

Back in the movie theater doorway they were establishing a crime-scene gestalt, which is to say they were hoping that the whole could be bigger than the sum of its parts.

Captain Anlauf had been shot twice in the neck and clearly had bled to death. He was about forty, heavyset, with a full face that had helped earn the Seventh Precinct commander his Pig Cheeks nickname. His weapon was still in his holster.

"It's too bad," said one of the other detectives. "His wife died three weeks ago."

"What did she die of?" I heard myself ask.

"A kidney ailment," said Heller. "This leaves three daughters orphaned."

"Someone's going to have to tell them," said someone.

"I'll do that." The man who spoke was in uniform, and everyone straightened up when we realized it was the commander of the Berlin Schupo, Magnus Heimannsberg. "You can leave that to me."

"Thank you, sir," said Heller.

"Who's the other man? I don't recognize him."

"Captain Lenck, sir."

Heimannsberg leaned down to take a closer look.

"Franz Lenck? What the hell was he doing here? This kind of police work wasn't his sort of thing at all."

"Every available man in uniform was summoned here," Heller said. "Anyone know if he was married?"

"Yes," said Heimannsberg. "No children, though. That's something, I suppose. Look, Reinhard, I'll tell her, too. The widow."

Lenck was also about forty. His face was leaner than Anlauf's, with deep smile lines that were no longer being used. A pince-nez was still on his face, just about, and the shako remained on his head, with the strap tight under his chin. He had been shot in the back and, like Anlauf, had his weapon holstered, a fact that Heimannsberg now remarked upon.

"They didn't even have a chance to get their weapons out," he said bitterly. Nodding at a Luger by his boot, he added, "I assume this is Sergeant Willig's gun."

"He got off a whole clip, sir," said Heller. "Before they ran in here."

"Hit anything?"

Heller looked at me.

"I don't think so, sir," I said. "Mind you, it's a little hard to tell in there. Everything's red. Carpet, walls, curtains, you name it. Hard to see any bloodstains. They ran out the rear exit on Hirtenstrasse. Sir, I'd like a couple of men with flashlights to help me search the length of the street. People have chucked away red flags and placards; it's possible they might have thrown the guns, too."

Heller nodded.

"Don't worry, lads," said Heimannsberg, who, having started his career as an ordinary patrolman, was enormously popular with everyone in the police. "We'll catch the bastards who did this."

A few minutes later, I was walking along Hirtenstrasse with a couple of uniformed men. As we went farther west toward Mulack Strasse and the territory of the Always True, a notorious Berlin gang, they started to become nervous. We stopped next to Fritz Hempel, the tobacconists. It was closed, of course. I pointed my flashlight one way and then the other. The two Schupo men came toward me, relaxing a little as, in the distance, a police armored car pulled up on the corner.

"This close to Mulack Strasse and the Always True, they must have figured they could hold on to their guns," said one of the bulls.

"Maybe." I started to retrace my steps along Hirtenstrasse, still searching the ground until my eyes caught sight of a drain cover in the gutter. It was a simple cast-iron grate, but someone had lifted it, and recently: The dirt was missing from two of the bars where someone might have grasped it. One of the Schupo men pulled it up while I was removing my jacket and my shirt; and then, inspecting the cobblestones around the open drain, I decided to remove my trousers as well.

"He was a dancer at the Haller Revue before he was police," said one of the cops, folding my clothes over his arm.

"Versatile, isn't he?"

"If Heimannsberg were here," I said, "he'd make you do it, so shut up."

"I'd put my whole fucking head down that drain if I thought it'd find the Jew bastard who killed Captain Anlauf."

I lay down next to the drain and plunged my arm into thick black water, right up to the shoulder.

"What makes you think it was a Jew?" I asked.

"Everyone knows that the Marxists and the Jews are one and the same," said the Schupo man.

"I wouldn't repeat that in front of Counselor Heller if I were you."

"This town is sick with Jews," said the Schupo man.

"Don't mind him, sir," said the other cop. "Anyone with a hat and a big nose is a Jew in his book. See if you can find any war reparations while you're down there."

"Funny," I said. "If I wasn't up to my shoulder in stagnant water, I might fucking laugh. Now put the cork back in."

I felt a hard, metallic object and fished out a pistol with a long barrel. I handed it to the cop who wasn't holding my clothes.

"Luger, is it?" he said, wiping some of the filth off the gun. "Looks like an artillery-corps version. That'll put an extra keyhole in your door."

I kept on searching the bottom of the drain. "No commies down here," I said. "Just this." I brought up the other gun, an automatic with a curious, irregular shape, as if someone had tried to break the slide from the muzzle.

We carried the two weapons over to a street water pump

and washed some of the filth away. The smaller automatic was a Dreyse .32.

I washed my arm and put my clothes back on and took the two guns back to the Seventh Street Precinct Station on Bülowplatz. Back in the detectives' room, Heller hailed my arrival with a verbal pat on the back.

"Well done, Gunther," he said.

"Thanks, sir."

Meanwhile, other cops were already gathering boxes of photo files to take over to the State Hospital for Sergeant Willig to look at when he came out of surgery. And after a while, I said, "You know, that's going to take a while. I mean, before he's conscious again. By then the killers will be out of the city. Maybe on their way to Moscow."

"Got a better idea?"

"I might. Look, sir, instead of showing Sergeant Willig a picture of every Red who's ever been arrested in this city, let's just pull a few."

"Like who? There are hundreds of these bastards."

"The chances are the attack was probably orchestrated from K.L. House," I said. "So how about we pull the records of just seventy-six Reds? Because that's how many Reds were arrested when we raided K.L. last January. Let's stick to those faces for now."

"Yes, you're right," agreed Heller. He snatched up the telephone. "Get me the State Hospital." He pointed at another detective. "Get onto IA. Find out who was on that raid. And tell the records boys in ED to find the arrest files and to meet us at the hospital."

Twenty minutes later we were on our way to the State Hospital in Friedrichshain.

They were just wheeling Willig into the operating theater when we arrived bearing the K.L. House arrest files. The wounded man had already received an injection, but in spite of the opposition of the doctors, who were anxious to operate as quickly as possible, Willig understood immediately the urgency of what was being asked of him. And it took the sergeant no time at all to pick out one of his attackers.

"Him, for sure," he croaked. "That one pulled the trigger on Captain Anlauf, for sure."

"Erich Ziemer," said Heller, and handed me the charge sheet.

"The other one was about the same age and build and coloring as this bastard. They might even have been brothers, they looked so alike. But he's not here. I'm certain of it."

"All right," said Heller. He spoke some words of encouragement to the sergeant before his doctors took the patient away.

"I recognize this man Ziemer," I said. "Back in May, I saw Ziemer in a car with three other men. They were outside K.L. House, and according to Sergeant Adolf Bauer, who was on patrol in Bülowplatz, one of those others was Heinz Neumann."

"The Reichstag deputy?"

I nodded.

"And the other two?"

"One of them I don't know. Perhaps Bauer will remember it."

"Yes, perhaps."

He paused expectantly. "And the Red that you do know?"

I told him about the day I had saved the life of Erich Mielke from a troop of SA intent on killing him.

"He was the fourth man in that car. And it's true what Sergeant Willig says. He looks a lot like Erich Ziemer."

"So. You believe that we're looking for two Erichs, yes?"

I nodded again.

"Gunther? I'd hate to be known around the Alex as the man who saved the life of a cop killer."

"I hadn't really thought about that, sir."

"Then perhaps you should. And from this moment on, my advice to you is this: that you make no further mention of exactly how you came to be acquainted with this Erich Mielke until he is safely in custody. Especially now. This is the kind of story the Nazis love to use to beat those of us in the police force who still count ourselves as democrats, is it not?"

"Yes, sir."

We drove west and north of the Ring to Biesenthaler Strasse, which was the address on Erich Ziemer's charge sheet. It was a dreary-looking building off Christiana Strasse and within snorting distance of the Löwen Brewery and the distinctive smell of hops that was always in the air over that part of Berlin.

Ziemer had rented a big gloomy room in a big gloomy house that was owned by an old man with a face like the Turin Shroud. He was unhappy to be roused from his bed at such an early hour, but hardly surprised that we were asking questions about his tenant, who was not in his room and, it seemed, was unlikely to be returning to it; but we asked to see the room anyway.

Up against the window was a dilapidated leather sofa that was the size and color of a slumbering hippo. On the dampish wall was a print of Alexander von Humboldt with a botanical specimen on an open book. The landlord, Herr Karpf, scratched his beard and shrugged and told us that Ziemer had disappeared like fog the previous day owing three weeks' rent—taking his belongings, not to mention a silver and ivory tankard worth several hundred marks. It was difficult to imagine Herr Karpf owning anything valuable, but we promised to do our best to recover it.

There was a police call box on Oskar Platz, near the hospital, and from there we telephoned the Alex, where another officer had been looking for a crime sheet and an address for Erich Mielke, but so far without success.

"That's that, then," said Heller.

"No," I said. "There's one more chance. Drive south, to the Electricity Works on Volta Strasse."

Heller's car was a neat little cream-colored DKW cabriolet

with a small two-cylinder, six-hundred-cc engine, but it had front-wheel drive and held on to the corners like a welded bracket, so we were there in no time at all. On Brunnen Strasse, opposite Volta Strasse, I told him to turn left on Lortzing Strasse and pull up.

"Give me ten minutes," I said, and, stepping over the DKW's little door, I walked quickly in the direction of a lofty-looking apartment building that was all red and yellow brick with window-box balconies and a mansard roof that resembled a small Moroccan fortress.

Elisabeth's shapeless landlady, Frau Bayer, was only a little surprised to see me at this early hour, as I had got into the habit of visiting the dressmaker whenever I came off duty. She knew I was a policeman, which was normally enough to silence her grumbling at being got out of bed. Most Berliners were always respectful of the law, except when they were communists or Nazis. And when it wasn't enough to silence her grumbling, I slipped a few marks into her dressing-gown pocket by way of compensation.

The apartment was a warren of shabby rooms full of old cherry-wood furniture, Chinese screens, and tasseled lampshades. As always, I waited in the living room for Frau Bayer to fetch her lodger; and as always when she saw me, Elisabeth smiled a sleepy but happy smile and took me by the hand to lead me to her room, where a proper welcome awaited me; only this time I stayed put on the living room sofa.

"What's the matter?" she said. "Is something wrong?"

"It's Erich," I said. "He's in trouble."

"What kind of trouble?"

"Serious trouble. Two policemen were shot and killed last night."

"And you think Erich might have something to do with it?"

"It looks that way."

"Are you sure?"

"Yes. Look, Elisabeth, I don't have much time. His best chance is if I find him before anyone else does. I can tell him what to say and, more importantly, what not to say. Do you see?"

She nodded and tried to stifle a yawn.

"So what do you want from me?"

"An address."

"You mean you want me to betray him, don't you?"

"That's one way of looking at it, yes. I can't deny that. But another way is this: that perhaps I can persuade him to make a clean breast of it. Which is the only thing that can save his life now."

"They wouldn't behead him, would they?"

"For killing a policeman? Yes, I think they would. One of the cops who was killed was a widower with three daughters who are now orphaned. The Republic would have no choice but to make an example of him, or else risk courting a storm of criticism in the newspapers. The Nazis would just love that. But if I am the arresting officer, I might be able to talk him into naming some names. If others in the KPD put him up to it, then he has to say so. He's young and impressionable, and that will help his case."

She pulled a face. "Don't ask me to turn him in, Bernie. I've known that boy for half his life. I helped bring him up."

"I am asking it. I give you my word I will do what I said and that I will speak up for him in court. All I'm asking for is an address, Elisabeth."

She sat down in a chair and clasped her hands tightly and closed her eyes, almost as if she were uttering a silent prayer. Perhaps she was.

"I knew something like this would happen," she said. "That's why I've never ever told him that you and I have been seeing each other. Because he would have been cross. And I'm beginning to understand why."

"I won't tell him that it was you who gave me an address, if that's what you're worried about."

"That's not what I'm worried about," she whispered.

"What, then?"

She stood up abruptly. "I'm worried about Erich, of course," she said loudly. "I'm worried about what's going to happen to him."

I nodded. "Look, forget it. We'll have to find him some other way. Sorry I bothered you."

"He lives with his father, Emil," she said dully. "Stettiner Strasse, number twenty-five. The top flat."

"Thanks."

I waited for her to say something else, and when she didn't I knelt down in front of her and tried to take her hand to give it a comforting squeeze, but she pulled it away. At the same time, she avoided my eye as if it had been hanging out of its socket.

"Just go," she said. "Go and do your duty."

It was almost dawn on the street outside Elisabeth's apartment building, but I felt that something important had happened between us: that something had changed, perhaps forever. I stepped into Heller's car and told him the address. From my expression I guess he knew better than to ask how I had come by it.

We sped north up Swinemünder Strasse onto Bellermann Strasse and then Christiana Strasse. Twenty-five Stettiner Strasse was a gray tenement building around a central courtyard that would have probably collapsed in on itself but for several large support timbers. Although it could just as easily have been moss or mold, a green rug was hanging out of an open window on one of the upper floors, and it was the only spot of color in that ghastly sarcophagus of raw brick and loose cobblestones. Even though this was fast becoming a bright summer's morning, no sun ever reached the lower levels of the tenements on Stettiner Strasse: Nosferatu could have spent the whole day quite comfortably in the twilight world of a ground-floor Stettiner Strasse apartment.

We pulled on a bell for several minutes before a gray-haired head appeared out of a dirty window.

"Yes?"

"Police," said Heller. "Open up."

"What's the matter?"

"As if you don't know," I said. "Open up, or we'll kick the door in."

"All right."

The head disappeared, and a minute or so later we heard the door open and we ran upstairs as if we actually believed there was a chance we might still apprehend Erich Mielke. In truth, neither of us thought there was much hope of that happening. Not in Gesundbrunnen. It was the kind of area where children were taught how to stay one step ahead of the cops before they learned long division.

At the top of the stairs, a man wearing trousers and a pajama jacket admitted us to a little flat that was a shrine to the class struggle. Every wall was hung with KPD posters, notices of strikes and demonstrations, and cheap portraits of Rosa Luxemburg, Karl Liebknecht, Marx, and Lenin. Unlike any of them, the man standing in front of us at least looked like a worker. He was around fifty, stocky and short, with a bull neck, a receding hairline, and an advancing waist. He stared at us suspiciously with small, close-set eyes that were like diacritical marks inside a naught. Short of wearing a towel and a silk dressing gown, he couldn't have looked any more rough and pugnacious.

"So what does the Berlin polenta want with me?"

"We're looking for a Herr Erich Mielke," said Heller. His punctiliousness was typical. You didn't get to be a counselor in the Berlin police without paying attention to detail, especially when you were also a Jew. That was probably the ex-lawyer in him. That was the part of Heller I didn't care for—the punctilious lawyer. The stocky little man in the pajama jacket didn't seem to like it either.

"He's not here," he said, barely concealing a smirk of pleasure.

"And who are you?"

"His father."

"When did you last see your son?"

"A few days ago. So what's he supposed to have done? Hit a policeman?"

"No," said Heller. "On this occasion, it seems that he's shot and killed at least one."

"That's too bad." But the man's tone seemed to suggest he didn't think that it was too bad at all.

By now the resemblance between father and son was all too obvious to me, and I turned and walked into the kitchen just in case the temptation to hit him grew too strong for me.

"You won't find him in there, either."

I put my hand on the gas ring. It was still warm. A pile of half-smoked cigarettes lay in an ashtray as if put there by someone who was feeling nervous about something. No one in Gesundbrunnen would have wasted tobacco like that. I pictured a man sitting in a chair by the window. A man who'd been trying to occupy his mind with a book, perhaps, while he waited for a car to come and take him and Ziemer to a KPD safe house. I picked up the book that lay on the kitchen table. It was *All Quiet on the Western Front*.

"Do you know where your son might be now?" asked Heller.

"I haven't a clue. Frankly, he could be anywhere. Never tells me anything about where he's been or where he's going. Well, you know what young men are like."

I came back into the room and stood behind him. "You KPD?"

He looked over his shoulder and smiled. "It's not illegal, is it? Yet?"

"Perhaps you were in Bülowplatz yourself last night." While I spoke, I turned the pages of the book.

He shook his head. "Me? No. I was here all night."

"Are you sure? After all, there were several hundred of your comrades there, including your son. Maybe as many as a thousand. Surely you wouldn't have missed something as fun-packed as that?"

"No," he said firmly. "I stayed at home. I always stay at home on a Sunday night."

"Are you religious?" I said. "You don't look religious."

"On account of the fact that I have to go to work in"—he nodded at the little wooden clock on the tiled mantelpiece—"yes, in just two hours from now."

"Any witnesses that you were here all night?"

"The Geislers, next door."

"Is this your book?"

"Yes."

"Good, isn't it?"

"I wouldn't have thought it was your taste," he said.

"Oh? Why's that?"

"I hear the Nazis want to ban it."

"Maybe they do. But I'm not a Nazi. And neither is the police counselor, here."

"All cops are Nazis in my book."

"Yes, but this isn't it. I mean your book." I turned the page and removed the Ringbahn ticket that was marking the reader's place. "This ticket says you're lying."

"What do you mean?"

"This ticket is for Gesundbrunnen Station, just a few minutes' walk from here. It was bought at Schönhauser Tor at eight-twenty this evening, which is about twenty minutes after two policemen were murdered on Bülowplatz. That's less than a hundred meters from the station at Schönhauser Tor. Which puts the owner of this book in the thick of it."

"I'm not saying anything."

"Herr Mielke," said Heller, "you're in enough trouble as it is without putting the brakes on your mouth."

"You won't catch him," he said defiantly. "Not now. If I know my Erich, he's already halfway to Moscow."

"Not nearly halfway," I said. "And not Moscow, either, I'll

bet. Not if you say so. That means it has to be Leningrad. Which in itself means he's probably traveling by boat. So the chances are he'll be heading to one of two German ports. Hamburg or Rostock. Rostock's nearer, so he'll probably figure to second-guess us and head for Hamburg. Which is what? Two hundred and fifty kilometers? They might be there by now if they left before midnight. My guess is that Erich's probably on the Grasbrook or Sandtor Dock at this very moment, sneaking onto a Russian freighter and boasting about how he shot a fascist policeman in the back. They'll probably give the little coward an Order of Lenin for bravery."

Some of this must have touched a nerve in Mielke's changeling body. One minute his beer-swilling troll's face was in ugly repose; the next the jaw had advanced belligerently and, growling abuse, he took a swing at me. Fortunately, I was half expecting it and I was already leaning back when it connected, but it still felt like I got hit by a sandbag. Feeling sick, I sat down hard on a soft chair. For a moment I had a new way of seeing the world, but it had nothing to do with Berlin's avant-garde. Mielke senior was grinning now, his mouth a gap-toothed, moon-gnawing rictus, his big trench mace of a fist already heading Heller's way; and when its orbit around Mielke's body was complete it crashed into the surface of Heller's skull like an asteroid, sending the police counselor sprawling onto the floor, where he groaned and lay still.

I got to my feet again. "I'm going to enjoy this, you ugly commie bastard."

Mielke senior turned just in time to meet my fist coming the other way. The blow rocked the big head on his meaty shoulders like a sudden bad smell in his nostrils, and as he took a step backward, I hit him again with a right that descended on the side of his head like a Borotra first service. That lifted his legs off the ground like a plane's undercarriage, and for a split second he actually seemed to fly through the air before landing on his knees. As he rolled onto his side I twisted one arm behind them, then the other, and managed to hold them long enough for a groggy-looking Heller to get the irons on his wrists. Then I stood up and kicked him hard, because I wasn't able to kick his son and because I was wishing I hadn't saved the young man's neck. I might have kicked him again, but Heller stopped me and, but for the fact that he was a counselor and I was still feeling sick, I might have kicked him, too.

"Gunther," he yelled. "That's enough." He let out a gasp and leaned heavily against a wall while he tried to recover all of his wits.

I shifted my jaw; my head felt larger on one side than the other and there was something singing in my ears, only it wasn't a kettle.

"With all due respect, sir," I said, "it's not nearly enough."

And then I kicked Mielke again before I staggered out of the apartment and onto the landing and, a minute or two later, puked over the banister.

13

GERMANY, 1954

I stopped talking. My throat felt tight, but not as tight as the handcuffs.

"Is that all there is?" demanded one of the two Amis.

"There's more," I said. "A lot more. But I can't feel my hands. And I need to use the lavatory."

"You saw Erich Mielke again."

"Several times. The last time was 1946, when I was a POW in Russia. You see, Mielke was—"

"No, no. Let's not get ahead of ourselves. We want everything in the correct order of appearance. That's the German way, isn't it?"

"If you say so."

"All right, then. You went to his home. You had a police witness. You found the murder weapons in the drain. I take it those were the murder weapons?"

"A long-barreled Luger and a Dreyse .32. That was the standard police automatic back then. Yes, they were the murder weapons. Look, I really do need a rest. I can't feel my hands—"

"Yes, you said that already."

"I'm not asking for apple pie and ice cream, just a pair of handcuffs off. That's fair, isn't it?"

"After what you just told us? About kicking Mielke's father when he was handcuffed and lying on the floor? That wasn't very fair of you, Gunther."

"He had it ordered, on room service. You hit a cop, you get trouble. I didn't hit you, did I?"

"Not yet."

"With these hands? I couldn't hit my own knees." I yawned inside the hood. "No, really, that's it. I've had enough of this. Now that I know what you want, that makes it easier for me keep my peep. Regardless of the legalities or illegalities of this situation—"

"You are in a place where there is no law. We are the law. You want to piss yourself, then go ahead and make yourself comfortable. Then see what happens to you."

"I'm beginning to understand—"

"I sure hope so, for your sake."

"You enjoy playing Gestapo. It's a little bit of a kick for you, doing it their way, isn't it? Secretly, you probably admire them and the way they went about extracting teeth and information."

They came close to me now, raising their voices beyond what was comfortable to hear.

"Fuck you, Gunther."

"You hurt our feelings with that remark about the Gestapo."

"I take it back. You're much worse than the Gestapo. They didn't pretend they were defending the free world. It's your hypocrisy that's offensive, not your brutality. You're the worst kind of fascists. The kind that think they're liberals."

One of them started knocking at my head with the knuckle on his finger; it wasn't painful so much as annoying.

"When are you going to get it into that fucking square head of yours—"

"You're right. I still don't understand why you're doing this when I'm perfectly willing to cooperate."

"You're not meant to understand. When are you going to understand that, asshole? We want more than your willingness to cooperate. That implies you have some choice in the matter. When you don't. It's up to us to assess your level of cooperation, not you."

"We want to know that when you're telling us the truth there's absolutely no question it could ever be anything else. The truth, the whole truth, and nothing but the truth. Which means that we'll decide when you need a rest, when you need to go to the lavatory, when you see the light of day. When you breathe and when you fart. So. Tell us some more about Erich Mielke. Did he go to Hamburg or Rostock?"

"With Mielke senior safely in custody, myself and another detective caught the first train to Hamburg."

"Why you? Why not someone else? Why were you so central to the investigation? Why not leave it to the Hamburg police?"

"I should have thought that was obvious. Or maybe you just weren't listening, Yank. I'd met Erich Mielke. I knew what he looked like, remember? Besides, I had a personal stake in seeing him arrested. I saved his life. Of course, the Hamburg police were alerted to pick up Ziemer and Mielke. The trouble was someone inside the Alex had tipped them off, and by the time Kestner and I reached Hamburg—"

"Kestner?"

"Yes. He was with the political police. A detective sergeant. We were old friends, Kestner and I. Later on, when the Nazis won the election of March 1933, he joined the party. Lots of people did. The March violets or March fallen, we called them. Anyway, that was when we stopped being friends, he and I.

"Later on, I learned that Mielke and Ziemer had been taken to

Antwerp by agents of the Comintern. There they were given false passports and, posing as crew members, they were put on a ship to Leningrad. From there they were taken to Moscow for training in the OGPU—Stalin's secret police."

"So there were communists as well as Nazis in the Berlin police."

"Yes. Eldor Borck—a retired police major I was friendly with—he estimated that as many as ten percent of the Berlin police sympathized with the Bolsheviks. But there were never the Red Schupo cells that the Nazis claimed existed. Most police were natural conservatives. Instinctive fascists rather than ideological ones. Anyway, Ziemer and Mielke spent the next five years in Russia."

"How do you know that?"

"I'll come to that. Of course, even though we didn't have the perpetrators of the murders of Anlauf and Lenck in custody, the Nazis were not about to allow a little fact like that stop them from making an example of people. There was a lot of propaganda value in making arrests and securing convictions."

"Of other commies?"

"Of course of other commies. And it can't be denied that Ziemer and Mielke did not act alone. Indeed, there was a strong case for believing that the whole riot on Bülowplatz had been engineered for the purpose of luring Anlauf and Sergeant Willig into a trap. As I said before, those two were really hated by the communists. Lenck was an accident, more or less. In the wrong place at the wrong time.

"Soon after I left the police to go and work at the Adlon hotel, an arrest was made. Fellow called Max Thunert. Very probably they put a bag over his head and persuaded him to name names. And name names he did. Fifteen men went to trial in June 1933, among them several prominent communists. Who knows? Maybe some of them had put Mielke and Ziemer up to the killing after all.

"Four received a death sentence. Eleven were sent to a concentration camp. But it was another two years before three of those death sentences were actually carried out. That was typical of the Nazis. To keep a man waiting for years before they executed him. I expect the Nazis could still teach you Ami bastards something about cruelty. It was in all the newspapers, of course. May 1935? I can't recall their names, the ones who went to the falling ax. But I often wondered how Mielke and Ziemer, safe in Moscow, felt about it. How much they were told. Oddly enough, it was the same month, May 1935, when Stalin decided that some of the many German and Italian communists who'd fled to Moscow after Hitler and Mussolini came to power could no longer be trusted. European communism was always too heterogeneous for Stalin's taste. Too many factions. Too many Trotskyites. I suspect that Mielke and Ziemer were more worried about what might happen to them than what was already happening to old comrades like Max Matern. Yes, I remember now. He was one who went to the guillotine.

"Most of the German communists in Moscow were lodged at a Comintern hotel called the Hotel Lux. There was a purge, and some of the more prominent German communists—Kippenberger, Neumann, ironically the very men who'd ordered the murders of Anlauf and Lenck—they were all shot. Kippenberger's wife was packed off to a Soviet labor camp and never seen again. Neumann's wife also went to a labor camp, but I think she survived. At least she did until Stalin's nonaggression pact with Hitler in 1939, at which point she was handed over to the Gestapo. I've no idea what happened to her after that."

"You're very well-informed. How come you know so much about this, Gunther? Mielke. The whole damned crew of German commies."

"For a while he was my beer," I said. "How do you say it? My pigeon. Up to 1946, there's not much I don't know about Erich Mielke."

"And then?"

"And then I hadn't really given him a thought until the lawyer from the Office of the Chief Counsel used the name. To be honest, I wish I'd never heard it."

"But you did. So here you are."

"The last time I saw him, he was—he was working for the OGPU after it became the MVD. That was seven years ago."

"Have you heard of the East German Secretariat for State Security?"

"No."

"Some Germans already call it the Stasi. Your friend Erich is the deputy chief of State Security. A secret policeman and probably one of the three most important men in the East German security apparatus, if not the whole country."

"He's survived Stalin, Beria, he even survived the downfall of Wilhelm Zaisser after last year's workers' uprising in Berlin. Survival is your friend Mielke's specialty."

"I think I'm going to faint," I said.

"The Allied Control Commission made an attempt to arrest him in February 1947, but the Russians were never going to let that happen."

I had stopped listening. I couldn't be bothered to pay attention. Only, that wasn't quite right. There wasn't anything to listen to unless you counted the singing in my ears from when Erich Mielke's father had hit me twenty-three years ago. Only, that wasn't it either. Something cold and heavy was lying on the side of my head, and it was a moment or two before I realized it was the floor. The numbness in my hands was spreading through my whole body like embalming fluid. The hood over my head grew thicker and tightened, as if there were a hangman's noose around my neck. It was difficult to breathe, but I didn't care. Not anymore. I opened the bag and climbed inside. Then someone threw the bag off a bridge. I felt myself drop through the air for twenty-three years. By the time I landed, I had forgotten who and what and where I was.

14

GERMANY, 1954

felt myself being carried. Then I fainted again. When I came to again, I was lying facedown on a bed and they had removed the manacles from one of my wrists and I could almost feel my hands again. Then they lifted me up and let me stand for a minute. I was thirsty, but I didn't ask for water. I just stood there waiting to be shouted at or struck on the head, so that I flinched a little when I felt a blanket on my shoulders and a chair behind my bare legs; and as I sat down again a hand held on to the bag, pulling it off my head.

I found myself in a larger, more comfortably appointed cell than my own. There was a table with a little sill around the edge that might have stopped a pencil from rolling onto the floor and not much else, and on it a small potted plant that was dead. On the wall above me was a mark where a picture had been hanging, and in front of the double window—which was barred—was a washstand with a jug and a porcelain washbasin.

There were two men in that room with me, and neither one of them looked much like a torturer. They were wearing double-breasted suits and silk ties. One of them had a pair of horn-rimmed glasses on his nose and the other had a cherrywood pipe clamped, unlit, between his teeth. The one wearing the pipe in his face picked up the water jug and poured some water into a dusty-looking glass and handed it to me. I wanted to throw the water in his face, but instead I tossed it down my throat. The one with the glasses lit a cigarette and threaded it between my lips. I sucked at the smoke like mother's milk.

"Was it something I said?" I grinned feebly.

Out of the first-floor window was a view of the garden and the conical roof of a little white tower in the prison wall. As far as I knew, it wasn't a view that any red jacket in Landsberg was accustomed to seeing. Blinking against the sun streaming in through the window and the smoke streaming into my eye, I rubbed my chin wearily and took the cigarette from my mouth.

"Maybe," said the man with the pipe. There was a mustache on his upper lip that matched the size and shape of his little blue bow tie. He had more chin than would have made him handsome, and while it wasn't exactly Charles V, there were some, myself included, who would have grown a short beard on it to make it seem smaller, perhaps. But in my eyes leprosy would have looked a lot better on him.

The door opened. No keys were required to open this cell. The door just swung open and a guard came in carrying some clothes, followed by another guard bearing a tray with coffee and a hot meal. I didn't much like the clothes, since these were the ones I'd been wearing the previous day, but the coffee and the food smelled like they'd been prepared in Kempinski's. I started to eat before they changed their minds. When you're hungry, clothes don't seem that important. I didn't use the knife and fork, because I couldn't yet hold them properly. So I ate with my fingers, wiping them on my thighs and backside. I certainly wasn't about to worry about my table manners. Immediately, I started to feel better. It's amazing how good even an American cup of coffee can taste when you're hungry.

"From now on," said the man with the pipe, "this is your cell. Number seven."

"Recognize that number?" The other Ami—the one wearing the glasses—had short gray hair and looked like any college professor. The arms of the glasses were too short for his head, and the hooks stood off his ears so that they looked like two small umbrellas. Maybe the glasses were too small for his face. Or maybe he'd borrowed them. Or maybe his head was abnormally large to accommodate all the abnormally unpleasant thoughts—most of them about me—that were in it.

I shrugged. My mind was a blank.

"Of course you do. It's the Führer's cell. Where you're eating your food is where he wrote his book. And I don't know which I find more disgusting. The thought of him writing down his poisonous thoughts, or you eating with your fingers."

"I'll certainly try not to let that thought spoil my appetite."

"By all accounts, Hitler had an easy time here in Landsberg."

"I guess you weren't working here back then."

"Tell me, Gunther. Did you ever read it? Hitler's book."

"Yes. I prefer Ayn Rand. But only just."

"Do you like Ayn Rand?"

"No. I think Hitler would have liked her, though. He wanted to be an architect, too, of course. Only, he couldn't afford the paper and the pencils. Not to mention the education. Plus he didn't have a large enough ego. And I think you've got to be pretty tough to make it in that world."

"You're pretty tough yourself, Gunther," said the one with the glasses.

"Me? No. How many tough guys do you have breakfast with when they're naked?"

"Not many."

"Besides, it's easy to look tough when you're wearing a bag

over your head. Even if it does get you wondering what it might be like to have nothing under your feet."

"Anytime you want to find out for sure, we can help you."

"Sure, you can take Klingelhöfer's place for the rehearsal."

"We were here when they executed those five war criminals in June 'fifty-one."

"I'll bet you've got an interesting scrapbook."

"They died quite calmly. Like they were resigned to their fate. Which was kind of ironic when you remember that's what they said about all those Jews they murdered."

I shrugged and pushed away my empty breakfast tray. "No man wants to die," I said. "But sometimes it just seems worse to go on living."

"Oh, I think they wanted to go on living, all right. Especially the ones who applied for clemency. Which was all of them. I read some of the letters that McCloy received. They were all predictably self-serving."

"Ah, well," I said. "That's the difference between me and them. It's just impossible for me to be self-serving. You see, I fired my own self a long time ago. These days I try to manage on my own."

"You say that like you don't want to go on living either, Gunther."

"And you say that like I should be impressed with your hospitality. That's the trouble with you Amis. You kick the shit out of people and then expect them to join in a couple of verses of 'The Star-Spangled Banner.'"

"We don't expect you to sing, Gunther," said the Ami with the pipe. Was he ever going to light it? "Just to go on talking. The way you've been talking until now." He tossed a packet of cigarettes onto the table where Hitler had written his bestselling book. "By the way. What happened to that sergeant who Ziemer and Mielke shot in the stomach?"

"Willig?" I lit a cigarette and remembered that he had lived; three months after the shooting he had made lieutenant. "I forget."

"You joined Kripo again in September 1938, is that right?"

"I didn't exactly join," I said. "I was ordered back in by General Heydrich. To solve a series of murders in Berlin. After the case was solved, I stayed on. Again, that's what Heydrich wanted. There's only one thing you have to understand about Heydrich: He almost always got what he wanted."

"And he wanted you."

"I had a certain reputation for getting the job done. He admired that."

"So you stayed on."

"I tried to get out of Kripo for good. But Heydrich made that more or less impossible."

"Tell us about that. About what you were doing for Heydrich."

"Kripo was part of Sipo, the State Security Police. I was promoted to Oberkommissar. A chief inspector. Most of the crime by then was politicized, but men carried on murdering their wives and professional criminals went about their business as normal. I conducted several investigations during that period, but in reality the Nazis cared very little about reducing crime in the usual time-honored way and most police could hardly be bothered to do what police do. This was because the Nazis preferred to "reduce" crime by declaring annual amnesties, which meant that most crimes never went to court at all. All the Nazis cared about was being able to say that the crime figures were down. In fact, crime—real crime—actually increased under the Nazis: Theft, murder, juvenile delinquency—it all got worse. So I carried on as normal at the Alex. I made arrests, prepared a case, handed the papers over to the Ministry of Justice, and in time the case was struck down, or dropped, and the accused walked free.

"One day in September 1939, not long after war was declared and Sipo became part of the RSHA—the Reich Main Security

Office—I went to see General Heydrich at his office in Prinz Albrecht-strasse. I told him I was wasting my time and asked his permission to put in my papers. He listened patiently but continued to write for almost a minute after I'd finished speaking before turning his attention to a rack of rubber stamps on his desktop. There must have been thirty or forty of these. He picked one up, pressed it onto an inkpad, and then carefully stamped the sheet of paper he'd been writing on. Then, still silent, he got up and closed the door. There was a grand piano in his office—a big black Blüthner—and, to my surprise, he sat down in front of it and started to play, and play rather well, I might say. While he was playing, he shifted his large arse on the piano stool—he'd put on some weight since last I'd seen him—and then nodded at the space he'd made to indicate that I should sit beside him.

"I sat down, hardly knowing what to expect, and for a while neither of us said a word as his thin, bony, dead Christ hands rippled over the shiny keyboard. I listened and kept my eyes on the photograph on the piano lid. It was a picture of Heydrich in profile, wearing a fencer's white jerkin and looking like the sort of dentist you might have nightmares about—the kind who would have pulled all of your teeth to improve your dental hygiene.

"Kuan Chung was a seventh-century Chinese philosopher," Heydrich said quietly. "He wrote a very great book of Chinese sayings, one of which is that 'even the walls have ears.'" Do you understand what I'm saying, Gunther?"

"Yes, General," I said, and, looking around, tried to guess where a microphone might be hidden.

"Good. Then I'll keep playing. This piece is by Mozart, who was taught by Antonio Salieri. Salieri was not a great composer. He's better known to us today as the man who murdered Mozart."

"I didn't even know he'd been murdered, sir."

"Oh yes. Salieri was jealous of Mozart, as is often the way

with lesser men. Would it surprise you to know that someone is trying to murder me?"

"Who?"

"Himmler, of course. The Salieri *de nos jours*. Himmler's is not a great mind. His most important thoughts are the ones I'm yet to give him. He is a man who goes to the lavatory and probably wonders what Hitler would like him to do while he's in there. But one of us will certainly destroy the other, and with any luck it will be him who loses the game to me. He is not to be underestimated, however. And this is the reason that I keep you in Sipo, Gunther. Because if by any chance Himmler wins our little game, I want someone to find the evidence that will help to destroy him. Someone with a proven track record in Kripo as an investigating detective. Someone intelligent and resourceful. That man is you, Gunther. You are the Voltaire to my Frederick the Great. I keep you close for your honesty and your independence of mind."

"I'm flattered, Herr General. And rather horrified. What makes you think I could ever destroy a man like Himmler?"

"Don't be a fool, Gunther. And listen. I said help to destroy. If Himmler succeeds and I am murdered, it will of course look like an accident. Or that someone else was responsible for my death. In those circumstances, there will have to be an inquiry. As head of Kripo, Arthur Nebe has the power to appoint someone to direct that inquiry. That someone will be you, Gunther. You will have the assistance of my wife, Lina, and of my most trusted confidante— a man named Walter Schellenberg, of the SS Foreign Intelligence Service. You can trust Schellenberg to know the most politic way to bring the evidence of my murder to the Führer's attention. I have enemies, it's true. But so does that bastard Himmler. And some of his enemies are my friends."

I shrugged. "So you see, he made it almost impossible for me to leave Kripo."

"And that's the real reason that Nebe ordered you back from Minsk to Berlin," said the Ami with the pipe. "What you told Silverman and Earp—about Nebe being worried you might land him in the shit—that was only half the story, wasn't it? He was protecting you, on Heydrich's personal instructions. Wasn't he?"

"I assume so, yes. It was only when I got back to Berlin and I met Schellenberg that I was reminded of what Heydrich had said. And also, of course, when he was assassinated in 1942."

"Let's get back to Mielke," said the Ami with the ill-fitting glasses. "Was it Heydrich who made him your pigeon?"

"Yes."

"When did that happen?"

"Following the conversation at the piano," I said. "A couple of days after the fall of France."

"So June 1940."

"That's right."

15

GERMANY, 1940

I was summoned back to Prinz Albrechtstrasse, where the scene was frenetic to say the least. People were scurrying around with files. Phones were ringing almost continually. Couriers were running along corridors carrying important dispatches. There was even a gramophone playing the song "Erika," as if we were actually with the motorized SS as they drove on toward the Normandy coast. And, most unusually, everyone was smiling. No one ever smiled in that place. But that day they did. Even I had a smile on my face. To defeat France as quickly as we did seemed nothing short of miraculous. You have to bear in mind that many of us sat in the trenches of northern France for four years. Four years of slaughter and stalemate. And then a victory over our oldest enemy in just four weeks! You didn't have to be a Nazi to feel good about that. And if I'm honest, the summer of 1940 was when I came the closest to thinking well of the Nazis. Indeed, that was the time when being a Nazi hardly seemed to matter. Suddenly, we were all proud to be German again.

Of course, people were also feeling good because they thought—we thought—that the war was over before it had even begun. Hardly anyone was dead in comparison with the millions who'd died in the Great War. And England would have to make peace. The Russian back door was secure. And America wasn't interested in getting involved, as usual. All in all, it seemed like some sort of miraculous reprieve. I expect the French felt very differently, but in Germany there was national jubilation. And frankly, the last person on my mind when I walked into Heydrich's office that morning was a stupid little prick like Erich Mielke.

Seated at a table beside Heydrich was another uniformed SS man whom I didn't recognize. He was about thirty, slightly built, with a full head of light brown hair, a fastidious, almost feminine mouth, and the sharpest pair of eyes I'd seen outside of the leopard's enclosure at the Berlin Zoo. The left eye was particularly cat-like. At first I assumed it was narrowed against the smoke from his silver cigarette holder, but after a while I saw that the eye was permanently like that, as if he had lost his monocle. He smiled when Heydrich introduced us, and I saw that there was more than a passing resemblance to the young Bela Lugosi, always supposing that Bela Lugosi had ever been young. The SS officer's name was Walter Schellenberg, and I think he was a major then—much later on he became a general—but I wasn't really paying attention to the pips on his collar patch. I was more interested in Heydrich's uniform, which was that of a reserve major in the Luftwaffe. More interesting still was the fact that his arm was in a sling, and for several nervous minutes I supposed that my presence there had something to do with an attempt on his life he wanted me to investigate. "Oberkommissar Gunther is one of Kripo's best detectives," Heydrich told Schellenberg. "In the new Germany, that's a profession not without some hazard. Most philosophers argue that the world is ultimately mind or matter. Schopenhauer states that the final reality is human will. But whenever I see Gunther I am reminded of the overriding importance to the world of human curiosity, too. Like a scientist or an inventor, a good detective must be curious. He must have his hypotheses. And he must always seek to test them against the observable facts. Is it not so, Gunther?"

"Yes, Herr General."

"Doubtless he is even now wondering why I am wearing this Luftwaffe uniform and hoping secretly that it heralds my departure from Sipo so that he might enjoy an easier, quieter life." Heydrich smiled at his little joke. "Come now, Gunther. Isn't that exactly what you were thinking?"

"Are you leaving Sipo, Herr General?"

"No, I'm not." He grinned like a very clever schoolboy.

I said nothing.

"Try to contain your obvious relief, Gunther."

"Very well, General. I'll certainly do my best."

"You see what I mean, Walter? He remains his own man at all times."

Schellenberg just smiled and smoked and watched me with his cat's eyes and said nothing. We had one thing in common, at least. With Heydrich, nothing was always the safest thing to say.

"Since the invasion of Poland," explained Heydrich, "I've been volunteering as aircrew on a bomber. I was a rear gunner in an air attack on Lublin."

"It sounds rather hazardous, Herr General," I said.

"It is. But believe me, there's nothing quite like flying down on an enemy city at two hundred miles an hour with an MG 17 in your hands. I wanted to show some of these bureaucratic soldiers what the SS is made of. That we're not just a bunch of asphalt soldiers."

I assumed he was referring to Himmler.

"Very commendable, sir. Is that how you injured your arm?"

"No. No, that was an accident," he said. "I've also been training as a fighter pilot. I crashed during takeoff. My own stupid fault."

"Are you sure about that?"

Heydrich's self-satisfied smile stalled midflight, and for a moment I wondered if I'd gone too far.

"Meaning what?" he said. "That it wasn't an accident?"

I shrugged. "Meaning only that I imagine you would want to find out everything that went wrong before flying again." I was trying to back up a little from what, unwisely perhaps, I'd already put in his mind. "What kind of plane was it, sir?"

Heydrich hesitated, as if debating the idea in his own mind. "A Messerschmitt," he said quietly. "The Bf 110. It's not considered a very agile plane."

"Well, there are you. I can't think why I mentioned such a thing. I certainly didn't mean to imply that you aren't a good pilot, General. I'm sure they wouldn't let you get in the cockpit unless they were quite satisfied the airplane was airworthy. Me, I've never even been off the ground, but I should still want to be quite sure it wasn't anything mechanical before I went up again."

"Yes, perhaps you're right."

Schellenberg was nodding now. "It certainly couldn't do any harm, Herr General. Gunther's right."

He had a curious, high-pitched voice with a slight accent I found hard to place; and there was something very neat and dapper about him that reminded me of a butler, or a menswear salesman.

An attractive-looking SS secretary—what we used to call a gray mouse—came in carrying a tray with three coffee cups and three glasses of water, just like we were in a café on the Ku-damm, and thankfully we were distracted from the subject of Heydrich's accident—Schellenberg by the woman herself and Heydrich by the sound of the gramophone that was coming through the open door. For a moment he stamped his boots on the floor in time with the song and grinned happily.

"That's a marvelous sound, isn't it?"

"Wonderful, Herr General," said Schellenberg, who was still eyeing Heydrich's secretary, and the comment might just as easily have been about her as the music.

I could see his point. Her name was Bettina and she seemed too nice by half to be working for a devil like Heydrich.

When she went out again, the three of us started to sing. It was one of the few SS songs I didn't mind at all, since it couldn't have had less to do with the SS or even fighting a war. And, for a moment, I forgot where I was and whom I was with.

"On the heath there grows a little flower
And its name is Erika.
A hundred thousand little bees
Swarm around Erika
Because her heart is full of sweetness
And her flowery dress gives off a tender scent
On the heath there grows a little flower
And its name is Erika."

We sang all three verses, and by the end we were in such a jolly mood that Heydrich told Bettina to fetch us some brandy. A few minutes later we were toasting the fall of France, and then Heydrich was explaining the real reason for my presence in his office. He handed me a file, waited for me to open it, and said:

"You recognize the name on the file, of course."

I nodded. "Erich Mielke. What about him?"

"You saved his life, and then he and an accomplice murdered two policemen. And then his arrest was bungled by the Jew in charge of the investigation."

"You mean Kriminal-Polizeirat Heller," I said. "Yes, I remember him. Wasn't it Heller who successfully investigated the murder of that young SA fellow in the Beussellkeitz? The one who was stabbed to death by some communist thugs. What was his name? Herbert Norkus?"

"Thank you for the history lesson, Gunther," said Heydrich patiently. "None of us is likely to forget Herbert Norkus."

This was hardly surprising, as the murder of Norkus had been the subject of the very first Nazi propaganda movie, about the Hitler Youth. I hadn't seen the movie myself, but I thought it unlikely that Heller's part had even made it into the script. All the same, I thought it best not to push this detail any further with Heydrich.

"You'll be glad to know that Foreign Intelligence has managed to keep track of Mielke since you and Heller allowed him to slip through your fingers," he said. "Walter, why don't you bring the chief inspector up to date with what we have on him now."

"I'd be delighted, sir," said Schellenberg. "In Moscow we know Mielke attended the Lenin School under the name Walter Scheuer. Then he was given the name Paul Bach, and we assume this was the same Paul Bach who gave evidence against many of the German communist cadres following the Stalinist purge at the Hotel Lux in May 1935. Naturally, the Gestapo was at the same time monitoring the Mielke family home; and soon after the murders of Anlauf and Lenck the family moved from the Stettiner Strasse apartment to an address in Grünthaler Strasse, where, in September 1936, Mielke's younger sister Gertrud received a postcard from Madrid. This seemed to confirm what we already suspected, which was that Mielke had gone to Spain as a Chekist. During the civil war, he was going by the name of Captain Fritz Leissner and was assigned to a General Gomez, whom we know rather better as Wilhelm Zaisser, another German communist. It seems these bastards spent more time killing other Republicans than they did killing any Nationalists; and it's no accident that the Thirteenth International Brigade, also known as the Dabrowski Brigade, mutinied soon after the Battle of Brunette in July 1937 because of the appalling casualties inflicted on them as a result of the incompetence of their officers.

"Following the Republican defeat in January 1939, Mielke was one of thousands who crossed the border into France. The French started locking them up almost immediately. In October 1939, one of our agents, who was posing as a member of the French

Communist Party—they were also interned in the same concentration camps as the German communists—met a man he believed to have been Erich Mielke at the Buffalo Sports Stadium, in the south of Paris, which the French were using as a provisional camp for undesirable aliens. He said that Mielke told him he'd been transferred from another provisional camp, the Roland Garros Tennis Stadium. Soon after that, Mielke was transferred again, to one of two rather more permanent concentration camps in the south of France: the camp at Le Vernet, in Ariège, near Toulouse, or to Gurs, which is in the region of Aquitaine. We believe he's still in one of these camps. He knows we're looking for him, so naturally he'll be using a false name. And while conditions in these camps are generally held to be abominable, nevertheless, since the Soviet Union signed the nonaggression pact with Germany, they might actually be the safest place for him. Stalin has already sent back here several German communists in order to demonstrate his goodwill toward the Führer. And it's quite likely he would do the same with Erich Mielke. So, with France now in the hands of the Third Reich, this is our best chance in almost a decade to capture him."

"And," said Heydrich, "since you're the only man in Sipo who's ever had the pleasure to have met Mielke, that makes you uniquely qualified to go to France and make the arrest. The French are already proving to be extremely cooperative in this regard. They're as anxious to get rid of some of their German undesirables as we are to get hold of them. And you certainly won't find that you're the only police officer making the journey down there to arrest a fugitive from German justice. Merely one of the most important ones. Because, make no mistake about it, Gunther, Erich Mielke is very near the top of our wanted list."

"I have some questions, sir," I said.

Heydrich nodded.

"First of all, I don't speak French."

"That's not a problem at all. In Paris you will liaise with

Hauptmann Paul Kestner, whom I believe you know from your time together in Kripo. Kestner is from Alsace and speaks fluent French. He's ordered to offer you any assistance that you require. The two of you will report to my own deputy, General Werner Best of the Gestapo. Together with Helmut Knochen, who's the senior commander of security in Paris, he'll assign you some French police to assist in your mission, code-named Fafnir."

I nodded. "Fafnir, right you are, sir. I'm glad you didn't say Hagen."

It didn't happen very often, but Heydrich looked puzzled.

"In the Ring cycle, sir," I explained, "Hagen kills Gunther."

Heydrich smiled. "Well, I'll kill you if don't find Mielke," he said. "Understand?"

I was glad he was smiling. "Yes, Herr General."

"He'll need a uniform, sir," said Schellenberg.

"Have you a uniform, Gunther?"

"No, Herr General. Not yet."

"I thought not. Good. That gives us an opportunity to talk privately. Come with me. And bring Mielke's file with you. You'll need it."

He stood up, collected his hat, and walked to the door. I followed him to the outer office, where he was already telling Bettina to have his car brought to the front door and collecting a briefcase from Schellenberg. He took the file from me and placed it inside the briefcase.

"Are we going somewhere?" I asked.

"My tailor," he said, and marched toward the huge marble staircase. "You can give me the clothing coupons later on."

As we came out of the building the guards on Prinz Albrecht-strasse came to attention, and for a moment we waited for the car to appear. Heydrich permitted me to light his cigarette and then handed me the briefcase.

"Everything you need for Operation Fafnir is in that briefcase," he said. "Money, passes, travel documentation, and more besides. Much more. Which is why I wanted to talk to you in private." He glanced around at the two SS guards as if making sure they were out of earshot and then said the most extraordinary thing:

"You see, Gunther, we have something in common, you and I. Years ago, both of us were denounced as mischlings because, allegedly, we have a Jewish grandparent. Nonsense, of course. But not unconnected with what I told you before."

"You mean about how someone is trying to kill you."

"Yes. Having failed to persuade the Führer that there was any truth in these wicked rumors, it is certainly Himmler's intention to have me assassinated. Of course, I am not without resources of my own. Certain records pertaining to my family's past in Halle, and which might be open to misinterpretation, have been erased. And the person who denounced me—a naval cadet I knew at the academy in Kiel—that man met an unfortunate accident. He was killed in the Deutschland Incident of 1937, when the Republican Air Force attacked the port of Ibiza. That's the official version, anyway."

The car arrived. It was a large, open-top, black Mercedes. The driver, an SS sergeant, sprang out, saluted, and then opened the big suicide door and tipped the front seat forward.

"What took you so long, Klein?" said Heydrich.

"I'm sorry sir, but I was filling her up when your call came through. Where are we going?"

"Holter's, the tailor."

"Sixteen Tauenzienstrasse. Right you are, sir."

We drove south, as far as the corner of Bulow Strasse, and then west.

"That briefcase I gave you," said Heydrich. "It also contains a file about the man who denounced you, Gunther. In fact, that file is not unconnected with Mielke's file, as you will discover. You see, the man who denounced you was Hauptmann Paul Kestner. Your former schoolmate and Kripo colleague."

"Kestner." I nodded. "I always thought that was someone else, sir. This girl I used to know, who also knew Mielke."

"But you don't look surprised that it was Kestner."

"No, perhaps I'm not, Herr General."

"He was a member of the KPD before he was a Nazi. Did you know that?"

I shook my head.

"It was Kestner who tipped off his friends in the KPD that you and he were traveling to Hamburg to arrest Mielke. After you left Kripo, he hoped to divert suspicion from himself by alleging that it was you who had tipped off Mielke. Something that was easier to do if it turned out that you were part Jew."

I shook my head.

"Oh, it's all in the file," said Heydrich.

"No, that's not it, Herr General. I'm just disappointed, that's all. As you say, I've known Paul Kestner since we were at the same gymnasium, here in Berlin."

"It's always disappointing when one discovers that one has been betrayed. But in a sense it's liberating, too. It serves as a reminder that ultimately one can only ever truly rely on oneself."

"There's something I don't understand," I said. "If you know all of this, why am I meeting up with Paul Kestner in Paris?"

Heydrich tutted loudly and looked away for a moment as we drove onto Nollendorf Platz. There he pointed at the Mozart Hall Movie Theater. *The Four Feathers,*" he said. "A marvelous picture. Have you seen it?"

"Yes."

"Quite right. It's one of the Führer's favorites. This is a movie about revenge, is it not? Albeit a very British and sentimental kind of revenge. Harry Favisham returns the four white feathers to the same men and woman who had accused him of cowardice. Absurd, really. Speaking for myself, I should have preferred to see my former comrades suffer a little more than they did. And perhaps die, although not without revealing myself as their nemesis. Do you follow me?"

"I'm beginning to, Herr General."

"As your superior officer, I should inform you that it's no crime to have been a Communist Party member before one saw the light and became a National Socialist. I should also inform you that Paul Kestner is not without connections in the Wilhelmstrasse, and that these people have decided to overlook his dishonest role in the Mielke affair. Frankly, if we were to cashier every Sipo officer with an unfortunate past, there would be no one left to wear the uniform."

"Does he know?" I asked. "That his superiors are aware of what he did?"

"No. We prefer to keep things like that in reserve. For when we need to bring a man into line and persuade him to do what he's told. However"—Heydrich flicked his cigarette into the street and lifted his injured arm—"as you can see, accidents happen. Especially in time of war. And if some harm were to befall Hauptmann Kestner while he was in occupied France, I doubt that anyone would be surprised. Least of all me. After all, it's a long road between Paris and Toulouse and I daresay there are still a few pockets of French resistance. It would be a tragedy of war, just like the death of Paul Baumer reaching to protect a fledgling bird on the last page of *All Quiet on the Western Front*." Heydrich sighed. "Yes. A tragedy. But hardly a matter for regret."

"I see."

"Well, it's entirely a matter for you, Hauptsturmführer Gunther. Your chief inspector rank in Kripo entitles you to the rank of SS captain. The same as Kestner. It makes no difference to me if he lives or dies. It's your choice."

The car purred along Tauenzienstrasse toward the stalagmite steeples of the Kaiser Wilhelm Memorial Church and came to a rumbling halt in front of a tailor's shop. In the window was a tailor's dummy, which looked like the torso at the scene of a crime, and several bolts of pewter-colored cloth. Pedestrians shot

Heydrich a curious look as he climbed out of the car and walked his bowlegged walk to the front door of Wilhelm Holter. You could hardly blame them for that. With all the medals and badges on his Luftwaffe tunic he looked like an accomplished Boy Scout, albeit a rather sinister one.

I followed him through the door with the shop bell ringing in my ears, as if warning other customers of the plague we brought with us. Something fearful, anyway.

An unassuming man wearing pince-nez, a black armband, and a stiff collar came toward us washing one hand in the other like Pontius Pilate and smiling an intermittent smile, as if he were functioning on half power only.

"Ah yes," he said quietly. "General Heydrich, isn't it? Yes, please come through."

He ushered us into a room that belonged in the Herrenklub. There were leather armchairs, a clock ticking on a mantelpiece, a pair of full-length mirrors, and several glass cases containing a variety of military uniforms. On the walls were an abundance of royal warrants and pictures of Hitler and Goering, whose fondness for wearing uniforms of all colors was well-known. Through a green velvet curtain I could see several men cutting cloth or pressing half-finished uniforms with a hot iron, and to my surprise one of these men was an Orthodox Jew. It was a nice example of Nazi hypocrisy to have a Jewish tailor making an SS uniform.

"This officer needs an SS uniform," explained Heydrich. "Field Gray. And it has to be ready in one week's time. Ordinarily, I should send him to the SS Quartermaster for an off-the-peg Hugo Boss uniform, but he'll be traveling on the Führer's personal train, so he'll need to look smart. Can you do it, Herr Holter?"

The tailor looked surprised even to be asked such a question. He uttered a polite little guffaw and smiled with quiet confidence. "Oh, certainly, Herr General."

"Good," said Heydrich. "Send the account to my office. "You'll receive the clothing coupons from my office by return of post. Gunther? I will leave you in Herr Holter's capable hands. And make sure you get your men. Both of them." Then he turned and left.

Holter produced a notebook and a pencil and began asking questions and noting the answers.

"Rank?"

"Hauptmann."

"Any medals?"

"Iron Cross, with Royal Citation. Great War Participation Medal, with swords and wound badge. That's it."

"Trousers or riding breeches?"

I shrugged.

"Both," he said. "Dress dagger?"

I shook my head.

"Hat size?"

"Sixty-two centimeters."

Holter nodded. "We'll have Hoffmann's in Gneisenaustrasse send over a couple for you to try on. Until then, perhaps you'd like to slip off your jacket and I'll take your measurements." He glanced at a little calendar on the wall. "It's always a hurry with General Heydrich."

"Yes, it's never a good idea to disagree with him." I said, slipping off my jacket. "I do know that feeling. Where Heydrich is concerned, your black armband could be catching."

It was after I'd been measured and I was on my way out of the door that I bumped into Elisabeth Gehler, who was coming into the tailor's shop with a uniform box under her arm. I hadn't seen her very much since that night in 1931 when she'd taken offense at my turning up at her apartment and asking for Mielke's address. But she greeted me warmly, as if all that was forgotten now, and agreed to come and meet me for a coffee after she had delivered the uniform to Herr Holter.

I waited around the corner at Miericke, on Ranke Strasse, where the chocolate cake was still the best in Berlin.

When she arrived, she told me that since the beginning of the war she'd had little or no time for making dresses; everyone wanted her for tailoring uniforms.

"This war is over before it even got started," I told her. "You'll be back to dressmaking in no time at all."

"I hope you're right," she said. "Even so, I suppose that's why you were there, at Holter's. To get yourself a uniform."

"Yes. I have a police job to do in Paris next week."

"Paris." She closed her eyes for a moment. "What I wouldn't give to be going to Paris."

"You know, I was just thinking of you about an hour ago."

She pulled a face. "I don't believe you."

"Honestly, it's true. I was."

"Why?"

I shrugged. I hardly wanted to tell her that I was being sent to Paris to hunt down her old friend Erich Mielke and that this was the reason she was in my mind again.

"Oh, I was just thinking that it would be nice to see you again, Elisabeth. Perhaps when I get back from Paris we could see a movie together."

"I thought you said you were going to Paris next week."

"I am."

"Then what's wrong with seeing a movie this week?"

"If it comes to that," I said, "what's wrong with tonight?"

She nodded. "Pick me up at six," she said, and kissed me on the cheek.

We were on our way out of the coffee shop when she said, "I nearly forgot. I'm living somewhere else now."

"No wonder I couldn't find you."

"As if you tried. Motzstrasse. Number twenty-eight. First floor. My name is on the bell."

"I'm already looking forward to ringing it."

FRANCE, 1940

At least it wasn't a black uniform. But in the Anhalter Bahnhof, waiting to board the Reich Railways train early that July morning, I felt oddly uncomfortable dressed as a Sipo captain in spite of the fact that almost everyone else was wearing a uniform. It was as if I'd signed a contract in blood with Hitler himself. In the event the great Mephistopheles chose not to visit the French capital by train. The Gestapo got wind of at least two plots to kill him while he was in Paris, and the word aboard the train was that Hitler had already returned from a flying visit to the jewel in his crown of conquest via Le Bourget, on June 23. Consequently, although quite luxurious in many respects—there were, after all, several senior Wehrmacht generals aboard—the train we traveled in was not the *Amerika,* the special train carrying the Führer headquarters and, by all accounts, the last word in Pullman-class comfort. That curiously named train—possibly it was a pun based on the Herms Niel song I had sung in Heydrich's office—was, it seemed, back at the Tempelhof Repair Depot in the southwest of Berlin. Since meeting Elisabeth again, I rather wished I could have been there myself, for although a small part of me was looking forward to seeing Paris, mostly I felt a distinct lack of enthusiasm for my mission. A lot of people in Sipo would have leapt at an all-expenses-paid trip to the most glamorous city in the world. And a little bit of murder along the way wouldn't have bothered them in the slightest. There were some on that train who looked like they'd been murdering people since 1933. Including the fellow sitting opposite me, an SS-Unterstürmführer—a lieutenant I half recognized from police headquarters in Alexanderplatz.

His little rat's eyes got there ahead of me, however.

"Excuse me, sir," he said politely. "But aren't you Chief Inspector Gunther? From the Homicide Division?"

"Have we met?"

"I was working Vice Squad at the Alex when I think I saw you last. My name is Willms. Nikolaus Willms."

I nodded silently.

"Vice isn't as glamorous as Homicide," he said. "But it has its moments."

He smiled without smiling—the sort of expression a snake has when it opens its mouth to swallow something whole. He was smaller than me, but he had the ambitious look of a man who might eventually swallow something larger than himself.

"So what takes you to Paris?" I asked without much interest.

"This isn't my first trip," he said. "I've been there for the last two weeks. I only came back to Berlin to attend to a family matter."

"You still have some work to do there?"

"There's plenty of vice in Paris, sir."

"So I'm led to believe."

"Although with any luck I won't be stuck in Vice for very long."

"No?"

Willms shook his head. He was small but powerful, and sat with his legs apart and his arms folded, as if watching a football match. He said:

"After the SD school in Bernau, I was sent on an exclusive leadership course in Berlin-Charlottenburg. It was the people who ran that course who organized this posting. I speak fluent French, you see. I'm from Trier originally."

"So that's what I can hear in your accent. French. I imagine that comes in handy in your line of work."

"To be honest with you, sir, it's rather dull work. I'm hoping for something a bit more exciting than a lot of French whores."

"There are about five hundred soldiers on this train who would disagree with that, Lieutenant."

He smiled, a proper smile this time, with teeth, only it didn't work any better, the way a smile was supposed to work.

"So what are you hoping for?"

"My father was killed in the war," Willms explained. "At Verdun. By a French sniper. I was two when that happened So I've always hated the French. I hate everything about them. I suppose I'd like a chance to pay them back for what they did to me. For taking my dad away from us. For giving me such a miserable childhood. My family should have left Trier, but we couldn't afford to go. So we stayed. My mother and my sisters. We stayed in Trier and we were hated." He nodded thoughtfully. "I should very much like to work for the Gestapo in Paris. Giving the Franzis a hard time sounds just about right to me. Cool a few, if you know what I mean, sir."

"The war's over," I said. "I should think your chances for cooling any French, as you put it, are rather limited now. They've surrendered."

"Oh, I should think there are some left who've still got a bit of fight in them. Don't you? Terrorists. We'll have to deal with them, surely. If you hear of anything in that line, sir, perhaps you'd let me know. I'm keen to get on. And to get out of Vice." He smiled his reptilian smile and patted the briefcase on the seat next to him. "Until then," he added, "perhaps I might do you a favor."

"Oh? How?"

"In this briefcase I've got a list of about three hundred Paris restaurants and seven hundred hotels that are to be declared off-limits because of prostitution. And a list of about thirty that are officially approved. Not that anyone will take a blind bit of notice either way. It's been my experience of vice that all the law in the world won't stop a fellow who's intent on having a bit of mouse or a whore who's ready to give it to him. Anyway, it's my considered opinion that if a man is looking for a good time in Paris then he could do a lot worse than go to the Hotel Fairyland on the place Blanche in Pigalle. According to the Prefecture of Police in the rue de Lutèce, the girls working in Fairyland are free of venereal disease. Of course, it might be asked how they know that, and I think the simple answer would have to be that it's Paris, and of course the police would know that." He shrugged. "Anyway, I just thought you might like to know that yourself, sir. Before the word gets around."

"Thanks, Lieutenant. I'll bear it in mind. But I think I'm going to be too busy to go looking for any more trouble than I already have. I'm on a case, see? An old case, and I figure I've got my work laid out in front of me. Anything else gets laid out, I'm liable to get even more distracted than seems reasonable, even in Paris. I'd like to tell you more about it, but I can't for security reasons. You see, the man I'm after got away from me before. And I don't intend to let that happen again. They could put hot and cold running Michèle Morgan in my hotel bedroom and still I'd have to behave myself."

Willms smiled his snake smile, the one he probably used when he wanted to get some poor little snapper to give him one for free. I knew what these bulls from Vice were like. But while he was loathsome, I didn't doubt that he might actually have been useful to my mission, and I suppose I could have offered him a job. I had a letter from Heydrich that would have compelled any man's commanding officer to offer me his full cooperation. But I didn't offer him a job. I didn't because you don't pick up a snake unless you really have to.

Arriving at Paris's Gare de l'Est in the late afternoon, I presented my taxi warrant to a wurst-faced NCO, who directed me to a military car already occupied by another officer. Petrol was scarce, and since we were to be billeted in the same hotel across the river, we were obliged to share a driver, an SS corporal from Essen who attempted to forestall our impatience at getting to the hotel by warning us that the speed limit was only forty kph.

"And it's worse at night," he added. "Then it's just thirty. Which is really crazy."

"Surely it's safer that way," I said. "Because of the blackout."

"No, sir," said the corporal. "Nighttime is when this city comes alive. That's when people really want to get somewhere. Somewhere important."

"Like where?" asked my brother officer, a naval lieutenant who was attached to the Abwehr—German military intelligence. "For example?"

The driver smiled. "This is Paris, sir. There's only one business of real importance here, sir. Or so you might think from the number of staff officers I drive to their liaisons, sir. The only business in Paris that's doing better than ever before, sir, is the business of male and female relations, sir. In a word, prostitution. This city is rife with it. And you'd think some of these Germans coming here have never seen a girl before, the way they go at it."

"Good God," exclaimed the Abwehr lieutenant, whose name was Kurt Boger.

"There will be plenty of German reinforcements on the way soon," said the driver. "Little Germans, that is. My advice to you both is to find yourselves a nice little girlfriend and get it for free. But if you're short of time, the best brothels in the city are Maison Chabanais, at number twelve rue Chabanais, and the One Twenty-two on rue de Provence."

"I heard the Fairyland was good," I said.

"No, that's rubbish, sir. With all due respect. Whoever told you that is talking out of their arse. The Fairyland is a real knock-ing shop. You want to keep away from there, sir, in case you wind up with a dose of jelly. If you'll forgive me for saying so. Maison Chabanais is for officers only. The madame, Mademoiselle Marthe, runs a very classy house."

Boger, hardly a typical sailor, was tutting loudly and shaking his head.

"But you'll be all right at the Hôtel Lutetia," said the driver, changing the subject. "It's a very respectable hotel. There's nothing going on there."

"I'm relieved to hear it," said Boger.

"All of the best hotels have been taken over by us Germans," said the driver. "The general staff with red stripes on their trousers and the party big guns are at the Majestic and the Crillon. But I reckon you're both better off here on the left bank."

Security near the Lutetia was tight. A protective zone of sand-bags and wooden barriers had been established around the hotel and armed sentries manned the entrance, to the general bewilder-ment of the hotel's doorman and porters. All traffic save German military vehicles was forbidden in the zone. There wasn't much traf-fic, however, since the last thing the French army had done before abandoning the city to its fate was to set fire to several fuel-storage depots to prevent them from falling into our hands. But the Paris Métro was still running, that much was evident. You could feel it underneath your feet in the Lutetia hotel lobby. Not that it was easy to see your feet, there were so many German officers milling around—SS, RSHA, Abwehr, Secret Field Police (the GFP)—and all goose-stepping on one another's toes, because there was no one I knew who could have told you for sure where the responsibilities of one security service ended and another's began. It wasn't exactly Babel, but there was plenty of confusion all around, and in turning men from the fear of God to a constant dependence on his own power, Hitler made a convincing Nimrod.

The Lutetia staff were no less confused than we were ourselves. When I asked the German-speaking porter to identify the cupola I could see from my window, he told me he wasn't sure; and, calling a maid over to the window, they debated the matter for a couple of minutes before, finally, they decided that the cupola was the dome of the church at Les Invalides where Napoleon was buried. A little later on I discovered that it was in fact the Pantheon, in the opposite direction. Otherwise, the service at the Lutetia was good, although hardly on a par with the Adlon in Berlin. And I couldn't help favorably contrasting my current French accommodation with what I'd endured in the Great War. Crisp, clean sheets and a well-stocked cocktail bar made a very pleasant change from a flooded trench and some warm ersatz coffee. The experience was almost enough to complete my conversion to being a Nazi.

I wasn't fond of the French. The war—the Great War—was much too recent in my mind to make me like them, but I felt sorry for them now that they were second-class citizens in their own country. They were forbidden the best hotels and restaurants; Maxim's was under German management; on the Paris Métro, first-class carriages were reserved for Germans; and the French, for whom good food was virtually a religion, found it was rationed and there were long lines for bread, wine, meat, and cigarettes. Of course, nothing was in short supply if you were German. And I enjoyed an excellent dinner at Lapérouse—a nineteenth-century restaurant that looked more like a brothel than the brothels.

The next day, Paul Kestner was waiting for me in the Lutetia lobby, as arranged. We shook hands like old friends and admired each other's tailoring. German officers did a lot of that in 1940, especially in Paris, where fine clothes seemed to matter more.

Kestner was tall and thin and round-shouldered like someone who had spent a lot of time behind a desk. His head was almost completely hairless apart from the dark eyebrows that softened his solidly cut features. It was a face engraved with integrity, and it was hard to believe that a man with a jaw as square as the Brandenburg Gate could have betrayed the police service and then me with such impunity. Kestner's was a head that belonged on a Swiss banknote, only I'd spent a large part of the rail journey from Berlin considering the idea of putting a bullet in it. Heydrich's myrmidons had done their homework well. The file he'd handed me in his car contained a copy of the anonymous letter Kestner had sent to the Jew desk denouncing me as a mischling, as well as a sample of Kestner's own identical handwriting, which, conveniently, he had also signed. There was even a photograph taken in March 1925—before he'd joined the Berlin police—of Kestner wearing the uniform of a Communist Party cadre and aboard a KPD election bus, with a placard over his shoulder on which was printed "You Must Elect Thalmann." At the very same moment I smiled and shook Kestner's hand and talked about the old times we shared, I wanted to punch his teeth in, and the only thing that seemed likely to stop me from doing it was the affection I still held for his little sister.

"How's Traudl?" I asked. "Has she finished medical school?"

"Yes. She's a doctor now. Working for something called the Charitable Foundation for Health and Institutional Care. Some government-funded clinic in Austria."

"You'll have to give me the address," I said. "So that I can send her a postcard from Paris."

"It's the Schloss Hartheim," he explained. "In Alkoven, near Linz."

"Not too near Linz, I hope. Hitler's from Linz."

"Same old Bernie Gunther."

"Not quite. You're forgetting this pirate hat I'm wearing now." I tapped the silver skull and crossbones on my gray officer's cap.

"That reminds me." Kestner glanced at his wristwatch. "We have an eleven-o'clock appointment with Colonel Knochen at the Hôtel du Louvre."

"He's not here at the Lutetia?"

"No. Colonel Rudolf of the Abwehr is in charge here. Knochen likes to run his own show. The SD is mostly at the Hôtel du Louvre, on the other side of the river."

"I wonder why they put me here."

"Possibly to piss Rudolf off," said Kestner. "Since almost certainly he knows nothing about your mission. By the way, Bernie, what is your mission? The Prinz Albrechtstrasse has been rather secretive about what you're doing in Paris."

"You remember that communist who murdered the two policemen in Berlin in 1931? Erich Mielke?"

To his credit, Kestner didn't even flinch at the mention of this name.

"Vaguely," he said.

"Heydrich thinks he's in a French concentration camp somewhere in the south of France. My orders are to find him, get him back to Paris, and then arrange his transport back to Berlin, where he's to stand trial."

"Nothing else?"

"What else could there be?"

"Only that we could have organized that on our own, without your having to come here to Paris. You don't even speak French."

"You forget, Paul. I've met Mielke. If he's changed his name, as seems likely, I might be able to identify him."

"Yes, of course. I remember now. We just missed him in Hamburg, didn't we?"

"That's right."

"Seems like a lot of effort for just one man. Are you sure there's nothing else?"

"What Heydrich wants, Heydrich gets."

"Point made," said Kestner. "Well. Shall we walk? It's a fine day."

"Is it safe?"

161

Kestner laughed. "From who? The French?" He laughed again. "Let me tell you something about the French, Bernie. They know that it's in their interest to get on with us Fridolins. That's what they call us. Quite a lot of them are happy we're here. Christ, they're even more anti-Semitic than we are." He shook his head. "No. You've got nothing to worry about from the French, my friend."

Unlike Kestner, I didn't speak a word of French, but it was easy to find your way around Paris. There were German direction signs on every street corner. It was a pity I didn't have a similar arrangement inside my own head; it might have made it easier to decide what to do about Kestner.

Kestner's French was, to my Fridolin ears, perfect, which is to say he sounded like a Frenchman. His father was a chemist who, disgusted by the Dreyfus affair, had left Alsace to live in Berlin. In those days, Berlin had been a more tolerant place than France. Paul Kestner had been just five years old when he came to live in Berlin, but for the rest of his life his mother always spoke to him in French.

"That's how I got this posting," he said as we walked north to the Seine.

"I didn't think it was because of your love of art."

The Hôtel du Louvre on the rue de Rivoli was older than the Lutetia but not dissimilar, with four façades and several hundred rooms; with an international reputation for luxury, it was a natural choice for the Gestapo and the SD. Security was every bit as tight as at the Lutetia, and we were obliged to sign in at a makeshift guardroom inside the front door. An SS orderly escorted us through the lobby and up a sweeping staircase to the public rooms, where the SD had established some temporary offices. Kestner and I were ushered into a tasteful salon with a rich red carpet and a series of hand-painted murals. We sat down at a long mahogany table and waited. A few minutes passed before three SD officers entered the room—one of whom I recognized.

The last time I had seen Herbert Hagen had been in 1937 in

Cairo, where he and Adolf Eichmann were attempting to make contact with Haj Amin, the Grand Mufti of Jerusalem. Hagen had been an SS sergeant then and a rather incompetent one. Now he was a major and aide to Colonel Helmut Knochen, who was a lugubrious officer of about thirty—about the same age as Hagen. The third officer, also a major, was older than the other two, with thick, horn-rimmed glasses and a face that was as thin and gray as the piping on his cap. His name was Karl Bömelburg. But it was Hagen who took charge of the meeting and came swiftly to the point without any reference to our former meeting. That suited me just fine.

"General Heydrich has ordered us to provide you with all available assistance in visiting the refugee camps at Le Vernet and Gurs," he said. "And in facilitating the arrest of a wanted communist murderer. But you will appreciate that these camps are still under the control of the French police."

"I was led to believe that they would cooperate with our extradition request," I said.

"That's true," said Knochen. "Even so, under the terms of the armistice signed on June 22 those refugee camps are in the non-occupied zone. That means we have to pay lip service to the idea that in that part of France, at least, they remain in charge of their own affairs. It's a way of avoiding hostility and resistance."

"In other words," said Major Bömelburg, "we get the French to do our dirty work."

"What else are they good for?" said Hagen.

"Oh, I don't know," I said. "The food at Lapérouse is quite spectacular."

"Good point, Captain," said Bömelburg.

"We shall have to involve the Préfecture de Police in your mission," said Knochen. "So that the French might persuade themselves that they are preserving French institutions and the French way of life. But I tell you, gentlemen, that the loyalty of the French police is indispensable to us. Hagen? Who's the Franzi that the *maison* has put up as liaison?" He looked my way. "The *maison* is what we call the *flics* in the rue de Lutèce. The Préfecture de Police. You should see the building, Captain Gunther. It's as big as the Reichstag."

"The Marquis de Brinon, sir," said Hagen.

"Oh yes. You know, for a republic, the French are awfully impressed by aristocratic titles. They're almost as bad as the Austrians in that respect. Hagen, see if the Marquis can suggest anyone to help the captain."

Hagen looked awkward. "Actually, sir, we're not entirely certain that the Marquis isn't married to a Jew."

Knochen frowned. "Do we have to worry about that sort of thing now? We've only just got here." He shook his head. "Besides, it's not his wife who's the liaison officer, is it?"

Hagen shook his head.

"All in good time we shall see who is a Jew and who isn't a Jew, but right now it seems to me the priority is the apprehension of a communist fugitive from German justice. A murderer. Isn't that right, Captain Gunther?"

"That's right, sir. He murdered two policemen."

"As it happens," said Knochen, "this department is already in the process of drawing up a list of wanted war criminals to present to the French. And in the establishment of a special joint commission—the Kuhnt Commission—to oversee these matters in the unoccupied zone. A German officer, Captain Geissler, has already gone down to Vichy to begin the work of this commission. And, in particular, to hunt for Herschel Grynszpan. You will perhaps recall that it was Grynszpan, a German-Polish Jew, who murdered Ernst vom Rath here, in Paris, in November 1938, and whose actions provoked such a strong outpouring of feeling in Germany."

"I remember it very well, sir," I said. "I live on Fasanenstrasse. Just off the Ku-damm. The synagogue at the end of my street was burned down during that strong outpouring of feeling you were talking about, Herr Colonel."

"A representative of the German Foreign Ministry, Herr Dr. Grimm, is also on Grynszpan's trail," said Knochen. "It seems that the little Jew was here in Paris, in the Fresnes Prison, until early June, when the French decided to evacuate all of the prisoners to Orléans. From there he was sent to prison in Bourges. However, he didn't arrive there. The convoy of buses transporting the prisoners was attacked by German aircraft, and after that the picture is rather confused."

"As a matter of fact, sir," said Bömelburg, "we rather think that Grynszpan might have gone to Toulouse."

"If that's the case, then what's Geissler doing in Vichy?"

"Setting up this Kuhnt Commission," said Bömelburg. "To be fair to Geissler, for a while there was also a rumor that Grynszpan was in Vichy, too. But Toulouse now looks like a better bet."

"Bömelburg? Karl. Correct me if I'm wrong," said Knochen. "But I seem to recall that this French concentration camp at Le Vernet—where Captain Gunther's quarry may be imprisoned—is in the Ariège *département*, in the mid-Pyrenees. That's near Toulouse, is it not?"

"Quite near, sir," agreed Bömelburg. "Toulouse is in the neighboring department of Haute-Garonne and about sixty kilometers north of Le Vernet."

"Then it strikes me," said Knochen, "that you and Captain Gunther should both get yourselves to Toulouse as quickly as possible. Perhaps the day after tomorrow. Bömelburg? You can remain in Toulouse and look for Grynszpan while Gunther here travels further south, to Le Vernet. Have the Marquis find someone to go with Gunther and Kestner to smooth over any ruffled French feathers. Meanwhile, I shall send a telegram to Philippe le Gaga in Vichy and inform him of what is happening. I daresay that by the time you get down there we will have a clearer idea of who to arrest and who to leave where they are."

"Any trains running down that way yet, sir?" This was Kestner. "I'm afraid not."

"Pity. That's rather a long drive. About six hundred kilometers. You know, it might be an idea to take a leaf out of the Führer's book and fly down there from Le Bourget. In a couple of hours we could be in Biarritz, where a motorized detachment from the SS-VT or secret GFP could take us on to Le Vernet and Toulouse."

"Agreed." Knochen looked at Hagen. "See to it. And find out if there are there any motorized detachments of SS operating that far south."

"Yes, sir, there are," said Hagen. "In which case the only question that remains is whether these men should be wearing uniforms when they cross the demarcation line into the French zone."

"An officer's uniform might lend us more authority, sir," argued Kestner.

"Gunther? What do you think?" asked Knochen.

"I agree with Captain Kestner. In a surrender situation, it's as well to be reminded that the surrender began with a war. After 1918, I think the French would do well to learn a little humility. If they'd treated us better at Versailles, then we might not be here at all. So I don't see any sense in trying to sugarcoat the pill they have to swallow. There's no getting away from the fact that they just got their arses kicked. The sooner they recognize it, the sooner we can all go home. But I came here to arrest a man who murdered two policemen. And I don't much care if some Franzi doesn't care for my manners while I'm doing it. Since I put on a uniform I don't much care for them myself. I can take the uniform off again and pretend to be something I'm not in order to get the job done, but I can't pretend to be diplomatic and charming. I never was one for French kissing. So to hell with their feelings, I say."

"Bravo, Captain Gunther," said Knochen. "That was a fine speech."

Maybe it was and maybe I even believed some of it, too. One

thing I said was certainly true: The sooner I went home, the better I was going to feel about a lot of things, especially myself. Mixing with anti-Semites like Herbert Hagen reminded me just why I'd never become a Nazi. And French victory or no French victory, I wouldn't ever be able to overcome my instinctive loathing of Adolf Hitler.

That afternoon I went to see Les Invalides. It was a very Nazi-looking monument. The front door had more gold than the Valley of the Kings, but the atmosphere was that of a public swimming bath. The mausoleum itself was a piece of mahogany-colored marble that resembled an enormous tea caddy. Hitler had visited Les Invalides just a couple of weeks before. And I can't have been the only person who wished that it had been he and not the Emperor Napoleon who was inside the six coffins that were contained in that overblown mausoleum. After his escape from Elba, I suppose they were worried the little monster might escape from his grave, like Dracula. Maybe they'd even put a stake through his heart just to be on the safe side. Burying Hitler in pieces looked like a better bet. With the Eiffel Tower through his heart.

Like every other German in Paris that summer, I'd brought a camera with me. So I walked around and took some photographs. In the Parc du Champ de Mars, I photographed some German soldiers getting directions from a gendarme. When he saw me the gendarme saluted smartly, as if a German officer's uniform really did command authority. But the way I saw it, the French police had an attitude problem. They didn't seem to mind the fact that they'd been defeated. Back in Germany, I'd seen cops look less happy when they failed to get elected to the Prussian Police Officers' Association.

I enjoyed another solitary dinner in a quiet restaurant on the rue de Varennes before returning to the Lutetia. The hotel was a mixture of Art Nouveau and Art Deco, but the swastika flag that appeared on the sinuous, broken-art pediment below the Lutetia's name was the clearest indication of the neobrutalism that afflicted its guests, me included.

The bar was busy and surprisingly inviting. A Welte-Mignon pianola was playing a selection of maudlin German tunes. I ordered a cognac and smoked a French cigarette and avoided the eye of the reptilian lieutenant who'd been on the train from Berlin. When he looked like he was headed my way, I finished my brandy and left. I rode the elevator up to the seventh floor and walked along the curving corridor to my room. A maid came out of another room and smiled. To my surprise, she spoke good German.

"Would you like me to turn down your bed linen for the night, sir?"

"Thanks," I said and, opening my door, complimented her German.

"I'm Swiss. I grew up speaking French and German and Italian. My father runs a hotel in Bern. I came to Paris to get some experience."

"Then we have something in common," I told her. "Before the war I worked at the Hotel Adlon, in Berlin."

She was impressed with that, which was of course my intention, as she was not without her charms. A little homely perhaps. But I was in the mood to think well of home and homely-looking girls. And when she finished her duties, I gave her some German money and the rest of my cigarettes for no other reason than I wanted her to think better of me than I thought of myself. Especially the man I saw in the mirror on the front of the wardrobe. In some pathetic little fantasy I imagined her coming back in the small hours, knocking on my door, and climbing into my bed. As things worked out, this wasn't so far from the mark. But that was later on, and when she left I wished I hadn't given her my last cigarettes.

"Well, at least you won't fall asleep with a cigarette in your hand and set the bed on fire, Gunther," I said, with one eye on the brass fire extinguisher that stood in the corner of the room next to the door. I closed the window, undressed, and went to bed. For a while I lay there feeling a little drunk, staring up at the blank ceiling and wondering if I should have gone to the Maison Chabanais after all. And perhaps I might even have got up and gone there if it hadn't been for the thought of putting on my riding boots again. Sometimes morality is just a corollary of laziness. Besides, it felt good to be back in the world of grand-hotel luxury. The bed was a good one. Sleep quickly came my way and put an end to all thoughts of what I might have been missing at the Maison Chabanais. A deep sleep that became unnaturally deeper as the night progressed and almost put an end to all thoughts of Maison Chabanais and Paris and my mission. The kind of sleep that almost put an end to me.

17

FRANCE, 1940

I told myself I must have dreamed the whole thing. I was back in the dugout. Had to be, or else why could I smell wintergreen ointment? We used it as a winter warmer for weathered or chapped hands in the colder months, and in the trenches, that was nearly all of them. Wintergreen was also an excellent chest rub for when you had a fever or a cough or a sore throat, which, because of the lice, overcrowding, and damp, was much of the time. Sometimes we even fingered a bit of the stuff inside our nostrils, just to keep the smell of death and decay at bay.

I had a sore throat. And I had a cough. The cold was on my chest and so was something else, only it wasn't wintergreen. It was a nurse and she was on top of me, and I was lifting her skirt so that she could mount me properly. Only, she wasn't a nurse at all but a hotel maid, a nice homely girl from Bern, and she'd come to keep me company after all. I reached for her breasts and she slapped me hard, twice, hard enough to make me catch my breath and then cough some more. Twisting away from underneath her, I retched onto the floor. She jumped off the bed and, coughing herself, went to the window and threw it open and hung her head outside for a moment before she came back to me, hauled me off the bed, and tried to drag me toward the door.

I was still coughing and retching when two men in white jackets came and carried me away on a stretcher. Outside the hotel, on the boulevard Raspail, I started to feel a little better as I managed to haul some of the fresh morning air into my lungs.

They took me to the Lariboisière Hospital on rue Ambroise-Paré. There they put a drip in my arm and a German army doctor told me I'd been gassed.

"Gassed?" I said wheezily. "With what?"

"Carbon tetrachloride," said the doctor. "It seems that the fire extinguisher in your room was faulty. But for the maid who detected the smell outside your room door, you'd probably be dead. The CTC converts to phosgene when it's exposed to air, which is how it puts the fire out. It suffocates it. You, too, very nearly. You're a lucky man, Captain Gunther. All the same, we'd like to keep you here for a while, to keep an eye on your liver and kidney functions."

I started coughing again. My head felt like the Eiffel Tower had collapsed on top of it. My throat felt like I'd tried to swallow it. But at least I was alive. I'd seen plenty of men gassed in France, and this wasn't anything like that. At least I wasn't bringing anything up. You've got to see a man retching two liters of yellow liquid every hour, drowning in his own mucus, to know how appalling it is to die from a gas attack. It was said that Hitler had been gassed and was temporarily blinded, and if that was so, it explained a lot. Whenever I saw him on a newsreel yelling his head off, gesticulating wildly, beating his breast, choking with his hatred of the Jews or the French or the Bolsheviks, he always reminded me of someone who had just been gassed.

In the early evening I started to feel better. Well enough to receive a visitor. It was Paul Kestner.

"They said you had an accident with a fire extinguisher. What did you do? Drink it?"

"It wasn't that type of a fire extinguisher."

"I thought there was only the one kind. The kind that puts out a fire."

"This one was the type that smothers a fire with chemicals. Takes away all the oxygen. That's kind of what happened to me."

"Someone catch you smoking in bed?"

"I've spent most of the day wondering that myself. And not liking any of the answers."

"Such as what, for instance?"

"I used to work in a hotel. The Adlon, in Berlin. And I learned a lot about what they do and what they don't do in hotels. And one of the things they don't do is to put fire extinguishers in the bedrooms. One reason is in case a guest gets drunk and decides to hose down the curtains. The other reason is that a lot of extinguishers are more dangerous than the fires they're meant to deal with. It's a funny thing, but when I arrived at the Lutetia I don't recall there being an extinguisher in my room. But there was one there last night. If I hadn't been drunk myself, I might have paid more attention to it."

"Are you suggesting someone tampered with it?"

"It seems so obvious to me that I wonder why you should sound surprised."

"Surprised? Yes, of course I'm surprised, Bernie. You're implying that someone tried to murder you in a hotel full of policemen."

"Tampering with a fire extinguisher is just the sort of thing a cop would know about. Besides, none of us at the Lutetia has a room key."

"That's because we're all on the same side. You can't mean a German tried to kill you."

"I do mean."

"But why not a Frenchman? We did just fight a war with these people, after all. Surely if it was anyone—and I'm not convinced it was anything but an accident—it would be one of them. A porter, perhaps. Or a patriotic waiter."

"And among all of the bastards he could have killed, he just chose me at random, is that it?" I shook my head, which seemed to provoke another violent fit of coughing.

Kestner poured a glass of water and handed it to me.

I drank it and caught my breath.

"Thanks. Besides. The kind of staff a grand hotel employs? It goes against everything they believe in to kill a guest. Even a guest they might despise."

Kestner went to the window and looked out. We were in a fourth-floor room in the high mansard roof of the hospital. You could see and sometimes hear the Gare du Nord just a few blocks away.

"But why would any German officer want to kill you? They would have to have a damn good motive."

For a moment I considered suggesting one: Anyone who had already denounced me to the Gestapo as a mischling would, I thought, have reason enough to kill me. Instead, I said:

"I wasn't always held in such good odor by our political masters. You remember what it was like in Kripo before 1933? Well, of course you do. You're about the one person in Paris I can talk to about this, Paul. Who I can trust."

"I'm relieved to hear it, Bernie. But just for the record, I spent most of last night at the One Twenty-two. The brothel."

"You forget," I said. "Everyone has to sign in and out of the hotel. I could easily check if you were in the hotel last night."

"Yes, you're right. I did forget that. You always were a better detective than I was." He came away from the window and sat on the edge of my bed.

"You're alive, that's the main thing. And you needn't worry about Mielke. I'm sure we'll find him. You can tell Heydrich that if he's in one of those French concentration camps, we'll find him as sure as there's an Amen in a church service. You can go back to Berlin confident in the knowledge that when we fly down there tomorrow, we'll take proper care of it."

"What makes you think I'm not coming with you?"

"Your doctor said that it would be several days before you were fit enough to resume your duties," said Kestner. "Surely you'll want to get home and recuperate."

"I'm working for Heydrich, remember? He's a bit like the God of Abraham. It's never a good idea to risk his wrath, because retribution is often direct. No, I'll be on that plane tomorrow even if you have to tie me on the undercarriage. Not a bad idea at that. The doc says I need plenty of fresh air."

Kestner shrugged. "All right. If you say so. It's your luck that's as black as pitch, not mine."

"Exactly. Besides, what would I do here in Paris except go to Maison Chabanais or One Twenty-two? Or one of those other puff houses."

"The car leaves the Hôtel du Louvre for Le Bourget at eight o'clock tomorrow morning." Kestner shot me an exasperated, weary sort of look and smacked the side of his thigh with his cap. Then he went away.

I closed my eyes for a moment and submitted to a long fit of coughing. But I wasn't worried. I was in a hospital. In hospitals people get better all the time. Some of them, anyway.

18

FRANCE, 1940

It was early the next morning when an SS staff car arrived to drive me back to the hotel, to collect my things, and then to the airport. Paris still wasn't awake, but for any decent Frenchman the city probably looked better with eyes closed. A detachment of soldiers was marching along the Champs-Élysées; German trucks were pouring in and out of the army garage that was located in the Grand Palais; and in case anyone was still in any doubt about it, on the façade of the Palais Bourbon they were erecting a large V for victory and a sign that read "Germany Is Everywhere Victorious." It was a bright, sunny summer's day, but Paris looked almost as depressing as Berlin. Still, I was feeling better. At my request, the hospital doctor had shot me full of dope to put some raspberry into my beer. Amphetamines, he said. Whatever it was, I felt like Saint Vitus was holding my hand. It didn't stop the pain in my chest and throat from all the retching I'd done, but I was ready to go flying. All I had to do was go back to the hotel, get into my uniform, and find a nice tall building for a takeoff.

The hotel manager was pleased to see me standing up. He'd have been glad to see me in a flower vase. It's bad for business when guests die in their rooms. I was alive and that was all that mattered. My old room was closed up because of the strong smell of chemicals in there, and my clothes had been taken to a suite on another floor. He seemed relieved when I told him I was going south to Biarritz for a few days. I said I was going up to my new room and that I wanted to say thanks to the maid who'd saved my life, and he said he'd arrange this immediately.

Then I went upstairs and took my field gray uniform out of the closet. It carried a strong smell of chemicals or gas and brought on a strong feeling of nausea as I recalled breathing the stuff. I opened the French window, hung my uniform there for a minute, and then rinsed my face with cold water. There was a knock at the door and I went to open it with shaking knees.

The maid was prettier than I remembered. Her nose wrinkled a little when she caught the smell of chemicals on my uniform, although it could just as easily have been the sight of it. But in truth it probably was the smell; in the summer of 1940 it was only Germans, Czechs, and Poles who had good reason to fear the field gray uniform of an SD captain.

"Thank you, mademoiselle. For saving my life."

"It was nothing."

"Nothing to you. But quite a bit to me."

"You don't look very well," she observed.

"I feel better than I look, I think. But that's probably down to what was in the needle I had for breakfast this morning."

"Which is all very well, but what's going to happen at dinnertime?"

"If I live that long, I'll let you know. Like I said, my life means quite a bit to me. So I'm going to do you a favor. Relax. It's not that kind of favor. Underneath this uniform I'm really not a bad fellow. How would you like to get some real hotel experience? I don't mean making beds and cleaning toilets. I mean in hotel management. I can fix that for you. In Berlin. At the Adlon. There's nothing wrong with this place, but it strikes me that Paris is going to be fine if you're German and not so fine if you're anything else."

"You'd do that? For me?"

"All I need from you is a little information."

She smiled a coy little smile. "You mean about the man who tried to kill you?"

"See what I mean? I knew you were too smart to be cleaning toilets."

"Smart enough. But a little confused. Why would one German officer want to murder another? After all, Germany is everywhere victorious."

I smiled. I liked her spirit. "That's what I mean to find out, mademoiselle . . . ?"

"Matter. Renata Matter." She nodded. "All right, Major."

"Captain. Captain Bernhard Gunther."

"Maybe they'll promote you. If they don't kill you first."

"There's always that possibility. Unfortunately, I think I'm a lot harder to promote than I am to kill." I started to cough again and kept it going for the sake of effect; at least that's what I told myself.

"I can believe that." Renata fetched me a glass of water. She moved gracefully, like a ballerina. Looked like one, too, being small and slim. Her hair was dark and quite short and a little boyish, but I liked that. What I previously saw as being homeliness now looked more like a very natural, girlish beauty.

I drank the water. Then I said, "So what makes you think someone tried to kill me?"

"Because there shouldn't have been a fire extinguisher in your room."

"Do you know where it is now?"

"The manager, Monsieur Schreider, he took it away."

"Pity."

"There's one the same on the wall along the corridor. Would you like me to fetch it for you?"

I nodded, and she went out of my room and returned a moment later carrying a brass extinguisher. Made by the Pyrene Manufacturing Company of Delaware, it had an integrated hand-pump that was used to expel a jet of liquid toward a fire and contained about nine liters of carbon tetrachloride. The container wasn't pressurized and was designed to be refilled with a fresh supply of chemical after use through a filling plug.

"When I found you, the filler cap had been removed," she said. "And the extinguisher was lying beside your bed. The chemical had poured onto the carpet beneath your nose. In other words, it looked deliberate."

"Have you mentioned this to anyone?"

"No one's asked me. Everyone believes it was an accident."

"For your own safety, it would be best if they continue to believe that, Renata."

She nodded.

"Did you see anyone enter or leave my room? Or hanging around in the corridor outside?"

Renata thought for a moment. "I don't know. To be honest, with everyone in uniform, all Germans look more or less alike."

"But not all of them are as handsome as me, surely?"

"That's true. Perhaps that's why they tried to kill you. Out of jealousy."

I grinned. "I never thought of that. As a motive, I mean."

She sighed. "Look, there's something I haven't told you. And I want your word that you'll leave my name out of it whenever you do what it is you're going to do. I don't want any trouble."

"It'll be fine," I said. "I'll look after you."

"And who looks after you? Maybe you were a champion when you walked into this hotel, but right now you look like you're in need of a good cornerman."

"All right. I'll keep you out of it. You have my word."

"As a German officer."

"What's that worth after Munich?"

"Good point."

"How about my word as someone who detests Hitler and all that he stands for, including this ridiculous uniform?"

"Better," she said.

"And who might wish the German army had never crossed the Rhine except for one thing."

"What's that?"

"I wouldn't have met you, Renata."

She laughed and looked away for a moment. She was wearing a black uniform and a little white pinafore. Hesitantly, she put a hand in the pocket of her pinafore and took out a brass plug about the size of a champagne cork. Handing it to me, she said, "I found this. The missing plug from the fire extinguisher in your room. It was in the wastepaper basket of the man in room fifty-five."

"Good girl. Can you find out the name of the officer who's in fifty-five?"

"I already did. His name is Lieutenant Willms. Nikolaus Willms." She paused. "Do you know him?"

"I met him for the first time on the train from Berlin. He's a cop specializing in vice. Hates the French. Face like a snake charmer, only without the charm. That's about all I know about him. I can't imagine why he would want to kill me. It doesn't make any sense."

"Perhaps he made a mistake. Got the wrong room."

"A French farce by Georges Feydeau doesn't normally include murder."

"What will you do now?"

"Nothing, for the moment. I have to leave Paris for a few days. Maybe I'll have thought of something by the time I come back. In the meantime, how would you like to earn some more German money?"

"Doing what?"

"Keep an eye on him?"

"And what am I supposed to look for?"

"You're a smart girl. You'll know. You found this top from the extinguisher, didn't you? Just bear in mind that he's dangerous and don't take any risks. I wouldn't like anything to happen to you."

I took her hand and, a little to my surprise, she let me kiss it.

"If I didn't think I'd start coughing, I'd kiss you."

"Then you'd better let me do it."

She kissed me, and in my weakened condition, I let her. But after a moment or two, I needed the air. Then I said, "When he gave me that shot this morning, the doc warned me that I might feel like this. A little euphoric. Like I was Napoleon."

I pressed myself hard against her belly.

"You're too big for Napoleon." She kissed me again and added, "And way too tall."

FRANCE, 1940

Le Bourget was about ten kilometers north of Paris. And so was I.
It's strange how physically and mentally restorative one or two
kisses can be. I felt like a new kind of fairy tale in which a sleeping
prince gets himself rescued by a plucky princess. Then again, that
could have been the dope.

At the entrance to the aerodrome was a statue of a nude woman
taking flight from her gray stone plinth. It was meant to commemorate Lindbergh's flight across the Atlantic, but the only memory
that was alive in my head was the feel of Renata's body and what it
might look like if ever I saw her out of that maid's uniform.

There were three of us—me, Kestner, and Bömelburg—pinned
in the back of the staff car like a collection of taupe-colored moths.
In the front was an SS driver and a handsome young chief inspector
from the Office of the Paris Prefect of Police. As we drove toward
the airport building, a four-engined FW Condor was landing on
the runway.

"Who do you suppose that is?" wondered Kestner.

"It's Dr. Goebbels," said Bömelburg. "Taking his cue from the
Führer to see the sights of Paris. Here to cause trouble, no doubt."

We were obliged to remain in our car for reasons of security until the Mahatma Propagandi had left the airport in an enormous beige Mercedes. I caught a glimpse of him as his car swept past ours. He looked like a malignant goblin on his best behavior.

When Goebbels had gone our car made for a smaller, two-engined plane that was awaiting us. I'd never flown before. Neither had Kestner or the Frenchman, and we were all a little nervous as we walked toward the plane's passenger door. Inside the fuselage we found another Frenchman waiting for us—an older, taller man with a Lautrec beard, pince-nez, and a quiet forensic manner. He was a commissioner of French police and his name was Matignon. The younger Frenchman was even taller than his commissioner. He wore an extremely well-cut charcoal-gray summer suit and a pair of thick rose-tinted glasses. His name was Philippe Oltramare. Neither of the two Frenchmen seemed to speak much German, but that was hardly a problem with French speakers like Kestner and Bömelburg on board.

The plane, a Siebel Fh 104, started its engines as soon as we were all aboard, and that was the cue for everyone except me to light a cigarette. Following the injury to my lungs, the insult of cigarettes seemed too much to bear, and it wasn't long before another fit of coughing had me in its grip, which prompted the others, politely, to extinguish their tobacco, and I enjoyed a smoke-free flight down to Biarritz without further irritation to my noisy breathing. I sounded like the audience at a dirty movie.

Mostly the conversation was in French, but there were several names I recognized, among them Rudolf Breitscheid, the former German minister of the interior, and Dr. Rudolf Hilferding, the former minister of finance. Both men had fled Germany after Hitler's election. I asked Bömelburg about them.

"We think the two Rudolfs are at a hotel in Arles," he said. "The Commissioner here has already applied for their arrest. But he seems to be encountering some local resistance."

I was pleased to hear it. The two Rudolfs had been the leading lights of the German Social Democratic Party, which I had voted for myself. Arresting a thug like Erich Mielke was one thing, but arresting Breitscheid and Hilferding was quite another.

"We trust the Commissioner's physical presence in Arles will overcome any opposition," added Bömelburg, and showed me a list he had compiled of other wanted men. Mielke's name was second from the top, underneath Willi Münzenberg, a former Comintern agent and leader of Germany's communist exiles. Other names were less familiar to me.

"I can't help noticing that this plane has only five seats," I told Bömelburg. "How am I supposed to get my prisoner back to Paris?"

"That all depends. If we manage to pick up Grynszpan and Mielke and some of these others, we may have to have the French deliver them first to Vichy and then apply to have them extradited across the border. At least that's what Commissioner Matignon thinks. So he's arranged for a French lawyer to meet us on the ground in Biarritz."

"It's already looking more complicated than we had supposed," complained Kestner. "It turns out that this damned Kuhnt Commission isn't supposed to go into the camps until the end of August. Of course, if we wait that long these commie Jew bastards might easily give us the slip. So we're treading on eggshells at the moment. We're not even supposed to be here."

The flight, at least, was much less complicated, and for the last forty minutes of a journey that lasted just under two hours we hugged the coastline of France and the Bay of Biscay. From the air the city of Biarritz appeared to be exactly what it was: a luxurious-looking seaside town. It was a hot day and the resort was packed with people intent on having a good time in spite of the new German government. I hadn't enjoyed the flight from Paris. There were too many potholes in the air for me to feel entirely comfortable with the experience of air travel. But when I saw the size of the waves rolling onto the banded agate that was the beach, I felt very glad I hadn't traveled there by boat. Under the cliff tops that adjoined the sand the ocean was like the milk in one enormous frothy cappuccino. Just looking at it made me feel seasick, although in truth that probably had a lot more to do with what I'd just learned about the two Rudolfs. That really made me feel sick.

"Münzenberg I can understand," I said. "Grynszpan, too. But why the Rudolfs?"

"Hilferding is one of these Jewish intellectuals," said Bömelburg. "Not to mention the fact that he was the finance minister who was in league with other bankers who helped bring about the Great Depression. Anyway, it's not our problem. It's a French problem. A test of their Vichy government's resolve to become a German ally. It'll be interesting to see what happens. Why? Do you have any objections to his being arrested?"

For a moment the plane dropped like a faulty elevator car. I felt my stomach rise in my chest. I wanted to puke right in the major's lap. He fumbled in his tunic and produced a hip flask.

"Me? No, I'm just an old-fashioned copper. You know? Short-sighted. I see all kinds of things and I never do anything about them."

Bömelburg took a bite of the flask and offered it to me. "Swallow?"

"That's the best thing I've heard since I got into this tin pigeon."

On the ground at Bayonne Airport there were four bucket wagons waiting for us, six SS storm troopers, and the French lawyer. The SS were good-humored and full of smiles, the way men are when they've won a war in less than six weeks. The lawyer had a big nose, thick glasses, and hair so curly it was almost absurd. To me he seemed like a Jew, but nobody was asking. Either way, he was jumpy and nervous. He lit a cigarette inside the lapel of this jacket to keep the wind off his match, and smoke billowed out of his sleeve.

It was a real bestiary that drove east from Biarritz. Something from the pages of Hesiod, with me in the leading bucket and moving at speed, as if the beauty of the French countryside meant not a thing to any of us. On the road we saw demobilized French soldiers, who regarded us with neither hostility nor enthusiasm. We also saw piles of abandoned military equipment—rifles, helmets, ammunition boxes, even a few pieces of artillery. Just beyond the village of St. Palais we crossed the demarcation line into what was Vichy France. Not that there was much love for the French so close to the Spanish border, as Chief Inspector Oltramare—who spoke better German than I had supposed—now told me:

"The bastards hate us French even more than they hate you Germans," he said. "They don't speak much French. They don't speak much Spanish. I'm not even sure they speak Basque."

Several times we overtook a family car heaped with luggage heading east along the main road to Toulouse.

"Why are they fleeing?" I asked Oltramare. "Don't they know about the armistice?"

Oltramare shrugged, but as we overtook the next car he leaned out of the bucket and asked the occupants where they were going; and when these answered he nodded politely and crossed himself.

"They're from Biarritz," he said. "They're going to Lourdes. To pray for France." He smiled. "For a miracle, perhaps."

"Don't you believe in miracles?"

"Oh yes. That is why I believe in Adolf Hitler. He's the one man who can save Europe from the curse of Bolshevism. That is what I believe."

"I suppose that's why he signed a deal with Stalin," I said. "To save us all from Bolshevism."

"But of course," said Oltramare, as if such a thing was obvious. "Don't you remember what happened in August 1914? Germany gambled on defeating France before Russia could mobilize and declare war. Which didn't happen. It's the same situation now, only the Molotov-Ribbentrop Pact meant that attacking France was much less of a gamble than it was before. And you mark my words, Captain. Now that France is defeated, the Soviet Union, the true enemy of Western democracy, will be next."

In the little town of Naverrenx we saw some German tanks and a couple of truckloads of SS and stopped to say hello and share cigarettes. Oltramare went to a shop to buy some matches and found there were none to be had. There was nothing to be had of anything—no food, no vegetables, no wine, and no cigarettes. He returned to the bucket, cursing the locals.

"You can bet these bastards are hiding what they've got and waiting for the prices to go up so that they can gouge us," he said.

"Wouldn't you do the same?" I said.

While he and I were talking, many women came out of the local town hall, and it turned out that nearly all of them were German internees from the nearby camp at Gurs, where they'd been taken from locations all over France. They were pretty bitter about the conditions there, but also because they'd been ordered to leave the area or face internment again as enemy aliens. And this was why the SS had stayed on in Naverrenx—to prevent this from happening. A truckload of SS and one of the women agreed to guide us to the camp at Gurs—which we were assured was not easily found—so that we might conduct our search for wanted persons. Meanwhile, the French lawyer Monsieur Savigny began to argue with Commissioner Matignon and Major Bömelburg about the presence of these SS troops in the French zone.

"In my opinion," Oltramare told Bömelburg afterward, "you should shoot that man. Yes, I think that would be best. Frankly, I am surprised you have not shot more. Myself, I would have shot a great many people. Especially the people who were in charge of this country. To punish them would have been a mercy. To let them go was barbarous and cruel. Frankly, I don't know why you bother to take prisoners back to Germany when you could just shoot them here by the roadside and save yourselves a lot of time and effort."

I frowned and shook my head at this display of pragmatic fascism. "Why are you here, Chief Commissioner?"

"I'm looking for someone, too," he said with a shrug. "A fugitive. Just like you, Captain. During the Spanish Civil War I fought on the Nationalist side. And I have a few scores to settle with some Republicans."

"You mean it's personal."

"When it involves the Spanish Civil War it's always personal, monsieur. Many atrocities were committed. My own brother was murdered by a communist. He was a priest. They burned him alive inside his own church, in Catalonia. The man in charge was a Frenchman. A communist from Le Havre."

"And if you find him? What then?"

Oltramare smiled. "I will arrest him, Captain Gunther."

I wasn't so sure about that. In fact, I wasn't sure about anything as we left Naverrenx and headed south to Gurs. The SS troops in the truck now leading the way were singing "Sieg Heil Viktoria." I was starting to have misgivings about everything.

My driver and the corporal in the bucket's front passenger seat were more interested in the woman seated beside Oltramare and me than in singing. Her name was Eva Kemmerich, and she was extremely thin, which seemed to make her mouth too wide and her ears too big. Under her eyes were shadows like bat wings, and she wore a pink handkerchief around her head to keep her hair tidy. It looked like the rubber on top of a pencil. In Gurs, she and the other women had suffered a tough time at the hands of the French.

"Conditions were barbaric," she explained. "They treated us like dogs. Worse than dogs. People talk about German anti-Semitism. Well, it's my considered opinion that the French just hate everyone who isn't French. Germans, Jews, Spanish, Poles, Italians—they were all treated equally badly. Gurs is a concentration camp, that's what it is, and the guards are absolute bastards. They worked us like slaves. Just look at my hands. My nails. They're ruined."

She looked at Oltramare with ill-concealed contempt. "Go on," she told him. "Look at them."

"I am looking at them, mademoiselle."

"Well? What's the idea of treating human beings like that? You're French. What's the big idea, Franzi?"

"I have no explanation, mademoiselle. And I have no excuse. All I can say is that before the war there were almost four million refugees living in France from countries all over Europe. That's ten percent of our population. What were we to do with so many people, mademoiselle?"

"Actually, it's madame," she said. "I had a wedding ring, but it was stolen by one of your French guards. Not that it ever stayed on my finger, after the diet I've endured. My husband is in another camp. Le Vernet. I hope things are better there. My God, it could hardly be any worse. You know something? I'm sorry the war is over. I just wish our boys could have killed a lot more Frenchmen before they were obliged to throw in the towel." She leaned forward and tapped the corporal and the driver on their shoulders. "Christ, I'm proud of you, boys. You really gave the Franzis a well-deserved kicking. But if you want to put the cherry on my cake, you'll arrest the criminal who's in charge of the camp at Gurs and shoot him down like the pig he is. Here, I tell you what. I'll sleep with whichever one of you puts a bullet in that bastard's head."

The corporal looked at the driver and grinned. I could tell that the idea was not without appeal for him, so I said:

"And I will shoot whoever takes this lady up on her generous offer." I took her bony hand in mine. "Please don't do that again, Frau Kemmerich. I appreciate that you've had a rough time of it, but I can't allow you to make things worse."

"Worse?" she sneered. "There isn't anything that's worse than Gurs."

The camp, situated in the foothills of the Pyrenees, was much larger than I had supposed, covering an area of about a square kilometer and split into two halves. A makeshift street ran the length of the camp, and on each side there were three or four hundred wooden huts. There seemed to be no sanitation or running water, and the smell was indescribable. I had been to Dachau. The only differences between Gurs and Dachau were that the barbed-wire fence at Gurs was smaller and not obviously electrified, and there were no executions; otherwise, conditions seemed to be much the same, and it was only after a parade was called in the men's half of the camp and we went in among the prisoners that it was possible to see how things were actually much worse than at Dachau.

The guards were all French gendarmes, each of whom carried a thick leather riding whip, although none of them seemed to own a horse. There were three "islets": A, B, and C. The islet C adjutant was a Gabin type with an effeminate mouth and narrow, expressionless eyes. He knew exactly where the German communists were held and, without offering any resistance to our requests, he took us to a dilapidated barrack containing fifty men who, paraded before us outside, exhibited signs of emaciation or illness or, more often, both. It was clear that they had been expecting us, or something like us, and, refusing to submit to a roll call, they started to sing "The Internationale." Meanwhile, the French adjutant glanced over Bömelburg's list and helpfully picked out some of our wanted men. Erich Mielke wasn't one of these.

While this selection was proceeding, I could hear Eva Kemmerich. She was standing in our bucket, which was parked on "the street," and shouting abuse at some of the prisoners who were still held in the camp. These and a few of the gendarmes on the women's side of the wire responded by laughing at her and making obscene remarks and gestures. For me, the sense of being involved in some nameless insanity was compounded when the inmates of another hut—the adjutant said they were French anarchists—began to sing "La Marseillaise" in competition with those who were singing "The Internationale."

We marched seven men out of the camp and into the buckets. All of them raised clenched fists in the communist salute and shouted slogans in German or Spanish to their fellow prisoners.

Kestner caught my eye. "Did you ever see anything like this place?"

"Only Dachau."

"Well, I never saw anything like it. To treat people this way, even if they are communists, seems disgusting."

"Don't tell me." I pointed at Chief Inspector Oltramare, who was marching a handcuffed prisoner toward the buckets at gunpoint. "Tell him."

"Looks like he got his man anyway."

"I wonder if I'll get mine," I said. "Mielke."

"Not here?"

I shook my head. "I mean, this fellow I'm after almost ruined my career, the Bolshie bastard. As far as I'm concerned, he's really got it coming."

"I'm sure he has. They all have. Communist swine."

"But you were a communist, weren't you, Paul? Before you joined the Nazi Party?"

"Me? No. Whatever gave you that idea?"

"Only, I seem to recall you campaigning for Ernst Thalmann in—when was that? Nineteen twenty-five?"

"Don't be fucking ridiculous, Bernie. Is this a joke?" He glanced nervously in Bömelburg's direction. "I think that phosgene gas has addled your brains. Really. Have you gone mad?"

"No. And actually, it's my impression that I'm probably the only sane one here."

As the day wore on, this was an impression that did not alter. Indeed, there was even greater madness to come.

20

FRANCE, 1940

It was late afternoon when our convoy took to the road again. We were headed to Toulouse, about one hundred fifty kilometers to the northeast, and thought that we could probably make it before dark. We took Eva Kemmerich with us so that she might look for her husband when we visited the camp at Le Vernet the following day. And, of course, our eight prisoners. I hadn't really looked at them. They were a miserable, malnourished, smelly lot and little or no threat to anyone, let alone the Third Reich. According to Karl Bömelburg, one of them was a German writer and another was a well-known newspaperman, only I hadn't heard of either of them.

Outside Lourdes, in sight of the River Gave de Pau, we stopped in a forest clearing to stretch our legs. I was pleased to see Bömelburg extend the same facility to our prisoners. He even handed out some cigarettes. I was feeling tired but better. At least my chest was no longer hurting. But I still wasn't smoking. I had another bite off Bömelburg's flask and decided that maybe he wasn't such a bad fellow after all.

"This whole area is full of caves and grottoes," he said, and pointed at an outcrop of rock that hung above our heads like a thick gray cloud.

We caught a glimpse of Frau Kemmerich disappearing into the rock. After a minute or two Bömelburg said, "Perhaps you would be good enough to go and inform Frau Bernadette that we shall be leaving in five minutes."

Instinctively, I glanced at my watch. "Yes, Herr Major."

I walked up the slope to fetch her, calling her name out loud in case she was answering a call of nature.

"Yes?"

I found her sitting on a rock in a leaf-lined grotto, smoking a cigarette.

"Isn't it lovely here?" she said, pointing over my head.

I turned to admire the view of the Pyrenees that she was enjoying.

"Yes, it is."

"Sorry if I was a bitch back there," she said. "You've no idea how bad the last nine months have been. My husband and I were in Dijon when war was declared. He's a wine merchant. They arrested us almost immediately."

"Forget it," I said. "What happened back there . . . You were justifiably upset. And the camp did look bloody awful." I nodded down the slope. "Come on. We'd better go back. There's still a long way to go before we get to Toulouse."

She stood up. "How long will it take to get there?"

I was about to answer her when I heard two or three loud bursts of machine-gun fire, none of them longer than a couple of seconds; but then, it takes only five seconds to empty an MP 40's thirty-two-round magazine. The sound and smell of it were still hanging in the air by the time I had sprinted down the slope into the clearing. Two storm troopers were standing a couple of meters apart, their jackboots surrounded with spent ammunition that looked like so many coins tossed to a couple of buskers. As well-trained soldiers, they were already changing the toylike magazines on their machine pistols and looking just a little surprised at their murderous efficiency. That's the thing about a gun: It always looks like a toy until it starts killing people.

A little farther away lay the bodies of the eight prisoners we had brought from Gurs.

"What the hell happened here?" I shouted, but I knew the answer already.

"They tried to make a run for it," said Bömelburg.

I went forward to inspect the bodies.

"All of them?" I said. "In a straight line?"

One of the shot men groaned. He lay on the forest floor, his knees collapsed under him, his torso lying back on his feet in an almost impossible position, like some old Indian fakir. But there was nothing to be done for him. His head and chest were covered in blood.

Angrily, I walked toward Bömelburg. "They would have run away in several directions," I said. "Not all of them down the same slope."

A pistol shot bored another hole through the still air of the forest and the groaning man's head. I turned on my boot heel to see Kestner holstering his Walther P38. Seeing my expression, Kestner shrugged and said:

"Best to finish him, I think."

"Back at the Alex, we'd have called that murder," I said.

"Well, we're not back at the Alex, are we, Captain?" said Bömelburg. "Look here, Gunther, are you calling me a liar? Those men were shot while trying to escape, do you hear?"

There was a lot I could have said, but the only thing that was true was the fact that I had no business being there. It wasn't just the bodies of fallen heroes that the Valkyries carried up to Valhalla but also those of Berlin chief inspectors who criticized their senior officers in remote French forests. After I remembered that, there seemed little point in saying anything; but there was still plenty I could do.

For his face and my neck I even offered an apology to Bömelburg when the toe of my boot would have seemed more appropriate. In my own defense, I should also add that the two MP 40 machine pistols were now reloaded and ready for lethal business.

We left the bodies where they lay and took our places in the buckets, only this time it was Kestner and not Oltramare who sat with me and Frau Kemmerich. Kestner could see I was upset about what had happened, and after my earlier remarks about his membership in the KPD he was in the mood to press home what he now perceived to be some kind of advantage over me.

"What's the matter? Can't bear the sight of blood? And I thought you were a tough guy, Gunther."

"Let me tell you something, Paul. Although it's none of your business. I've killed people before. In the war. After that I thought the whole world had learned a lesson, but it hasn't. If I have to kill someone again, I'm going to make sure I make a good start by killing someone I want to kill. Someone who needs killing. So keep chirruping in my ear and see what happens, comrade. You're not the only man in this bucket who can put a bullet in the back of another man's head."

He was quiet after that.

The evening turned to dusk. I kept my eyes on the trees above the road, and if I stayed silent it was because the noise inside my head was indescribable. I suppose it was the echo of those machine pistols. I would hardly have been surprised to find the ghosts of the men we had slain sitting in the buckets beside us. Silent and motionless, withdrawn into my own ego, I waited for the nightmare that was our journey to end.

Toulouse was called the Rose City. Almost all the buildings in the center of town, including our hotel, Le Grand Balcon, were pink, as if we had been looking through the chief inspector's rose-colored spectacles. I decided to adopt this as a persona to help me achieve what I now needed to achieve. And my breathing was easier now, which also helped. So the following morning at breakfast, I greeted Major Bömelburg and the two French policemen warmly. I was even courteous to Paul Kestner.

"My apologies for yesterday," I said generally. "But before I left Paris, the doctor at the hospital gave me something to help me carry out my duties. And he warned me that after it wore off I might behave in a peculiar way. Perhaps I shouldn't have come at all, but as you can probably imagine, I was rather anxious to carry out the mission given to me by General Heydrich, at almost any cost to myself."

Bömelburg was looking rather more thin and gray than the day before. Kestner might have spent the whole night polishing his bald head, so shiny did it seem. Oltramare said something in French to the commissioner, who put on his pince-nez and regarded me with indifference before nodding his apparent approval.

"The commissioner says you look much better," said Oltramare. "And I must say, I agree."

"Yes, indeed," said Bömelburg. "Much better. Yesterday can't have been easy for you, Gunther. All that traveling when you were clearly not yourself. It's commendable that you wanted to come at all, under the circumstances. I shall certainly say so to Colonel Knochen when I make my report in Paris. What with the good news I just had from Commissioner Matignon, this is turning out to be a very good day. Don't you agree, Kestner?"

"Yes, sir."

"What good news is that?" I asked, smiling with Toulouse-colored optimism.

"Why, that we've got the Jew who assassinated vom Rath," said Bömelburg. "Grynszpan." He chuckled. "Apparently, he knocked on the door of the prison here in Toulouse and asked to be let in."

Oltramare was laughing, too. He said, "Apparently he speaks very little French, had no money, and thought that we might be able to protect him against you fellows."

"The stupid kike," muttered Kestner. "I'm on my way to the prison now. With the Commissioner and Monsieur Savigny. To organize Grynszpan's extradition back to Paris and then Berlin."

"The Führer wants a trial, apparently," said Bömelburg. "At all costs there must be a trial."

"In Berlin?" I tried not to sound surprised.

"Why not in Berlin?" said Bömelburg.

"It's just that the murder took place in Paris," I said. "And it was my understanding that Grynszpan's not even a German citizen. He's a Pole, isn't he?" I smiled. "I'm sorry, sir, but sometimes it's hard for me to stop being a cop and thinking about little things like jurisdiction."

Bömelburg wagged his finger at me. "You're just doing your job, old fellow. But I know this case better than anyone. Before I joined the Gestapo I was with our foreign service in Paris, and I spent three months working on this case. For one thing, Poland is now a part of the Greater German Reich. As is France. And for another, the murder took place in the German Embassy here in Paris. Technically, diplomatically that was German soil. And that makes a big difference."

"Yes, of course," I said meekly. "That does make a big difference."

Certainly, it had made a big difference to Germany's Jews. Herschel Grynszpan's murder of a junior official in the Paris embassy in November 1938 had been used as an excuse by the Nazis to launch a massive pogrom against Germany's Jews. Until the night of November 10, 1938—Kristallnacht—it was almost possible to imagine that I still lived in a civilized country. The trial was certain to be the kind the Nazis liked: a show trial, with the verdict a foregone conclusion. But if Bömelburg was being honest, at least Grynszpan wasn't about to be murdered by the roadside.

Leaving Kestner, Matignon, and Savigny to go to the Prison St. Michel in Toulouse, Bömelburg and I, accompanied by six SS men, set off on the sixty-five-kilometer drive south to Le Vernet. Frau Kemmerich did not come with us, as it seemed her husband was after all in another French concentration camp at Moisdon-la-Rivière, in Brittany.

Le Vernet was near Pamiers and the camp was a short way south of the local railway station, which Bömelburg described as "convenient." There was a cemetery to the north of the camp, but he neglected to mention if that was convenient, too, although I was sure it would be: Le Vernet was even worse than Gurs. Surrounded by miles of barbed wire in an otherwise deserted patch of French countryside, the many huts looked like coffins laid out after some giant's battle. They were in a deplorable state, as were the two thousand men who were imprisoned there, many of them emaciated and guarded by well-fed French gendarmes. The prisoners labored to build an inadequate road between the railway station and the cemetery. There were four roll calls a day, each of them lasting half an hour. We arrived just before the third, explained our mission to the French policeman in charge, and he handed us politely over to the care of a vile-looking officer who smelled strongly of aniseed, and his yellow-faced Corsican sergeant. They listened as Oltramare translated the details of our mission. Monsieur Aniseed nodded and led the way into the camp.

Bömelburg and I followed, pistols in hand, as we had been warned that the men of hut 32, the "Leper Barrack," were considered the most dangerous in Camp Le Vernet. Oltramare followed at a distance, also armed. And the three of us waited outside while several French gendarmes entered the pitch-black barrack and drove the occupants outside with whips and curses.

These men were in a disgraceful condition—worse than at Gurs, and even worse than Dachau. Their ankles were swollen and their bellies distended from starvation. They wore cheap-looking galoshes on their feet and the same ragged clothing they'd probably been wearing since the winter of 1937 when they had fled the advance of Franco's Nationalist Army. Some of them were half naked. They were all infested with vermin. They knew what was coming but were too beaten to sing "The Internationale" in defiance of our presence.

It took several minutes for the barrack to empty and the men to line up again. Just when you thought the barrack couldn't contain any more men, others came out until there were 350 of them paraded in front of us. The judgment line from purgatory to hell could not have looked more abject. And with every second I was confronted with their emaciated, unshaven faces, the more I wanted to shoot Monsieur Aniseed and his fat gendarmes.

While the Corsican called the roll, Bömelburg checked his clipboard, looking for names that tallied; and while they did that I walked between their ranks, like the Kaiser come to hand out a few Iron Crosses to the bravest of the brave, looking to see if I could pick out a man I hadn't seen in nine years. But I never saw him there, and I never heard his name called out. Not that I put much faith in a name. From everything I'd read about him in Heydrich's file, Erich Mielke was too smart to have been arrested and interned using his real name. Bömelburg knew this, of course. But there were others who had not been possessed of the same presence of mind as the German Comintern agent; and as these few men were identified they were led away to the administration barracks by the gendarmes.

"He's not in this barrack," I said finally.

"The adjutant says there's another all-German barrack in this section," said Oltramare. "This one is all International Brigade and it would make sense for Mielke to keep away from them, especially now that Stalin has closed his doors to them."

The men from barrack 32 were driven back inside and we

repeated the whole exercise with the men from barrack 33. According to the yellow-faced Corsican—he looked like a careless tanner— these were all communists who had fled from Hitler's Germany only to find themselves interned as undesirable aliens when war was declared in September 1939. Consequently, these men were in rather better shape than their comrades from the International Brigades. That wouldn't have been difficult.

Once again, I walked up and down the lines of prisoners while Bömelburg and the Corsican called the roll. These faces were more defiant than the others and most of the men met my eye with unshifting hatred. Some were Jews, I thought. Others were more obviously Aryan. Once or twice I paused and stared levelly at a man, but I never identified any of the prisoners as Erich Mielke.

Not even when I recognized him.

As the Corsican finished the roll call, I walked back to Bömelburg's side, shaking my head.

"No luck?"

"No. He's not there."

"Are you sure? Some of these fellows are a shadow of their former selves. After six months in this place, I doubt my own wife would recognize me. Have another look, Captain."

"All right, sir."

And while I looked at the prisoners again, I made an announcement, for the sake of impressing Bömelburg.

"Listen," I said. "We're looking for a man called Erich Fritz Emil Mielke. Perhaps you know him by a different name. I don't care about his politics—he's wanted for the murders of two Berlin policemen in 1931. I'm sure many of you read about it in the newspapers at the time. This man is thirty-three years old, fair-haired, medium height, brown eyes, Protestant, from Berlin. He attended the Kollnisches Gymnasium. Probably speaks Russian quite well, and a bit of Spanish. Maybe he's good with his hands. His father is a woodworker."

All the time I was speaking I could feel Mielke looking at me, knowing I'd recognized him the way he'd recognized me and doubtless wondering why I didn't arrest him straightaway and what the hell was going on. I holstered my pistol and took off my officer's cap in the hope I might look a little less like a Nazi.

"Gentlemen, I make you this promise. If any one of you identifies Erich Mielke to me now, I will personally speak to the camp commander with a view to organizing your release as soon as possible."

It was the kind of promise that a Nazi would have made. A shifting promise that no one would have trusted. I hoped so. Because after what had happened to the prisoners from Gurs in the forest near Lourdes, the last thing I wanted to do was help the Nazis arrest any more Germans, even a German who had murdered two policemen. I couldn't do anything about the other men who were on Bömelburg's list, but I was damned if I was going to finger any more Germans for Heydrich. Not now.

Once again I met Erich Mielke's eye. He didn't look away, and I suppose he guessed what I was doing. He was older than I remembered him, of course. Broader and more powerful-looking, especially across the shoulders. He wore a light beard, but there was no mistaking the surly-looking mouth, the watchful ruthless eyes, or the coxcomb of unruly hair on top of his largish head. He must have thought I was a beefsteak Nazi: brown on the outside, red on the inside. But he couldn't have been more wrong. The murders of Anlauf and Lenck had been just about the most cowardly I'd ever seen, and nothing would have pleased me more than to have snapped him for it and for the Berlin courts to have sent him for a permanent haircut; but as much as I disliked him now, I disliked the casual, instinctive brutality of the Nazi police state even more. I almost wanted to tell him that but for the murders of eight men on a country road the day before he'd have been on his way to a date with a man wearing white gloves and a top hat.

I turned away and walked back to Bömelburg with a shrug.

"It was worth a shot," he said.

Neither of us expected what happened next.

"I don't know an Erich Mielke," said a voice.

The man was small and Jewish-looking, with short, dark, curly hair and shifty brown eyes. A lawyer's face, which could have been why there was a large bruise on his cheek.

"I don't know an Erich Mielke," he repeated, now that he had our attention, "but I would like to become a Nazi."

Some of the other prisoners laughed, some whistled, but the man kept going.

"I was arrested by the French because I was a German communist," he said. "I wasn't an enemy of France then, but I am now. It's true, I really hate and despise these people worse than I used to hate the Nazis. I spend all day moving latrine bins, and for the rest of my life I'm forever going to associate France with the smell of shit."

The Corsican's eyes narrowed and he moved toward the man with his whip raised.

"No," said Bömelburg. "Let the fellow speak."

"I'm glad France was defeated," said the prisoner. "And since I'm declaring myself to be an enemy of France, I'd also like to join the German army and become a loyal soldier of the fatherland and a follower of Adolf Hitler. Who knows? I know the war's over, but I might just get the chance to shoot a Franzi, which would really make me very happy."

His fellow prisoners started to jeer, but I could see that Major Bömelburg was impressed.

"So, if you don't mind, sir, when you leave this shit hole, I'd like to come with you."

Bömelburg smiled. "Well," he said. "I think you'd better."

And he did. But it said a lot about the rest of the Germans in barrack 33 that there was no one else who followed his example. Not one.

21

GERMANY, 1954

"Jesus Christ, Gunther," exclaimed one of my American interrogators. "Are you trying to tell us that you had that communist bastard Mielke in your power and you let him go?"

"Yes. I am."

"What, are you crazy? That's twice you saved his bacon. Did you ever think about that? Jesus."

"Of course I thought about it."

"I mean, didn't you ever regret that?"

"I don't think I could have made myself clear," I said. "Even while I was doing it, even while I was pretending I didn't recognize him, I regretted it. Captain Anlauf's murder left three orphaned daughters. You see, what you've got to remember is that for a while back there, in the dog days of Weimar, the communists were every bit as loathsome as the Nazis. Maybe more so. After all, it was the Comintern that ordered the German Communist Party to treat the country's governing SPD as the main enemy, not the Nazis. Can you imagine it? In the Red Referendum of July 1931, the KPD and the Nazis marched together and voted together. That was the nonaggression pact in miniature. I always hated them for that. It was the Reds who really destroyed the Republic, not the Nazis." I helped myself to another of the Ami's cigarettes. "And if that wasn't enough, there's my own experience of Soviet hospitality to take into account as well. For why I hate the communists."

"Well, we all hate the Reds," said the man with the pipe.

"No. You hate the Reds because you've been told to hate them. But for five years they were your Allies. Roosevelt and Truman shook hands with Stalin and pretended he was different from Hitler. Which he wasn't. I hate the Reds because I've learned to hate them the way a dog learns to hate the man who beats it regularly. During Weimar. During the war. On the Russian front. But most of the reason I hate them is because I spent almost two years in a Soviet labor camp. And until I met you boys I thought that was about as much hate as I could have for any one race of people."

"We're not so bad." The man with the pipe took it out of his mouth and started to refill it. "When you get to know us."

"You can get used to anything, it's true," I said.

The man with the glasses tutted loudly. By now I vaguely recognized him from seven years earlier, at the Stiftskaserne hospital in Vienna.

"After all the trouble we had getting you this exclusive suite," he said. He started to clean his glasses with the end of his tie. "I'm hurt."

"When you're done cleaning your glasses," I said, "the windows in here could use a wipe, too. I'm particular about windows. Particularly when I know who's been breathing on them. There's nothing about this cell I like, now that I know who was in here last."

The man with the pipe was finally lighting up. Hitler would have hated his pipe. It looked as if I'd found one reason at last to like Adolf Hitler.

The Ami sucked at the stem, blew out some sweet smoke, and said, "I watched an old newsreel the other day. Of Hitler making a speech at Tempelhof Field in Berlin. There were one million people that day. Apparently, it took twelve hours just to get everyone in there, and another twelve to get them all out again. I guess you were the only Berliner who stayed home that night."

"Berlin nightlife was much better before the Nazis," I said.

"That's what I hear. People say it was quite something. Degenerate but lively. All those clubs. Striptease dancers. Naked ladies. Open homosexuality. What were you people thinking? I mean, no wonder the Nazis got an in." He shook his head. "On the other hand. Munich's kind of dull, I think."

"It has some advantages," I said. "There are no Ivans in Munich."

"Is that why you lived there after you were in that POW camp? Instead of Berlin?"

"One reason, I suppose."

"You were in and out of that camp relatively quickly." He had finished cleaning his glasses and put them back on his head. They were still too small for him, and I wondered if American heads were like American stomachs and kept on growing faster than those in Europe. "In comparison with a lot of other guys. I mean, some of your old comrades are only just coming home now."

"I was lucky," I said. "I escaped."

"How?"

"Mielke was involved."

"Then we'll pick it up there tomorrow, shall we? In here. Ten o'clock."

"You'd better clear that with my secretary," I said. "Tomorrow's the day when I start writing my book."

"What did I tell you? You know, this is a great room for a writer. Maybe the spirit of Adolf Hitler will come and help you out with a few pages."

"Seriously, though," said the other Ami. "If you need pen and paper to make a few notes about Mielke, just ask the guard. Might help to jog your memory if you wrote a few things down."

"Why now? Why not before?"

"Because things are starting to become more important. Mielke starts to become more important. So the more details you can remember, the better."

"I know one spirit that might help a lot," I said. "And it isn't Hitler's."

"Yeah?"

"I'm a little bit like Goethe," I said. "When I'm writing a book, I find that a bottle of good German brandy usually helps."

"Is there such a thing as a good German brandy?"

"I'll settle for some cheap vodka, only a man needs a hobby when he's got his feet in the cement. Something to take his mind off the present and put it somewhere in the past. About seven years ago, to be more accurate."

"All right," said the man with the glasses. "We'll get you a bottle of something."

"And I would like to catch up on my smoking. I'd given up until I left Cuba. Since I met you I've got a much better reason to kill myself."

They left me alone after that. Pencils and paper, a bottle of brandy, a clean glass, a couple of packets of cigarettes and some matches, and even a newspaper arrived, and I placed them all on the table and just watched them for a while, enjoying the freedom to have a drink or not have a drink. It's the little things that can make prison tolerable. Like a door key. By all accounts, they'd let Hitler have the run of Landsberg and he'd treated the place more like a hotel than a penitentiary. Not that he was in any way penitent about the putsch of 1923, of course.

I lay down on the bed and tried to relax, but it wasn't easy in that cell. Was this why they'd put me in here? Or was it just an American idea of a joke? I tried not to think about Adolf Hitler, but he kept on getting up from the desk and, full of impatience, going to the window and staring out through the bars in that way he had of always looking like a man chosen by destiny.

The curious thing was I'd never really thought about Hitler. For years when he was still alive I tried not to think of him at all, dismissing him as a crank before he was elected chancellor of Germany and, after that happened, merely wishing him dead. But now that I was lying on the bed where, for nine months, he had dreamed his autocratic dreams, it seemed impossible not to pay attention to the man with blue eyes at the window.

As I watched he sat down at the desk again, picked up the pen, and started to write, covering the sheets of paper with furious scribbling, and sweeping each page off the table and onto the floor as he finished so that I might pick them up and read what was written. At first, the sentences made no sense at all; but gradually these became more coherent, affording glimpses into the extraordinary phenomenon that was Hitler's mind. Whatever he wrote was based on his own incontrovertible logic and served as a perfect guide for the commission of evil, worked out to the most minute detail. It was like sitting in the same asylum cell as the insane Dr. Mabuse, together with the ghosts of all those he had exterminated and watching him write his last criminal testament.

At last he stopped writing and, leaning back on the chair, turned to look at me. Feeling this was my chance to put him on the spot, I tried to frame a question of the kind that Robert Jackson, the chief American prosecutor at Nuremberg, might have asked. But this was more difficult than I might have imagined. There wasn't any single question beyond a simple "Why?" that I could have asked, and I was still wrestling with this realization when he spoke to me:

"So, what happened next?"

I tried to stifle a yawn. "You mean when I left Le Vernet?"

"Of course."

"We went back to Toulouse," I said. "From there we drove to Vichy and handed our prisoners to the French. Then we drove to the border of the occupied zone—Bourges, I think it was—and waited for the French to deliver them back to us. A ridiculous arrangement, but one that seemed to suit the hypocrisy of the French. These prisoners included poor Herschel Grynszpan. From Bourges we drove back to Paris, where the prisoners were locked up before being flown to Berlin. Well, you probably know better than me what happened to Grynszpan. I know he was in Sachsenhausen for a while. And there never was a show trial, of course."

"A trial was unnecessary," said Hitler. "His guilt was obvious. Besides, it might have been embarrassing for Pétain. Just like the Riom trial, when that Jew André Blum gave evidence against Laval."

I nodded. "Yes, I can see that."

"I didn't hear anything about what happened to him," said Hitler. "At any rate, I cannot recollect. At the end, I had quite a lot on my mind. Himmler probably dealt with him. I daresay he was one of those whose hash got settled by the SS at Flossenburg in the last days of the war. But, you know, Grynszpan had it coming. After all, there's no doubt that he really did murder Ernst vom Rath. No doubt at all. The Jew just wanted to kill an important German, and vom Rath was merely the unlucky man he killed. There were plenty of witnesses to the murder who came forward and told the truth about what happened. Not that you would know the meaning of truth. Your behavior at Le Vernet was a gross act of deceit and betrayal. To me and your fellow officers."

"Yes, it was," I said. "But I'll live with it."

"Did you go straight back to Berlin?"

"No, I stayed on in Paris for a while, pretending to make further inquiries about Erich Mielke. A lot of other German communists and men from the International Brigade had volunteered for the French Foreign Legion to escape from the Gestapo in France. The Legion never paid much attention to a man's past. You enlisted in Marseilles and served in the French colonies, with no questions asked. It was easy to suggest in my report to Heydrich that this was how he had escaped us. The truth is rather more interesting."

"Not to me," said Hitler. "What I'm rather more interested in is what you did about the officer who tried to murder you."

"What makes you think I did anything at all?"

"Because I know men. Go on. Admit it. You got even with him, didn't you? This Lieutenant Nikolaus Willms."

"Yes, I did."

Hitler was triumphant. "I knew it. You sit there with your kangaroo court, Robert Jackson questions, but underneath you're no different from me. That makes you a hypocrite, Gunther. A hypocrite."

"Yes, that's true."

"So what did you do? Denounce him to the Gestapo? The same way you helped denounce that other fellow? The Gestapo captain from Würzburg. What was his name again?"

"Weinberger." I shook my head. "No, that's not what happened."

"Of course. You had Heydrich take care of him. Heydrich was always very good at getting rid of people. Considering he was a mischling, he was an excellent Nazi. I suppose he felt he had to try that much harder to prove himself to me." Hitler laughed. "That's the only reason we ever kept him on."

"No, it wasn't like that either. I didn't involve Heydrich."

Hitler turned his chair around to face me and rubbed his hands. "I want to hear it all. Every sordid detail."

I yawned again. I was feeling tired. My eyes kept on closing. All I really wanted to do was go to sleep and dream of somewhere different.

"I order you to tell me."

"Is that a Führer order?"

"If you like."

I gave a little jolt, the way you do when sleep takes you for a ride and instead you get the crazy idea you just died. This little death is a wonderful sensation. It reminds you why it is that breathing feels so good.

22

FRANCE, 1940

It certainly felt good in the summer of 1940. And there was no better place to be breathing air than Paris. Especially when I had the little maid from the Lutetia hotel to keep me amused. Not that I took advantage of her. As a matter of fact, I was rather scrupulous where Renata was concerned. It was one of the ways I had of convincing myself I wasn't as big a rat as the field gray said I was. This wasn't Onegin's sermon. I mean, I wanted her. And eventually I had her. But I took my time about it the way you do when you like what's between a girl's ears as much as you want what's between her legs. And when it happened, it felt like it was something shaped by a higher motive than simple lust. It wasn't love, exactly. Neither of us wanted to get married. But it was romance: courtship, desire, fear, and dread. Yes, there was fear and dread, too, because Renata always knew I would go and slay my fire-extinguishing dragon just as soon as I knew why he'd sought to put me out for good.

While I'd been away in the south of France, Renata had searched Willms's room and once or twice even followed him to discover that he ate at Maxim's almost every other night. On a general's pay this would have been unusual enough, but for a mere lieutenant it was nothing short of miraculous, and I resolved to visit the restaurant myself in the hope that this might provide me with some clue as to why he had tried to kill me. And, in this respect, it was fortunate for me that Maxim's was now run by Otto Horcher, who owned a restaurant in Berlin-Schöneberg. In the spring of 1938, Otto Horcher had been a client of mine when I'd been running a successful business as a licensed private investigator. I'd worked undercover as a waiter in his place for a couple of weeks in order to find out who was stealing from him. As it turned out, everyone was stealing from him, but one man, the majordomo, was stealing a lot more than all of the others put together. After that we were friends, and even though he was a Nazi and a good friend of Goering's—which was how he came to be managing the most famous restaurant in Paris—I could always count on him for a table when I needed to impress someone, because after Borchardt, Horcher's was the best restaurant in Berlin.

Maxim's was in the rue Royale, in the Eighth Arrondissement and a shrine to Art Nouveau, red velvet, and *grande cuisine*. Parked outside were several German staff cars, but you didn't need to be German to eat at Maxim's. When I went along there with Renata, Pierre Laval, one of Vichy's leading politicians, was there; and so was Fernand de Brinon. All you needed was money—quite a lot of money—and some bismuth tablets. In 1940, Maxim's was a good place for men and women who knew what they wanted and how to get it, no matter what the price. Probably still is.

We went through the door and were shown straight to a table—or at least as straight as the oleaginous and fawning waiter could manage.

"Can you afford this?" asked Renata, glancing over the menu with widening eyes.

"It makes me feel young again," I said. "That was the last time I felt this poor."

"So what are we doing here?"

"Looking for the one thing that's not on this menu. Information."

"About your friend Willms?"

"You know, if you keep on calling him that, even in the spirit of jest, I'm going to have to show you how much I dislike him."

She shuddered visibly. "No, please. I don't want to know." She glanced around the restaurant. "I don't see him in here." She did a double take on Laval. "All the same, he should be. There are more snakes in here than in the whole of Africa."

"I didn't know you were so well traveled."

"No, just traveled. Obviously, you haven't seen Africa."

"I'm beginning to think I made a mistake about you, Renata. I had the quaint idea that you were the girl next door."

"Where my parents live, in Bern, if you'd ever met the girl next door, you know why I came to Paris."

The maître d' arrived with two menus and more attitude than a professor of aeronautics. Renata found him a little intimidating. Me, I'd been intimidated before, and usually by someone holding something more deadly than a wine list.

"What's your name?" I asked him.

"Albert, monsieur. Albert Glaser."

"Well, Albert, it was my impression that Germany had stopped paying France war reparations, but I can see from the prices on this menu that I was wrong about that."

"Our prices don't seem to bother most of the other German officers who come in here, monsieur."

"That's what victory does for Nazis, Albert. It makes them profligate. Careless. Arrogant. Me? I'm just a humble German from Berlin who's anxious to renew my acquaintance with a certain Monsieur Horcher. Do me a favor, will you, Albert? Go and whisper in his ear that Bernie Gunther is in the store. Oh, and bring us a bottle of Mosel. The nearer the Rhine, the better."

Albert bowed stiffly and went away.

"You don't like the French, do you?" said Renata.

"I'm doing my best," I said. "But they make it so difficult. Even in defeat, they seem to persist in the belief that this is the best country in the world."

"Maybe it is. Maybe that's why they didn't have the best army."

"If you're going to be a philosopher, you're going to have to grow an enormous beard or a silly mustache. Those are the only people we take seriously in Germany."

Horcher arrived bearing a bottle of Mosel and three glasses. "Bernie Gunther," he said, shaking my hand. "Well, I'll be."

"Otto. This is Fräulein Renata Matter, a friend of mine."

Horcher kissed her hand, sat down, and then poured the wine.

"So this is you teaching the hen to be as clever as an egg, is it, Otto?"

"You mean me, here in Paris?" Horcher shrugged. He was a big man with a face like a German general's. Bavarian or Viennese by origin—I forget which—he always had the air of a man in search of a beer and a brass band. "If Fat Hermann asks you to do something for him, then you don't say no, right?" He chuckled. "He likes this place a lot. It's the snooty French waiters he's got a problem with. Which is why I'm here. To make him and the red stripes feel at home. And to cook some of their favorite dishes."

"I'm interested in one of your lower-ranking customers," I explained. "Lieutenant Nikolus Willms. Know him?"

"He's one of my regulars. Always pays cash."

"You can't get many lieutenants in here. Did he win the German lottery? Must have been the South German and the Sachsen with a first-class ticket at these prices, Otto."

Horcher looked around and leaned toward me.

"This place gets a lot of joy girls, Bernie. High-end. Courtesans, they call them here in Paris. But they're whores just the same. Your pardon, Miss Matter. It's not a subject to discuss in front of a lady."

"Don't apologize, Herr Horcher," she said. "I came to Paris for an education. So, please, speak frankly."

"Thank you, miss. This fellow Willms seems to know an awful lot of these girls, Bernie. So I ask some questions. I mean, I like to know the customers. That's just good business. Anyway, it seems this Willms has the power to close down any *maison de plaisir* in Paris. Apparently, he used to be a vice cop in Berlin and can bounce the ball off all the cushions. The word I heard was that the ones that pay he leaves open and the ones that don't he closes down. A good old-fashioned shakedown."

"That's a nice little gold mine," I said.

"There's more," said Horcher. "You see, there's a diamond mine, too. Have you heard of the One Twenty-two and the Maison Chabanais?"

"Sure. They're high-class houses that only the Germans can go to. I guess they paid up."

Horcher nodded. "Like it was the Winter Relief. But Willms was clever. There's a third high-class house where you need a code word to get through the door and which is by invitation only."

"And Willms is printing the stationery?"

Horcher nodded. "Guess who got an invitation when he was on a flying trip to Paris?"

"The Mahatma Propagandi?"

"That's right." Horcher sounded surprised that I had guessed. "You should have been a detective, do you know that?"

"Surely Willms can't be doing this on his own?"

"I don't know if he is or not. But I do know who he often has dinner with. They're both German officers. One of them is General Schaumberg. The other is a Sipo captain like yourself. Name of Paul Kestner."

"That's interesting." I let that one sink in a long way before my next question. "Otto, you wouldn't happen to have an address for this puff house, would you?"

"Twenty-two rue de Provence, opposite the Hôtel Drouot, in the Ninth Arrondissement."

"Thanks, Otto. I owe you one."

After dinner there was still an hour before the midnight curfew, and I told Renata to take the Métro back to her tiny apartment in the rue Jacob.

"Be careful," she said.

"It's all right," I said. "I shan't go in. I'll just—"

"I didn't say be good. I said be careful. Willms has already tried to kill you once. I don't think he'd hesitate to try again. Especially now that you're onto his racket."

"Don't worry. I know what I'm doing."

It would have been nice if this had been true. But I didn't know what I was doing for the simple reason I still didn't have a clue why Willms had tried to kill me.

I decided to walk to the rue de Provence in the hope that the exercise and the summer air might help me to figure things out. For a while I was racking my brains for something I might have said to Willms on the train from Berlin—something that might have made him think I was a threat to his nefarious little organization. And gradually I formed the conclusion that it was nothing I had said; it was what I was that might have alarmed him. At the Alex it was generally supposed that I was Heydrich's spy, and Willms, who worked there for a while, would have known that; even if he didn't, Paul Kestner would certainly have said as much. For his part, Kestner had hardly believed that I'd come all the way from Berlin to arrest just one man. If the two of them were partners, then getting rid of me might have looked like a wise precaution, and Willms was just the type to have taken the matter in hand. Of greater concern, perhaps, was how General Schaumberg was involved, and before my theory was complete I was going to need to know something more about him. This seemed more urgent when, arriving outside 22 rue de Provence, I discovered even more staff cars than had been parked in front of Maxim's.

For several minutes I stood at a distance, in a doorway on the opposite side of the street, watching the comings and goings at what, on the face of it, was a smart address with a liveried doorman. Twice I saw a German officer arrive, utter a single word to the doorman, and be admitted inside, and it seemed obvious that unless I uttered the code word I had no chance of getting into the *maison*. I was just about to give up and return to my hotel when a staff car turned the corner and I caught a glimpse of the officer in the backseat. He was unremarkable in every way save the red and gold patches on his collar and the Blue Max he wore around his neck. The Pour la Merité— popularly known as the Blue Max—isn't a common decoration and led me to think that this could be none other than the commandant of Paris, General Alfred von Vollard-Bockelburg himself. And seeing him headed to the *maison* gave me an idea. What you have to remember is that many of the general staff in Paris in 1940 were tremendous Francophiles, that relations with the French were good, and that German officers all went out of their way to avoid giving offense to the French or to tread on their administrative toes.

By now, the general, who couldn't have been more than five feet tall, even in his boots, had got out of the car and was repeating the code word to the doorman.

I took off my hat and sprinted toward this diminutive hero as the puff house door opened. Seeing me near the general, an aide-de-camp blocked my path. This man was a colonel with a monocle.

"General," I said. "General von Vollard-Bockelburg."

I put on my cap and saluted smartly.

"Yes," said the general, and returned my salute. His head was almost hairless. He looked like a baby with a mustache.

"Thank God, sir."

"Willms, is it?"

This was better than I had hoped for. I glanced nervously at the doorman, wondering if he spoke much German, and risked clicking my heels, which, to a German officer at least, always meant "Yes."

"I'm so glad I caught you, Herr General. Apparently, there's a detachment of French gendarmes on their way here to raid this place."

"What? General Schaumberg assured me that this establishment was beyond reproach."

"Oh, I'm sure the general is right, sir. But the Prefecture of Paris has been given orders by the German Morality Commission that *maisons de plaisir* employing coloreds or Jews are to be closed down, the women arrested, and any German officers found on the premises checked for venereal disease."

"I signed that order myself," said the general. "That order was for the protection of the ordinary rank and file. Not for senior German officers. Not for *maisons* like this."

"I know, sir. But the French, sir. It would appear that they didn't appreciate that, sir. Or at least have chosen not to appreciate it, if you receive my meaning." I glanced urgently at my watch.

"What time is this raid to take place?" asked the general.

"Well, that all depends, sir. Not everyone in Paris has bothered to set clocks to German time, as per your orders, sir. And that includes the French police. If the raid takes place according to Paris time, then it might happen at any minute. But if it's Berlin time, then there might yet be time to get everyone else in the *maison* out before an embarrassing incident occurs."

"He's right, sir," said the aide. "There are still a great many French paying no attention to official German time."

The little general nodded. "Willy," he said to the aide. "Go in there and discreetly inform all general staff officers you can find that the story is out on this place. I'll wait for you in the car."

"Would you like me to help, Herr Colonel?"

"Yes, thank you, Captain Willms. And thank you for your presence of mind."

I clicked my heels again and followed the colonel through the door while the little general explained things to the doorman in what sounded like excellent French.

I went up a curving cast-iron staircase and found myself in a tall, elegant room with a chandelier as big as the underside of an iceberg, and several rococo murals that might have been painted by Fragonard if ever he'd been asked to illustrate the memoirs of Casanova with extreme obscenity. The vaulted gilt ceiling looked like the inside of a Fabergé egg. There were plenty of chairs and sofas that had been upholstered with the aid of an air compressor; they had long legs and narrow ankles with ball-and-claw feet. The girls seated on the chairs and sofas had long legs and narrow ankles and, for all I knew, ball-and-claw feet as well, only I wasn't paying that much attention to their feet because there were other details of their appearance that commanded my attention first. All of them were naked. The angle of this gold-plated puff house was that every man with a red stripe on his trouser leg might sit in leisurely judgment of these Olympian beauties, like Paris with his specially inscribed apple. There was even a bowl of fruit on the table.

These were attractive thoughts, but I was in a hurry, and before the *temps-perdu patronne* could give me her couple-mother spiel, I had grabbed a natural blonde and herded her toward a bedroom with a couple of well-placed slaps on her well-placed derriere. It wasn't that I was interested in having her, but I was in urgent need of a door to lock and wait behind while the general's aide set about raising the alarm. Already I could hear him warning other officers that the police were on their way to raid the place. And it wasn't very long before the sound of many boots was heard on the stairs as the *maison*'s exclusive clientele left the building hurriedly. Meanwhile, I tried to reassure my beautiful naked companion that there was nothing at all to worry about and asked her questions about Willms, Kestner, and Schaumberg. Her name was Yvette and she spoke excellent German, as did nearly all of the girls at number twenty-two. Probably that was why they'd been selected to work there in the first place.

"General Schaumberg is the deputy commander of Berlin," she

explained. "He seems to spend most of his time touring Parisian brothels. Him and his adjutant, who's a German count. The Graf Waldersee. And there's a prince in tow as well: the Prince von Ratibor. The prince and his dog are here at least twice a week. All brothel certificates are issued by Schaumberg's office, and together with Kestner and Willms they've already made it into a nice little racket. The Germans win both ways. They get paid off for a certificate. They get laid by the best whores. But the brains of the outfit is Willms. He used to be a *flic*, so he knows how a *maison* works. A bastard, too. Takes a slice of everything. Most evenings he's in his office here up on the top floor, cooking the books to show Schaumberg."

"Is he here now?"

"He was. I expect he's already on the phone to Schaumberg's office trying to find out what the hell's going on. What is going on?"

I thought it best not to tell her any more than she needed to know.

After about half an hour, I went upstairs. There was no one to be seen, but I could hear someone on the floor above shouting in French. I quickened my steps and arrived on a landing outside an open office door. Willms was on the telephone behind a desk. He was sitting next to an open safe as if he thought it might keep him warm. Perhaps it would have done, too—there was enough money in it.

Seeing me there, he put down the phone and nodded.

"I suppose it was you," he said. "The person who gave out that the gendarmerie was coming to raid this place."

"That's right. I didn't want to embarrass any of those red stripes when I put you under arrest, Willms."

"Me? Under arrest?" He chuckled. "It's you who's going to be in trouble, Gunther. Not me. Half of the general staff in Paris are sharing in this particular bottle, my friend. Some very important heads are going to feel sore about what you've done here tonight."

"They'll get over it. In a few days those Wehrmacht counts and princes will forget a rat like you ever even existed, Willms."

"The amount of coal they're raking back from this place? I don't think so. See, you're trying to flood a very nice little money pit here. The only question is, why? Or maybe you've got something against your brother officers having a thump now and again."

"I'm not arresting you for being a pimp, Willms. Though that's what you are. Personally, I've got nothing at all against pimps. A man can't help what he is. No, I'm arresting you for attempted murder."

"Oh? And whose murder is it that I'm supposed to have attempted?"

"Mine."

"You can prove that, can you?"

"I'm a detective, remember? I've got a little thing called evidence. Not to mention a witness. And if I'm right, a motive, too. Not that I'll need any of these things when Himmler finds out what you've been up to here in Paris, Willms. He's rather less understanding than me when it comes to the conduct of men wearing the uniform of his beloved SS. Somehow I get the feeling that his opinion of your conduct is going to matter a lot more than General Schaumberg's."

"You're serious, aren't you?"

"I always take it seriously when someone tries to gas me with the contents of a chemical fire extinguisher. And by the way, I checked back with the Alex. It seems that before you joined the police, you worked for the fire brigade."

"I don't see that that proves a thing."

"It proves you know something about fire extinguishers. And it would account for how it was that the missing plug from the extinguisher that almost killed me was found in your hotel room."

"Says who?"

"The witness."

"You think that a court-martial will accept the word of a Frenchman against the word of a German officer?"

"No. But they might accept it against the word of a greasy little pimp."

"You might be right," said Willms. "We'll have to see, won't we?"

Uttering a weary sort of sigh, he sat back in his chair and, in the same movement, pulled open the drawer of his desk. Even before I saw the gun I knew it was there, and after that it was simply a question of who could shoot first, him or me. On my SS soft-shell holster there was just a brass stud to keep the flap down, but even so I was no Gene Autry and the Luger was in his hand before the Walther P38 was in mine. It was the Walther's double-action trigger that probably saved my life. Like most policemen, I was in the habit of carrying it with one in the chamber and the hammer down. All I had to do was squeeze the trigger. Willms ought to have known that. The toggle-lock action on his Luger was much more cumbersome, which was why cops didn't carry them, and by the time his pistol was ready to fire I was already shouting a warning. I might have finished the warning, too, if he hadn't started to straighten his arm and point the gun at me, at which point I fired at the side of his head.

For a moment I thought I'd missed.

Willms sat down, only he didn't sit on the chair but on the floor, like a Boy Scout dropping onto his backside beside a campfire. Then I saw the blood boiling out of his skull like hot mud. He collapsed onto his side and lay still except for his legs, which straightened slowly, like someone trying to get comfortable enough to die; and all the time his head painted the beige carpet a very dark shade of red as if an indifferent claret had been poured onto the floor by a truculent guest in an unsatisfactory restaurant.

With shaking hands, I made my Walther safe and then holstered it, asking myself if I couldn't have aimed at something other than his head. At the same time, I told myself that one of the easiest ways to end up dead is to leave your wounded adversary with an opportunity to shoot you.

I bent down and made sure the Luger was safe, too, and it was then I started to see how much of a jam I was in, what with all the generals and counts and princes who were in league with Willms. And thinking it might be better if Willms's death at least looked a bit less like a murder, I swapped the Luger for my own Walther. Then, seeing Willms's tunic and belt, I took his Walther and put it in my holster before replacing the cold Luger in the desk drawer. Things only looked like a mess. Suicide was actually a nice, tidy solution for the French police, for Sipo, and for the red stripes over at the Majestic hotel. I wondered if they'd even bother to look for a powder burn on Willms's head. Because cops all over the world love suicides; they're nearly always the easiest homicides to solve. You just lift the rug and brush them underneath.

I picked up the telephone and asked the operator for the Préfecture de Police, in the rue de Lutèce.

23

GERMANY, 1954

I sat up and blinked hard in the near darkness of cell number seven, wondering how long I'd been asleep. The shade of Hitler was gone, at least for now, and I was glad about that. I didn't much like his questions or the mocking assumption that, deep down, I was as big a criminal as him. It was true that I might have shot Nikolaus Willms somewhere less lethal than his head, and that even when I'd been trying to put him under arrest, secretly I had probably wanted to kill him. Perhaps if Paul Kestner had pulled a gun on me I'd have shot him, too. But as it was I never saw him again, and the last I heard of him he'd been part of a police battalion in Smolensk, murdering Jews and communists.

I opened my window and put my face in the cool breeze of the Landsberg dawn. I couldn't see the cows, but I could smell them in the fields across the river to the southwest and I could hear them, too. One, anyway; it sounded like a lost soul in a place far, far away. Like my own soul, perhaps. I almost felt like blowing my own breath in a solitary hot blast by way of an answer.

The Paris of 1940 seemed equally far away. What a summer that had been, thanks to Renata. The prefecture in the person of

Chief Inspector Oltramare had accepted without demur my story of finding Willms dead after going to the *maison* with the intention of arresting him, although it was as plain as the Eiffel Tower that he believed not a word of it. Sipo proved only a little more troublesome, and I was summoned to the Hôtel Majestic, in the avenue des Portugais, to explain myself to General Best, the head of RSHA in Paris.

A dark-eyed, severe-looking man from Darmstadt, Best was in his late thirties and bore a strong resemblance to the Nazi Party's deputy leader, Rudolf Hess. There was some bad blood between him and Heydrich, and because of that, I half expected Best to give me a rougher ride. Instead, he confined himself to delivering a light reprimand for my declared intent to arrest Willms without consulting him. Which was fair enough, and my apology seemed to put an end to the matter; as things turned out, he was much more interested in picking my brains for a book he was writing about the German police. On several occasions we met at his favorite restaurant, a brasserie on the boulevard de Montparnasse called La Coupole, and I told him all about life at the Alex and some of the cases I had investigated. Best's book was published the following year and sold very well.

In fact, he turned out to be something of a benefactor. He and his damn book were the main reason I managed to stay on in Paris until June 1941, and so it was Best who effectively ensured I missed out on going to Pretzsch and Himmler's pep talk for the SS and SD. I might have stayed on a bit longer and avoided going to the Ukraine altogether but for Heydrich. Now and then he liked to tug the line a little just to remind me that he had his hook in my mouth.

I lit a cigarette and lay down on the bed again, waiting for the gray light to strengthen and the room to take shape and the uncaring guards to rouse Landsberg's inmates for exercise, breakfast, and then what was called "free association." To my surprise, I was now allowed back into the general prison population. But to avoid

Biberstein and Haensch with their worries about what I was telling the Americans and how that might affect their own chances of parole, I found myself seeking out the company of Waldemar Klingelhöfer. Since he had been cut by everyone else at Landsberg, my speaking to him was the best way of ensuring I was left alone—at least for the duration of our conversation. We talked in the garden, with the sun warming our faces.

Klingelhöfer had not aged well since our time together at Lenin House in Minsk, and he was perhaps the only prisoner at WCPN1 of whom it could have been said that he had some sort of conscience about what he had done. He looked like a man haunted by his actions with the Moscow commando. Martin Sandberger, watching us from a short distance away, merely looked psychopathic.

Looking at Klingelhöfer's twitching, bespectacled face, it was hard to imagine the former opera tenor who owned it singing anything except perhaps the "Dies Irae." But I was more interested in talking to him about what had happened in Minsk after I had returned from there to Berlin.

"Do you remember a man called Paul Kestner?" I asked him.

"Yes," said Klingelhöfer. "He was active with a murder commando in Smolensk when I got there in 1941. I was supposed to obtain furs to use for German military winter clothing. Kestner had been in Paris, I think, and was bitter about his being posted to Russia. He seemed to be taking it out on Jews, that much was obvious, and my impression was that he was a really cruel man. After that I heard he got posted to the death camp at Treblinka. That must have been about July of 1942. He was the deputy commander, I think. There was some talk about Kestner and Irmfried Eberl, who was in charge, running the camp for their own pleasure and profit, using Jewish women for sex and embezzling Jewish gold and jewelry that was properly the property of the Reich. Anyway, the bosses found out about it and by all accounts dismissed the pair of them and some others besides before putting in a new man to clean the stables. Fellow named Stangl. Meanwhile, Eberl and Kestner were dismissed from the SS and, in 1944, I heard they joined the Wehrmacht in an attempt to redeem themselves. The Amis got Eberl a few years ago, and I believe he hanged himself. But I've no idea what became of Kestner. They say Stangl's in South America."

"Well, if he is, it's not Argentina," I said. "Or Uruguay."

"You're lucky," said Klingelhöfer. "To have been to those places. Me, I expect I'll die here."

"You must be the only prisoner in Landsberg who believes that, Wally. Everyone else seems to be expecting a parole. They've already let go men who, in my opinion, were worse than you."

"Thanks. Nice of you to say so. But I just hope that if I do die in here, they'll allow my family to have my body. I wouldn't want to be buried here in Landsberg. It would mean a lot to them. Nice of you to say so, yes. I mean, I'm not looking to get out. I mean, what would I do? What can any of us do?"

I left Klingelhöfer talking to himself. He did a lot of that in Landsberg. It looked easier than talking to the Americans. Or Biberstein and Haensch. Or Sandberger, who cornered me on the way back to my cell.

"Why do you speak to a bastard like that?" he demanded.

"Why not? I speak to you. Really, I'm not that particular."

"Funny guy. I heard that about you, Gunther."

"I don't see you laughing. Then again, you used to be a judge, didn't you? Before you went to Estonia? Not many laughs there, either, from what I heard."

Sandberger had a ruffian's face, with a jaw like a flat tire and a boxer's hostile eyes. It was hard to imagine how anyone could have become a lawyer or a judge with a face like that. It was easier to imagine him murdering sixty-five thousand Jews. You didn't need to be a criminologist to figure out a physiognomy like Sandberger's.

"I hear the Amis have been giving you a hard time of it," he said.

"You hear good with those things on the side of your head."

"So I took the liberty of mentioning you to the evangelical bishop of Württemburg," he said. "In my last letter to him."

"As long as there are prisons there will be prayers."

"There's a lot more he can do than just pray."

"A cake would be nice. Lots of cream and fruit, and a Walther P38 filling."

Sandberger smiled a lopsided smile that wasn't provoking any second thoughts in my mind about the descent of man.

"He doesn't do prison breaks," said Sandberger. "Just letters to influential people here and in America."

"I wouldn't want to put him to any trouble," I said. "Besides, I just came back from America myself. But I certainly didn't make any friends while I was there."

"Which part?"

"The southern half. Argentina, mainly. You wouldn't like Argentina, Martin. It's hot. Lots of insects. Plenty of Jews. But you're only allowed to kill the insects."

"But lots of Germans, too, I hear."

"No. Just Nazis."

Sandberger grinned. Probably he meant it well, but it felt like seeing something unpleasant and atavistic toward the end of a séance. Evil flickering on and off like a faulty lightbulb.

"Well," he said, full of patient menace. "Let me know if I can help. My father is a friend of President Heuss."

"And he's trying to help free you?" I tried to contain the surprise in my voice. "To get you a parole?"

"Yes."

"Thanks." I walked away before he could see the look of horror on my face. It was beginning to look as if the only way I was ever going to have any friends in the new Germany was to have friends I really didn't like.

My American friends, both of them, were in cell seven when,

after breakfast, I was returned there by one of the guards. This time they'd brought a little tape recorder in a leather case with a microphone not much bigger than a Norelco shaver. One was filling his pipe from a pouch of Sir Walter Raleigh; the other was adjusting his clip-on bow tie against his reflection in my cell window. There was a short-brimmed Stetson on my bed and both men smelled lightly of Vaseline hair tonic.

"Make yourself at home," I said.

"Thanks, we already did."

"If you're here to record my singing voice, I should warn you fellows I already made a deal with Parlophone."

"This is for our listening pleasure," said the one puffing some heat into his Sir Walter Raleigh. "We're not planning on a general release. Not this Christmas."

"We think we're getting to the interesting part," said the other. "About Erich Mielke. At long last. The part that affects us now." He snapped on the machine and the spools began to turn. "Say something for recording level."

"Like what?"

"I dunno. But let's just hope that the oral tradition is not yet dead in Germany."

"If it isn't, it must be the only thing in Germany that's not dead."

A few seconds later, I heard for the first time the sound of my own voice uttered by someone other than myself. There was something about it I didn't like. Mostly it was the laconic way I had of speaking. It was five years since I'd seen my home city, but I still sounded as unhelpful as a Berlin grave digger. It was easy to see why people didn't like me very much. If ever I was going to make a useful contribution to society I was going to have to fix that. Maybe take some lessons in courtesy and charm.

"Think of us like the Brothers Grimm," said the Ami smoking the pipe. "Gathering material for a story."

"I try not to think of you at all if I can help it. But the Brothers Grimm works for me. I never liked their stuff very much. I especially hated the story about the village idiot with the pipe and the bow tie and his wicked Uncle Sam."

"So, then. After Paris. You went home to Berlin."

"Briefly. I organized Renata a job at the Adlon and lived to regret it. The poor kid was killed in the first big bombing raid on Berlin, in November 1943. Some help I was."

"And Heydrich?"

"Oh, he was killed much earlier than 1943. Only, he had it coming and on a silver salver. But that's another story."

"Did he believe you? About not finding Mielke?"

"Maybe. Maybe not. You never knew with Heydrich. We talked it over in his office at the Prinz Albrechtstrasse. Next thing I knew, I had orders to go to the Ukraine. I might have taken that personally except for the fact that everyone had the same orders." I shrugged. "Well, I expect your friends Silverman and Earp told you all about that. Then I was in Berlin for a while before going to Prague. That was the summer of 1942. Let's see, now. A year later, I was in Smolensk with the War Crimes Bureau. As an Oberleutnant. But after the Battle of Kursk we were out of that whole theater pretty quickly. The Red Army was in the driver's seat, you might say. I got a leave. I got married. To a schoolteacher. Then I was recruited into the Abwehr—military intelligence—and promoted to captain again."

"Why were you demoted?"

"Because of what happened in Prague. I stepped on someone's corns, I guess." I shrugged. "Anyway, February 1944, I joined General Schörner's Northern Army as an intelligence officer. I spoke a fair bit of Russian by then. And a bit of Polish, too. The work was mostly interpreting. At least it was until the fighting started. Then it was just fighting. Kill or be killed. Tell me something. Did either of the Brothers Grimm see combat?"

"Nope," said the man with the pipe. "I was flying a desk for the whole of the war."

"I was too young," said the man with the bow tie.

"I didn't think so. You get to recognize that in a man's eye. It might interest you to know that by 1944 there was no such thing as 'too young' for the German army. There was no 'too old,' either. And no one was left flying a desk, as you put it, when they could fly a plane, or sit in a tank, or man an antiaircraft battery. Boys of thirteen marched alongside men aged sixty-five and seventy. You see, it wasn't until the Red Army reached East Prussia that German civilians began to suffer in the way Russian civilians had suffered. This meant that there was more for us to fight for; and it was why men and boys of all ages were conscripted into the army. Nothing and no one was to be spared, least of all ourselves. Total war was what Goebbels called it. And it means what it says, which was rare for him. Total means everything. All in, nothing left out.

"You Amis talk about this Cold War of yours with no understanding of what it means to fight a cold, pitiless war without mercy and against an enemy who never stops coming. Oh, believe me, I know. I was killing Ivans for fourteen months and I can tell you this—there's no end to them. As many as you can kill, they keep on coming. So remember that if the time ever comes when you have to do the same. Not that anyone believes you'll stop them. Why would you fight to save Europe, to save Germans? That's the only reason we fought. To stop the Ivans from slaughtering the population of East Prussia. You might say that this was what we had done to the Jews, and you'd be right. But there were no war crimes trials for Soviet officers, no Ivans here in Landsberg. You would have to see what happens to a crowd of civilians when a Russian tank drives straight through its middle, or watch a fighter strafe a line of civilian refugees, to know what I'm talking about. Sepp Dietrich and his men shot how many Americans at Malmédy? Ninety? Ninety. A war crime you call it. For the Russians in East

Prussia, ninety wasn't even an infraction, it was a misdemeanor. Except that it's hardly a misdemeanor when the general demeanor of your soldiery is one of barbarous cruelty."

I was silent for a moment.

"Something wrong?"

"I never talked about this before," I said. "It's not easy. What does Goethe say? About sun and worlds I can tell you but little. All that I can see is the suffering of humanity. Still, it's right that you should hear it. The trouble with you Amis is that you think it was you who won the war when everyone knows it was the Ivans. Without you and the British, they'd have taken longer to beat us. But they'd have beaten us all the same. Stalin's maths, we used to call it. When there were just five of us left, there would be twenty Russians. And that was how Stalin was going to win. You'd better remember that if the Ivans ever invade West Berlin."

"Sure, sure. Let's talk about Königsberg. You were taken prisoner at Königsberg."

"Don't rush me. I have to tell this in my own way. When something has been asleep for this long, you don't just shake it by the shoulder and shout in its ear."

"Take your time. You've got plenty of time."

24

GERMANY AND RUSSIA, 1945–1946

Königsberg is, was, important to me. My mother was born in Königsberg. When I was a child, we used to go on vacation to a seaside town near there called Cranz. Best vacation we ever had. My first wife and I went there on our honeymoon, in 1919. It was the capital of East Prussia—a land of dark forests, crystal lakes, sand dunes, white skies, and Teutonic knights who built a fine old medieval city with a castle and a cathedral and seven good bridges across the River Pregel. There was even a university founded in 1544, where the city's most famous son, Immanuel Kant, would one day teach.

I arrived there in June 1944. As part of Army Group North. I was attached to the 132nd Infantry Division. My job was to gather intelligence on the advancing Red Army. What type of men were they? What condition were they in? How well armed were they? Supply lines—all the usual stuff. And from the German civilians who fled their homes ahead of the Russian advance, the intelligence I had was of well-equipped, ill-disciplined, drunken Neanderthals who were bent on rape, murder, and mutilation. Frankly, a lot of this seemed like hysterical nonsense. Indeed, there was a lot of Nazi propaganda to this effect that was designed to dissuade everyone from surrendering. And so I resolved to discover the true situation for myself.

This was made more difficult when, at the end of August, the Royal Air Force bombed the city to rubble. And I do mean rubble. All of the bridges were destroyed. All of the public buildings lay in ruins. So it was a while before I was able to verify the reports of atrocities. And I was left in no doubt as to the truth of these when our troops retook the German village of Nemmersdorf, about a hundred kilometers east of Königsberg.

I'd seen some terrible things in the Ukraine, of course. And this was as bad as anything we'd done to them. Women raped and mutilated. Children clubbed to death. The whole village murdered. All seven hundred of them. You've got to see it to believe it, and now I believed it and I could have wished I didn't. I made my report. The next thing, the Ministry of Propaganda had it and was even broadcasting parts of it on the radio. Well, that was the last time they were honest about our situation. The only part of my report they didn't use was the conclusion: that we should evacuate the city by sea as soon as possible. We could have done it, too. But Hitler was against it. Our wonder weapons were going to turn the tide and win the war. We had nothing to worry about. Plenty of people believed that, too.

That was October 1944. But by January the following year, it was painfully clear to everyone that there were no wonder weapons. At least none that could help us. The city was encircled, just like at Stalingrad. The only difference was that as well as fifty thousand German soldiers there were three hundred thousand civilians. We started to get people out. But in the process, thousands died. Nine thousand died in just fifty minutes when a Russian submarine sank the *Wilhelm Gustloff* outside the port of Gotenhafen. And we kept on fighting, not because we obeyed Hitler, but because for every day that we fought, a few more civilians managed to escape. Did I say it was the coldest winter in living memory? Well, that hardly helped the situation.

For a short while, the artillery and the bombing stopped as the

Ivans prepared their final assault. When it came, in the third week of March, we were thirty-five thousand men and fifty tanks against perhaps one hundred fifty thousand troops, five hundred tanks, and more than two thousand aircraft. Me, I was in the trenches during the Great War and I thought I knew what it was to be under a bombardment. I didn't. Hour after hour the shells fell. Sometimes, there were as many as two hundred fifty bombers in the sky at any one time.

Finally, General Lasch contacted the Russian High Command and offered our surrender in return for a guarantee that we would be well treated. They agreed, and the next day we laid down our arms. That was fine if you were a soldier. But the Russians were of the opinion that the guarantee had never applied to Königsberg's civilian population and the Red Army proceeded to exact a terrible revenge on it. Every woman was raped. Old men were murdered out of hand. The sick and wounded were thrown out of hospital windows to make room for Russians. In short, the whole Red Army got drunk and went crazy and did what it liked to civilians of all ages before finally they set on fire what remained of the city and their victims. Those they didn't kill they let fend for themselves in the countryside, where most of them starved to death. There was nothing any of us in the army could do about this. Those who did protest were shot on the spot. Some of us said this was justice—that we deserved it for what had been done to them—and this was true, only it's hard to think of justice when you see a naked woman crucified on a barn door. Maybe we all deserved crucifixion, like those mutinous gladiators in ancient Rome. I don't know. But every man who saw that wondered what lay in store for us. I know I did.

For several days we were marched east of Königsberg, and as we walked we were robbed of wedding rings, wristwatches, even false teeth. Any man refusing to hand over an object of value in a Russian's eyes was shot. At the railway station, we waited patiently in a field for transport to wherever we were going. There was no food and no water, and all the time more and more German soldiers joined our host.

Some of us boarded a train that took us to Brno in Czechoslovakia, where at last we were given some bread and water; and then we boarded another train headed southeast. As the train left Brno we caught sight of the city's famous St. Peter and Paul Cathedral, and for many men this was almost as good as seeing a priest. Even those who didn't believe took the opportunity to pray. The next time we stopped we got out of the cattle cars, and finally we were given some hot soup. It was the thirtieth of April, 1945. Twenty days after our surrender. I know this because the Russians made a point of telling us the news that Hitler was dead. I don't know who was more pleased to hear this, them or us. Some of us cheered. A few of us wept. It was the end of one hell, no doubt. But for Germany and us in particular, it was the beginning of another—hell as it really is, perhaps, being a timeless place of punishment and suffering and run by devils who enjoy inflicting cruelty. Certainly, we were judged by the book that was open, and that book was *Mein Kampf*, and for what was written in that book we were all going to suffer. Some more than others.

From that transit camp in Romania—someone claimed it was a place called Secureni, from where Bessarabian Jews had been sent to Auschwitz—there was another train traveling northeast, right through the Ukraine, a country I had hoped never to see again, to a stop in the middle of nowhere where MVD guards drove us from the cattle cars with whips and curses. Standing there, faint from lack of food and water, blinking in the spring sunshine like unwanted dogs, we awaited our orders. Finally, after almost an hour, we were marched along a dirt road between two infinite horizons.

"Bistra!" shouted the guards. "Hurry up!"

But to where? To what? Would any of us ever see home again? Out there, so far away from any sign of human habitation, it seemed unlikely; even more so when those who had only just survived the journey found they could walk no farther and were shot where they fell at the side of the road by mounted MVD. Four or five men were shot in this way like horses that had outlived their usefulness. No man was allowed to carry another, and in this way only the strongest of us were permitted to survive, as if Prince Kropotkin had been in charge of our exhausted company.

Finally, we arrived at the camp, which was a selection of dilapidated gray wooden buildings surrounded by two barbed-wire fences, and remarkable only because next to the main gate was the steeple of a nonexistent church—one of those sharp, metallic-roofed Russian church edifices that looked like some old Junker's *Pickelhaube* helmet. There was nothing else for miles around—not even a few huts that might once have been served by the church to which the steeple had once belonged.

We trooped through the gate under the silent, hollow eyes of several hundred men who were the remains of the Hungarian Third Army; these men were on the other side of a fence, and it seemed we were to be kept separate from them, at least until we had been checked for parasites and diseases. Then we were fed, and having been pronounced fit for labor, I was sent to the sawmill. I might have been an officer, but no one was excused from work—that is, no one who wanted to eat—and for several weeks I spent every day loading and unloading wood. This seemed like a hard job until I spent a whole day shoveling lime, and returning the next day to the sawmill, half blinded by the stuff blowing in my face, and blood streaming from my nose, I told myself I was lucky that a few splinters in my hands and a sore back were the worst I had to suffer. In the sawmill I befriended a young lieutenant called Metelmann. Really he was not much more than a boy, or so it seemed to me; physically he was strong enough, but it was mental strength that was needed more and Metelmann's morale was at a very low ebb. I'd seen his type in the trenches—the kind who awakes every morning expecting to be killed, when the only way of dealing with our predicament was to give the matter no thought at all, as if we were dead already. But since caring for another human being is often a very good means of ensuring one's own survival, I resolved to look after Metelmann as best I could.

A month passed. And then another. Long months of work and food and sleep and no memories, for it was best not to think about the past and, of course, the future was something that had no meaning in the camp. The present and the life of a *voinapleni* was all there was. And the life of the *voinapleni* was *bistra* and *davai* and *nichevo*; it was *kasha* and *klopkis* and the *kate*. Beyond the wire was the death zone, and beyond that there was another wire, and beyond that there was just the steppe, and more of the steppe. No one thought of escape. There was nowhere to go, that was the real communist *pravda* of life in Voronezh. It was as if we were in limbo waiting to die so that we could be sent to hell.*

But instead we—the German officers at Camp Eleven—were sent to another camp. No one knew why. No one gave us a reason. Reasons were for human beings. It happened without warning early one August evening, just as we finished work for the day. Instead of marching back to camp, we found ourselves on the long march somewhere else. It was only after several hours on the road that we saw the train and we realized we were off on another journey and, very likely, we would never see Camp Eleven again. Since none of us had any belongings, this hardly seemed to matter.

"Do you think we could be going home?" asked Metelmann as we boarded the train and then set off.

I glanced at the setting sun. "We're headed southeast," I said, which was all the answer that was needed.

"Christ," he said. "We're never going to find our way home."

He had an excellent point. Staring out of a gap in the planks on the side of our cattle car at the endless Russian steppes, it was the sheer size of the country that defeated you. Sometimes it was so big and unchanging that it seemed the train wasn't moving at all, and the only way to make sure that we weren't standing still was

---

* *Voinapleni* = POW; *bistra* = hurry up; *davai* = go on, or all right; *nichevo* = it doesn't matter; *kasha* = barley broth; *klopkis* = lice; *kate* = hut or barracks; *pravda* = truth; Voronezh is a Russian province.

to watch the moving track through the hole in the floor that served as our latrine.

"How did that bastard Hitler ever think we could conquer a country as big as this?" said someone. "You might as well try to invade the ocean."

Once, in the distance, we saw another train traveling west, in the opposite direction, and there was not one of who didn't wish we were on it. Anywhere west seemed better than anywhere east.

Another man said: " 'Sing to me of the man, Muse, the man of twists and turns, driven time and again off course, once he had plundered the sacred heights of Troy. Many cities of men he saw and learned their ways, many places he endured, heartsick on the open sea, struggling to save his life and bring his comrades home.' "

He paused for a moment and then, for the benefit of those who'd never done the classics, said, "Homer's *Odyssey*."

To which someone else said, "I only hope that Penelope is behaving herself."

The journey took two whole days and nights before, finally, we disembarked beside a wide, steel-gray river, at which point the classics scholar, whose name was Sajer, began to cross himself religiously.

"What is it?" asked Metelmann. "What's wrong?"

"I recognize this place," said Sajer. "I remember thanking God I'd never see it again."

"God likes his little jokes," I said.

"So what is this place?" demanded Metelmann.

"This is the Volga," said Sajer. "And if I'm right, we're not far south of Stalingrad."

"Stalingrad." We all repeated the name with quiet horror.

"I was one of the last to get out before the Sixth Army was encircled," explained Sajer. "And now I'm back. What a fucking nightmare."

From the train we marched to a larger camp that was mostly

SS, although not all of them German: There were French, Belgian, and Dutch SS. But the senior German officer was a Wehrmacht colonel named Mrugowski, who welcomed us to a barrack with proper bunk beds and real mattresses, and told us that we were in Krasno-Armeesk, between Astrakhan and Stalingrad.

"Where have you come from?" he asked.

"A camp called Usman, near Voronezh," I said.

"Ah yes," he said. "The one with the church steeple."

I nodded.

"This place is better," he said. "The work is hard, but the Ivans are relatively fair. Relative to Usman, that is. Where were you captured?"

We exchanged news, and like all the other Germans at K.A., the colonel was anxious to hear something about his brother, who was a doctor with the Waffen SS, but no one could tell him anything.

It was the height of the summer on the steppe, and with little or no shade, the work—excavating a canal between the Don and the Volga rivers—was hard and hot. But for a while at least, my situation was almost tolerable. Here there were Russians working, too—*saklutshonnis** convicted of a political crime that, more often than not, was hardly a crime at all, or at least none that any German—not even the Gestapo—would have recognized. And from these prisoners I began to perfect my knowledge of the Russian language.

The site itself was an enormous trench covered with duckboards and walkways and rickety wooden bridges; and from dawn until dusk it was filled with hundreds of men wielding picks and shovels, or pushing crudely made wheelbarrows—a regular Potsdamer Platz of *pleni* traffic—and policed by stone-faced "Blues," which was what we called the MVD guards with their *gimnasterka* tunics, *portupeya* belts, and blue shoulder boards. The work was not without hazard. Now and then, the sides of the canal would

---

Saklutshonni = a convict, as opposed to a POW.

collapse in upon someone and we would all dig frantically to save his life. This happened almost every week, and to our surprise and shame—for these were not the inferior people that the Nazis had told us of—it was usually the Russian convicts who were quickest to help. One such man was Ivan Yefremovich Pospelov, who became the nearest thing I had to a friend at K.A., and who thought he was well off, although his forehead, which was dented like a felt hat, told a different story from the one he told me:

"What matters most, Herr Bernhard, is that we are alive, and in that we are indeed fortunate. For right now, at this very moment, somewhere in Russia, someone is meeting his undeserved end at the hands of the MVD. Even as we speak, a poor Russian is being led to the edge of a pit and thinking his last thoughts about home and family before the pistol fires and a bullet is the last thing to travel through his mind. So who cares if the work is hard and the food is poor? We have the sun and the air in our lungs and this moment of companionship that can't be taken away from us, my friend. And one day, when we're free again, think how much more it will mean to you and me just to be able to go and buy a newspaper and some cigarettes. And other men will envy us that we live with such fortitude in the face of what only appear to be the travails of life. You know what makes me laugh most of all? To think that ever I complained in a restaurant. Can you imagine it? To send something back to a kitchen because it was not properly cooked. Or to reprimand a barman for serving warm beer. I tell you, I'd be glad to have that warm beer now. That's happiness right there, in the acceptance of that warm beer and remembering how it's enough in life to have that and not the taste of brackish water on cracked lips. This is the meaning of life, my friend. To know when you are well off and to hate or envy no man."

But there was one man at K.A. whom it was hard not to hate or envy. Among the Blues were several political officers, *politruk*s, who had the job of turning German fascists into good anti-fascists. From time to time, these *politruk*s would order us into the mess to hear a speech about Western imperialism, the evils of capitalism, and what a great job Comrade Stalin was doing to save the world from another war. Of course, the *politruks* didn't speak German and not all of us spoke Russian, and the translation was usually handled by the most unpopular German in the camp, Wolfgang Gebhardt.

Gebhardt was one of two anti-fascist agents at K.A. He was a former SS corporal, from Paderborn, a professional footballer who once had played for SV 07 Neuhaus. After being captured at Stalingrad in February 1943, Gebhardt claimed to have been converted to the cause of communism and, as a result, received special treatment: his own quarters, better clothing and footwear, better food, cigarettes, and vodka. There was another anti-fa agent called Kissel, but Gebhardt was by far the more unpopular of the two, which probably explains why sometime during the autumn of 1945, Gebhardt was murdered. Early one morning he was found dead in his hut, stabbed to death. The Ivans were very exercised about it, as converts to Bolshevism were, despite the material benefits of becoming a Red, rather thin on the ground. An MVD major from the Stalingrad Oblast came down to K.A. to inspect the body, after which he met with the senior German officer and, by all accounts, a shouting match ensued. Following this, I was surprised to find myself summoned to see Colonel Mrugowski. We sat on his bed behind a curtain that was one of the few small privileges allowed to him as SGO.

"Thanks for coming, Gunther," he said. "You know about Gebhardt, I suppose."

"Yes. I heard the cathedral bells ringing."

"I'm afraid it's not the good news that everyone might imagine."

"He didn't leave any cigarettes?"

"I've just had some MVD major in here shouting his head off. Making me into a snail about it."

"Show me a Blue who doesn't like to shout and I'll show you a pink unicorn."

"He wants me to do something about it. About Gebhardt, I mean."

"We could always bury him, I suppose." I sighed. "Look, sir, I think I ought to tell you. I didn't kill him. And I don't know who did. But they should give whoever did it the Iron Cross."

"Major Savostin sees things differently. He's given me seventy-two hours to produce the murderer, or twenty-five German soldiers will be selected at random to stand trial at an MVD court in Stalingrad."

"Where an acquittal seems unlikely."

"Exactly."

I shrugged. "So you appeal to the men and ask the guilty man to step up for it."

"And if that doesn't work?" He shook his head. "Not all of the *pleni*s here are German. Just the majority. And I did remind the major of this fact. However, he's of the opinion that a German had the best motive to kill Gebhardt."

"True."

"Major Savostin has a low opinion of German moral values but a high opinion of our capacity for reasoning and logic. Since a German had the best motive for the murder, he thinks it seems reasonable that we should have the most to lose if the killer is not identified. Which he believes is now the best incentive for us to do his job for him."

"So what are you telling me, sir?"

"Come on, Gunther. Everyone in Krasno-Armeesk knows you used to be a detective at Berlin's Alexanderplatz Praesidium. As the SGO, I'm asking you to take charge of a murder investigation."

"Is that what this is?"

"Maybe none of this will be necessary. But you should at least take a look at the body while I parade the men and ask the guilty man to step forward."

I walked across the camp in the stiffening wind. Winter was

coming. You could feel it in the air. You could hear it, too, as it rattled the windows of Gebhardt's private hut. A depressing sound it was, almost as loud as the noise of my own rumbling belly, and I was already reproaching myself for not exacting a price for my forensic services. An extra piece of *chleb*. A second bowl of *kasha*. No one at K.A. volunteered for anything unless there was something in it for him, and that something was nearly always food.

A *starshina*, a Blue sergeant named Degermenkoy, standing in front of Gebhardt's hut, saw me and walked slowly in my direction.

"Why aren't you at work?" he yelled, and hit me hard across the shoulders with his walking stick.

Between blows I explained my mission, and finally he stopped and let me get up off the ground.

I thanked him and went into the little hut, closing the door behind me in case there was anything in there I could steal. The first things, I saw were a bar of soap and a piece of bread. Not the *shorni* that we *pleni*s received, but *belii*, the white bread, and before I even looked at Gebhardt's body I stuffed my mouth full of what should have been his last meal. This would have been reward enough for the job I was doing, except that I saw some cigarettes and matches, and as soon as I had swallowed the bread I lit one and smoked it in a state of near ecstasy. I hadn't smoked a cigarette in six months. Still ignoring the body on the bed, I looked around the hut for something to drink and my eyes fell on a small bottle of vodka. And finally, smoking my cigarette and taking little bites off Gebhardt's bottle, I started to behave like a real detective.

The hut was about ten feet square, with a small window that was covered with an iron grille meant to keep the occupant safe from the rest of us *pleni*s. It hadn't worked. There was a lock on the wooden door, but the key was nowhere to be seen. There was a table, a stove, and a chair, and feeling a little faint—probably from the cigarette and the vodka—I sat down. On the wall were two propaganda portraits—cheap, frameless posters of Lenin and

Stalin—and, collecting some phlegm at the back of my throat, I let the great leader have it.

Then I drew the chair up to the bed and took a closer look at the body. That he was dead was obvious, since there were stab wounds all over his body, but mainly around the head, neck, and chest. Less obvious was the choice of murder weapon—a piece of elk horn that was sticking out of the dead man's right eye socket. The ferocity of the attack was remarkable, as was the brutal instrumentality of the elk horn. I'd seen violent crime scenes before in my time as a detective, but rarely as frenzied as this. It gave me a new respect for elks. I counted sixteen separate stab wounds, including two or three protective wounds on the forearms, and from the blood spatter on the walls it seemed clear that Gebhardt had been murdered on the bed. I tried to raise one of the dead man's hands and discovered rigor had already well set in. The body was quite cold, and I formed the conclusion that Gebhardt had met his well-deserved death between the hours of midnight and four o'clock in the morning. I also discovered some blood underneath his fingernails, and I might even have taken a sample of this if I'd had an envelope to put it in, not to mention a laboratory with a microscope that might have analyzed it. I did, however, take the dead man's wedding ring, which was so tight and the finger so badly swollen that I had to use the soap to get it off. Any other man's ring would have fallen off his finger, but Gebhardt drew better rations than any of us and was a normal weight. I weighed the ring in the palm of my hand. It was gold and would certainly come in useful if I ever needed to bribe a Blue. I looked closely at the inscription on the inside, but it was too small for my weakened eyes. I didn't put it in my pocket, however; for one thing, the trousers of my uniform were full of holes, and for another, there was the *starshina* outside the door who might take it upon himself to search me. So I swallowed it, in the certainty that with my bowels as loose as vegetable soup I could easily retrieve the ring later.

By now I could hear the SGO addressing the German *pleni*s outside. There was a cheer as he confirmed what most of them knew: that Gebhardt was dead. This was followed by a loud groan as he told them how the MVD were planning to handle the matter. I got up and went to the window in the hope that I might see one brave soul identify himself as the culprit, but no one moved. Fearing the worst, I took another bite off the vodka bottle and laid my hand on the stove. It was cold, but I opened it all the same, just in case the killer had thought to burn his signed confession; but there was nothing—just a few pages from an old copy of *Pravda* and some bits of wood, ready for when the weather turned colder.

A shallow closet, no deeper than a shoe box, was fixed against the corner of the hut and in it I found the Waffen SS uniform that Gebhardt had ceased wearing when he'd switched sides. It would hardly have done for an anti-fascist officer to have carried on wearing an SS uniform. His new Russian *gimnasterka* was hanging on the back of the chair. Quickly, I searched the pockets and found a few kopecks, which I pocketed, and some more cigarettes, which I also pocketed.

With time growing short now, I took off my own threadbare uniform jacket and tried on Gebhardt's. Ordinarily it wouldn't have fitted, but I'd lost so much weight that this was hardly a problem, so I kept it on. It was a great pity his boots were too small, but I took his socks—those were an excellent fit and, as with the jacket, in much better condition than my own. I lit another cigarette and, on my hands and knees, went hunting around the floor for something other than the dust and the splinters I found down there. I was still searching for clues when the hut door opened and Colonel Mrugowski came in.

"Did anyone come forward?"

"No. As a result, I can't believe it was a German who did this. Our men aren't so lacking in honor. A German would have given himself up. For the good of the others."

"Hitler didn't," I observed.

"That was different."

I pushed Gebhardt's cigarettes across the table. "Here," I said. "Have one of the dead man's cigarettes."

"Thanks. I will." He lit one and glanced uncomfortably at the dead body. "Don't you think we should cover him up?"

"No. Looking at it helps to give me ideas as to how it happened."

"And have you any? Ideas about who killed him?"

"So far I'm considering the possibility that it was an elk with a grudge." I showed him the murder weapon. "See how sharp it is?"

Gingerly, Mrugowski touched the bloodied end with his forefinger. "Makes a hell of a shiv, doesn't it?"

I shook my head. "Actually, I think it was probably meant to be decorative. In here. There's a couple of nails and a mark on the wall facing the window that's consistent with this having been part of a small trophy set of horns. But I can't say for sure, since I've never been in here before."

"So where's the rest of it?"

"Maybe he realized how effective a weapon it was and took the rest of it with him. I rather imagine there was an argument. The killer grabbed the trophy, broke it over Gebhardt's skull, and found himself holding just a piece of it. A conveniently sharp piece. There are some smaller punctures on Gebhardt's head that are consistent with that possibility. Gebhardt collapsed onto the bed. The killer then went at him with the point. Finished him off. Then he went outside and caught the U-Bahn home. As to who and why, your guess is as good as mine. If this was Berlin, I'd be telling the uniforms to look for a man with bloodstains on his jacket, but of course here that's not so unusual. There are fellows out there who are still wearing uniforms stained with the blood of comrades at Königsberg. And I expect the killer knows that, too."

"Is that all you've got?"

"Look, if this was Berlin I could pick up the rugs and beat them, you know? Interview some witnesses, some suspects. Speak to a few informers. There's nothing like an informer in my business. They're the flies who know their shit, and that's the detective work that nearly always pays a dividend."

"So why not speak to Emil Kittel? The other anti-fa agent? It's in his interest to cooperate with your inquiry, wouldn't you say? He might wind up being the killer's next victim, after all."

"That might work. Of course, speaking to Kittel means I have to speak to Kittel, and if that happens, I don't want anyone in this camp thinking it's because I'm turning Ivan like him."

"I'll make sure that people know the score."

"But that's only one objection. You see, Kittel's already one of my suspects. He's left-handed. And one of the only things I can tell you about the murderer is that he's probably left-handed."

"How do you figure that?"

"The stab wounds on Gebhardt's body. They're mostly on his right side. Less than ten percent of the population is left-handed. So out of more than a thousand men in this camp, I've got about a hundred suspects. And one of them is Kittel."

"I see."

"Somehow I've got to clear ninety-nine of them in less than seventy-two hours, with nothing more to go on than the fact they disliked the victim only a little less than the man who actually killed him. All of this would be more than enough to do if there wasn't already a wheelbarrow with my name on it and several tons of sand ready for shifting around this canal. That's not a tall order, it's a tall order standing on a box."

"I'll speak to Major Savostin. See if I can't get you off the work detail until this thing is sorted."

"You do that, sir. Appeal to his sense of fair play. He probably keeps it in a matchbox alongside his sense of humor. And now I think about it, that's another objection I have to this so-called investigation. I don't like the Ivans knowing anything more about me than they already do. Especially the MVD."

The SGO smiled.

"Did I say something funny, sir?"

"Before the war, I was a doctor," said the SGO.

"Like your brother."

He nodded. "In a mental asylum. We treated a lot of people for something called paranoia."

"I know what paranoia is, sir."

"Why are you so paranoid, Gunther?"

"Me, I suppose it's because I have a problem trusting people. I should warn you, Colonel, I'm not the persistent type. Over the years I've learned it's better to be a quitter. I find that knowing when to quit is the best way of staying alive. So don't expect me to be a hero. Not here. Since I put on a German uniform I find that the hero business has been put back thirty years."

The SGO gave me a disapproving look. "Perhaps," he said stiffly, "if we'd had more heroes we might just have won the war."

"No, Colonel. If we'd had more heroes the war might never have got started."

I went back to work, filling my wheelbarrow with sand, pushing it up a gangplank, emptying it, and then pushing it back down again. Endless and unavailing, it was the kind of work that gets your picture on the side of a Greek amphora, or in a story that illustrates the dangers of betraying the secrets of the gods. It wasn't as dangerous as the kind of work the SGO wanted me to do, and but for the vodka inside me and the nicotine in my lungs, I might have been feeling a little less than inspired about the prospect of saving twenty-five of my comrades from a little show trial in Stalingrad. I've never been the type to mistake intoxication for heroism. Besides, it's not heroes you need to win a war, it's people who stay alive.

I was still feeling a little intoxicated when the SGO and the MVD major came to fetch me from my Sisyphean labor. And this can be the only explanation for the way I spoke to the Ivan. In Russian. That was a mistake all on its own. The Russians liked it a lot when you spoke Russian. In that respect they're like anyone else. The only difference is that Russians think it means you like them.

The MVD major, Savostin, dismissed the SGO with a wave of his hand as soon as Mrugowski had pointed me out. The Russian waved me toward him impatiently.

"Bistra! Davai!"

He was about fifty, with reddish hair and a mouth as wide as the Volga that looked as if it had been exaggerated for the purpose of a vindictive caricature. The pale blue eyes in his pale white head had been inherited from the gray she-wolf who'd littered him.

I dropped my shovel and ran eagerly toward him. The Blues liked you to do everything at the double.

"Mrugowski tells me that you were a fascist policeman before the war."

"No, sir. I was just a policeman. Generally, I left the fascism to the fascists. I had enough to do just being a policeman."

"Did you ever arrest any communists?"

"I might have done. If they broke the law. But I never arrested anyone for being a communist. I investigated murders."

"You must have been very busy."

"Yes, sir, I was."

"What is your rank?"

"Captain, sir."

"Then why are you wearing a corporal's jacket?"

"The corporal to whom it belonged wasn't using it."

"What function did you have during the war?"

"I was an intelligence officer, sir."

"Did you ever fight any partisans?"

"No, sir. Only the Red Army."

"That is why you lost."

"Yes, sir, that is certainly why we lost."

The pale blue wolf eyes stayed on me, unblinking, obliging me to snatch my cap off while I stared back at him.

"You speak excellent Russian," he said. "Where did you learn it?"

"From Russians. I told you, Major, I was an intelligence officer. That generally means you have to be something more than just intelligent. With me it was the fact that I'd learned Russian. But it wasn't the same standard of Russian you've described until I came here, Your Honor. I have the great Stalin to thank for that."

"You were a spy, Captain. Isn't that right?"

"No, sir. I was always in uniform. Which means if I had been a spy I'd have been a rather stupid one. And as I told you already, sir, I was in intelligence. It was my job to monitor Russian radio broadcasts, read Russian newspapers, speak to Russian prisoners . . ."

"Did you ever torture a Russian prisoner?"

"No, sir."

"A Russian would never give information to fascists unless he was tortured."

"I expect that's why I never got any information from Russian prisoners, sir. Not once. Not ever."

"So what makes the SGO think that you can get it from German *pleni*s."

"That's a good question, sir. You would have to ask him that."

"His brother is a war criminal. Did you know that?"

"No, sir."

"He was a doctor at the Buchenwald concentration camp," said Major Savostin. "He carried out experiments on Russian POWs. The colonel claims not to be related to this person, but it's my impression that Mrugowski is not a common name in Germany."

I shrugged. "We can't choose the people to whom we are related, sir."

"Perhaps you are also a war criminal, Captain Gunther."

"No, sir."

"Come, now. You were in the SD. Everyone in the SD was a war criminal."

"Look, sir, the SGO asked me to look into the murder of Wolfgang Gebhardt. He gave me the strange idea that you wanted to find out who did it. That if you didn't find out, then twenty-five of my comrades were going to be picked out at random and shot for it."

"You were misinformed, Captain. There is no death penalty in the Soviet Union. Comrade Stalin has abolished it. But they will stand trial for it, yes. Perhaps you yourself will be one of these men picked at random."

"So it's like that, is it?"

"Do you know who did it?"

"Not yet. But it sounds like you just handed me an extra incentive to find out."

"Good. We understand each other perfectly. You're excused from work for the next three days in order that you may solve the crime. I will inform the guards. How will you start?"

"Now that I've seen the body, by thinking. That's what I normally do in these situations. It's not very spectacular, but it gets results. Then I'd like permission to interview some of the prisoners, and perhaps some of the guards."

"The prisoners, yes, the guards, no. It wouldn't be right to have a good communist being cross-questioned by a fascist."

"Very well. I'd also like to interview the surviving anti-fa agent, Kissel."

"This I will have to think about. Now, then. It would not be appropriate for you to interview the other prisoners while they're working. So you can use the canteen for that. And for thinking, yes, it might be best if you were to use Gebhardt's hut. I'll have the body removed immediately if you're finished with it."

I nodded.

"Very well, then. Please follow me."

We walked to Gebhardt's hut. Halfway there Savostin saw

some guards and barked some orders in a language that wasn't Russian and, noticing my curiosity, told me that it was Tatar.

"Most of these pigs who guard the camp are Tatars," he explained. "They speak Russian, of course. But to make yourself clear you really have to speak Tatar. Perhaps you should try to learn."

I didn't answer that. He wasn't expecting me to. He was too busy looking around at the huge building site.

"Just think," he said. "All of this will be a canal by 1950. Extraordinary."

I had my doubts about that, which Savostin seemed to sense. "Comrade Stalin has ordered it," he said, as if this were the only affirmation needed.

And in that place, and in that time, he was probably right.

When we reached Gebhardt's hut, he supervised the removal of the body.

"If you need anything," he said, "come to the guardhouse." He looked around. "Which is where exactly? I'm not at all familiar with this camp."

I pointed to the west, beyond the canteen. I felt like Virgil pointing out the sights in hell to Dante. I watched him walk away and went back into the hut.

The first thing I did was to turn over the mattress, not because I was looking for something but because I intended to have a sleep and I hardly wanted to lie on top of Gebhardt's bloodstains. No one ever had enough sleep at K.A., but thinking's no good if you're tired. I took off his jacket, lay down, and closed my eyes. It wasn't just lack of sleep that made me tired but the vodka, too. The deflated football that was my stomach wasn't used to the stuff any more than my liver was. I closed my eyes and went to sleep wondering what the Soviet authorities were likely to do to me and twenty-four others if the death penalty had indeed been abolished. Was it possible there was a worse camp than the ones I had already seen?

A while later—I've no idea how long I slept, but it was still light outside—I sat up. The cigarettes were still in my jacket pocket so I lit another, but it wasn't like a proper cigarette; there was a paper holder and only about three or four centimeters of tobacco— what the Ivans called a *papirossi* cigarette. These were Belomor- kanal, which seemed only appropriate since that was a Russian brand introduced to commemorate the construction of another canal, this one connecting the White Sea to the Baltic. The Abwehr's opinion of the Belomorkanal was that it had been a disaster: too shallow, making it useless to most seagoing vessels, not to mention the tens of thousands of prisoners sacrificed in its construction. I wondered if this particular canal would fare any better.

I finished the cigarette and aimed the butt at Stalin, and some- thing about the way it struck the great leader's nose made me get up and take a closer look at the paper portrait; and when I tugged it off the wall, I was surprised to see that the picture had neatly concealed a small shelved alcove about the size of a book. On the shelf were a notebook and a roll of banknotes. It wasn't a wall safe, but in that place it was perhaps the next-best thing.

The roll of banknotes was almost 405 "gold" ruble notes— about three or four months' wages for a Blue. This wasn't a fortune unless you were a *pleni*. Two thousand rubles plus a gold wedding band might just be enough to bribe some better treatment inside an MVD jail in Stalingrad. I looked at the rubles again, just to make sure, and to my relief they all had that greasy, authentically Russian feel about them. I even held the bills up to the light coming through the window to check the watermark before folding them into the back pocket of my uniform breeches, which was the only one with a button and without a large hole.

The notebook had a red cover and was about the size of an iden- tity card. It was full of cheap Russian paper that looked more like something flattened by a heavy object and that contained a surprise all of its own, for on one page there was a name beneath which were written some dates and some payment details, and these seemed to indicate that the *pleni* named was in the pay of Gebhardt. Not that this made the *pleni* a murderer, exactly, but it did help to explain how it was that the Blues were able to police the POWs so effectively.

But the date of one particular payment caught my eye: Wednesday, August 15. This was the Feast of the Assumption of Mary, and for some Catholic Germans, especially those from Saarland or Bavaria, it was also an important public holiday. But nearly everyone in camp remembered this as the day when Georg Oberheuser—a sergeant from Stuttgart—had been arrested by the MVD. Angry that this date was to be treated as a normal working day, Oberheuser had loudly denounced Stalin to everyone in our hut as a "wicked, godless bastard." There were other, no less slanderous epithets he used as well, and all of them well deserved, no doubt, but we were all a little bit shaken when Oberheuser was taken away and never seen again, and by the knowledge that with no Ivans in our hut, Oberheuser had been betrayed to the Blues by another German.

The name in Gebhardt's notebook was Konrad Metelmann—the young lieutenant I had naïvely resolved to look out for. It appeared that he'd been doing a better job of looking out for himself.

I did a bit of thinking after that and remembered how the Blues were always ordering our hut to appear in the canteen for an identity check. They would ask each man his name, rank, and serial number in the hope—we had supposed—of catching one of us out, for it was certainly the case that there were several SS officers who, believing themselves to be wanted for war crimes, were pretending to be someone else, someone who had been killed in the war. We were always questioned alone, with Gebhardt translating, and any one of us could have used such an opportunity to give the MVD information. The only reason none of us had connected this with Oberheuser was that there had been no identity check on the day of his arrest, which meant that Metelmann and Gebhardt must also have been using some kind of dead-letter drop.

The Russians had a saying: The best way to keep your friends in the Soviet Union is never to betray them. I'd never much liked Georg Oberheuser, but he didn't deserve to be betrayed by one of his own comrades. According to Mrugowski, Oberheuser was tried by a People's Court and sentenced to twenty years of labor and correction. Or at least that was what the camp commander had told Mrugowski. But I saw no reason to believe what Major Savostin had told me: that the great Stalin had abolished the death penalty. I'd seen far too many of my fellow countrymen shot at the side of the road on the long march out of Königsberg to accept the idea that summary execution was no longer routine in the Soviet Union. Maybe Oberheuser was dead and maybe he wasn't. Either way, it was up to me to make things up to him. That's the debt we owe the dead. To give them justice if we can. And a kind of justice if we can't.

The rest of the *pleni*s were coming back from work, and I went straight over to the canteen to beat the rush. Seeing Metelmann, I fell in behind him and waited for some indication that he was anxious. But Sajer spoke first:

"Are you really going to finger someone for the Ivans, Gunther?"

"That all depends," I said, shuffling forward in the line.

"On what?"

"On me finding out who did it. Right now I haven't got a clue. And by the way, I've been told that I'm one of the twenty-five the Ivans are going to pick if they don't get a name. Just so you know that I'm taking this seriously."

"Do you think they mean it?" asked Metelmann.

"Course they mean it," said Sajer. "When do the Ivans ever issue an idle threat? You can always depend on them in that way at least. The bastards."

"What are you going to do, Bernie?" asked Metelmann.

"How should I know?" I glared at Mrugowski. "This is all his fault. But for him, I'd have the same chance as everyone else."

"Maybe you'll find out something," said Metelmann. "You were a good detective. That's what people say."

"What do they know? Believe me, I'd have to be Sherlock Holmes to solve this case. My only chance is to bribe that MVD major and get myself off the list. Here, Metelmann, have you got any money you can lend me?"

"I can let you have five rubles," he said.

"It'll take a lot more than five rubles to bribe that major," said Sajer.

"I've got to start somewhere," I said as Metelmann gave me a five from his pocket. "Thanks, Konrad. How about you, Sajer?"

"Suppose I need to bribe someone myself?" He grinned unpleasantly at Metelmann. "If it's you they pick, you might regret giving him that five, you silly bastard."

"Fuck you, Sajer," said Metelmann.

"Where does someone like you get five rubles, anyway?" asked Sajer.

Metelmann sneered and reached for his chunk of *chleb*. With his left hand.

I also noted the livid-looking scar on his forearm. He might have got the injury on-site. But all things considered, I thought it more likely that he'd got it while murdering Gebhardt.

I spent the next three days alone in Gebhardt's hut catching up on my sleep. I knew what I was going to do, but I saw little point in doing it before the MVD's allotted time had elapsed. I was determined to enjoy every minute of my holiday at K.A. while it was there to be had. After months of hard labor on starvation rations, I was exhausted and a little feverish. Once a day the SGO came over and asked how my inquiry was progressing, and I told him that despite any evidence to the contrary I had made good progress. I could see he didn't believe me. But I didn't care. It wasn't like I was going to lose my army pension because of his opinion. Besides, the SGO and I were two different heads on the same imperial eagle— me looking left and him looking to the right. Even in a Soviet POW camp he could seldom leave a room without clicking his heels. Oh yes, our Colonel Mrugowski was a regular Fred Astaire.

On the third day, I rolled the stone away from the front door and went to the site to find Metelmann. I handed him back his five rubles. "Here," I said, "you might as well keep this. I shan't be needing it where I'm going."

Quickly pocketing the note in case one of the guards should see it, Metelmann tried not to look relieved at my obvious disappointment. "No luck, huh?"

"My luck ran out on me a long time ago," I said. "It was going so fast, it must have been wearing running shoes."

"You know, maybe that MVD major was bluffing," he said.

"I doubt it. The thing I've noticed about people with power is that they always use it even when they say they don't want to." I started to walk away.

"Good luck," said Metelmann.

Major Savostin was playing chess when I found him in the guardhouse. With himself. Colonel Mrugowski was there, too. They were waiting for my report.

"There's no one here that plays," said the major. "Perhaps we should have a game, you and I, Captain."

"I'm sure you're much better than me, sir. After all, it's virtually your national game."

"Why is that, do you suppose? One would think as logical a game as chess would suit the German character rather well."

"Because it's black and white?" I suggested. "Everything is black and white in the Soviet Union. And perhaps because the game involves making sacrifices of smaller, less important pieces. Besides, sir, with you I should worry how to win without losing." I snatched off my cap. "As a matter of fact, sir, I've been worried about that for the last three days. I mean, how to solve this case without pissing you off. And I'm still not satisfied I know the answer to that question."

"But you do know who killed Gebhardt, don't you?"

"Yes, sir."

"Then I fail to understand your difficulty."

I wondered if I had misjudged him—if he wasn't quite as intelligent as I'd thought. Then again, there is a whole earthwork of understanding between someone who is hungry and someone who is not. I could see no way of identifying Metelmann as the culprit without putting my own head in the lion's mouth.

"I mean, you're not suggesting it was a Russian, I trust," he said, fiddling with his queen.

"Oh no, sir. A Russian would never have murdered a German and not owned up to it. Besides, why kill a *pleni* in secret when you could just as easily kill him in the open? Even if he was an anti-fascist agent. No, you were right, sir. It was a German who killed Gebhardt."

I cast my eye over the board in the hope that I might see some evidence of intelligence there, but all I could tell was that the right pieces were on the right squares and that the major needed a manicure like I needed a hot bath. They probably didn't care about manicures in the Soviet workers' paradise. They certainly didn't care about hot baths. It was a little hard to be sure, but I had the idea that the major smelled almost as bad as I did.

"The murder was not premeditated," I said. "It happened on the spur of the moment. Frenzied stabbings are often like that where there's no sexual aspect involved. Of course, it's hard to say much with certainty at a crime scene that I've had to work without a thermometer to take the body's temperature. And there were certainly fingerprints that could have been recovered from the murder weapon and the brass door handle. What can be said with confidence, however, is that the murderer was left-handed. Because of the pattern of wounds on the dead man's body. Now, at the canteen, I observed all of the men in this camp and drew up a list of all the left-handed *plenis*. This was my initial pool of suspects. Since when I have identified the murderer, I will not say his name. As a German officer, it would be wrong for me to do so. But there is no need, since his name appears in Gebhardt's notebook."

I handed the red notebook to the major.

"Metelmann," he said quietly.

"As you will see, this page contains details of payments that were made to this particular officer in return for information. In other words, the culprit was acting as the murdered man's paid informer. I believe the two men argued about money, sir. Among other things. Possibly Gebhardt refused to pay the murderer five rubles—his usual rate—for information received. After the murder, the culprit took the money anyway."

I handed Savostin a hundred of the five-ruble notes I had found behind the poster of Stalin. Savostin handed the notebook to the SGO.

"I found these bills hidden in Gebhardt's hut. As you can see, all of the bills are marked in the top right-hand corner with a small pencil mark, which I believe is a Russian Orthodox cross."

Savostin examined one of the notes and nodded. "All of them?" he said.

"Yes, sir." I knew this because I had marked every one of the bills myself. "It's my guess that if you were to search the officer named in that notebook, you would find him in possession of one or more five-ruble notes with the same penciled cross in the top right-hand corner, sir. The same officer is left-handed, and his arm currently bears a livid scar that was most probably sustained during the attack on Gebhardt."

Still clutching my cap, I rubbed my shaven head with my knuckle. It sounded like something happening to a piece of wood in the camp workshop. "If I might speak frankly, sir?"

"Speak, Captain."

"I don't know what you're going to do with this man, sir. Given who and what he is, I can appreciate that it might leave you with a problem. After all, he's your man's man. But he's no good to you now, sir, is he? Not now that we know who and what he is. I suppose you could always use him to replace Gebhardt, as the antifa officer, although his Russian isn't up to much. And you'd have to take him away anyway, for political reeducation. Either way, he's finished in this camp. I just wanted to let you know that, sir."

"Aren't you jumping the gun a little, Gunther? You haven't proved anything yet. Even if I do find this marked money on Metelmann, there's nothing to prove he didn't receive the money before Gebhardt was murdered. And have you considered the possibility that if this man is an informer, then it might suit me better to leave him here and have you and the colonel transferred to another camp?"

"I have considered that, yes, sir. It's true there's nothing to stop you doing that. But you can't be sure that we haven't told all our comrades what I've told you. That's one reason why it wouldn't suit you to send us to another camp. Another reason is that the colonel is doing an excellent job as SGO. The men listen to him. With all due respect, sir, you need him."

Major Savostin looked at the colonel. "Perhaps I do, at that," he said.

I shrugged. "As for proving anything to your satisfaction, Major, that's your affair. I've handed you the gun. You can't expect me to pull the trigger as well. However, if you do decide to search Metelmann, you might ask him the name of his wife, sir."

"Meaning?"

"Konrad Metelmann's wife is called Vera, sir." I handed Savostin the ring I had found, which I had assumed was Gebhardt's wedding ring. "There's an inscription inside."

Savostin's eyes narrowed as he read what was engraved on the inside of the gold band. " 'To Konrad, with all my love, from Vera. February 1943.' " He looked at me.

"That was on Gebhardt's ring finger, sir. The finger was broken, I think, because Metelmann tried to get the ring off Gebhardt's finger after he killed him and failed. Possibly he even broke the finger, I don't know. But I had to use soap to get it off myself."

"Perhaps Gebhardt bought this from Metelmann."

"Gebhardt bought it, all right. But I'm pretty sure it wasn't from Metelmann. Metelmann hid that ring up his arse for weeks. Then he got a bad dose of diarrhea and had to wear it on a piece of string around his neck. But one of the guards found it and made him hand it over. As a matter of fact, I saw it happen."

"Who?"

"Sergeant Degermenkoy. My guess is that Gebhardt bought it back from him and promised to return it to Metelmann but never did. Possibly he may have used the ring as leverage to obtain information from Metelmann. Either way, I'm certain this ring is what the fight was about. And I'm sure the sergeant will confirm what I've said, sir. That he sold the ring to Gebhardt."

"Degermenkoy is a lying pig," said Major Savostin. "But I don't doubt that you are correct about what must have happened. You've done very well, Captain. I shall question both men in due course. For now, I thank you, Captain. You, too, Colonel, for recommending this man. You may go back to work now. Dismissed."

Mrugowski and I went out of the guardhouse. "Are you sure about all of this?"

"Yes."

"Suppose Savostin searches Metelmann and he doesn't have that five-ruble note."

"He had it half an hour ago," I said. "I know that because it was me who gave it to him. And it's marked with a lot more than just a Russian Orthodox cross. There's a thumbprint in blood on it, too. Rather a good one, as it happens, although I daresay the Ivans won't be looking to make a match."

"I don't understand," said Mrugowski. "Whose thumbprint?"

"Gebhardt's. I put the print on the bill using his dead hand. And I borrowed five rubles from Metelmann the day before yesterday, just so that I could repay him with a marked bill. I marked the bills with the cross myself. The thumbprint was merely for added effect."

"I still don't understand."

"I chalked him out for it. Metelmann. Framed him, so that he could take the bath out."

Mrugowski stopped and stared at me with horror. "You mean he didn't kill Gebhardt?"

"Oh, he killed him all right. I'm almost sure of that. But proving it is something else. Especially in this place. Anyway, I don't much care. Metelmann was a point. A lousy informer, and we're well rid of him."

"I do not like your methods, Captain Gunther."

"You wanted a detective from the Alex, Colonel, and that's what you got. You think those bastards always play fair? By the book? Rules of evidence? Think again. Berlin cops have planted more evidence than the ancient Egyptians. This is how it works, sir. Real police work isn't some gentleman detective writing notes on a starched shirt-cuff with a silver pencil. That was the old days, when the grass was greener and it only snowed on Christmas Eve. You make the suspect, not the punishment, fit the crime, see? It was always thus. But more especially here. Here most of all. That Major Savostin isn't the laughing policeman. He's from the Ministry of Internal Affairs. I just hope you didn't sell me too hard to that coldhearted bastard, because I tell you this. It's not Lieutenant Metelmann I'm worried about, it's me. I've been useful to Savostin. He likes that. The next time he gets cold hands, he's liable to treat me like a pair of gloves."

Konrad Metelmann was taken away by the Blues the same day and life at Krasno-Armeesk resumed its awful, gray, unrelentingly brutal routine. Or at least I thought it did until it was pointed out to me by another *pleni* that I was receiving double rations in the canteen. People always noticed things like that. At first none of my comrades seemed to mind, as everyone was now aware that I had uncovered an informer and saved twenty-five of us from a show trial in Stalingrad. But memories are short, especially in a Soviet labor camp, and as winter arrived and my preferment continued— not just more food, but warmer clothes, too—I began to encounter some resentment among the other German prisoners. It was Ivan Yefremovich Pospelov who explained what was happening:

"I've seen this before," he said. "And I'm afraid it will end badly unless you can do something about it. The Blues have picked you out for the Astoria treatment. Like the hotel? Better food, better clothes, and in case you hadn't noticed, less work."

"I'm working," I said. "Like anyone else."

"You think so? When was the last time a Blue shouted at you to hurry up? Or called you a German pig?"

"Now you come to mention it, they have been rather more polite of late."

"Eventually, the other *pleni*s will forget what you did for them and remember only that you are preferred by the Blues. And they'll conclude that there's more to it than meets the eye. That you're giving the Blues something else in return."

"But that's nonsense."

"I know it. You know it. But do they know it? In six months from now you'll be an anti-fascist agent in their eyes, whether you are or not. That's what the Russians are gambling on. That as you are shunned by your own people you have no choice but to come over to them. Even if that doesn't happen one day, you'll have an accident. A bank will give way for no apparent reason and you'll be buried alive. But your rescue will come too late. And if you are rescued, then you'll have no choice but to take Gebhardt's place. That is, if you want to stay alive. You're one of them, my friend. A Blue. You just don't know it yet."

I knew Pospelov was right. Pospelov knew everything about life at K.A. He ought to have done. He'd been there since Stalin's Great Purge. As the music teacher to the family of a senior Soviet politician arrested and executed in 1937, Pospelov had received a twenty-year sentence—a simple case of guilt by association. But for good measure the NKVD—as the MVD was then called—had broken his hands with a hammer to make sure that he could never again play the piano.

"What can I do?" I asked.

"For sure you can't beat them."

"You can't mean that I should join them, surely?"

Pospelov shrugged. "It's odd where a crooked path will sometimes take you. Besides, most of them are just us with blue shoulder boards."

"No, I can't."

"Then you will have to watch out for yourself, with all three eyes, and by the way, don't ever yawn."

"There must be something I can do, Ivan Yefremovich. I can share some of my food, can't I? Give my warmer clothing to another man?"

"They'll simply find other ways to show you favor. Or they'll try to persecute those that you help. You must really have impressed that MVD major, Gunther." He sighed and looked up at the gray-white sky and sniffed the air. "Any day now it will snow. The work will be tougher then. If you're going to do anything, it would be best to do it before the snow, when days and tempers are shorter and the Blues hate us more for keeping them outside. In a way, they're prisoners just like we are. You've got to remember that."

"You'd see the good in a pack of wolves, Pospelov."

"Perhaps. However, your example is a useful one, my friend. If you wish to stop the wolves from licking your hand, you will have to bite one of them."

Pospelov's advice was hardly welcome. Assaulting one of the guards was a serious offense—almost too serious to contemplate. And yet I didn't doubt what he had told me: If the Ivans kept on giving me special treatment, I was going to meet with a fatal accident at the hands of my comrades. Many of these were ruthless Nazis and loathsome to me, but they were still my fellow countrymen, and faced with the choice of keeping faith with them or joining the Bolsheviks to save my own skin, I quickly formed the conclusion that I'd already stayed alive for longer than I might otherwise have expected and that maybe I had no choice at all. I hated the Bolsheviks as much as I hated the Nazis; under the circumstances, perhaps more than I hated the Nazis. The MVD was just the Gestapo with three Cyrillic letters, and I'd had enough of everything to do with the whole apparatus of state security to last me a lifetime.

Clear in my mind what I had to do, and in full view of almost every *pleni* in the half-excavated canal, I walked up to Sergeant Degermenkoy and stood right in front of him. I took the cigarette from the mouth in his astonished-looking face and puffed it happily for a moment. I discovered I didn't have the guts to hit him but managed to find it in me to knock the blue-banded cap off his ugly tree stump of a head.

It was the first and only time I heard laughter at K.A. And it was the last thing I heard for a while. I was waving to the other *pleni*s when something hit me hard on the side of my head—perhaps the stock of Degermenkoy's machine gun—and probably more than once. My legs gave way and the hard, cold ground seemed to swallow me up as if I'd been water from the Volga. The black earth enveloped me, filling my nostrils, mouth, and ears, and then collapsed altogether, and I fell into the dreadful place that the Great Stalin and the rest of his murderous Red gang had prepared for me in their socialist republic. And as I fell into that endless, deep pit they stood and waved at me with gloved hands from the top of Lenin's mausoleum, while all around me there were people applauding my disappearance, laughing at their own good fortune, and throwing flowers after me.

I suppose I should have been used to it. After all, I was accustomed to visiting prisons. As a cop, I'd been in and out of the cement to interview suspects and take statements from others. From time to time I'd even found myself on the wrong side of the Judas hole: once in 1934, when I'd irritated the Potsdam police chief; and again in 1936, when Heydrich had sent me into Dachau as an undercover agent to gain the trust of a small-time criminal. Dachau had been bad, but not as bad as Krasno-Armeesk, and certainly not as bad as the place I was in now. It wasn't that the place was dirty or anything; the food was good, and they even let me have a shower and some cigarettes. So what was it that bothered me? I suppose it was the fact that I was on my own for the first time since leaving Berlin in 1944. I'd been sharing quarters with one or more Germans for almost two years, and now, all of a sudden, there was only myself to talk to. The guards said nothing. I spoke to them in Russian and they ignored me. The sense of being separated from my comrades, of being cut off, began to grow and, with each day that passed, became a little worse. At the same time, I had an awful feeling of being walled in—again, this was probably a corollary of having spent so much of the last six months outside. Just as the sheer size of Russia had once left me feeling overwhelmed, it was the very smallness of my windowless cell—three paces long and half as wide—that began to weigh on me. Each minute of my day seemed to last forever. Had I really lived for as long as I had with so little to show for it in the way of thoughts and memories? With all that I had done I might reasonably have expected to have occupied myself for hours with a remembrance of things past. Not a bit of it. It was like looking down the wrong end of a telescope. My past felt wholly

265

insignificant, almost invisible. As for the future, the days that lay ahead of me seemed as vast and empty as the steppes themselves. But the worst feeling of all was when I thought of my wife; just thinking of her at our little apartment in Berlin, supposing it was still standing, could reduce me to tears. Probably she thought I was dead. I might as well have been dead. I was buried in a tomb. And all that remained was for me to die.

I managed to mark the passing time on the porcelain tile walls with my own excrement. And in this way I noted the passing of four months. Meanwhile, I put on some weight. I even got my smoker's cough back. Monotony dulled my thinking. I lay on the plank bed with its sackcloth mattress and stared at the caged lightbulb above the door, wondering how long they gave you for knocking a Blue's hat off. Given the immensity of Pospelov's crime and punishment, I came to the conclusion that I might expect anything between six months and twenty-five years. I tried to find in me something of his fortitude and optimism, but it was no good: I couldn't help recalling something else he had said, a joke he made once, only with each passing day it felt less and less like a joke and more like a prediction:

"The first ten years are always the hardest," he'd said.

I was haunted by that remark.

Most of the time, I hung on to the certainty that before I was sentenced there would have to be a trial. Pospelov said there was always a trial of sorts. But when the trial came, it was over before I knew it.

They came and took me when I least expected it. One minute I was eating my breakfast, the next I was in a large room being fingerprinted and photographed by a little bearded man with a big box range-finder camera. On top of the polished wooden box was a little spirit level—a bubble of air in a yellow liquid that resembled the photographer's watery, dead eyes. I asked him several questions in my best, most subservient Russian, but the only words he used were "Turn to the side" and "Stand still, please." The "please" was nice.

After that I expected to be taken back to my cell. Instead, I was steered up a flight of stairs and into a small tribunal room. There was a Soviet flag, a window, a large hero wall featuring the terrible trio of Marx, Lenin, and Stalin, and, up on a stage, a table behind which were sitting three MVD officers, none of whom I recognized. The senior officer, who was seated in the middle of this troika, asked me if I required a translator, a question that was translated by a translator—another MVD officer. I said I didn't, but the translator stayed anyway and translated, badly, everything that was said to or about me from then on. Including the indictment against me, which was read out by the prosecutor, a reasonable-looking woman who was also an MVD officer. She was the first woman I'd seen since the march out of Königsberg, and I could hardly keep my eyes off her.

"Bernhard Gunther," she said in a tremulous voice. Was she nervous? Was this her first case? "You are charged—"

"Wait a minute," I said in Russian. "Don't I get a lawyer to defend me?"

"Can you afford to pay for one?" asked the chairman.

"I had some money when I left the camp at Krasno-Armeesk," I said. "While I was being brought here, it disappeared."

"Are you suggesting it was stolen?"

"Yes."

The three judges conferred for a moment. Then the chairman said: "You should have said this before. I'm afraid these proceedings may not be delayed while your allegations are investigated. We shall proceed. Comrade Lieutenant?"

The prosecutor continued to read out the charge: "That you willfully and with malice aforethought assaulted a guard from Voinapleni camp number three, at Krasno-Armeesk, contrary to martial law; that you stole a cigarette from the same guard at camp number three, which is also against martial law; and that you committed these actions with the intent of fomenting a mutiny among the other prisoners at camp three, also contrary to martial law. These are all crimes against Comrade Stalin and the peoples of the Union of Soviet Socialist Republics."

I knew I was in trouble now. If I hadn't realized it before, I realized it now: Knocking a man's hat off was one thing; mutiny was something else. Mutiny wasn't the kind of charge to be dismissed lightly.

"Do you have anything you wish to say in your defense?" said the chairman.

I waited politely for the translator to finish and made my defense. I admitted the assault and the theft of the cigarette. Then, almost as an afterthought, I added: "There was certainly no intention of fomenting a mutiny, sir."

The chairman nodded, wrote something on a piece of paper— probably a reminder to buy some cigarettes and vodka on his way home that night—and looked expectantly at the prosecutor.

In most circumstances, I like a woman in uniform. The trouble was, this one didn't seem to like me. We'd never met before, and yet she seemed to know everything about me: the very wicked thought processes that had motivated me to cause the mutiny; my devotion to the cause of Adolf Hitler and Nazism; the pleasure I had taken in the perfidious attack upon the Soviet Union in June 1941; my important part in the collective guilt of all Germans in the murders of millions of innocent Russians; and, not happy with this, that I'd intended to incite the other *pleni*s at camp three to murder many more.

The only surprise was that the court withdrew for several minutes to reach a verdict and, more important, have a cigarette. Smoke was still trailing from the nostrils of one member of the tribunal as they came back into the room.

The prosecutor stood up. The translator stood up. I stood up. The verdict was announced. I was a fascist pig, a German bastard, a capitalist swine, a Nazi criminal; and I was also guilty as charged.

"In accordance with the demands of the prosecutor and in view of your previous record, you are sentenced to death."

I shook my head, certain the prosecutor had made no such demands—perhaps she had forgotten—nor had my previous record been so much as mentioned. Unless you counted the invasion of the Soviet Union, and that much was true.

"Death?" I shrugged. "I suppose I can count myself lucky I don't play the piano."

Oddly, the translator had stopped translating what I was saying. He was waiting for the chairman to finish speaking.

"You are fortunate that this is a country founded on mercy and a respect for human rights," he was saying. "After the Great Patriotic War, in which so many innocent Soviet citizens died, it was the wish of Comrade Stalin that the death penalty should be abolished in our country. Consequently, the capital punishment handed down to you is commuted to twenty-five years of hard labor."

Stunned at my declared fate, I was led out of the court to a yard outside where a Black Maria was waiting for me, its engine running. The driver already had my details, which seemed to indicate that the court's verdict had been a foregone conclusion. The Black Maria was divided into four little cells, each of them so cramped and low you had to bend over double just to get inside one. The metal door was perforated with little holes, like the mouthpiece of a telephone. They were considerate like that, the Ivans. We set off at speed—you might have thought the driver was in charge of a getaway car after a bank robbery—and when we stopped, we stopped very suddenly, as if the police had forced us to stop. I heard more prisoners being loaded into the Black Maria and then we were off, again at high speed, with the driver laughing loudly as we skidded around one corner and then another. Finally we stopped, the engine was switched off, the doors were flung open, and all was made plain. We were beside a train that was already under steam and making strongly exhaled hints that it was impatient to leave, but to where, no one said. Everyone in the Black Maria was ordered to climb aboard a cattle car alongside several other Germans whose faces looked as grim as I was feeling. Twenty-five years! If I lived that long, it was going to be 1970 before I went home again! The door of the cattle car slid shut with a bang, leaving us all in partial darkness; the bogies shifted a little, throwing us all into each other's arms, and then the train set off.

"Any idea where we're going?" said a voice.

"Does it matter?" said someone. "Hell's the same whichever fiery pit you're in."

"This place is too cold to be hell," said another.

I peered through an airhole in the wall of the cattle car. It was impossible to see where the sun was. The sky was a blank sheet of gray that was soon black with night and salted with snow. At the other end of the wagon, a man was crying. The sound was tearing us all apart.

"Someone say something to that fellow, for God's sake," I muttered loudly.

"Like what?" said the man next to me.

"I dunno, but I'd rather not listen to that sound unless I have to."

"Hey, Fritz," said a voice. "Stop that crying, will you? You're spoiling the party for some fellow at the other end of the carriage. This is supposed to be a picnic, see? Not a funeral cortege."

"That's what you think." This accent was unmistakably Berlin. "Take a look out of this airhole. You can see the Kirchhof Cemetery."

I moved toward the Berliner and got talking to him, and soon afterward we discovered that everyone in the wagon had been tried in the same court on some trumped-up charge, found guilty, and sentenced to a long term of hard labor. I seemed to be about the only man who had committed a real offense.

The Berliner's name was Walter Bingel, and before the war

he'd been a park keeper in the gardens of the Sansouci Palace in Potsdam.

"I was at a camp next to the Zaritsa Gorge, near Rostov," he explained. "I was sad to leave, as a matter of fact. The potatoes I planted were about ready to pull up. But I managed to bring some seeds with me, so maybe we won't go hungry at wherever it is we're going."

There was much speculation about where this might be. One man said we were going to a coal-mining camp at Vorkuta, north of the Arctic Circle. Then another mentioned the name of Sakhalin, and that silenced everyone, including myself.

"What's Sakhalin?" asked Bingel.

"It's a camp in the easternmost part of Russia," I said.

"A death camp," said someone else. "They sent a lot of SS there after Stalingrad. Sakhalin means 'black' in one of those sub-human languages they use out there. I met a man who claimed he'd been there. An Ivan prisoner."

"No one really knows if it exists or not," I added.

"Oh, it exists all right. Full of Nips, it is. The place is so far east, it's not even attached to the fucking mainland. They don't bother with a barbed-wire fence at Sakhalin. Why would they? There's nowhere else to go."

The train rolled on for almost three whole days, and there was relief when finally they broke the ice on the locks and the door of the wagon opened, because the faces of the guards who greeted us were vaguely European and not Oriental, which seemed to indicate that we'd been spared Sakhalin. Not all of us had been spared, however. As men jumped down from the wagon, it was clear that one man had managed to hang himself from a wooden peg. It was the man who had been crying.

Several hundred of us lined up beside the track awaiting our new orders. Wherever we were now was cold, but not nearly as cold as Stalingrad; perhaps it was the weather, but a new rumor—that we were home—quickly murmured its way through the ranks like a Hindu's mantra.

"This is Germany! We're home."

Unlike most of the rumors to which we German *pleni*s were often prey, there was some truth in this one, for it seemed that we were just across the border in what many of my more rabidly Nazi comrades probably still thought of as the German Protectorate of Bohemia, otherwise known as Czechoslovakia.

And excitement mounted as we marched into Saxony.

"They're going to let us go! Why else would they have brought us all the way from Russia?"

Why else indeed? But it wasn't long before our hopes of an early release were dashed.

We marched into a little mining town called Johannesgeorgenstadt and then out the other side, up a hill with a fine view of the local Lutheran church and several tall chimneys, and through the gates of an old Nazi concentration camp—one of almost a hundred subcamps in the Flossenburg complex. Most of us imagined that all of Germany's KZs had been closed, so it was a bit of a shock to discover one still open and ready for business. A greater shock awaited us, however.

There were almost two hundred German *pleni*s already living and working at the Johannesgeorgenstadt KZ, and even by the poor standards of Soviet prisoner welfare, none of these looked well. The SGO, SS General Klause, soon explained why:

"I'm sorry to see you here, men," he said. "I wish I could have been welcoming you back to Germany with pleasure, but I'm afraid I can't. If any of you are familiar with the Erzgebirge mountains, you will know that the area is rich with pitchblende, from which uranium ore is extracted. Uranium is radioactive and has a number of uses, but there's only one use for it that the Ivans are interested in. Uranium in large quantities is vital for the Soviet atom bomb project, and it's no exaggeration to say that they perceive the development of such a weapon as a matter of the highest priority. And certainly a much higher priority than your health.

"We're uncertain what effect prolonged exposure to unrefined pitchblende has on the human body, but you can bet it's not good—for two reasons. One is that Marie Curie, who discovered the stuff, died from its effect; and the other is that the Blues come down the mine shaft only when they have to. And even then only for short periods and wearing face masks. So if you're down the pit, try to cover your nose and mouth with a handkerchief.

"On the positive side, the food here is good and plentiful and brutality is kept to a minimum. There are good washing facilities—after all, this was a German camp before it was a Russian one—and we're allowed a day off once a week; but only because they have to check the lifting gear and the gas levels. Radon gas, I'm told. Colorless, odorless, and that's about all I know about it, except I'm sure it's also hazardous. Sorry, that's another negative. And since we're back on the side of the debits, I may as well mention now that in this camp the MVD employs a number of Germans as recruiting officers for some new people's police they're planning to create in the Soviet zone of occupied Germany. A secret police designed to be a German arm of the MVD. The establishment of such a police force in Germany is banned by the rules of the Allied Control Commission, but that doesn't mean they're not going to do it under the table, by subterfuge. But they can't do it at all if they don't have the men to do it, so be careful what you say and do, for they will most certainly interrogate and interview you at length. D'you hear? I want no renegades under my command. These Germans the Ivans have working for them are communists. Veteran communists from the old KPD. What we were fighting against. The ugly face of European Bolshevism. If there were some among you who doubted the truth of our National Socialist cause, I imagine you have learned that it was you who were mistaken, not the leader. Remember what I've said and watch yourself."

was one of the lucky ones, in that I wasn't ordered down the pit immediately. Instead, I was put on the sorting detail. Wagonloads of rock were brought up from the mine and emptied onto a large conveyor belt that was running between two lines of *plenis*. Someone showed me how to inspect the pieces of brownish-black rock for veins of the all-important pitchblende. Rocks without veins were thrown away, the others graded by eye and tossed into bins for further selection by a Blue holding a metal tube with a mica window at one end: The better the quality of the ore, the more electric current that was reproduced as white noise by the tube. These higher-quality rocks were taken away for processing in Russia, but the quantities considered useful were small. It seemed that tons of rock would be needed to produce just a small quantity of ore, and none of the men working at the Johannesgeorgenstadt mine were of the opinion that the Ivans would be building an atom bomb anytime soon.

I'd been there almost a month when I was told to report to the mine office. This was housed in a gray stone building next to the pithead winding gear. I went up to the first floor and waited. Through the open door of the office I could see a couple of MVD officers. I could also hear what they said, and I realized that these were two of the Germans General Klause had warned us about.

Seeing me standing there, they waved me inside and closed the door. I glanced up at the clock on the wall. It was eleven a.m. There was a microphone on the table and, I imagined, somewhere a large tape machine ready to record my every word. Next to the microphone was a spotlight, but it wasn't switched on. Not yet. There was an undrawn black curtain beside the window. They invited me to sit down on a chair in front of the desk.

"The last time I did this, I got twenty-five years hard labor," I said. "So, if you'll forgive me, I really don't have anything to say."

"If you wish," said one of the officers, "you may appeal the verdict. Did the court tell you that?"

"No. What the court did tell me was that the Soviets are every bit as stupid and brutal as the Nazis."

"It's interesting you say that."

I didn't reply.

"It seems to support an impression we have of you, Captain Gunther. That you're not a Nazi."

Meanwhile, the other officer had picked up a telephone and was saying something in Russian that I could not hear.

"I'm Major Weltz," said the first officer. He looked at the man now replacing the telephone receiver. "And this is Lieutenant Rascher."

I grunted.

"Like you, I am also from Berlin," said Weltz. "As a matter of fact, I was there just last weekend. I'm afraid you'd hardly recognize it. Incredible the destruction that was inflicted by Hitler's refusal to surrender." He pushed a packet of cigarettes across the table. "Please. Help yourself to a cigarette. I'm afraid they're Russian, but they're better than nothing."

I took one.

"Here," he said, coming around the desk and snapping open a lighter. "Let me light that for you."

He sat down on the edge of the table and watched me smoke. Then the door opened and a *starshina* came in, carrying a sheet of paper. He laid it on the table next to the cigarettes and left again without saying a word.

Weltz glanced at the sheet of paper for a moment and then turned it to face me.

"Your appeal form," he said.

My eyes flicked across the Cyrillic letters.

"Would you like me to translate it?"

"That won't be necessary. I can read and speak Russian."

"Very well, too, by all accounts." He handed me a fountain pen and waited for me to sign the sheet of paper. "Is there a problem?"

"What's the point?" I said dully.

"There's every point. The government of the Soviet Union has its forms and formalities like every other country. Nothing happens without a piece of paper. It was the same in Germany, was it not? An official form for everything."

Again, I hesitated.

"You want to go home, don't you? To Berlin? Well, you can't go home unless you've been released, and you can't be released unless you appeal your sentence first. Really, it's as simple as that. Oh, I'm not promising anything. But this form puts the process into motion. Think of it like that pithead winding gear outside. That piece of paper makes the wheel start to move."

I read the form forward and then backward: Sometimes, things in the Soviet Union and its zones of occupation made more sense if you read them backward.

I signed it, and Major Weltz drew the form toward him.

"So at least we know that you do want to get out of here," he said. "To go home. Now that we've established that much, all we have to do is figure out a way of making that happen. I mean, sooner rather than later. To be exact, twenty-five years from now. That is, if you survive what anyone here will tell you is hazardous work. Personally, I don't much care to be even this close to large deposits of uraninite. Apparently, they turn it into this yellow powder that glows in the dark. God only knows what it does to people."

"Thanks, but I'm not interested."

"We haven't told you what we're offering yet," said Weltz. "A job. As a policeman. I would have thought that might appeal to a man with your qualifications."

"A man who was never a member of the Nazi Party," said

Lieutenant Rascher. "A former member of the Social Democratic Party."

"Did you know, Captain, that the KPD and the SDP have joined together?"

"It's a bit late," I said. "We could have used the support of the KPD in December 1931. During the Red Revolution."

"That was Trotsky's fault," said Weltz. "Anyway. Better late than never, eh? The new party—the Socialist Unity Party, the SED—it represents a fresh start for us both to work together. For a new Germany."

"Another new Germany?" I shrugged.

"Well, we can hardly make do with the old one. Wouldn't you agree? There's so much that we have to rebuild. Not just politics, but law and order, too. The police force. We're starting a new force. For the moment, it's being called the Fifth Kommissariat, or K-5. We hope to have it up and running by the end of the year. And until then we're looking for recruits. A man such as yourself, a former Oberkommissar with Kripo, with a record for honesty and integrity, who was chased out of the force by the Nazis, is just the sort of principled man we need. I think I can probably guarantee reinstatement at your old rank, with full pension rights. A Berlin-weighted allowance. Help with a new apartment. A job for your wife."

"No, thanks."

"That's too bad," said Lieutenant Rascher.

"Look, why don't you think it over, Captain," said Weltz. "Sleep on it. You see, to be perfectly honest with you, Gunther, you're at the top of our list in this camp. And, for obvious reasons, we'd rather not stay here longer than we have to. I'm already a father, but the lieutenant here has no wish to damage his chances of having a son if and when he marries. Radiation does something to a man's ability to procreate. It also affects the thyroid and the body's ability to use energy and make proteins. At least, that's what I think it does."

"The answer is still no," I said. "May I go now?"

The major adopted a rueful expression. "I don't understand you," he said. "How is it that you, a Social Democrat, were prepared to go and work for Heydrich? And yet you won't work for us. Can you explain that, please?"

It was now I realized who the major reminded me of. The uniform might have been different, but with the white-blond hair, blue eyes, high forehead, and even loftier tone—I was already thinking of Heydrich before he mentioned the name. Probably Weltz and Heydrich would have been about the same age, too. If he hadn't been murdered in June 1942, Heydrich would have been about forty-two now. The younger lieutenant was rather more gray-haired, with a face as wide as the major's was long. He looked like me before the war and a year in a POW camp.

"Well, Gunther? What have you to say for yourself? Perhaps you were always just a Nazi in all but name. A party fellow traveler. Is that it? Did it take you this long to understand what you really are?"

"You and Heydrich," I said to the major. "You're not so very different. I never wanted to work for him either, but I was afraid to say no. Afraid of what he might do to me. You, on the other hand, have shot your bolt there. You've already done your worst. Short of shooting me, there's not much more you can actually do to me. Sometimes it's a great comfort to know that you've already hit rock bottom."

"We could break you," said Weltz. "We could do that."

"I've broken a few men myself in my time," I said. "But there has to be some point to it. And with me, there isn't, because if you break me, then you'd be doing it just for the hell of it, and what's more, I'd be no good to you when you were finished. I'm no good to you now, only you just don't know it, Major. So let me tell you why: I was the kind of cop who was too dumb to act smart and look the other way, or to kiss someone's behind. The Nazis were cleverer than you. They knew that. The only reason Heydrich brought me back to Kripo was because he knew that even in a police state there are times when you need a real policeman. But you don't want a real policeman, Major Weltz, you want a clerk with a badge. You want me to read Karl Marx at bedtime and people's mail during the day. You want a man who's eager to please and looking for advancement in the Communist Party." I shook my head wearily. "The last time I was looking for advancement in a party, a pretty girl slapped my face."

"Pity," said Weltz. "It seems you're going to spend the rest of your life dead. Like all of your class, Gunther, you're a victim of history."

"We both are, Major. Being a victim of history is what being a German is all about."

But I was also a victim of my environment. They made sure of that. Soon after my meeting with the boys from K-5, I was transferred off the sorting detail and into the mine shaft.

It was a world of constant thunder. There was the rumble of underground explosions that broke the rock into manageable chunks; and there was the crash of the cage doors before it slid down the guides and into the shaft. There was the din of rocks we split with pickaxes and then threw into the wagons, and the continual barrage as these moved backward and forward along the rails. And with each detonating noise there was dust and more dust, turning my own snot black and my sweat into a kind of gray oil. At night, I coughed great gritty gobs of saliva and phlegm that looked like burned fried eggs. It all felt like a high price to pay for my principles. But there was a camaraderie in the shaft that wasn't to be had anywhere else in Johannesgeorgenstadt, and an automatic respect from the other *pleni*s who heard our coughing and recognized their own comparative good fortune. Pospelov had been right about that. There's always someone worse off than yourself. I hoped to get a chance to meet that someone before the work killed me. There was a mirror in the washroom. Mostly we avoided it, for fear that we'd see our own grandfathers or, worse, their decomposed bodies looking back at us; but one day I inadvertently caught sight of myself and saw a man with a face like the pitchblende rock we were mining. It was brownish black, lumpy and misshapen, with two dull opaque spaces where my eyes had once been, and a row of dark gray excrescences that might have been my teeth. I'd met a lot of criminal types in my life, but I looked like Mr. Hyde's black-sheep brother. Acted like him, too. There were no Blues in the shaft, and we settled our differences with a maximum of violence. Once, Schaefer, another *pleni* from Berlin who didn't much like cops, told me that he'd cheered when the leaders of the SDP had been chased out of Berlin in 1933. So I punched him hard in the face, and when he tried to hit me with a pickax, I hit him with a shovel. It was a while before he got up, and in truth, he was never quite the same again after that—another victim of history. Karl Marx would have approved.

But after a while I stopped caring about anything very much, including myself. I would squeeze into tight spaces in the black rock to work in solitude with my pick, which was the most dangerous thing to do, since cave-ins were common. But there was less dust to breathe this way than when they used explosives.

Another month passed. And then one day I was summoned to the office again, and I went along expecting to find the same two MVD officers and hear them ask me if my time in the mine shaft had helped to change my mind about K-5. It had changed my mind about a lot of things, but not German communism and its secret police force. I was going to tell them to go to hell, and perhaps sound like I meant it, too, even though I was ready for someone to come and put some plaster of Paris on my face. So I was a little disappointed that the two officers weren't there, the way you are when you've worked up a pretty good speech about a lot of noble things that don't add up to very much that's important when you're lying in the morgue.

There was only one officer in the room, a heavyset man with receding brown hair and a pugnacious jaw. Like his two predecessors, he wore blue breeches and a brown *gimnasterka* tunic but was better decorated; as well as the veteran NKVD soldier badge and Order of the Red Banner, there were other medals I didn't recognize. The insignia on his collar tabs and the stars on his sleeves seemed to indicate that he was at least a colonel, or perhaps even a general. His blue officer's cap, with its squarish visor, lay on the table alongside the Nagant revolver in its bucket-sized holster.

"The answer is still no," I said, hardly caring who he was.

"Sit down," he said. "And don't be a bloody fool."

He was German.

"I know I've put on a bit of weight," he said. "But I thought you of all people would recognize me."

I sat down and rubbed some of the dust from my eyes. "Now you come to mention it, you do seem kind of familiar."

"You I wouldn't have recognized at all. Not in a million years."

"I know. I should lay off the chocolates. Get myself a haircut and a manicure. But I never do seem to have the time. My job keeps me pretty busy."

The officer's pork-butcher's face cracked a smile. Almost. "A sense of humor. That's impressive in this place. But if you really want to impress me, then stop playing the tough guy and tell me who I am."

"Don't you know?"

He tutted impatiently and shook his head. "Please. I can help you if you'll let me. But I have to believe you're worth it. If you're any kind of detective, you'll remember who I am."

"Erich Mielke," I said. "Your name is Erich Mielke."

25

GERMANY, 1946

You knew all along."

"There was a moment when I didn't. The last time I saw you, Erich, you looked like me."

For a moment Mielke looked grim, as if he was remembering. "Fucking French," he said. "They were as bad as the Nazis in my book. It still sticks in my throat they get to be one of the four victorious powers in Berlin. What did they do to defeat the fascists? Nothing."

"We can agree on something, anyway."

"Le Vernet was the second time you pulled my bread out of the oven. Why'd you do it?"

I shrugged. "It seemed like a good idea at the time."

"No, that won't do," he said firmly. "Tell me. I want to know. You were dressed like a Gestapo officer. But you didn't act like one. I didn't get it then and I don't get it now."

"Between you and me and these four walls, Erich, I'm afraid the Gestapo were rather a bad lot." I told him about the murders committed by Major Bömelburg and the SS storm troopers on the road to Lourdes. "You see, it's one thing taking a man back to stand trial. It's something completely different just to shoot him in a ditch at the side of the road. It was just your good fortune that we went to the camp at Gurs first, otherwise it might have been you who was shot while trying to escape. But given what I've seen since of your friends in the MVD, it's probably what you deserved. Rats are still rats whether they're gray, black, or brown. I just wasn't cut out to be much of a rat myself."

"Maybe a white rat, eh?"

"Maybe."

Mielke chucked a packet of Belomorkanal across the table at me. "Here. I don't smoke myself, but I brought these for you." He tossed some matches after the cigarettes. "It's my opinion that smoking is bad for your health."

"My health has got more important things to worry about." I lit one and puffed it happily. "But maybe you didn't know. Russian nails are better for your health than American ones."

"Oh? Why's that?"

"Because there's so little tobacco in them. Four good puffs and they're gone."

Mielke smiled. "Talking about your health, I don't think this place is good for you. If you stay here long enough, you're liable to grow two heads. That would be a waste, in my opinion." He came around the table and sat on the corner, swinging one of his polished riding boots carelessly. "You know, when I was in Russia, I learned to look after my health. I even won the sports medal of the Soviet Union. I was living in a little town outside Moscow called Krasnogorsk, and I used to go hunting at the weekend on a sporting estate once owned by the Yusupov family. Prince Yusupov was one of those aristocrats who murdered Rasputin. There was all sorts of rubbish talked about the death of Rasputin, you know. That they had to kill him three or four times before he was actually dead. That they poisoned him, shot him, beat him to death, and then drowned him. In fact, they made it all up to make their futile deed seem more heroic. And the prince didn't even do the deed himself. The truth was that Rasputin was shot through the forehead by a member of the British Secret Service. Now, I mention all of this to make the point that a man, even a strong man like Rasputin, or you perhaps, can survive almost anything except being killed. You, my friend, will die here. You know it. I know it. Perhaps you will be poisoned by the uraninite. Perhaps you will be shot, attempting to escape. Or when the mine floods, as I believe sometimes it does, then you will drown. But it doesn't have to be that way. I want to help you, Gunther. Really, I do. But you'll need to trust me."

"I'm all ears, Erich. Just two of them at the last count."

"We both know that you would make a very poor officer in the Fifth Kommissariat. First, you would have to attend the Anti-Fascist School in Krasnogorsk. For reeducation. To be turned into a believer. From our one meeting and everything I've read about you, Gunther, I'm quite convinced that it would be a waste of time trying to convert you into a communist. However, that still remains your best way out of here. To volunteer for K-5 and reeducation."

"It's true, I've rather neglected my reading of late, but . . ."

"Naturally, this would only be a smoke screen for your escape."

"Naturally. I suppose there's no chance of me being shot through this smoke screen."

"There's a chance of us both being shot, if you really want to know. I'm sticking my neck out for you, Gunther. I hope you appreciate that. Over the last ten or twelve years, I've become something of an expert at saving my own skin. I imagine it's something we have in common. Either way, it's not something I do lightly."

"Why do it at all? Why take the risk? I don't get it the same way you didn't get it."

"You think you're the only rat that's not cut out for it? You think a Gestapo officer is the only man who can develop a conscience?"

"I was never a believer. But you—you believed it all, Erich."

"It's true. I did believe. Absolutely. Which is why it comes as a shock to discover that party loyalty can count for nothing, and everything can be taken away again at the stroke of a pen."

"Why would they do that to you, Erich?"

"We all have our little secrets, that's why."

"No, that won't do," I said, parroting his earlier speech once more. "Tell me. I want to know. And then maybe I'll trust you."

Mielke stood up and walked around the room with his arms folded around himself in thought. After a while, he nodded and said:

"Did you ever wonder what happened to me after Le Vernet?"

"Yes. But I told Heydrich you joined the Foreign Legion. I'm not sure if he believed me."

"I was interned at Le Vernet for another *three* years after I saw you in 1940. Can you imagine that? Three years in hell. Well, perhaps you can now—yes, I suppose you can. I was posing as a German Latvian called Richard Hebel. Then, in December 1943, I was conscripted as a laborer into Speer's Ministry for Armaments and War Production. I became what had previously been known as a Todt worker. Effectively, I and thousands of others were slave labor for the Nazis. I myself was a woodcutter in the Ardennes Forest, supplying fuel for the German army. That's where I became the man you see now. These are woodcutter's shoulders. Anyway, I remained a so-called relief volunteer, working twelve hours a day until the end of the war, when I made my way back to Berlin and walked into the newly legalized KPD headquarters on Potsdamer Platz to volunteer my services to the party. I was extremely lucky. I met someone who told me to lie about what I'd been doing during the war. He advised me to say that I hadn't been a prisoner at all, and certainly not a relief volunteer for the fascists."

Mielke frowned a big, puzzled frown, like a bear gradually realizing that it had been stung by a bee. He shook his head.

"Well, this didn't make any sense to me. After all, it was hardly my fault that I'd been forced to work for the Nazis. But I was told that the party wouldn't see it that way. And against all of my instincts, which were to have faith in Comrade Stalin and the party, I decided to put my trust in this one man. His name was Victor Dietrich. So I told them I'd been lying low in Spain and then fighting with the French partisans. It was just as well I did say this, for without Dietrich's advice my honesty would have been fatal. You see, back in August 1941, Comrade Stalin, as People's Commissar for Defense, had issued an infamous order—order number two-seventy—which, in essence, said that there were no Soviet prisoners of war, only traitors." Mielke shrugged. "Of almost two million men and women who returned from German and French incarceration to the Soviet Union and its zones of control—many of them loyal party members—a very large percentage have been executed or sent to labor camps for between ten and twenty years. These included my own brother. That's why I no longer believe, Gunther. Because at any moment my past might catch up with me and I could be where you are now.

"But I want a future. Something concrete. Is that so unusual? I'm seeing this woman. Her name is Gertrud. She's a seamstress in Berlin. My mother was a seamstress. Did you know that? Anyway, I'd like us to feel that we might have a life together. I don't know why I'm telling you all this. I don't have to justify why I'm helping you, surely. You saved my life. Twice. What kind of man would I be if I forgot that?"

I stayed silent for a moment. Then his face darkened with impatience.

"Do you want my help or not, damn it?"

"How is it going to happen?" I asked. "That's what I'd like to know? If I'm going to put my soul in your hands, you can hardly be surprised if I want to check that your fingernails are clean."

"Spoken like a true Berliner. And fair enough. Now, then. The Central Anti-Fa School is in Krasnogorsk. Every month, we send them a bag of Nazis on a plane from Berlin for reeducation. There's quite a number of them there now. Members of the National Committee for a Free Germany, they call themselves. Field Marshal Paulus is one of them. Did you know that?"

"Paulus, a collaborator?"

"Ever since Stalingrad. Also there is von Seydlitz-Kurzbach. Of course, you'd remember his propaganda broadcasts in Königsberg. Yes, it's quite a little German colony over there. A regular Nazi home away from home. Once you're on the plane to Krasnogorsk from Berlin, there's no getting off. But on the train between here and Berlin—or better still, between here and Zwickau—that's where you could make your escape. Just think. From this camp to the Ami zone of occupation is less than sixty kilometers. If my lady friend, Gertrud, was not in East Berlin, I might be tempted myself. So what I propose is this: I will inform Major Weltz that I've persuaded you to change your mind. That you are prepared to undergo reeducation at the Anti-Fa School. He'll speak to the camp commander, who'll take you out of the pit and put you back on the sorting. Otherwise, everything else will appear as normal until the day you leave this place, when a clean uniform and new boots will be provided for you to wear. By the way, what size boots do you take?"

"Forty-six."

Mielke shrugged. "A man's body weight can fluctuate dramatically, but his feet always stay the same size. All right. There will be a gun inside the leg of the boot. Some papers. And a key for your manacles. You'll probably be accompanied on your journey by that young MVD lieutenant and a Russian *starshina*. But be warned. They won't give up easily. The penalty for allowing a *pleni* to escape is to take the prisoner's place in the labor camp. And the chances are you'll have to use the gun and kill them both. But that shouldn't be a problem for you. The train won't be like previous convict trains you've been on. You'll be in a compartment. As soon as you're moving, ask to use the toilet. And come out shooting. The rest is up to you. The best thing would be if you took the uniform of one of your escorts. Since you speak Russian, that shouldn't be a problem either. Jump the train and head west, of course. If you're caught, I shall deny everything, so please spare me the embarrassment. If they torture you, blame Major Weltz. I never liked him anyway."

Mielke's ruthlessness made me smile. "There's just one problem," I said. "The other *pleni*s. My comrades. They'll think I sold out."

"They're Nazis, most of them. Do you really care what they think?"

"I didn't think I would. But oddly, I do, yes."

"They'll find out you escaped soon enough. That kind of news travels fast. Especially if that major gets the rap for it. And I'll make sure he does. There's just one more thing. When you get to the Ami zone, I want you to do me a favor. I want you to go to an address in Berlin and give someone I know some money. A woman. As a matter of fact, you met her once. You probably don't remember, but you gave her a lift in your car that same day you saved me from those SA storm troopers."

"I wouldn't want to make helping you a habit, Erich. But sure. Why not?"

How much of what Erich Mielke told me was true was neither here nor there. He was certainly right that if I remained at the camp in Johannesgeorgenstadt I would probably die. What Mielke didn't know when he offered me a way to escape was that I had been about ready to throw in the towel and join K-5 in the hope that much later on, after I had become a good communist, I might find an opportunity to escape.

Almost immediately after my meeting with Mielke, I was, as he'd promised, transferred back to the sorting of the rock. This raised some suspicions that I'd agreed to collaborate with the German communists and I was subjected to some close questioning by General Krause and his adjutant, an SS major named Dunst; however, they seemed to accept my assurances that I remained "loyal to Germany," whatever that meant. And as the days passed, their earlier suspicions began to diminish. I had no idea when I would be summoned to the office and given my clean uniform and the all-important boots, and as yet more time passed, I began to wonder if Mielke had deceived me or even if he had been arrested himself. Then, one cold spring day, I was ordered to the showers, where I was allowed to wash and then given another uniform. It had been boil-washed and all of the badges and insignia removed, but after my own lousy clothes it felt like it had been tailored at Holter's. The *pleni* who gave it to me was a Russian *besprisorni*— an orphaned boy who'd grown up in the Soviet labor camp system and was regarded by the Blues as a trusted prisoner who needed no supervision. He handed me my boots, which were made of rather fine soft leather, and then kept a lookout for me.

The money was rubles and, in an envelope addressed to Mielke's friend, several hundred dollars. The papers included a pink pass, a ration card, a travel permit, and a German identity card— everything I'd need if I was stopped on the road to Nuremburg in the Ami zone. There was a small key for a set of manacles. And there was a loaded gun that was almost as small as the key: a six-shot Colt .25 with a two-inch barrel. Not much of a gun, but enough to make you think again about disagreeing with the person who might be holding it. But only just. It was a joy girl's gun, hammerless so as not to snag her stockings.

I tucked the papers and the money inside my boots, the gun under my waistband, and walked toward the gate, where Lieutenant Rascher and a Blue sergeant were waiting for me, as predicted. The only trouble was that Major Weltz was waiting for me as well. Killing two men was going to be hard enough. Three looked like a much taller order. But there was no going back now. They were standing beside a black ZIM saloon that looked more American than Russian. I was halfway there when I heard someone call my name. I glanced around to see Bingel nod at me.

"Sign the pact in blood, did you, Gunther?" he asked. "Your soul. I hope you got a good price for it, you bastard. I just hope I live long enough to have the chance to send you to hell myself."

I felt pretty low at this. I went to the car and held out my wrists for the manacles. Then we got in and the Blue drove us away.

"What did that man say?" asked Rascher.

"He wished me all the best."

"Really?"

"No, but I reckon I can live with it."

In the little railway station in Johannesgeorgenstadt there was a train already waiting. The steam locomotive was black with a red star on the front, like something from hell, which, in the circumstances, was entirely suitable. I couldn't rid myself of the feeling that even though I was planning to escape, I was doing something inherently shameful. I almost couldn't have felt worse if I really had been intending to join the Fifth Kommissariat.

The four of us climbed up into a carriage with the word for Berlin in Cyrillic chalk-marked on the side. We had it all to ourselves. The train had no central corridor. All of the carriages were separate. So much for coming out of the toilet with all guns blazing. The rest of the carriages were full of Red Army soldiers headed for Dresden, which hardly made things any easier.

Our own Russian sergeant was sweating and nervous-looking, and before he boarded the train behind me I noticed that he crossed himself. Which seemed a little curious, as even in the Soviet zone, rail travel was really not that hazardous. By contrast, the two German MVD officers appeared composed and relaxed. As we sat down and waited for the train to move, I asked the *starshina* if he spoke any German. He shook his head.

"The fellow's Ukrainian, I think," said Major Weltz. "He doesn't speak a word of German."

The Ivan lit a cigarette and stared out of the window, avoiding my eye.

"He's an ugly sonofabitch, isn't he?" I remarked. "I imagine his mother must have been a whore, like all Ukrainian women."

The Ivan didn't flinch at any of that.

"All right," I said. "I really do think he doesn't speak German. So. It's probably safe to talk."

Weltz frowned. "What on earth are you driving at?"

"Listen. Sir. All our lives could depend on us trusting each other now. We three Germans. Don't look at him. But how much do you know about our smelly friend here?"

The major glanced at the lieutenant, who shook his head. "Nothing at all," he said. "Why?"

"Nothing?"

"He was posted to the camp at Johannesgeorgenstadt just a few days ago," said Rascher. "From Berlin. That's really all I know about him."

"And he's going back already?"

"What's all this about, Gunther?" said Weltz.

"There's something about him that's not quite right," I said. "No. Don't look at him. But he's nervous when he shouldn't be nervous. And I saw him crossing himself a minute ago—"

"I don't know what you think you're playing at, Gunther, but "

"Shut up and listen. I was an intelligence officer. And before that I worked for the War Crimes Bureau in Berlin. One of the crimes we investigated was the murders of twenty-six thousand Polish officers, four thousand of them at a place I'm not going to mention in case it makes this dog prick up his ears. They were all of them murdered and buried in a forest clearing by NKVD."

"Oh, that's nonsense," insisted the major. "Everyone knows that was the SS."

"Look, it's vital you believe that they weren't killed by the SS. I know. I saw the bodies. Look, this man, this Blue sitting next to us, is wearing several medals on his chest, one of which is the Merited NKVD Worker medal. Like I said, I was an intelligence officer, and I happen to know that this medal was commissioned by the Council of the People's Commissars of the USSR—in other words,

Uncle Joe himself—in October 1940, as a special thank-you to all of those who did the killings in April of that same year."

The major tutted loudly and rolled his eyes in exasperation. Outside our carriage, the stationmaster blew his whistle and the locomotive expelled a loud cloud of steam. "Where are you going with this conversation?"

"Don't you get it? He's an assassin. I wouldn't mind betting that Comrade General Mielke has placed him on this train to kill all three of us."

The train started to move.

"Ridiculous," said Weltz. "Look, if this is the beginning of an attempt at escape, it's a pretty clumsy one. Everyone knows that those Poles were murdered by the fascists."

"You mean everyone except everyone in Poland," I said. "There's not much doubt there who was responsible. But if you don't believe that, then maybe you'll believe this: Mielke's already screwed you in the ass, Major. He gave me a gun that I'm supposed to use to help make my escape. But my bet is that the gun isn't going to work."

"Why would the comrade general do such a thing?" asked Weltz, shaking his head. "It makes absolutely no sense."

"It makes a lot of sense if you know Mielke as well as I do. I think he wants me dead because of what I could tell you about him. And he probably wants you both dead in case I already have."

"It couldn't hurt to see if he's telling the truth about the gun, sir," said Lieutenant Rascher.

"All right. Stand up, Gunther."

Staying exactly where I was, I glanced quickly at the Russian sergeant. He had a large Stalin-size mustache and one continuous matching eyebrow; the nose was round and red, almost comical-looking; the ears had more hair on and in them than a wild pig's.

"If you search me, Major, the Ivan will figure something's wrong and draw his gun. And it will be too late for us all when he's done that."

"What if Gunther's right, sir?" said Lieutenant Rascher. "We don't know anything about this fellow."

"I gave you an order, Gunther. Now do as you're told."

The major was already unbuttoning the flap on his holstered Nagant. There was no telling if he was about to pull the gun on me or the MVD *starshina,* but the Ivan saw it and then met my eye, and when he met my eye he saw what I had seen in his—something lethal. He reached for his own pistol, and this prompted Lieutenant Rascher to abandon the idea of searching me and fumble for his own gun.

Still wearing handcuffs and with no time to decide if the major was with me or not, I swung my fists at the Ivan as if I had been driving a golf ball, connecting hard with the outside of his porcine head. The blow knocked him onto the floor between the two rows of seats, but the big thirty-eight was already in his greasy fist. Someone else fired and the glass in the carriage door above him shattered. A split second later, the Ivan fired back. I felt the bullet zip past my head and hit something or someone behind me. I kicked at the Russian's face and turned to see the major dead on the seat, the lieutenant aiming his revolver at the Ivan with both hands but still hesitating to pull the trigger, as if he'd never shot anyone before.

"Shoot him, you idiot!" I yelled.

But even as I spoke, the more experienced Ukrainian fired again, punctuating the young German's forehead with a single red full stop.

Gritting my teeth, I stamped at the Russian's face with the heel of my boot, and this time I kept on going, as if I were stamping on something verminous. One last uppercut of a kick caught him under the jaw and I felt something give way. I stamped again, and his throat seemed to collapse under the force of my boot. He made a loud choking noise that lasted as long as my next kick, and then he stopped moving.

I collapsed back onto the seat of the railway carriage and surveyed the scene.

Rascher was dead. Weltz was dead. I didn't need to check for a pulse to know that. When he's shot dead, a man's face wears a certain look that's a mixture of surprise and repose—as if someone stopped a movie in the very middle of an actor's big scene, with his mouth agape and his eye half open. There was that and there was the fact that their brains and what these had been swimming in were all over the floor.

The MVD *starshina* made a long, slow gurgling noise, and adjusting my balance against the movement of the railway carriage, I kicked him hard—as hard as I could—against the side of his head. There had been enough shooting for one day.

My ears were still ringing from the shots and the carriage smelled strongly of cordite. But I wasn't disturbed by any of this. After the Battle of Königsberg, nothing like that bothered me much, and my mind was disposed to interpret the ringing in my ears as an alarm and a call to action. If I kept my nerve, I could still complete my escape. In other circumstances, I might easily have panicked, jumped off the train, and tried to make for the American zone, as I'd originally intended; but a better plan was already presenting itself, and this depended on my acting quickly, before the blood spreading on the floor spoiled everything.

Both the German MVD officers had luggage. I opened up the bags and found that each man had brought a spare *gimnasterka*. This was just as well, as there was blood on both of their tunics. But the all-important blue trousers were still unmarked. First I emptied their pockets and removed their decorations, their blue shoulder boards, and their *portupeya* cross-belts. Then I pulled their tunics up and wrapped their shattered heads in the thick cloth to help staunch the blood. Weltz's skull felt like a bag full of marbles.

You have to be a certain type of man to clean up efficiently after a murder, and no one does that better than a cop. Maybe what I was planning wouldn't work, maybe I'd get caught, but the two Germans had bigger problems. They were both as dead as Weimar.

I took off their boots, unlaced the legs of their blue breeches, and then hauled those off, too. I put both pairs carefully up on the luggage rack, well out of the way of what I was going to do next.

It would have been a mistake to have opened the carriage door. A Red Army soldier in one of the other carriages might have seen me doing it. So I slid down the window, balanced the major's naked body on the sill, and waited for a tunnel. It was fortunate that we were traveling through the Erzgebirge. There are lots of tunnels for the railway line that runs through the Erzgebirge.

By the time I had defenestrated the two dead Germans I was exhausted, but working down in the mine shaft had given me the capacity to go beyond the limits of my own exhaustion, to say nothing of a wiry muscularity in my arms and shoulders, and in this respect I was also fortunate. I might add that I was also desperate.

I wasn't sure if the Ukrainian was dead, but I hardly cared. His NKVD assassin's badge did not inspire my sympathy. In his pockets I found some money—quite a lot of money—and, more interesting, a piece of paper bearing an address in Cyrillic, and a note in German; it was the same address as on the envelope Mielke had given me for his friend, and I guessed that, my assassin once he had killed me, was detailed to deliver the dollars and the note in the envelope himself. That envelope had been a nice touch, partly allaying any fears of a double cross on Mielke's part. After all, who would give an envelope full of money to a man he intended to have killed? There was also an identity document that gave the Ukrainian's name as Vasili Karpovich Lebyediev; he was stationed at MVD headquarters in Berlin, at Karlshorst, which I remembered better as a villa colony with a racecourse. He worked not for the MVD but for the Ministry of Military Forces—the MBC—whatever that was. The Nagant revolver in his apparently lifeless hand was dated 1937 and had been well looked after. I wondered how many innocent victims of Stalin it had been used to kill. For that reason, I took a certain pleasure in pushing his naked body out of the carriage window. It felt like a kind of justice.

I used the Ivan's tunic and my old uniform to mop the floor

and wipe the walls of any remaining blood and brain tissue, then threw them out of the window. I put the pieces of glass into the Russian's cap alongside his decorations and threw that out of the window, too. And when everything apart from me looked almost respectable, I dressed carefully in the lieutenant's blue breeches— the major's were too big around the waist—and his spare tunic, and prepared to face down any Ivans who might come aboard at Dresden. I was ready for that.

What I wasn't ready for was Dresden. The train went straight past the ruins of the city's eighteenth-century cathedral. I could hardly believe my own eyes. The bell-shaped dome was completely gone. And the rest of the city was no better. Dresden had never seemed like an important town or one with any strategic significance, and I began to worry about what Berlin might look like. Did I even have a hometown that was worth returning to?

The Red Army sergeant who came aboard the carriage at Dresden and asked to see my papers glanced at the broken window with mild surprise.

"What happened in here?" he asked.

"I don't know, but it must have been some party."

He shook his head and frowned. "Some of these young lads they have in uniform now. They're just *kolkhoznik*s. Peasants who don't know how to behave. Half of them have never even seen a proper passenger train, let alone traveled on one."

"You can't blame them for that," I said generously. "And for letting off a bit of steam now and again. Especially when you consider what the fascists did to Russia."

"Right now I'm more concerned about what they've done to this train." He glanced at Lieutenant Rascher's identity document and then at me.

I met his gaze with steady-eyed innocence.

"You've lost a bit of weight since that picture was taken."

"You're right," I said. "I hardly recognize myself. Typhus

does that to a man. I'm on leave back to Berlin after six weeks in hospital."

The sergeant inched back a little.

"It's all right," I said. "I'm over the worst of it now. I picked it up in the POW camp at Johannesgeorgenstadt. Full of fleas and lice, it was." I started to scratch for added effect.

He handed me back the documents and nodded a quick good-bye. I expect he washed his hands quite soon afterward. I know I would have.

I dropped down on the seat and opened the major's bag again. There was a bottle of Asbach brandy I'd been looking forward to all morning. I opened it, took a swig, and searched through the rest of his stuff. There were some clothes, some smokes, a few papers, and an early edition of poems by Georg Trakl. I'd always rather admired his work, and one particular poem, "In the Eastern Front," now seemed to match the time and, more especially, the place. I can still remember it by heart.

The ominous anger of the People
Is like the furious organ of the winter storm,
The purple wave of battle,
Like the leafless stars.
With broken brows and silver arms,
The night winks to dying soldiers.
In the shade of an autumn ash tree
The ghosts of the dead are sighing
A desert crown of thorns surrounds the city.
From the bleeding stairs
The moon chases the shocked women
Wild wolves break through the door.*

---

*Author's translation.

26

GERMANY, 1954

"A nd you think that Erich Mielke wanted you dead because he owed his life to you?"

My American friend tapped his pipe and let the burned tobacco fall onto the floor of my cell. I wanted to scold him for it, to remind him that these were my quarters and to show a little respect. But what was the point? It was an American world I was living in now, and I was just a pawn in a never-ending game of intercontinental chess with the Russians.

"Not just that," I said. "Because I could connect him with the murders of those two Berlin policemen. You see, Heydrich always suspected that Mielke felt a certain amount of embarrassment that he'd committed a crime as serious as the murders of policemen. That it was somehow unworthy of him. He thought it was almost certainly Mielke who fingered the two Germans who put him up to it—Kippenberger and Neumann—during Stalin's Great Purge of 1937. They both died in the labor camps. Their wives, too. Even Kippenberger's daughter was sent to a labor camp. Mielke really tried to clean house there.

"But I also knew about Mielke's work in Spain. His work as

a Chekist, with the military security service, torturing and killing those Republicans—anarchists and Trotskyites—who deviated from the party line as dictated by Stalin. Again, Heydrich strongly suspected that Mielke used his position as a political commissar with the International Brigade in Spain to eliminate Erich Ziemer. If you remember, Ziemer was the man who helped Mielke murder the two cops. And I think Heydrich was probably right. I think that Mielke may even have planned some political role for himself in Germany after the war; and he reasoned, quite rightly, that the German people—and more especially Berliners—would never take to a man who'd murdered two policemen in cold blood."

"There was an attempt by the West Berlin courts in 1947 to prosecute him for those murders," said the Ami with the bow tie. "A judge called Wilhelm Kühnast issued a warrant for Mielke's arrest. Did you know about that?"

"No. By then, I wasn't living in Berlin."

"It failed, of course. The Soviets closed ranks in front of Mielke to shield him from further inquiry and tried their best to discredit Kühnast. The criminal records that Kühnast used to build up his case disappeared. Kühnast was lucky not to disappear himself."

"Erich Mielke has survived numerous party purges," said the Ami with the pipe. "He survived the death of Stalin, of course, and, rather more recently, the death of Lavrenty Beria. We think that he was never a relief volunteer for the Todt organization. That was just a story he gave you. If he had worked for them, he'd be dead like all the rest who came back and found a cold welcome from Stalin. To us it seems much more likely that Mielke got out of that French camp at Le Vernet quite soon after you saw him there, in the summer of 1940, and got himself back to the Soviet Union before Hitler invaded Russia."

"Why not?" I shrugged. "He never struck me as the George Washington, 'I cannot tell a lie' type. So I'll contain my obvious disappointment that he might have misled me."

"Today, your old friend is East Germany's deputy chief of the secret police. The Stasi. Have you heard of the Stasi?"

"I've been away for five years."

"Okay. When Stalin died last year, there was this big workers' strike in East Berlin, and then throughout the whole of the DDR. As many as half a million took to the streets to demand free and fair elections. Even policemen defected to the side of the protesters. This was the first big test of the Stasi as run by Mielke. And effectively, he broke the strike."

"Big-time," said the other Ami.

"At first martial law was declared. The Stasi opened fire on the protesters. Many were killed. Thousands were arrested and are still in prison. Mielke himself arrested the minister of justice, who'd questioned the legality of those arrests. Since then, Comrade Erich has been consolidating his position within the East German hierarchy. And he continues to expand the Stasi's network of secret informers and spies, and to build the organization into the image of the Soviet KGB. The MVD, that was."

"He's a bastard," I said. "What more can I tell you? I have nothing else to say about the man. That day in Johannesgeorgenstadt was the last time I saw him."

"You could help us to get him."

"Sure. Before lockdown tonight, I'll see what I can do for you."

"Seriously."

"I've told you everything."

"And it's been very interesting. Most of it, anyway."

"Don't think we're not grateful, Gunther. Because we are."

"Might that gratitude stretch as far as letting me go?"

Bow Tie glanced at the Pipe, who nodded vaguely and said, "You know? It might. It just might. Provided you agree to work for us."

"Oh." I yawned.

"'Sa matter, Bernie boy? Don't you want to get out of the stir?"

"We'll put you on the payroll. We can even get your money back. The money you had when the Coast Guard picked you up in the sea off Gitmo."

"That's very generous of you," I said. "But I'm tired of fighting. And frankly, I can't see this Cold War of yours being any more worthwhile than the last two I took part in."

"I'd say it could end up being the most crucial war of all," said Bow Tie. "Especially if it gets any warmer."

I shook my head. "You guys make me laugh. The people you want to work for you. Do you always treat them like this?"

"Like what?"

"My mistake. The other day, when I was handcuffed with a hood over my head, I formed the distinct impression you didn't like my face."

"That was then."

"You don't see us ill-treating you now, do you?"

"Hell, Gunther, you've got the best fucking room in the place. Cigarettes, brandy. Tell us what else you need and we'll see if we can get it for you."

"They don't sell what I want in the army PX."

"And what's that?"

I shook my head and lit a cigarette. "Nothing. It doesn't matter."

"We're your friends, Gunther."

"With American friends, who needs enemies?" I pulled a face. "Look, gentlemen, I've had American friends before. In Vienna. And there was something about the experience I didn't like. Even so, I knew their names. And mostly this is a given with the people who claim to be my friends."

"You're taking this way too personally, Gunther."

"Nothing's been broken that can't be fixed. We can do this. I'm Mr. Scheuer and this is Mr. Frei. Like we said before, we work for the CIA. At a place called Pullach. You know Pullach?"

"Sure," I said. "It's the American part of Munich. Where you kennel all of the tame German shepherds who look after the flock for you in this part of the world. General Gehlen and his pals."

"Unfortunately, those dogs are not coming to heel the way they used to," said Scheuer. He was the one with the pipe. "We suspect Gehlen made a private deal with Chancellor Adenauer and that the Germans are about to run their own show from now on."

"Very ungrateful," said Frei. "After all we did for them."

"Gehlen's new intelligence outfit—the GVL—is mostly ex-SS. Gestapo, Abwehr. Some very nasty people. Much worse than you. And it's probably riddled with Russian spies."

"I could have told you that seven years ago in Vienna," I said. "In fact, I think I did."

"So it looks like we're going to have to start again from scratch. And that means we're going to have to be rather more certain of the kind of people we recruit. Which is why we were so rough on you from the start. We wanted to make quite sure of who and what you are. The last thing we want working for us this time is a bunch of die-hard Nazis."

"Imagine how we felt when we discovered that the GVL was helping to train Egyptians and Syrians for a war with the state of Israel. With the Jews, Gunther. Talk about history repeating itself. I would think a man like you, someone who wasn't ever anti-Semitic himself, might want to do something about that. Israel is our friend."

"You've got to ask yourself a question, Bernie. Do you really want to stay here and let those two jokers from the OCCWC, Silverman and Earp, decide your fate?"

"I thought you said they cleared me."

"Oh, they did. Since then the French have put in a request for your extradition to Paris. And you know what the French are like."

"The French haven't got anything on me."

"That's not what they think," said Scheuer. "That's not what they think at all."

"You have to hand it to the French," said Frei. "Their capacity for hypocrisy is nothing short of breathtaking. France was a fascist country during the war. Even more so than Italy or Spain. But even now, they like to portray themselves as victims. To hold others responsible for their crimes and misdemeanors. Others like you, perhaps. Right now there's a big trial under way in Paris. Your old friend, Helmut Knochen. And Carl Oberg. It's quite the cause célèbre. Really. It's in all the newspapers, every day."

"I don't see what that has to do with me," I said. "Those people, Knochen and Oberg, they were big fish. I was just a minnow. I never even met Oberg. So what the hell's all this about?"

"The Brits tried Knochen in 1947. In Wuppertal. They found him guilty of the murders of some British parachutists and sentenced him to death. But the sentence was commuted and now the French want their kilo of flesh. They're looking for scapegoats, Gunther. Someone to blame. And of course, so is Knochen. Which apparently is how your name came up. He made a statement to the French Sûreté that it was you who murdered all those prisoners from Gurs on the road to Lourdes in 1940."

"Me? There must be some mistake."

"Oh, sure," said Frei. "I think there has been a mistake. But that's not going to stop the French. They've made a formal application for your extradition to Paris. Perhaps you would care to read Knochen's statement?"

He reached into his jacket pocket and fished out several folded sheets of paper, which he handed to me. Then he and Scheuer stood up and moved toward the cell door.

"You read that over and then decide whether working for Uncle Sam is such a bad thing after all."

HELMUT KNOCHEN, interviewed March 1954

My name is Helmut Knochen. I was the senior commander of the security police in Paris during the Nazi occupation of

France between 1940 and 1944. My jurisdiction extended from northern France to Belgium. Until the appointment of Carl Oberg as supreme leader of the SS and the German police in France I had full responsibility for keeping order and upholding the rule of law. As a policeman I tried to ensure that relations between the French and the Germans were without friction and that the proper administration of justice was unhindered by the occupation. This was not easy. I was not always made privy to senior policy decisions. And the most profound tragedy of my life has been the fact that, in an indirect way, and without being aware of it, I was involved in the persecution of the Jews of France. At no point did I know or even suspect that Jews deported to the east were to be exterminated. If I had known this I should never have gone along with their deportation. Let me say that the greatest crime in history was the systematic murder of Jews by Adolf Hitler.

Of course, there were many other crimes inflicted upon the French people and I always saw my job as being to help restrain some of my colleagues from acting with excessive zeal, not least because I was always fearful of the impact of heavy-handed policing on French public opinion, and on those Vichy officials whose willing collaboration was needed in all security matters. I was always reluctant to provoke an embarrassing confrontation. For example, in September 1942, I thwarted an early attempt to round up prominent French Jews in Paris. There were other occasions when this happened, but that was the largest, I think, involving as many as five thousand Jews. This often brought me into conflict with Heinz Röthke, who was chief of the Gestapo's Jewish office in France. But my relationship with other fanatical elements in the SS and SD was no less fractious and difficult. Frequently I had to censure those officers who, arriving from

Berlin, believed that the SD uniform permitted them to deal summarily with the French. I remember one junior officer from Berlin, Hauptsturmführer Bernhard Gunther, who, in the summer of 1940, was dispatched to the refugee camps at Gurs and Le Vernet in order to arrest a number of French and German communists and bring them back to Paris for questioning. But instead this officer ordered the men to be shot at the side of a French country road. When I heard about this I was shocked, then furious. When he subsequently murdered another German officer, Hauptsturmführer Gunther was sent back to Berlin.

HELMUT KNOCHEN, interviewed April 1954

My name is Helmut Knochen and I have been asked to make a statement concerning information I gave regarding another German officer, Captain Bernhard Gunther, in a previous statement.

I first met Captain Gunther in Paris in July 1940. The meeting took place at the Hôtel du Louvre, or possibly the HQ of the French Gestapo at 100 avenue Henri-Martin. Other officers present at this meeting included Herbert Hagen and Karl Bömelburg. Gunther had arrived in Paris as the special emissary of SS General Reinhard Heydrich and he was ordered to track down a number of French and German communists who were wanted by the Nazi government back in Berlin. Gunther struck me as typical of the type who found favor with Heydrich: cynical, ruthless, and not at all a gentlemen. He made clear his own detestation of the French and, in spite of my efforts to rein him in, he insisted on flying to the south of France and collecting a detachment of motorized SS to drive him to Gurs and Le Vernet, to search those two camps for Heydrich's wanted men. It was my own feeling there was nothing to be lost by delaying matters until the end of summer, largely out of sensitivity to the defeated armies of France. But Gunther was most insistent. He was ill, I recall—I don't remember why, later on there was talk of his involvement with a Swiss prostitute—but in spite of this, he still traveled south to carry out his mission, to which Heydrich had given top priority. In fairness to Captain Gunther, it may have been this illness that prompted his summary action in regard to the prisoners. He was accompanied by another German officer, Hauptsturmführer Paul Kestner, and it was him who informed me of what had happened on the road from Gurs to Lourdes.

Almost a dozen men were arrested in Gurs. Among these was the head of the French Communist Party in Le Havre, Lucien Roux. It seems terrible to think it, but apparently these men knew what Captain Gunther had in store for them. The SS drove a few kilometers out of Gurs and stopped in a forest clearing. There Gunther ordered everyone out of the trucks. The prisoners were lined up, offered a last cigarette, and then shot. Gunther delivered the coup de grâce to several men who showed signs of life and then they all went on their way, leaving the bodies where they fell.

Frankly, when Captain Kestner told me exactly what had happened down there I thought seriously about making a formal complaint against Captain Gunther; but I was advised against it: Gunther was Heydrich's man and this made him all but untouchable. Even when he murdered another officer at a brothel in Paris and it might reasonably have been expected that Gunther would be court-martialed, he managed to evade all charges. He was merely recalled to Berlin, from where he was immediately dispatched to the Ukraine, most likely to carry out the kind of dirty work for which the SS is now notorious. It's not given to every German officer to behave like a gentleman. Later on, I met Heydrich and expressed my own reservations about Gunther, and his response was typical of the man. He said that he rather agreed with Schopenhauer that all honor ultimately rests on considerations of expediency. Heydrich was of course strongly influenced by Schopenhauer, and I don't just mean his anti-Semitism. Anyway, I didn't argue with him. That was never wise. Like Kant, I believe that honor and morality contain their own imperatives. And this is, of course, why I was part of Count Stauffenberg's plot to kill Adolf Hitler. And why I was arrested by the Nazis in July 1944.

HELMUT KNOCHEN, interviewed May 1954

My name is Helmut Knochen and I have been asked to provide a description of SS-Hauptsturmführer Bernhard Gunther for the record. I met Gunther in 1940. He was older than me, I think. Perhaps forty years old. I recall also that he was a Berliner. I myself am from Magdeburg and I have always had a fascination for the Berlin accent. Well, it wasn't so much his accent that marked him out as a Berliner as his manner. This might be described as rude and uncompromising; cynical and unfriendly. It's no wonder that Hitler disliked Berlin so much. Well, this man Gunther was doubly typical, because he was also a policeman. A detective. I always think that the character of Doubting Thomas in the Bible must have been a Berliner. This fellow would only have believed Christ had risen from the dead if he could have looked through the holes in his hands and feet and seen a judge and a research physicist on the other side.

He was very German-looking. Fair-haired, blue-eyed, about one-ninety centimeters tall and powerful in the arms and shoulders, even a little heavy. His face was pugnacious.

Yes, he was very much the kind of man I didn't like at all. A real Nazi, you know?

[The witness, Knochen, was subsequently shown a photograph of a man and positively identified him as the wanted war criminal Bernhard Gunther.]

FRANCE, 1954

From the grimy window in the holding cell at Paris's Cherche-Midi prison I could just see the front of the Hôtel Lutetia, and for a long while I stood pressed into the cobwebbed corner, watching the hotel closely, as if I almost expected to see myself coming out of the door with poor little Renata Matter on my arm. It was hard to know whom I felt more sorry for, her or me, but eventually she edged it. She was dead, after all, when she would have had every reason to expect that she might still be alive. But for me. I didn't spare myself anything in the way of reproach or blame. If only I hadn't fixed her up with a job at the Adlon, I told myself, then she wouldn't have been killed. If only I had left her here in Paris, then there would have been a small but nonetheless real possibility that she could have turned left out of the Lutetia, crossed the boulevard Raspail, and come to see me in the Cherche-Midi. It would have been easy enough. The Cherche-Midi was, after all, no longer a prison but a court, and like many others in Paris—most of them journalists—she might have gone there to see the trial of Carl Oberg and Helmut Knochen and seen me there, too, my hosts in the SDECE—a French counterespionage service—having thought it necessary to remind me that I was in their power, and that like Dreyfus, who had also been imprisoned in the Cherche-Midi, they could do what they liked with me now that I had been extradited to their custody.

Not that custody in Paris was such an enormous hardship. Not after everything else. Not after Mainz and the French Sûreté. They had been a little rough. And it was true that La Santé Prison, where I was currently held, wasn't exactly the Lutetia, but the SDECE wasn't so bad. Probably not as bad as the CIA, anyway; and certainly not as bad as the Russians. Besides, the food at La Santé was good and the coffee even better; the cigarettes were tasty and plentiful; and most of the interrogations at the Caserne Mortier—nicknamed "the Swimming Pool"—were conducted politely, often with a bottle of wine and some bread and cheese. Sometimes the French even gave me a newspaper to take back to La Santé. None of this was what I'd been expecting when I left WCPN1 in Landsberg. My French improved—enough to understand what was in the newspapers and a little of the proceedings on the day I went to court, which just happened to be the day when the military tribunal brought in its verdict and handed down the sentences. My hosts in French intelligence had a point they wanted to make, after all. I could hardly blame them for that.

We sat in the public gallery, which was full. A civil judge, M. Boessel du Bourg, and six military judges came into court and took their places in front of a large blackboard, so that I half expected them to write out the verdict and sentence with a piece of chalk. The civil judge wore robes and an extremely silly hat. The military judges were all wearing lots of medals, although it was unclear to me what any of these could have been for. Then the two accused were led into the dock. I hadn't seen Oberg before, except on the German newsreels during the war. He wore a smart, double-breasted pin-striped suit and light-framed glasses. He looked like Eisenhower's older brother. Knochen was thinner and grayer than I remembered: Prison does that to a man—that and a death sentence from the British hanging over your head. Knochen looked straight at me without showing any sign of his having recognized me. I wanted to shout at him that he was a damned liar, but, of course, I didn't. When a man's on trial for his life, it's not good manners to bend his ear about something else.

At considerable length M. Boessel du Bourg read the verdict and then delivered the sentence, which was death, of course. This was the cue for lots of people in court to begin shouting at the two defendants, and—a little to my surprise—I found I was almost sorry for them. Once the two most powerful men in Paris, they now looked like two architects receiving the news that they hadn't won an important contract. Oberg blinked with disbelief. Knochen let out a loud sigh of disappointment. And amid more abuse and jeers from all around me, the two Germans were led out of court. One of my SDECE escorts leaned toward me and said:

"Of course, they will appeal the sentences."

"Still, I do get the point," I said. "I am encouraged by Voltaire's example."

"You've read Voltaire?"

"Not as such, no. But I'd like to. Especially when one considers the alternative."

"Which is?"

"It's hard to read anything when your head is lying in a basket," I said.

"All Germans like Voltaire, yes? Frederick the Great was a great friend of Voltaire, yes?"

"I think he was. At first."

"Germans and French should be friends now."

"Yes. Indeed. The Schuman plan. Exactly."

"For this reason—I mean, for the sake of Franco-German relations—I think the appeal will be successful."

"That's good news," I said, although I could hardly have cared less about Knochen's fate. All the same, I was surprised at this conversational turn of events and I spent the drive back to the Swimming Pool feeling encouraged. Perhaps my prospects were improving after all. Despite the trial of Oberg and Knochen, and the verdict, there was perhaps good reason to imagine that the SDECE was keener on cooperation than coercion, and this suited me very well.

From the Cherche-Midi we drove east to the outskirts of Paris. The Caserne Mortier in the barracks of the Tourelles was a traditional-looking set of buildings near the boulevard Mortier in the Twentieth Arrondissement. Made of red brick and semirusticated sandstone, the C.M. held no obvious affinity with a swimming pool beyond an echo in the corridors and an Olympic-sized courtyard, which, when it rained, resembled an enormous pool of black water.

My interrogators were quiet-spoken but muscular. They wore plain clothes and did not give me their names. No more did they accuse me of anything. To my relief, they weren't much interested in the events that had happened on the road to Lourdes in the summer of 1940. There were two of them. They had intense, birdlike faces, five-o'clock shadows that appeared just after lunch, damp shirt collars, nicotine-stained fingers, and espresso breath. They were cops, or something very like it. One of the men, the heavier smoker, had very white hair and very black eyebrows that looked like two lost caterpillars. The other was taller, with a whore's sulky mouth, ears like the handles on a trophy, and an insomniac's hooded, heavy eyes. The insomniac spoke quite good German, but mostly we spoke in English, and when that failed I took a shot at French and sometimes managed to hit what I was aiming at. But it was more of a conversation than an interrogation, and save for the holsters on their broad shoulders, we could have been three guys in a bar in Montmartre.

"Did you have much to do with the Carlingue?"

"The Carlingue? What's that?"

"The French Gestapo. They worked out of rue Lauriston. Number ninety-three. Did you ever go there?"

"That must have been after my time."

"They were criminals recruited by Knochen," said Eyebrows. "Armenians, Muslims, North Africans, mostly."

I smiled. This, or something like it, was what the French always said when they didn't want to admit that almost as many Frenchmen as Germans had been Nazis. And given their postwar record in Vietnam and Algeria, it was tempting to see them as even more racist than we were in Germany. After all, no one had forced them to deport French Jews—including Dreyfus's own granddaughter— to the death camps of Auschwitz and Treblinka. Naturally, I hardly wanted to hurt anyone's feelings by saying so directly, but as the subject remained on the table, I shrugged and said:

"I knew some French policemen. The ones I've already told you about. But not any French Gestapo. Now, the French SS, that's something else again. But none of them were Muslims. As I recall, they were nearly all Catholics."

"Did you know many from the SS-Charlemagne?"

"A few."

"Let's talk about the ones you did know."

"All right. Mostly they were Frenchmen captured by the Russians during the battle for Berlin in 1945. They were men in the POW camps, like I was. The Russians treated them the same way they treated us Germans. Badly. We were all fascists, as far as they were concerned. But really there was only one Frenchman in the camps I got to know well enough to call him a comrade."

"What was his name?"

"Edgard," I said. "Edgard de something or other."

"Try to remember," one of the Frenchmen said patiently.

"Boudin?" I shrugged. "De Boudin? I don't know. It was a long time ago. A lifetime. Not a good lifetime, either. Some of those poor bastards are only just coming home now."

"It couldn't have been de Boudin. *Boudin* means 'sausage' or 'pudding.' That couldn't have been his name." He paused. "Try to think."

I thought for a moment and then shrugged. "Sorry."

"Maybe if you told us something of what you can remember of him, the name will come back to you," suggested the other Frenchman. He uncorked a bottle of red wine, poured a little into a small round glass, and then sniffed it carefully before tasting it and pouring some more for me and the two of them. In that room, on that dull summer's day, this small ritual made me feel civilized again, as if, after months of incarceration and abuse, I amounted to something more than just a name chalked on a little board by a cell door.

I toasted his courtesy, drank some wine, and said, "I first met him here in Paris in 1940. I think it must have been Herbert Hagen who introduced us. Something to do with the policy on Jews in Paris, I don't know. I never really cared about that sort of thing. Well, we all say that now, don't we? The Germans. Anyway, Edgard de something or other was almost as anti-Semitic as Hagen, if such a thing was possible, but in spite of that, I quite liked him. He had been a captain in the Great War, after which he'd failed in civvy street, and this had led him to join the French Foreign Legion. I think he was stationed in Morocco before being sent to Indochina. And of course, he hated the communists, so that was all right. We had that much in common, anyway.

"Well, that was 1940, and when I left Paris I didn't expect to see him again, and certainly never as soon as November 1941 in the Ukraine. Edgard was part of this French unit in the German army—not the SS, that was later, but the Legion of French Volunteers against Bolshevism, or some such nonsense. That's what the French called it. I think we just called it the something infantry. The 638th. Yes. That was it. Mostly, the men were Vichy fascists, or even French POWs who didn't fancy being sent to Germany as forced labor with the Todt organization. There were probably about six thousand of them. Poor bastards."

"Why do you say that?"

I sipped some wine and helped myself to a cigarette from the packet on the table. Outside the window, in the central courtyard, someone was trying to start a motorcar without success; somewhere farther away, de Gaulle was waiting or sulking, depending on how you looked at it; and the French army was licking its wounds after getting its ass kicked—again—in Vietnam.

"Because they couldn't have known what they were letting themselves in for," I said. "Fighting partisans sounds fair enough back here in Paris. But out there, in Byelorussia, it meant something very different." I shook my head sadly. "There was no honor in it. No glory. Not what they were looking for, anyway."

"So what *did* it mean?" asked Eyebrows. "On the ground."

I shrugged. "That kind of action was, quite often, nothing more than murder. Mass murder. Of Jews. All sorts of police actions and antipartisan activities were merely a euphemism for killing Jews. To be frank with you, the Wehrmacht High Command in Russia wouldn't have trusted the 638th with any other kind of task but murder."

"The name of the unit commander. Can you remember that?"

"Labonne. Colonel Labonne. After the winter of 1941, I lost touch with Edgard." I clicked my fingers. "De Boudel. That was his name. Edgard de Boudel."

"You're quite sure of that?"

"I'm sure."

"Go on."

"Well, then. Let's see. A couple of years later, I was briefly back in that theater to investigate an alleged war crime. That was when I heard that the 638th was now attached to an SS division in Galicia. And that it was pretty bad there. But I didn't see de Boudel again until 1945, when the war was over and we were both at a Soviet prisoner-of-war camp called Krasno-Armeesk. As a matter of fact, there were quite a few French and Belgian SS there. And Edgard told me something of what he'd been up to. How the 638th ended up as a part of a French brigade of the SS and that kind of thing. Apparently, there was a recruiting drive here in Paris in July 1943. The French who joined had to prove the usual Himmler rubbish about not having any Jewish blood, and then they were in. A few weeks of basic training in Alsace and then at a place near Prague. By the late summer of 1944, the war in France was almost over, but there was a whole brigade of French SS ready to fight the Ivans. About ten thousand of them, he said. And they were called the SS-Charlemagne.

"The brigade got sent by train to the Eastern Front, in Pomerania, which wasn't very far from where I was. Edgard said that as the train carrying the brigade pulled into the railhead at Hammerstein they came under attack by the Soviet First Byelorussian and were divided up into three groups. One group, commanded by General Krukenberg, made it north to the Baltic coast, near Danzig. Of these, quite a few managed to get themselves evacuated to Denmark. But some, like Edgard, fought on until they were captured. The rest were wiped out or fell back to Berlin.

"There were other French at Krasno-Armeesk who'd been captured at Berlin. I can't say I remember any names. By all accounts, it was the SS-Charlemagne who were the last defenders of Hitler's bunker in Berlin. I think they were the only SS happy to be caught by the Soviets rather than the Americans, because the Amis handed them over to the Free French, who shot them immediately."

"Tell us about Edgard de Boudel."

"In the camp?"

"Yes."

"He was a decorated lieutenant colonel. In the SS, I mean. Easy to be with. Charming, even. Good-looking. Unscathed by the war, you might even say. He was one of those types who looked like he was always going to survive pretty much anything. He spoke good Russian. Edgard was the kind for whom languages are easy. His German was perfect, of course. Even I couldn't have guessed that he was French if I hadn't already known that about him. I think he might have spoken Vietnamese, too. It was his facility with languages that made him especially interesting to the MVD. In the beginning, they made life pretty difficult for him. And, of course, once they had got their hooks into you it was very difficult for any man to resist them. I know that from my own experience with them."

"What specifically did they want him for? Do you know?"

"Well, it wasn't K-5. That's for sure."

"That's the forerunner of the Stasi."

"Yes. I don't know what they had in mind for him. But the next thing I knew, he'd been sent to the Anti-Fa School in Krasnogorsk for reeducation. As you know, I almost ended up there myself. They'd have got me, too, but for the fact that the MVD officer who interrogated me was a man I'd known from before the war. A man named Mielke. Erich Mielke. He was the German political commissar in charge of recruiting us *pleni*s for K-5."

The French asked me some more questions about Edgard de Boudel and then took me back to La Santé. It means "health," but that didn't have much to do with what went on inside the prison. It was called La Santé because of the prison's proximity to a psychiatric hospital, the Sainte-Anne on the rue de la Santé, which was just east of the boulevard Raspail.

In La Santé I kept to myself as much as possible. I didn't see Helmut Knochen, which suited me just fine. I read my newspaper, which reported that things in North Africa were as bad for the French as they had been in Vietnam. In spite of my new friends in the SDECE, this news was not displeasing to me. There were times when I was never very far away from the trenches. Especially given all the rats there were at La Santé. Real rats. They walked along the landings as coolly as if they'd been carrying keys.

Back at the Swimming Pool the next day, the French asked me about Erich Mielke.

"What do you want to know?" I asked, as if unaware of what my audience would best like to hear—or, to be more accurate, what it was best they were told. "It's all ancient history. Surely you don't want me to go over all that."

"Everything you can tell us."

"I can't see how it's at all relevant to my being here in Paris."

"You should allow us to be the judge of that."

I shrugged. "Perhaps if I knew why you were interested in him, I could be more specific. After all, it's not like this is a story that takes only a couple of minutes to tell. Christ, some of this stuff is twenty years old. Or even older."

"We've got plenty of time. Perhaps if you went from the beginning. How you first met and when. That kind of thing."

"You mean the whole novel, with a beginning, a middle, and an end."

"Precisely."

"All right. If you really want to know this stuff. I'll tell you everything."

Of course, I hardly wanted to do that. Hell, no. Not all over again. So I gave them an edited, more entertaining version of what I'd already told the Amis. A French version. A smooth-tongued précis, if you like, that was not spoiled by the inclusion of too many facts and that, like the French themselves, was the result of an exhausted conscience wrestling with simple pragmatism and being very quickly overcome. A story that was the best kind of story being better told than believed.

"The decision was made in the Ministry of the Interior to let Mielke make his escape. Despite the fact that he had participated in the murders of two cops. It came about like this. Department IA had been brought into being to protect the Weimar Republic against conspirators on the left and on the right, and we decided that the best way to do this was to cultivate a few informers on both sides. But on the face of it, that hardly applied to a man like Mielke.

We had arrested him and fully intended to send him to the guillotine. However, the Abwehr—German intelligence—persuaded the ministry that they might turn Mielke into their agent. And this is what happened. We were persuaded to let him escape so that he might become our long-term agent, the Abwehr's Moscow mole. In return, we looked after his family. The Abwehr kept him going all the way through the thirties and the Spanish Civil War. As well as passing us some very important information on Republican troop movements that was extremely helpful to the Condor Legion, he was able to initiate several political purges of some of their best men, on the grounds that they were Trotskyites or anarchists. In that respect, Mielke was doubly useful.

"When the war broke out, the SD and the Abwehr decided to share Mielke. The trouble was, we'd lost him. So Heydrich sent me to France in the summer of 1940 to get him out of Gurs or Le Vernet, which is where we thought he must be. Which is what happened. I got him out of Le Vernet and across the sea to Algeria. From there, German agents managed to facilitate his return to Russia. I was his case officer at the SD for the next three years as he worked his way up through the party hierarchy. I lost contact with him in 1945, at the end of the war. However, he managed to track me down at the same time that he was recruiting German officers for the Stasi, and he helped me to escape back to Germany, where I negotiated a deal with some Amis in the Counterintelligence Corps on behalf of both of us."

"What kind of a deal?"

"Money, of course. Lots of money. After that, I helped handle him in Berlin and Vienna until the CIC came to the conclusion that my SS background made me a possible embarrassment to them. So they assigned Mielke a new controller and got me out of the country on a ratline, via Genoa, to Argentina. And then Cuba. I'd still be in Havana but for American incompetence. Having gone to all that trouble to spirit me out of Germany, they sent me back there.

A case of the left hand not knowing what the right hand is doing. And now here I am with you."

"Is Mielke still working for the Americans?"

"I can't imagine why not. Someone that highly placed? He was the mother lode of all their intelligence on the GDR. But they weren't sharing. Even the GVL had no idea that Mielke was spying for the Amis. Gehlen knew the Amis had a very highly placed agent. When the Amis refused to reveal who this was, Gehlen decided to quit and throw in his lot with the West Germans."

"So why would they risk letting you go to tell us?"

"Well, for one thing, they don't know everything about me and Mielke. There were certain things I've told you that I never told them. But now it hardly seems to matter. Not anymore. I haven't had any contact with Mielke since 1949, when I went to Argentina. Since then, Mielke has become the second or third most powerful man in the GDR, so who would believe me? How could I prove anything of what I've told you? It's just my word, right? Besides, I have other things on my mind. In case you've forgotten, I'm rather more concerned that you believe it wasn't me who shot those prisoners from Gurs on the road to Lourdes in 1940. I don't think it's even crossed their minds that you might be interested in Mielke. As far as they're concerned, you're only interested in settling old scores against people like me. If you'll forgive me for saying so, gentlemen, they think your intelligence is snagged on the fence of Muslim extremism in Algeria and wholly irrelevant in their Cold War against Russian communism. You're a sideshow. Even the British look more relevant to them than you do."

None of this was what the French wanted to hear, of course; but it was what they expected to hear. The French were nothing if not pragmatic; facts were always of lesser importance than experience. It was, of course, the only way the French could live with themselves.

Later on, our conversation returned again to the subject of

Edgard de Boudel, and one of the two SDECE men asked me the same question that Heydrich had posed about Mielke in 1940:

"Do you think you would recognize him again?"

"Edgard de Boudel? I don't know. It's been seven years. Maybe. Why?"

"We want to arrest him and put him on trial."

"In the Cherche-Midi? How many trials have there been in that court? Hundreds, isn't it? How many war criminals and collaborators have you sentenced to death? Let me tell you how many. It was in the newspaper. Six thousand five hundred. Four thousand of those sentences handed down in absentia. Don't you think that's enough? Or do you really mean it to feel like the French Revolution?"

They said nothing while I lit a cigarette.

"Why do you want to put him on trial? For being in the SS? Well, I'm not buying that. France is full of ex-Nazis. Besides, I liked him. I liked him a lot. Why should I betray him? Even if I could."

"Since the death of Stalin last year, your President Adenauer has been negotiating the release of the last German POWs. These last are, perhaps, the worst of the worst—or merely the most important and, in Soviet eyes, the most culpable. Many of these men are wanted for war crimes in the West. Including Edgard de Boudel. We have received information that he plans to make his way back to Germany as part of one of these repatriations from the Soviet Union. From Germany we think he will, eventually, make his way back to France."

"I don't get it," I said. "If he was working for the KGB, why is he coming back as a POW?"

"Because, in his current role, he's outlived his usefulness to them. The only way he can worm his way back into their favor is by doing what they tell him to do. And what they want him to do is pose as someone else. A German. A German who's probably already dead. You said yourself he's a fluent German speaker, that even you couldn't fault his German. Many of these returning POWs are treated as heroes. A returning hero is a good place to begin rebuilding a career in German society. Perhaps in German politics. And then, one day, he'll be useful again."

"But what can I do?"

"You know the man. Who better than you to recognize if someone or something doesn't look quite right?"

"Perhaps." I shook my head. "If you say so."

"All of the returning POWs arriving back in West Germany come through the station in Friedland. The next train is due in four weeks."

"What do you want me to do? Stand at the end of the platform with a bunch of flowers in my hand, like some pathetic widow who doesn't know her old man's never coming home?"

"Not exactly, no. Have you heard of the VdH?"

I shrugged. "Something to do with the German government compensating returning German POWs, yes?"

"It's the Association of Returnees. And that's one of the things it's about, yes. According to the West German POW Compensation Law passed in January of this year, there's a flat rate payable to all POWs of one mark for every day spent in captivity after January first, 1946. And two marks for every day after January first, 1949. But the VdH is also a citizens' association that advertises the advantages of German democracy to former Nazis. It's denazification of Germans, by Germans."

"Your background," said the other Frenchman, "makes you ideally suited to be a part of this association. Not that this would be a problem. The Lower Saxony branch of the VdH is under our control. The chairman and several of his members are in the service of the SDECE. And working for us, it goes without saying you'll be well paid. You're probably even entitled to some of that POW compensation yourself."

"And what's more, we can make all this business with Helmut

Knochen go away." The Insomniac clicked his fingers. "Like that. We'll put you up at a little boardinghouse in Göttingen. You'll like Göttingen. It's a nice town. From there it's a short car ride down to Friedland." He shrugged. "If things work out, we could perhaps make the arrangement more permanent."

I nodded. "Well, it's been a long time since I saw de Boudel. And naturally, I would like to get out of La Santé. Göttingen's nice, as you say. And I do need a job. It all sounds very generous, yes. But there is something else I'd like. There's a woman in Berlin. Perhaps the only person in the whole of Germany who means anything to me. I'd like to go and see her. Make sure she's all right. Give her some money, perhaps."

The Insomniac picked up a pencil and prepared to write. "Name and address?"

"Her name is Elisabeth Dehler. When I was last in Berlin, about five years ago, her address was twenty-eight Motzstrasse, off the Ku-damm."

"You never mentioned her before."

I shrugged.

"What does she do?"

"She was a dressmaker. Still is, for all I know."

"And you and she were—what?"

"We were involved for a while."

"Lovers?"

"Yes, lovers, I suppose."

"We'll check out the address for you. See if she's still at that address. Save you the trouble if she's not."

"Thanks."

He shrugged. "But if she is, we have no objections. It will be difficult. It's always difficult going in and out of Berlin. Still, we'll manage."

"Good. Then we have a deal. If I knew the words, I'd sing 'The Marseillaise.'"

"A signature on a piece of paper will do for now. We're not much for singing here at the Swimming Pool."

"There's one question I have. Everyone calls this place the Swimming Pool. Why?"

The two Frenchmen smiled. One of them stood up and opened a window. "Can't you hear it?" he said after a moment. "Can't you smell it?"

I got up and went to his side and listened carefully. In the distance I could hear what sounded like a school playground.

"You see that turreted building over the wall?" he explained. "That is the largest swimming pool in all of Paris. It was built for the 1924 Olympics. On a day like today, half the children in the city are there. We go there ourselves sometimes when it's quieter."

"Sure," I said. "We had the same thing in the Gestapo. The Landwehr Canal. We never went swimming there ourselves, of course. But we took lots of others there. Communists, mostly. That is, provided they couldn't swim."

28

FRANCE AND GERMANY, 1954

From La Santé I was transferred to the Pension Verdin at 102 avenue Victor Hugo in the suburbs of Sainte-Mandé, which was about a five-minute drive south from the Swimming Pool. It was a quiet, comfortable place with polished parquet floors, tall windows, and a lovely garden, where I sat in the sun awaiting my return to Germany. The pension was a sort of safe house and hotel for members of the SDECE and its agents, and there were several faces I half recognized from my time in the Swimming Pool, but no one bothered me. I was even allowed out—although I was followed at a distance—and spent a day walking northeast along the Seine as far as the Île de la Cité and Notre Dame Cathedral. It was the first time I'd seen Paris without the Wehrmacht everywhere, or without hundreds of signs in German. Bicycles had given way to a great many cars, which did little to make me feel any safer than I'd felt as an enemy soldier in 1940. But a lot of this was just nerves—cement fever after spending the last six months in one prison or another: I couldn't have felt more like a big-house brother if I'd been carrying a ball and chain. Or looked like one. That was why they took me to Galeries Lafayette on boulevard Haussmann to get some new clothes. It would be an exaggeration to say that my new clothes made me feel normal again: Too much water had run off the mountain for that to happen. However, I did feel partly restored. Like an old door with a new lick of paint.

The French had not exaggerated the difficulty of traveling to Berlin. The inner German border between West and East Germany—the Green Border—had been closed since May 1952, with transport links between the two halves of the country mostly severed. The only place where East Germans were able to cross freely into the West was in Berlin itself; and getting in or out of the East was restricted to a few points along a heavily guarded and fortified fence, of which the largest and most frequently used was the Helmstedt-Marienborn crossing at the edge of the Lappwald. First, however, we had to go to Hannover, in the British zone of occupation.

We left the Gare du Nord on the overnight train—me and my two French handlers from the SDECE. They had names now—names and passports—although it seemed unlikely that their names were real, especially as I now had a passport myself—French—in the name of Sébastien Kléber, a traveling salesman from Alsace. The Frenchman with the eyebrows went by the name of Philippe Méntelin; the Insomniac was calling himself Émile Vigée.

We had a sleeping compartment to ourselves, but I was too excited to sleep, and when, nine and a half hours later, the train pulled into Hannover Railway Station, I uttered a quiet little prayer of thanks that I was back in Prussia. The equestrian statue of King Ernst August was still in front of the station, and City Hall with its red roofs and green cupolas looked much the same as I remembered, but elsewhere the city was very different. Adolf Hitler Strasse was now Bahnhofstrasse; Horst Wessel Platz was now Königswerther Platz; and the Opera House was no longer occupying Adolf Hitler Platz but Opern Platz. The Aegidienkirche on the corner of Breite Strasse was a bombed-out ruin, overgrown with ivy and left that way as a memorial to those who had died during the war. Elsewhere, the city was hardly recognizable. One thing hadn't changed, however: It's said that the purest German is spoken in Hannover; and that's certainly what it sounded like to me.

The safe house was in the east of Hannover, in a large wooded area called the Eilenriede on Hindenburg Strasse, close to the zoo. The house was a largish villa in a smallish garden. It had a red mansard roof and an octagonal corner tower with a silver-steel cupola. This tower contained my room, and although my door wasn't locked, it was hard to rid myself of the impression that I was still a prisoner. Especially when I mentioned to Émile Vigée that I'd seen two suspicious-looking men from my Rapunzel-like vantage point.

"Look there," I said, inviting him into my room and over to the window. "On Erwinstrasse, is it?"

He nodded.

"Those two men in the black Citroën," I said. "They've been there for at least an hour. From time to time, one of them gets out, smokes a cigarette, and watches this house. And I'm pretty sure he's armed, too."

"How can you tell from here?"

"It's a warm day, but all three buttons on his suit are done up. And every so often he adjusts something on his breast."

"You have keen eyes, Monsieur Kléber."

Every time Vigée spoke to me now he called me Kléber, or Sébastien, to help me become accustomed to hearing this name.

"I used to be a cop, remember?"

"Nothing to worry about. They're both with us. As a matter of fact, they're going to drive you to Berlin and back here before going on to Göttingen and Friedland. They're both German and they've made the drive many times before, so there shouldn't be a problem. They both work for the VdH here in Hannover. He glanced at his watch. "I invited them both for dinner tonight. To give you a chance to meet them. They're a little early, that's all."

We went to dinner at the nearby Stadthalle, formerly the

Hermann Goering Stadthalle—a very large round building that was a bit like Fat Hermann himself. With its green roof the place was half concert hall and half circus tent, but according to Vigée, there was also a good restaurant.

"Not as good as Paris, of course," he said. "But not bad for Hannover. With quite a reasonable wine list." He shrugged. "I expect that's why Goering liked it, eh?"

As we arrived for dinner, everyone else was leaving to go to the Friday-night concert, and I decided the French had probably timed it that way so we could talk without fear of being overheard. The music helped, of course. It was Mendelssohn's Third Symphony, the *Scottish*.

The two Frenchmen were disappointed with the food, but to me, after months of prison fare, it was delicious. My two fellow Germans had also brought hearty appetites, although little in the way of conversation. They wore gray suits to match their gray skin. Neither was very tall. One of them had bright blond hair that must have come out of a bottle; the other might have come out of a bottle himself, he drank so much, although it appeared not to affect him at all. The blonder man was called Werner Grottsch; the other called himself Klaus Wenger. Neither seemed inclined to try to find out anything about me. Perhaps they were already well-informed on that subject by Vigée, but I thought it more likely that they knew better than to ask, and if so, it was a compliment I repaid by making no inquiries of them.

Eventually, Vigée brought the conversation around to the true purpose of our acquaintance.

"Sébastien's not crossed the border before," he said. "At least not since the implementation of the DDR's special regime. Werner, perhaps you'd like to put him in the picture about what will happen tomorrow. You'll be in a car with French diplomatic number plates. Even so, it's always useful to know how to behave. What to expect."

Grottsch nodded politely, extinguished his cigarette, leaned forward, and clasped his hands, as if he were going to lead us in prayer.

"It's called the special regime because the measures are intended to keep out spies, diversionists, terrorists, and smugglers. In other words, people like us." He smiled at his own little joke. "We'll be crossing at Checkpoint Alpha. At Helmstedt. It's the largest and busiest crossing point because it allows for the shortest land route between West Germany and West Berlin. It's one hundred and eighty-five kilometers through East Germany to Berlin. The road runs through a fenced corridor that's heavily guarded. A bit like No Man's Land, if you remember that, and almost as dangerous, so if we have a breakdown, on no account get out of the car. We wait for assistance, no matter how long that takes. If you get out, you risk being shot, and people do get shot. The border police—the Grepos—are particularly trigger-happy. Do I make myself clear?"

"Abundantly clear, Herr Grottsch. Thank you."

"Good." Grottsch cocked an ear at the air and nodded his appreciation. "What a pleasure, to listen to Mendelssohn again. And not to be worried that one was being unpatriotic."

"He was German, wasn't he?" I said. "From Hamburg."

"No, no," said Grottsch. "Mendelssohn was a Jew."

Wenger nodded and lit a cigarette. "That's right," he said. "He was. A Jew from Leipzig."

"Of course," Grottsch went on, "going in is one thing. Getting out is quite another. Inspection pits, mirrors, there's even a mortuary where they can look inside coffins to check if an occupant who wanted to be buried in West Germany is really dead. Even Mendelssohn couldn't leave these days without the proper paperwork. And he's been dead for a hundred years."

"Your lady friend," said Wenger. "Fräulein Dehler. You'll be pleased to know she's still at the same address. But she's no longer a dressmaker. She now runs a nightclub called The Queen on Auguste-Viktoria Strasse."

"A straight kind of place?"

"As straight as they go."

Helmstedt was an attractive little medieval town of brightly colored towers and unusual churches. The town hall looked like an enormous organ from a cathedral that, typically, no longer existed. The redbrick university building resembled a military barracks. I might have seen more of it, but my two companions were keen to get through Checkpoint Alpha so that we might reach Berlin before dark. And I could hardly fault them for that. From Marienborn, Berlin was a three-hour drive through an inhospitable landscape of barbed wire and, on the other side of the fence, men with dogs, and mines. But nothing compared with the inhospitable faces of the Grepos at Checkpoint Alpha. In their jackboots, cross-belts, and long leather coats, the border police reminded me strongly of the SS, and the long wooden huts from which they emerged were like something from a concentration camp. The swastikas were gone, replaced by the red stars and the hammer and sickle, but everything else felt the same. Except for one thing: Nazism had never looked quite so permanent as this. Or thorough.

Grottsch and Wenger shared the driving, which was straightforward enough; if you drive east on the A2 for long enough, you arrive in Berlin. But they remained wary of asking questions, as if the French had warned them against the answers. So when we spoke at all, it was concerning nothing of any real consequence: the weather, the scenery, the Citroën versus the Mercedes, life in the DDR, and, as we got nearer our destination, the Four Powers and their continuing occupation of the former German capital, which, we all agreed, none of us liked. It went without question that we thought the Russians the worst of all, but we spent at least an hour arguing which of the other three was going to take the silver medal. It seemed my two colleagues were of the opinion that the British had the same faults as the Americans—arrogance and ignorance—without any of their virtues—money—that made their arrogance and ignorance easier to ignore. The French, we decided, were simply the French: not to be taken seriously and, therefore, beneath any real contempt. Personally, I had my doubts about the British; and if I had any lingering doubts about my silver-plated dislike of the Americans, they were soon to be dispelled. Just southwest of Berlin, at the Dreilinden border crossing into the city in Zehlendorf, we were obliged to stop to present our papers again, and entering the American zone we parked our car and went into a shop to buy some cigarettes. I was used to seeing, and smoking, mostly American brands. It was all the other American brands in the shop that brought me up short: Chex breakfast cereal, Rexall toothpaste, Sanka caffeine-free coffee, Ballantine beer, Old Sunnybrook Kentucky whiskey, Dash dog food, Jujyfruits, Appian Way pizza mix, Pream, Nescafé, and 7Up. I might have been back in Berlin, but not so as you would have noticed.

We drove into the French sector, to a safe house on Bernauer Strasse that overlooked the Russian sector, which is to say the French controlled the north sidewalk and the Russians controlled the south. It hardly mattered. Even if it didn't look like the Berlin I remembered—on the Soviet side of the street the bombed-out buildings remained in an appalling state of disrepair—it still felt and smelled much the same: cynical, mongrel—perhaps more mongrel than ever. In my head and heart, an orchestra the size of a division was playing "Berliner Luft" and I was clapping and whistling in all the right places for a true citizen. In Berlin it wasn't about being German—Hitler and Goebbels never understood that—it was being a Berliner first and telling anyone who wanted to change that to go to hell. One day we would surely be rid of the rest of them, too. The Ivans, the Tommies, the Franzis, and yes, even the Amis. Friends are always harder to get rid of than enemies; especially when they believe they're good friends.

The following day, the two Germans drove me to Motzstrasse in the American sector.

We drew up outside number twenty-eight. The building was in a much better state of repair than it had been the last time I was there. For one thing, it had been painted canary yellow; there were several window boxes filled with geraniums; and, in front of the heavy oak door, someone had planted a thriving lime tree. The whole area looked like it was doing well. Across the street was an expensive porcelain shop, and below Elisabeth's first-floor apartment was an equally pricey restaurant called Kottler's, where my two escorts elected to wait for me.

The street door was open. I went upstairs and rang the bell and listened. Inside Elisabeth's apartment I could hear music, and then it stopped. A moment later, the door opened and she was standing in front of me. Five years older and at least seven kilos heavier. Before she'd been a brunette. Now she was a blonde. The weight suited her more than the hair color, which didn't really match her widening brown eyes, but I hardly minded that, as it was six months since I'd even spoken to a woman, let alone one in her dressing gown. Just seeing Elisabeth like that reminded me of a more innocent time before the war, when sex still seemed like a practical proposition.

Her jaw dropped and she blinked deliberately, as if she really didn't believe her own eyes.

"Oh, my God, it's you," she said. "I was afraid you were dead."

"I was. Eternal life has its advantages, but it's amazing how quickly you get bored. So here I am again. Back in the city of mahogany and marijuana."

"Come in, come in." She vacuumed me inside, closed the door, and hugged me fondly. "I don't have any marijuana," she said, "but I have good coffee. Or something stronger."

"Coffee will be fine." I followed her along a corridor and into the kitchen. "I like what you've done with the place. You've put furniture in it. The last time I was here, I think you'd sold everything. To the Amis."

"Not everything." Elisabeth smiled. "I never sold that. Lots did, mind. But not me." She set about making the coffee and then said: "How long has it been?"

"Since I was last here? Six or seven years."

"It seems longer. Where have you been? What were you doing?"

"None of that matters now. The past. Right now, the only thing that matters is right now. Everything else is irrelevant. Or at least that's how it seems to me."

"You really were dead, weren't you?"

"Mmm hmm."

She made coffee and led the way into a small but comfortable sitting room. The furniture was solid but unremarkable. Outside, the copper-colored leaves of the linden tree helped to shade the window from the bright autumn sun. I felt quite at home. As much at home as I was likely to feel anywhere.

"No sewing machine," I observed.

"There's not much call for expensive tailoring anymore," she said. "Not in Berlin, anyway. Not since the war. Who can afford such things? These days I run a club called The Queen. On Auguste-Viktoria Platz. Number seventy-six. Drop by sometime. Not today, of course. We're closed on Sundays. Which is why I'm here."

"Is it a Sunday? I don't know."

"Dead and just coming back to life. That's hardly respectable. But the club is. Probably too respectable for a man like you, but that's what the customers want nowadays. No one wants the old Berlin anymore. With the sex clubs and the whores."

"No one?"

"All right. The Americans don't seem to want them. At least not officially."

"You surprise me. In Cuba, they couldn't get enough of the sex clubs. Every night there was a long line outside the most notorious club of all. The Shanghai."

"I don't know about Cuba. But here we get some very Lutheran Americans. Well, this is Germany, after all. It's as if they think the Russians might use any sign of depravity as an excuse to invade West Berlin. They seem to want to make the Cold War as cold as possible for everyone involved. Did you know that you can get yourself arrested for nude sunbathing in the parks?"

"At my age, that's hardly a concern." I sipped her coffee and nodded my appreciation.

Elisabeth lit a cigarette. "So it was you. The person who sent me that money from Cuba. I thought it must be."

"At the time, I had more than enough to spare."

"And now?"

"I'm sorting things out."

"You don't look like someone who's just back from the sun."

"Like I said. At my age. I was never one for lying around in the sun."

"Me, I love it. Whenever I can. After all, the winters we get. What sort of things are you sorting out?"

"The Berlin kind."

"Hmm. That sounds suspicious. This used to be a city of whores. And you don't look like a whore. Now it's a city of spies. So—" She shrugged and sipped her coffee.

"I expect that's why they don't like joy ladies and sex clubs. Because they want their spies honest. And as for nude sunbathing, well, it's difficult being something you're not when you've got your clothes off."

"I'll bear that in mind. As a matter of fact, we get lots of spies in the club. American spies."

"How can you tell?"

"They're the ones not wearing uniforms."

She was joking, of course. But that didn't mean it wasn't true.

I glanced over at a radiogram the size of a drinks cabinet from which a low murmur was emanating. "What are we almost listening to?"

"RIAS," she said.

"I don't know that station. I don't know any of the Berlin stations."

"It stands for 'Radio in the American Sector.'" She said it in English. Good English, too. "I always listen to RIAS on a Sunday morning. To help my English. No, to improve my English."

I pulled a face. On the coffee table was a copy of *Die Neue Zeitung*. "American radio. American newspapers. Sometimes I think we lost a lot more than just a war."

"They're not so bad. Who's paying your rent?"

"The VdH."

"Of course. You were a prisoner yourself, weren't you?"

I nodded.

"A couple of years ago, I went to one of those exhibitions put on by the VdH," she said. "On the POW experience. They had reconstructed a Soviet POW camp, complete with a wooden watchtower and a four-meter-high barbed-wire fence."

"Was there a gift shop?"

"No. Just a newspaper."

"*Der Heimkehrer.*"

"Yes."

"It's a rag. Among other things, the VdH leadership believes that a free people cannot renounce in principle the protection of a new German army."

"But you don't believe that?"

I shook my head. "It's not that I don't think military service is a good idea. In principle." I lit a cigarette. "It's just that I don't trust our Western allies not to use us as cannon fodder in a new war that some lunatic Confederate American general thinks he can safely fight on German soil. Which is to say, a long way from America. But which in reality no one can win. Not us. Not them."

"Better Red than dead, huh?"

"I don't think the Reds want a war any more than we do. It's only the men who fought the last war, not to mention the one before that, who can really know how many human lives were wasted. And how many comrades were sacrificed needlessly. People used to talk about the phony war. Remember that? In 1939. But if you ask me, this war, this Cold War, that's the phoniest war of the lot. Something dreamed up by the intelligence people to scare us and keep us all in line."

"There's a waiter at the club," she said, "who'd disagree with you. He's a former POW, too. He came home last year, still a rabid Nazi. Hates the Bolsheviks." She smiled wryly. "I'm none too fond of them myself, of course. Well, you remember what it was like when the Red Army turned up in Berlin with a hard-on for German women." She paused for a moment. "I had a baby. Did I ever tell you that?"

"No."

"Well, he—the baby—died, so it didn't seem important, I guess. He got influenza meningitis, and the penicillin they used to treat it turned out to be fake. That was—God, February 1946. They got the men who sold the stuff, I'm happy to say. Not that it really matters. Made in France, it was. Glucose and face powder dissolved in genuine penicillin vials. Of course, by the time anyone knew it was fake it was too late." She shook her head. "It's hard to remember what it was like back then. People would do or sell anything to make money."

"I'm sorry."

"Don't be, darling. It was a long time ago. Besides, even after I had it, the baby, I was never really sure I wanted it."

"Under the circumstances, that's hardly surprising," I said. "You never told me this before."

"Well, you had your own problems, didn't you?" She shrugged. "And that, of course, is the real reason I never sold my body to the Amis, of course. Gang rape. It tends to take away your sexual appetite for quite a while. By the time I did start feeling inclined that way again, it was too late. I was on the shelf, more or less."

"Nonsense."

"Too late to find a husband, anyway. German men are still in rather short supply, in case you hadn't noticed. Most of the good ones were in Soviet POW camps. Or Cuba."

"I'm sure that's not true. You're a fine-looking woman, Elisabeth."

She took my hand and squeezed.

"Do you really think so, Bernie?"

"Of course I do."

"Oh, there have been men, all right. I'm not completely clapped out, it's true. But it's not like it used to be. Nothing ever is, of course. But . . . There was an American who worked for the U.S. State Department at HICOG, in the Headquarters Compound on Saargemünder Strasse. But he went home to his wife and children in Wichita. And there was a guy, a sergeant, who ran Club 48—that's the U.S. Army's NCO club. It was him who helped me to get the job at The Queen. Before he went home, too. That was six months ago. My life." She shrugged. "It's not exactly *Effi Briest*, is it. Oh, I do okay at the club. Pays well. The customers behave. Good tippers, I'll say that for the Amis. At least they show their appreciation. Not like the British. Worst tippers in the world. Hell, even the French tip better than the British. You wouldn't think they'd won the war, they're so tight with their money. They say that even the mousetraps are empty in the British sector. I tell you, this fellow Nasser, I'm on his side. And when Uruguay beat England, I think I was even more happy than I was when West Germany won the actual trophy."

"Talking of West Germany, Elisabeth, do you go there ever?"

"No. I'd have to cross the Green Border. And I don't like to do that. I did it once. I felt like a criminal in my own country."

"And East Berlin. Do you ever go there?"

"Sometimes. But there's less and less cause to go. There's not much there for those of us who live in West Berlin. Just before Jimmy—my American sergeant—went back to America, we took a trip around old Berlin. He wanted to buy a camera, and you can still get a good one for not much money in East Berlin. We got a camera, too, but not in a shop. On the black market. The only shop we visited, a department store the communists call H.O., had very little in it. And as soon as I saw it, I realized why so many East Germans turned up here last year to get a food parcel. And why quite a few of them never went back."

"But you wouldn't say it was dangerous."

"For someone like me? No. You read about the odd person getting snatched by the Soviets. Injected with something and then bundled into a car. Well, I suppose if you were important, that might happen. But then, you wouldn't go there in the first place if you were someone like that, would you? All the same, I wouldn't have thought you would want to go across to the Russian sector. You having escaped from a POW camp and all."

"Look, Elisabeth, there's nobody left in Berlin I can really trust. If it comes to that, there's no one left I even know. And I need a favor. If there was anyone else I could ask, I would."

"Go ahead and ask."

I handed her an envelope. "I was hoping I could ask you to deliver this. I'm afraid I don't know the correct address, and I thought—well, I thought you might help. For old times' sake."

She looked at the name on the envelope and was silent for a moment.

"You don't have to," I said. "But it would help me a lot."

"Of course I'll do it. Without you, without that money you sent, I don't know how I'd ever have hung on to this place. Really I don't."

I finished my coffee and then my cigarette. I must have looked as if I was about to leave, because she said, "Will I see you again?"

"Yes. Only, I'm not sure when. I'm not living in Berlin at the moment. For the foreseeable future, I'll be staying in Göttingen." She looked puzzled at that. So I explained: "With the VdH? Göttingen is near the Friedland Transit Camp for returning POWs. They're there for only a couple of weeks, during which time they receive food, clothing, and medical aid. They're also given army-discharge certificates, which they need to obtain a residency permit, a food-ration card, and a travel warrant to get home."

"Poor devils," she said. "How bad was it, really?"

"I'm not about to sit here and tell any woman from Berlin about suffering," I said. "But maybe, because of it, we'll know how and where to find each other."

"I'd like that."

"Do you have a telephone?"

"Not here. If I want to make a call, I always use the telephone at the club. If you ever need to get in contact with me, that's the best place to do it. If I'm not there, they'll take a message." She found a pencil and paper and scribbled down the number: *24-38-93.*

I put the number in my empty wallet.

"Or you could write to me here, of course. You should have written before to let me know you were coming. I'd have prepared something. A cake. I wouldn't have been in my dressing gown. And you should have sent me an address in Cuba. So that I could have written back to thank you."

"That might have been a little difficult," I confessed. "I was living there under a false name."

"Oh," she said, as if such an idea had never occurred to her. "You're not in any trouble, are you, Bernie?"

"Trouble?" I smiled ruefully. "Life is trouble. Only the naïve and the young imagine that it's anything else. It's only trouble that finds out if we're up to the task of staying alive."

"Because if you are in trouble . . . ,"

"I hate to ask you another favor. . . ."

She took my hand and kissed the fingers, one by one. "When are you going to get it through your thick Prussian head," she said. "I'll help you in any way I can."

"All right." I thought for a moment and then, taking her pencil and paper, I started to write. "When you get to the club, I want you to make a call to this number in Munich. Ask for a Mr. Kramden. If Mr. Kramden isn't there, tell whoever it is that you will call back in two hours. Don't leave your name and number, just tell them that you want to leave a message from Carlos. When you get to speak to Kramden, tell him I'll be staying with my uncle François in Göttingen for the next few weeks at the Pension Esebeck, until I've met Monsieur Voltaire off the train from the Cherry Orchard. Tell Mr. Kramden that if he and his friends need to contact me I'll be going to the St. Jacobi Church each day I'm in Göttingen, at around six or seven o'clock in the evening, and to look for a message under the front pew."

She looked over my notes. "I can do that." She nodded firmly. "Göttingen's quaint. Pretty. What Germany used to look like. I've often thought it would be nice to live there."

I shook my head. "You and me, Elisabeth. We're Berliners. Hardly cut out for fairy-tale living."

"I suppose you're right. What will you do after Göttingen?"

"I don't know, Elisabeth."

"It seems to me," she said, "that if there's no one else in Berlin you know, or who you can trust, then you should think yourself free to come and live here. Like you did before. Remember?"

"Why else do you think I sent you that money from Cuba? I hadn't forgotten. Lately, I've had to do quite a bit of remembering one way or another. Telling my story to—well, it doesn't matter who. A lot of stuff I'd rather forget. But I don't forget that. You can depend on it. I never forgot about you."

Of course, not everything had been told back at Landsberg.

A man should keep some secrets, after all, especially when he's talking to the CIA.

Special Agents Scheuer and Frei might have opened a file in Elisabeth Dehler's name if I'd told them every little detail about what happened on the train from the *pleni* camp in Johannesgeorgenstadt to Dresden, and then Berlin, in 1946.

I hadn't wanted them bothering her, so I hadn't mentioned the fact that the address on the envelope containing the several hundred dollars Mielke had given me was Elisabeth's.

29

GERMANY, 1946

Instead of pocketing this money, I'd resolved to deliver it to her myself—as the MVD assassin would have done if I hadn't killed him first. Besides, I needed somewhere to stay, and where better to stay than with a former lover? So, when I got off the train from Dresden in the no-less-depressing ruin of Anhalter Station in Berlin, I'd quickly boarded a westbound tram and headed straight for the Kurfürstendamm.

From there I walked south, convinced that at least one of Hitler's predictions had come true. In the early days of his success, he had told us that "in five years you will not recognize Germany," and this was certainly true. Kurfürstendamm, formerly one of Berlin's most prosperous streets, was now little more than a series of ruins. Even for me, a former policeman, it was hard to find one's way around. Once, forgetting the uniform I was wearing, I asked a woman for directions and she hurried away without reply, as if I'd been the carrier of plague. Later on, when I heard about what the Red Army had done to the women of Berlin, I wondered why she'd not picked up a rock and thrown it at me.

Motzstrasse was not as badly damaged as some. Even so, it

was hard to imagine anyone safely living there. One decent earth-mover could probably have leveled the entire street. It was like walking through a scene from the apocalypse. Piles of rubble. Buttressed façades. Moon-sized craters. The prevailing smell of sewage. The road underfoot as uncertain as a mountain path. Burned-out armored vehicles. The occasional grave.

The window on the landing in front of Elisabeth's apartment was gone and boarded over, but the weather-beaten door looked secure enough. I knocked at it for several minutes until a voice shouted down the stairs and told me that Elisabeth was out until five. I glanced at the dead major's watch and realized I needed to kill some time without drawing too much attention to myself. It wasn't that an MVD officer was unusual in the American sector, but I thought it best to avoid contact with anyone official, who might have asked what I was doing.

I walked until I found a church I almost recognized, on Kieler Strasse, although given the state of Kieler Strasse it might just as easily have been Düppelstrasse. The church was Catholic and strangely tall and angular, like a castle on a mountaintop. Inside there was a fine mosaic basilica that had escaped the bombs. I sat down and closed my eyes, not from reverence but sheer fatigue. But this was hardly the quiet sanctuary I had expected. Every few minutes an American serviceman would come in with loud, polished shoes, genuflect to the altar, and then wait patiently on a pew near the confessional. Business was brisk. After the day I'd had, I might have confessed myself, but I wasn't feeling particularly sorry about that. I'd been wanting to kill a Russian—any Russian—ever since the Battle of Königsberg. I told Him that myself. I didn't need a priest to come between us in what was, by now, an old argument.

I stayed there for a long time. Long enough to make peace with myself, if not God, and when I left the Rosary Church—for that was its name—I put a few of the MVD major's coins into a collection box, for his sins, if not mine. Then I walked north again. And this time Elisabeth was at home, although she regarded my uniform with horror.

"What the hell are you doing here dressed like that?" she demanded.

"Ask me in and I'll explain. Believe me, it's not at all what it looks like."

"It better not be, or you can be on your way again. I don't care who you are."

I entered her apartment, and it was immediately clear from the bed and the gas ring that she was living in just the one room. Seeing my eyebrows flex their surprise, she said, "It's easier to heat like this."

I dropped Major Weltz's bag onto the floor and took the envelope of money from inside my *gimnasterka* tunic and handed it over. Now it was Elisabeth's turn to exercise her eyebrows. She fanned herself with several hundred American dollars and then read Mielke's note, which made everything clear.

"Did you read this?"

"Of course."

"So where's the Russian who was supposed to give me this?"

"Dead. This is his uniform I'm wearing." I thought it best to keep things as simple as possible.

"Why didn't you keep this for yourself?"

"Oh, I would have," I said, "if it had been anyone else's name on that envelope. After all, it's not like we're strangers."

"No," she said. "All the same, it's been a long time. I thought you must be dead."

"Why not? Everyone else is." I told her, as briefly as possible, that I'd been in a Soviet POW camp and that I'd escaped. "I was supposed to be on my way to Berlin and then to the Anti-Fascist School near Moscow. All arranged by our mutual friend, of course. But I think he figured I knew too much about his past and decided the safer thing was to have me eliminated. So here I am. I thought that the woman named on that envelope might be prepared to overlook the fact that I left her for another woman and let me lie low for a couple of days. Especcially when she saw those dollars."

She nodded thoughtfully. "How is Kirsten?"

"I don't know. I haven't seen or heard from Frau Gunther since Christmas 1944. Earlier on today, I took a walk down my old street and found it isn't there anymore."

"I guess if it had been, then you wouldn't be here now and I wouldn't have this."

"Anything's possible."

"Well, that's honest, anyway." She thought for a moment. "People who were bombed out usually leave a little red card on the ruins, with some sort of address, in case a loved one turns up."

"Well, maybe that's it. Loved one. Kirsten never was what you'd call loving. Unless you mean herself, of course. She always loved herself." I shook my head. "There wasn't any little red card. I looked."

"There are other ways of contacting relatives," said Elisabeth.

"Not looking like this there aren't. It's only a matter of time before I'm picked up. And shot. Or sent back to the POW camp, which would be worse."

"It's true. Maybe it's the uniform, but you don't look so good. I've seen healthier skeletons." She shrugged. "Very well. You can stay here. The first time you try any funny stuff, you're on your toes. Meanwhile, I'll see what I can find out about Kirsten."

"Thanks. Look, I have a little money of my own. Perhaps you could find or even buy me some clothes, too."

She nodded. "I'll go to the Reichstag first thing in the morning."

"The Reichstag? I was thinking of something a little less formal, perhaps."

"That's where the black market is," she said. "The biggest in the city. Believe me, there's nothing you can't get there. From a pair of nylons to a fake denazification certificate. Perhaps I can get you one of those, too. Of course, it'll mean I'm late for work."

"Tailoring?"

She shook her head grimly. "I'm a servant, Bernie," she said. "Like nearly everyone left alive in Berlin. I'm the housekeeper for a family of American diplomats in Zehlendorf. Hey, perhaps I can find you a job, too. They need a gardener. I can go into the labor office at McNair on my way back from work tomorrow."

"McNair?"

"McNair Barracks. Just about everything to do with the U.S. Army in Berlin takes place at McNair."

"Thanks," I said, "but if you don't mind, I'd rather not have a proper job at this moment. I've spent the last eighteen months working harder than a donkey with three masters. If I never see another pick and shovel again, it will be too soon."

"Rough, huh?"

"Only by the standards of a Russian serf. Now that I've lived and almost died in the Soviet Union, it's easy to see where they learn their manners. And where they find their sunny outlook on life. There's not an Ivan I met who could ever be mistaken for an optimist." I shrugged. "Still, our mutual friend seems to be well in with them." I nodded at the envelope she was still holding. "Erich."

"You have no idea how much I need this money."

"Presumably he did, though. I wonder why he didn't give it to you himself."

"He has his reasons, I suppose. Erich doesn't forget his friends."

"I couldn't argue with that, Elisabeth."

"Did he really try to have you killed?"

"Only a bit."

She shook her head. "He was a hothead when he was younger, it's true. But he never struck me as a cold-blooded killer. Those two cops. I never believed he did that, you know. And I can't believe he ordered someone to murder you."

"The two Germans I was traveling with aren't here to tell you you're wrong, Elisabeth. They weren't as lucky as me."

"You mean they're dead."

"Right now that's my working definition of unlucky." I shrugged. "I don't know. Probably it always was."

GERMANY, 1954

On Monday morning, we drove out of East Germany and back to Hannover, where I spent another night in the safe house. And early the next day we drove south to Göttingen and checked into an old pension overlooking the canal on Reitstallstrasse. The pension was damp, with hard wooden floors, even harder furniture, high ceilings, and dusty brass chandeliers; and about as homely as Cologne Cathedral. But from there it was only a short walk to the VdH office in a half-timbered building on Judenstrasse that looked like it was home to a family of three bears. Everywhere in Göttingen was a bit like that, and quite a few of the people, too. The director of the local VdH, Herr Dr. Winkel, was a mild, bespectacled type who might once have been the court librarian to some ancient king of Saxony. And he informed me what we already knew, that a train carrying a thousand German *pleni*s was due in Friedland the following week. For form's sake we decided—I, Grottsch, and Wenger—to pay a visit to the refugee camp at Friedland.

Previously a research farm owned by Göttingen University, the Friedland Camp was in the British zone and composed of a series of what were called Nissen huts. If Nissen was a synonym of "grim

and inhospitable," then these half-cylindrical corrugated-iron struc-
tures were well named. The camp was a miserable-looking place,
especially in the rain, an impression that was underscored by the
muddy roads and the goose-shit green that everything was painted.
And it was all too easy to give credence to the rumor that the Friedland Refugee Camp had been the location for anthrax experiments
conducted by Nazi scientists during the war. As a reintroduction to
homeland, freedom, and all things wholesomely German, the camp
left a great deal to be desired and, in my expert opinion, was almost
as bad as any of the labor camps that these German POWs had
left behind. I might have succeeded in feeling sorry for these men
had it not been for the fact that I was rather more concerned for
my own welfare, as the prospect of mixing with a large number of
*pleni*s was not without its hazards. Even after an interval of six or
seven years, it was possible I might be recognized and denounced as
some sort of "comrade-killer," a renegade or a collaborator. After
all, as far as anyone back at the camp in Johannesgeorgenstadt
was concerned, I had sold out to the Reds and gone to Russia for
anti-fascist training at Krasnogorsk. And I was reminded of the
precariousness of my position when I asked one of the Friedland
camp police why they were needed at all.

"Surely," I said, "Germans who have come back home know
how to behave themselves."

"That's just the point," said the policeman. "They're not back
home, are they? At least not *at* home. Some of them get a bit pissed
off when they find out they're going to be here, sometimes for as
long as six to eight weeks. But it can take that long to get them
sorted out with everything they're going to need for life in the new
republic. Then there are the prisoners intent on settling old scores
with each other. Men who have denounced other men to the Ivans.
Informers. That kind of thing. Deprivation of liberty, we call that
kind of behavior if it leads to someone getting more ill-treatment
from the Ivans, and we charge them under section 239 of the

German Criminal Code. At the present moment, there are over two hundred pending cases involving ex-POWs. Of course, that's just the ones we find out about, and just as often someone in the camp turns up dead, his throat cut, and no one saw or heard a thing. That's not at all uncommon, sir. In this camp, we reckon on as many as one murder a week."

Of course, I hardly wanted to inform the French Intelligence Service of my own fears. I had no appetite for an early return to La Santé, or indeed any other of the five prisons I'd been in since leaving Havana. And I was resigned to hoping that, come what may, the Franzis would protect me just as long as they thought I was their best chance of identifying and arresting Edgard de Boudel.

The fact that I had never seen or even heard of someone called Edgard de Boudel was neither here nor there. I was doing what I had been told to do by the Americans in Landsberg. And when I returned to my room at the Pension Esebeck in Göttingen, I wrote a note to my CIA handlers describing the full extent of my progress: how the French had listened to me paint a picture of de Boudel at the same time I had also been painting another picture, of Erich Mielke; and that they appeared to accept everything I had told them about Mielke—all of which was false—because of everything I had told them about Edgard de Boudel, which was true. This operation was what Scheuer called "the beautiful twin." The French—and, more important, the Soviet agent whom the Americans knew to be at the heart of the SDECE in Paris—would, it was supposed, be more inclined to believe my lies and misrepresentations about Mielke if everything they were told about de Boudel coincided with what they knew about him, or strongly suspected. And the icing on this rich cake was a tip-off (supplied to them by the British, who, of course, had received it from the Americans) that Edgard de Boudel was arriving back in Germany as a returning POW, having served out his usefulness to the Russians in Indochina, where, as a political commissar, he had assisted the Viet Minh in the interrogation and torture of many captured French soldiers, most of whom still remained, until the Geneva negotiations were complete, prisoners of war in Indochina. All I had to do was identify de Boudel and the French would, it was supposed, treat me and my information about Mielke as gold-plated; and to this end, before my "deportation" from Landsberg to Paris, I had carefully studied the only known photographs of de Boudel. It was hoped that these two pictures, along with my own familiarity with the life of a German POW— not to mention my background as a Kripo detective—would help me spot him for the French, who forever thereafter would be in thrall to me as an intelligence source. Because Edgard de Boudel was one of the most wanted men in France.

Naturally, I was a little concerned about what might happen to me if I failed to identify de Boudel, so I wrote about that, too, mentioning my continuing concern that he might have changed more than just his name and identity if, as the Americans believed, the Russians were intent on infiltrating him back into West German society in the hope of reactivating him as their agent at some later date. I had little or no chance of success if de Boudel had undergone plastic surgery. I also mentioned what by then would have been obvious: that I was being watched closely.

When I finished writing, I went into the sitting room to speak to Vigée, who was the French officer in charge of the SDECE's Göttingen operation.

"If you please," I said, "I'd like to go to church."

"You didn't say you were religious," he said.

"Did I need to?" I shrugged. "Look, it's not mass, or even confession. I just want to go and sit in church for a while and pray."

"What are you? Catholic? Protestant? What?"

"Lutheran Protestant," I said. "Oh yes, and I'd like to buy some chewing gum. To stop me from smoking so much."

"Here," he said, and handed me a packet of Hollywood. "I have the same problem."

I put one of the green chlorophyllic sticks in my mouth.

"Is there a Lutheran church near here?" he asked.

"This is Göttingen," I said. "There are churches everywhere."

St. Jacobi was a strange-looking church. Eccentric, even. The body of the building was ordinary enough, made of a handsome pinkish stone with darker pink perpendiculars. But the steeple, the tallest in Göttingen, was anything but ordinary. It was as if the lid of a pink toy box had burst open to permit the egress of a green object on top of a giant gray spring. As if some lazy Jack had tossed a handful of magic beans onto the floor of the church and these had grown so quickly that the stalk had forced its way through the simple church roof. As a metaphor of Nazism, it was perhaps unsurpassed in the whole of Germany.

The candy-striped interior was no less like a fairy tale. As soon as you saw the pillars you wanted to lick them, or to break off a piece of the medieval altar triptych and eat it, like sugarloaf.

I sat down in the front pew and bowed my head to the amnesiac gods of Germany and pretended to pray, because I'd prayed before and knew exactly what to expect of it.

After a while I glanced around, and observing that Vigée was occupied in the admiration of the church, I fixed the note for my CIA handlers underneath the pew with my Hollywood gum. Then I stood up and walked slowly to the door. I waited patiently for Vigée to follow, and then we went outside into the Rumpelstiltskin streets.

GERMANY, 1954

Things were quiet at the Pension Esebeck, and there was little to do except eat and read the newspapers. But *Die Welt* was the only paper I was keen to read. I was especially interested in the small ads at the back, and on my second morning in Göttingen I found the message for Field Gray that I had been waiting for. It was some verses from the Gospel according to Saint Luke, 1:44, 49; 2:3; 6:1; 1:40; 1:37; and 1:74.

I took the Bible from the shelf in the sitting room, and went to my own room to reconstruct the message. It read as follows:

For lo, as soon as the voice of Thy salutation sounded in my ears, the babe leaped in my womb for joy.

For He that is mighty hath done to me great things; and holy is His name.

And all went to be taxed, every one into his own city.

And it came to pass on the second Sabbath after the first, that he went through the cornfields; and His disciples plucked the ears of corn, rubbing them in their hands, and did eat.

And entered into the house of Zacharias, and saluted Elisabeth.

For with God nothing shall be impossible.

That He would grant unto us, that we being delivered out of the hand of our enemies might serve Him without fear.

Having burned the note I'd made of the message, I went to look for Vigée and found the Frenchman in a little walled garden overlooking the canal. As usual, he looked as if he hadn't slept; his eyes were half closed against the smoke from his cigarette, and there was a little cup of coffee in the palm of his hand, like a coin. He regarded me with his usual indifferent expression, but, as before, when he spoke it was frequently with the added emphasis of a firm nod or a quick shake of the head.

"You made your peace with God, yes?" His German was halting but grammatical.

"I needed some time to reflect," I said. "On something that happened in Berlin. On Sunday."

"With Elisabeth, yes?"

"She wants to get married," I said. "To me."

He shrugged. "Congratulations, Sébastien."

"Soon."

"How soon?"

"She's waited five years for me, Émile. And now that I've seen her again . . . well, she doesn't propose to wait any longer. In short, she gave me an ultimatum. That she would forget all about me unless I married her before the weekend."

"Impossible," said Vigée.

"That's what I said, Émile. However, she means it. I'm certain of it. I never knew this woman to say anything she didn't mean." I took one of his offered cigarettes.

"That's hardly civilized," he said.

"That's women," I said. "And it's me, too. Up until now,

everything in the world I ever wanted was never quite as good as I thought it would be. But I've a strong feeling that Elisabeth's different. In fact, I know she is."

Vigée picked a piece of tobacco off his tongue and for a moment regarded it critically, as if it might have been the answer to all our problems.

"I was thinking, Émile. The POW train won't be here until next Tuesday night. If I could spend Sunday with Elisabeth, in Berlin . . . Just a few hours."

Vigée put down his coffee cup and started to shake his head.

"No, please listen," I said. "If I could spend a few hours with her, I'm sure I could persuade her to wait. Especially if I arrived with a few presents. A ring, perhaps. Nothing expensive. Just a token of my feelings for her."

He was still shaking his head.

"Oh, come on, Émile, you know what women are like. Look, there's a shop full of inexpensive jewelry on the corner of Speck-strasse. If you could advance me a few marks—enough to buy a ring—then I'm sure I could persuade her to wait for me. If this wasn't my last chance, I wouldn't ask. We could be back here by Monday evening. A full twenty-four hours before the train is even due in Friedland."

"And what if you chose not to come back?" he said. "It's very difficult bringing people out of Berlin across the Green Border. What's to stop you from just staying there? She doesn't even live in the French sector."

"At least say you'll think about it," I said. "I mean, it would be a real shame if I allowed my own disappointment to cloud my eyes next Tuesday evening."

"Meaning?"

"I want to help you find Edgard de Boudel, Émile. Really I do. But there has to be a little give-and-take, especially in a situation like this. If I'm to work for you, then surely it's best that I'm completely in your debt, monsieur. That there's nothing unpleasant between us."

He smiled a nasty little smile and threw his cigarette over the wall and into the canal. Then he quickly gathered the lapels of my jacket in his fist and smacked me hard across both cheeks.

"Maybe you've forgotten La Santé," he said. "Your boche friends, Oberg and Knochen, and their death sentences." He slapped me again for good measure.

I took it as calmly as I was able and said: "That might work on your wife and your sister, Franzi, but not on me, see?" I caught the hand he was waving near my ear and twisted it hard. "No one gets to slap me unless I've got my hand in her panties. Now, take your paws off this cheap French suit before I teach you the Method on tough."

I looked him in the eye and saw that he seemed to relax a little, so I let go his hand in order to prize his fingers off my coat, and that was when he punched me with a right hook that rocked my head like a balloon on a stick. Probably he'd have punched me again but for my own presence of mind, which is another way of saying that I banged its hard bony covering firmly against the bridge of his long hooked nose.

The Frenchman yelped with pain, and finally letting go of my coat, he pressed his fingers to the side of his nose and took several steps back until he reached the garden wall.

"Look," I said, "stop trying to polish my chin and take it easy, Émile. I'm not asking for the return of Alsace-Lorraine, just one lousy Sunday afternoon with the woman I love. Some compassionate leave, that's all. And none of that gets in the way of me helping you find your traitor. I help you, you help me. Unless you want me to enroll in a course at the university, it's not like I have anything much to do before next Tuesday evening."

"I think you broke my nose," he said.

"No, I didn't. There's not nearly enough blood. Take it from someone who's broken a few noses in his time. Although nothing on the scale of that Eiffel Tower on your face." I shook my head. "Hey, I'm sorry I hit you, Émile, but for the last nine months a lot of people have been getting tough with me and I've had enough of it, see? I have to look at my face every morning, Frenchman. It's not much of a face, but it's the only one I've got. And it's got to last me for a while yet. So I don't like it when people think they can knock it around. I'm sensitive like that."

He wiped his nose and nodded, but the incident hung strong in the air between us like the smell of burned hops from a brewery. And for a moment we both stood there stupidly, wondering how to proceed.

It could have been worse, I told myself. There had been a brief moment when I had actually contemplated tipping him over the wall and into the canal.

He lit a cigarette and smoked it as if he thought it might improve his humor and take his mind off his nose, which, now that he had wiped away the blood, was already looking better than he might have supposed.

"You're right," he said. "There's no reason at all why this thing can't be fixed. After all, it is, as you say, just one Sunday afternoon, yes?"

I nodded. "Just one Sunday afternoon."

"Very well. We will fix it. Yes, I tell you, I would do anything to get de Boudel."

Including lie to me, I thought. After I had served my purpose and identified de Boudel, there was no telling what the French might do with me: send me back to La Santé, to the Amis, even the Russians. France was, after all, cozying up to the Soviet Union in its foreign policy, and the return of an escaped prisoner was not beyond its perfidy.

"And a ring?" I asked, as if such a bauble really mattered to me or to Elisabeth.

"Yes," he said. "I'm sure that can be arranged also."

GERMANY, 1954

On Saturday, Grottsch and Wenger drove me back to Berlin, as agreed; and on Sunday, I returned to Motzstrasse, only this time my two companions insisted on accompanying me to Elisabeth's door.

I let her kiss me chastely on the cheek, and then made the introductions.

"This is Herr Grottsch. And Herr Wenger. They're responsible for my safety while I'm in Berlin, and they insist on looking around your apartment, just to make sure everything is kosher."

Elisabeth frowned. "Are they policemen?"

"Yes. Kind of."

"Are you in any trouble?"

"I can assure you it's nothing to worry about," I said smoothly. "It's not much more than a formality. But they certainly won't leave us alone until they've had a good look around."

Elisabeth shrugged. "If you think it's really necessary. But there's no one else here. I can't imagine what you think you'll find, gentlemen. This isn't Hohenschönhausen, you know."

Grottsch stopped and frowned. "What do you know about Hohenschönhausen?" he asked suspiciously.

"I can see your friends aren't from Berlin, Bernie," said Elisabeth. "My dear man, everyone in Berlin knows about Hohenschönhausen."

"Everyone except me," I said truthfully.

"Well," she said. "You remember the Heike factory?"

"The meat-processing factory? On the corner of Freienewelder Strasse."

She nodded. "That whole area is now occupied by the State Security Service of the DDR."

"I thought that was in Karlshorst," I said.

"Not anymore," she said.

"You seem to know a lot about it, Fräulein," said Wenger.

"I'm a Berliner. The communists pretend the place doesn't exist and the rest of us pretend not to see it. It's an arrangement that suits us all very well, I think. A very Berlin kind of arrangement. It was the same with Gestapo headquarters on Prinz Albrechtstrasse. Remember?"

I nodded. "Of course. It was the building that no one saw."

Elisabeth looked at Grottsch and Wenger and frowned. "So? Go ahead and search."

The two men walked through the apartment and found nothing. When they were quite satisfied at finding nothing, Grottsch said, "We'll be outside the door." And then they left.

I moved her away from the door in case they were listening and into the kitchen, where we embraced fondly.

"What were you thinking of?" I said. "Mentioning the Stasi like that?"

"I don't know. It just sort of came out."

"Still, you recovered it pretty well, I thought. I'd forgotten about Heike's meat. In the army, we lived on that stuff."

"That's probably why they shot him. Richard Heike."

"Who? The Russians?"

She nodded. "Who are those two characters?"

"Just a couple of thugs who work for French intelligence."

"But they were German, weren't they?"

"I think the French rather enjoy making us do their dirty work."

"So that's what you're doing."

"Actually, I don't know what I'm doing."

"That's a comforting thought."

"I told the French I had to come here and ask you to marry me. That you'd given me an ultimatum."

"Not a bad idea at that, Gunther." She pulled away from my embrace and started to make us coffee. "I don't much like living on my own. To be alone in Berlin is not like being alone anywhere else. Even the trees here look isolated."

"You mean you really would like to be married?"

"Why not? You were kind to me, Gunther. Once in 1931. Again in 1940. A third time in 1946. And then a fourth time last year. That makes four times in twenty-three years. My father left home when I was ten. My husband—well, you remember what he was like. Very free with his fists was my Ulrich. I have a brother who I haven't seen in years." Elisabeth took out a handkerchief and dabbed her eyes. "God, I hadn't realized it until now, but you've been one of the only constant figures in my life, Bernie Gunther. Perhaps the only one." She sniffed loudly. "Shit."

"What about your Americans?"

"What about them? Are they here, drinking coffee in my kitchen? Are they? Do they send me money from America? No, they don't. They fucked me while they were here, the way Amis do, and then they went home to Wichita and Phoenix. Oh, yes, there was another one I didn't tell you about. Major Winthrop. Now, he did give me money, only it wasn't like I asked for it or wanted it, if you know what I mean. He used to leave it on the dresser, so that when he went back to his wife in Boston, it meant he went with a clear conscience because we'd never had a proper relationship. At least, not according to him. I was just some little choco-lady he saw when he wanted someone to suck his pipe." She blew her nose, but the tears kept on coming. "And you ask me why I want to get married, Gunther. It's not just Berlin that's an enclave, it's me, too. And if I don't do something about it, soon, then I don't know what's to become of me. You want an ultimatum? Well, there it is. You want to me to help you? Then help me. That's my price."

I nodded. "Then it's lucky I came prepared." I handed her the ring box Vigée had given me. Bought, he said, from a secondhand shop in Göttingen, but for all I knew, he might have stolen it from the dwarf, Alberich.

Elisabeth opened the box. The ring was not Rhinegold, but it did at least look like something valuable, although in truth I'd seen better diamonds on a playing card. Not that it seemed to matter to her. In my experience, women like the idea of jewelry no matter what it looks like. If they like you, then they're almost always pleased to see a ring of any size and color.

She gasped and snatched it out of the box.

"If it doesn't fit," I said lamely, "then I suppose there's a way of fixing that."

But the ring was already on her finger and seemed to fit well enough, which was her cue to start crying again. There could be no doubt about it. I had a real talent for making women happy.

"Just so you know," I said. "My wife died, twice. The first one after the first war and the second one soon after the second. That's not a record you can be proud of as a husband. If there's another war, you should probably take the precaution of divorcing me quickly. But frankly, I've always been better at finding other people's husbands or sleeping with their wives. What else? Oh yes, I'm a born loser. That's important for you to know, I think. This, at least, explains my current situation, which is not without its hazards, angel. I daresay you've gathered that. A man doesn't work for his enemies unless he has little choice in the matter. Or no choice at all. I'm just a cheap paper knife. People pick me up when they need to open an envelope, and then they put me down again. I don't have any say in the matter. As far back as I can remember, that's all I've been when I thought I was more than that. The truth is that we're just what we've done and what we do, and not what we ever want to be."

"You're wrong," she said. "It doesn't matter what we've done or what we do. What matters is what others think we are. If you're looking for meaning, then here it is. Let me supply that for you. To me you'll always be a good man, Gunther. In my brown eyes, you'll always be the man who was there for me when I needed someone to be there. Maybe that's all any of us need. You want a plan or a purpose, then look no further than me, mister."

I grinned, liking her resilience. You could tell she was a Berliner, all right. Probably she'd been one of those women with a bucket who'd cleared the city of rubble in 1945. Raped one day, rebuilding it the next, like some Trojan princess in a play by some marble-headed Greek. Made of the same stuff as that German aviatrix who used to fly missiles for Hitler. You could say that's why I kissed her—properly this time—but it might just as easily have been because she was as sexy as black stocking tops. Especially when her eyes were fixed on me. Besides, most German men prefer a woman who looks like she has a healthy appetite. Which is not to say Elisabeth was fat, or even large, just well-endowed.

"I expect you're wondering if there was a reply to your letter," she said.

"It was beginning to itch a little."

"Good. At the very least, I want to see some scratch marks for what you put me through to get this. I've never been so scared."

She opened a kitchen drawer and took out a letter, which she now handed to me. "I'll finish making that coffee while you read it."

GERMANY, 1954

To the west there was the town; to the east there were just green open fields; and in the middle was the railway line. The station, immediately south of the refugee camp, was—like every other building in Friedland—unremarkable. It was made of red bricks and had two red roofs—three if you counted the wizard's-hat roof on top of the square corner tower that was the stationmaster's house. A neat little flower garden was laid out by the front door of the house, and at the two upper-floor arched windows a neat set of flowery curtains hung. There was also a clock, a notice board with a timetable, and a bus stop. Everything was neat and orderly and just as sleepy as it should have been. Except today. Today was different. The capital of West Germany might have been the unlikely town of Bonn, but today—and no less unlikely than that—all German eyes were focused on Friedland in Lower Saxony. For today saw the homecoming of one thousand German prisoners of war from Soviet captivity, aboard a train that had left its remote destination more than twenty-four hours earlier.

The late-evening mood was one of high expectation, even celebration. A brass band was assembled in front of the station, and it was already playing a selection of patriotic music that was at the same time politically acceptable to the ears of the British, whose zone of occupation this was. Of the train there was as yet no sign, but that autumn evening several hundred people were assembled on the platform and around the station to greet the returnees. You would have thought we were expecting to see West Germany's FIFA World Cup team arriving home, victorious, from the "miracle of Bern" and not a train carrying SS and Wehrmacht, none of whom had expected ever to be released from Russia and who were all of them entirely ignorant of the fact that Germany had won the World Cup or even that Konrad Adenauer, the former mayor of Cologne, to whom they owed their freedom, was now chancellor of another German republic—this time the Federal Republic of Germany. But some local men, keen to remind the returnees of the chancellor's crucial role in their delivery from captivity, were carrying a sign that read "We Thank You, Doctor Adenauer." I wouldn't have argued with that, although it sometimes seemed to me that the Herr Doktor was intent on becoming another uncrowned king of Germany.

Other signs were much more personal, even pathetic. Between ten and twenty men and women were carrying signs on which were written details of a missing loved one, and of these, that of an old bespectacled lady who reminded me of my own late mother, seemed typical:

Do you know him? Untersturmführer Rudolf (Rolf) Knabe. Second 9th SS Panzer Division "Hohenstaufen" (1942) & Second SS Panzerkorps (1943). Last heard of at Kursk, July 1943.

I wondered how much she knew about what had happened at Kursk—that this place had been the scene of the largest and bloodiest tank battle in history and had probably marked the beginning of the end for the German army.

Others, perhaps less optimistic, were holding little candles or what looked like miners' lamps, which I took to be memorials for those who weren't ever coming back.

On the actual platform of the station were those, like myself, Grottsch, Vigée, and Wenger, whose role was more official. VdH and others veterans' organizations, policemen, churchmen, Red Cross volunteers, British army soldiers, and a large contingent of nurses, several of whom caught my bored eye. All were facing south, down the track toward Reckershausen and beyond, to the DDR.

"Now, now," said Vigée, noticing my interest in the nurses. "You're almost a married man."

"There's something about nurses that always attracts me. I used to think it was the uniform, but now I don't know. Maybe it's just sympathy for anyone who has to do someone else's dirty work."

"Is it so dirty? To help someone who needs it?"

I glanced at the German policeman whom Vigée had brought along, so that if I did identify de Boudel, he might be arrested immediately and then extradited to France.

"Forget it," I growled. "I just never had to blow the whistle on anyone before, that's all. I guess there's something about it I don't like. Who knows?" I started on a new stick of gum. "If I see this fellow, what do you want me to do, anyway? Kiss him on the cheek?"

"Just point him out to us," Vigée said patiently. "The police inspector will do the rest."

"Why so squeamish, Gunther?" asked Grottsch. "I thought you used to be a policeman."

"I was a cop, it's true," I said. "Several thousand midnights ago. But it was one thing arresting some old lag. It's something else when it's an old comrade."

"A nice distinction," said the Frenchman. "But hardly correct. It's not much of an old comrade who sells his soul to the other side."

There was a loud cheer along the platform as, in the distance, we heard the whistle of an approaching steam locomotive.

Vigée made a fist and pumped his biceps excitedly.

"Who gave you this tip, anyway?" I asked. "That de Boudel would be on this train?"

"The English Secret Service."

"And how did they find out?"

The train was now in sight, a shiny black locomotive wreathed in gray smoke and white steam, as if a kitchen door in hell had been flung open. It was hauling not cattle wagons, as would have been more typical of a Russian POW train, but passenger carriages; and it was immediately plain to me that upon entering Germany, the prisoners had been transferred onto a German train. Men were already leaning out of open windows, waving to the people running alongside the track or catching bunches of flowers thrown up into their arms.

The train whistled again and halted in the station, and men in patched and threadbare uniforms stretched out to touch those on the platform amid shouts and cheers. The Russians had not provided names of the POWS on the train, and before anyone was allowed to get off they had to wait patiently while officials from the Red Cross entered each carriage and collected a list of names for the benefit of the police, the commander of the refugee camp, and the VdH. Only when, after almost half an hour, this task was completed were the men finally allowed to step down from the train. A trumpet sounded, and for a moment it seemed as though the hour had truly arrived when those who had been in their graves were truly resurrected. And when they came forth from the train in their battered field gray they did indeed resemble recently interred corpses—so thin were their bodies, so gap-toothed were their smiles, so white their hair, and so old their weather-beaten faces. Some were filthy and shoeless. Others appeared stunned to be in a place that was not filled with cruelty or surrounded with barbed wire and empty steppe. Quite a few had to be carried from the train on stretchers. A great stink of unwashed bodies filled the clean air of Friedland, but no one seemed to mind. Everyone was smiling.

Even a few of the POWs were, but mostly they were crying like stolen children now returned to their aged parents after many years in a dark forest.

D. W. Griffith or Cecil B. DeMille could not have directed a more moving crowd scene than that which was taking place on a railway platform at a small town in Germany. Even Vigée appeared moved to the verge of tears. Meanwhile, the brass band started to play the "Deutschlandlied"—a few of the crazier-looking prisoners started to sing the forbidden words—and, across the fields, a couple of kilometers to the north in Gros Schneen, the local church bells rang out.

I heard one of the POWs tell someone on the platform that it was only the day before that they'd learned they were to be released.

"These men," said Vigée. "They look like they're back from hell."

"No," I told him. "In hell they tell you what's happening to you."

I had my eyes peeled, but I knew there was little real chance of seeing de Boudel in the crowds of people at the station. Vigée knew this, too. He was expecting us to have better luck when the POWs paraded back at the camp the next morning; it seemed that I was going to have to repeat my Le Vernet experience and inspect the men at close quarters. I was not looking forward to this and was hoping against hope that we might get lucky and spy de Boudel at the station—that I might see him before one of my old comrades saw me. To this improbable end, I went into the station and climbed the stairs to lean out of an upper-floor window in order to gain a better view of this mass of jubilant German soldiery. Vigée followed, then Grottsch, Wenger, and the detective.

I had not seen so many uniforms since the labor camp at Johannesgeorgenstadt. They swept across the platform like a sea of gray. Wearing his chain of office and dispensing schnapps from a double-sized earthenware bottle, the mayor of Friedland moved among the returnees like some Hamelin burgomaster surrounded by a plague of rats and mice. I could hear him shouting, "Your health!" and "To your freedom!" and "Welcome home!" at the top of his voice. Next to him a large Wehrmacht sergeant stood enfolding an old woman in his arms; both were weeping uncontrollably. His wife? His mother? It was hard to tell, the sergeant looked so old himself. They all did. It was hard to believe that these old men had once been the proud storm troopers who had carried Hitler's mad Operation Barbarossa into Russia.

A woman standing next to me was throwing carnations onto the gray heads below. "Isn't it wonderful?" she said. "I never thought I'd live to see the day our boys finally came home. Germany's heart beats in Friedland. They're back. Back from the godless world of Bolshevism."

I nodded politely but kept my eyes on the faces in the crowd below the window.

"This is chaos," said the detective, whose name was Moeller. "How the hell are we supposed to find anyone in this? The next time we have prisoners arriving here, they'd do better to bring them on buses from the border station at Herleshausen. That way we might at least establish some kind of order. You'd think this was Italy, not Germany."

"Let them have their chaos," I said. "For fourteen years these men have endured discipline and order. They've had a belly full of it. So let them enjoy a moment of disorder. It might help to make them feel like human beings again."

Flowers, fruit, candies, cigarettes, schnapps, hot coffee, hugs and kisses—every sign of affection was showered on these men. I hadn't seen so much joy on the faces of so many Germans since June 1940. And two things were clear to me: that only the Federal Republic could claim to be the legitimate representative of the German nation; and that no one regarded any of these men—whatever crimes and atrocities they might have committed in Russia and the Ukraine—as anything other than heroes.

But equally clear was the reality of the problem now facing me.

For among the lined, grinning faces of the men underneath my gaze was one I recognized from Johannesgeorgenstadt. A Berliner named Walter Bingel whom I had befriended on the train from the MVD prison near Stalingrad. The same Bingel who had seen me leaving the camp in a ZIM saloon, accompanied by two German communists from K-5, and who assumed that I'd made a deal with them to save my skin. And if Bingel was on the train, then quite probably there were others from Johannesgeorgenstadt who, thanks to him, would have the same memory of me. It was beginning to look as if Inspector Moeller might be obliged to arrest me, too.

Vigée's keen eyes saw mine lingering nervously on Bingel's face. "Recognize anyone?" he asked.

"Not so far," I lied. "But to be honest, these men seem older than their years. I'm not sure I'd recognize my own brother down there. If I had a brother."

"Well, that's good for us, isn't it?" said the Frenchman. "A man who has spent the last six or seven years working for the MVD ought to stick out from the rest of these uncles. After all, de Boudel is merely posing as a POW. He hasn't been in a labor camp, like them."

I nodded. The Frenchman had a point.

"Can we get a copy of that list of names made by the Red Cross?" I asked.

Vigée nodded at Moeller, who went away to fetch one. "All the same," he said, "I don't think he'll be using his real name, do you?"

"No, of course not. But one has to start somewhere. Most police work starts with a list of something or other, even if it's a list of what you don't know. Sometimes that's as important as what you do know. Really, detective work is simple, it's just not very easy."

"Don't sweat it," said Vigée. "We always knew that finding de Boudel at the station would be a long shot. Reveille at the refugee camp tomorrow morning. That's where I'm pinning my hopes."

"Yes, I think you're right," I said.

We watched Moeller struggling through the crowd of men to one of the Red Cross officials. He said something, and the official nodded back.

"Where did you find him?" I asked.

"Göttingen," said Vigée. "Why?" He lit a cigarette and flicked his match onto the heads of the men below, as if he wished to express his contempt for them. "Do you think he's not up to this?"

"I couldn't say."

"Maybe he's not the detective you were, Gunther." Vigée blew out his cheeks and sighed. "All he has to do is arrest the man you identify. There's not much to being that kind of a cop, *n'est-ce pas?*" he sneered. "Perhaps you should give him some tips. Tell him your forensic secrets."

"They're quite simple, too," I said. "I used to get up in the morning and go to bed at night. And in between I'd try to keep myself busy and out of mischief."

"Really? Is that all you have to offer? After how many years of being a detective?"

"Any fool can solve a crime, Frenchman. It's proving it that wears you out."

Moeller started back through the crowd to the station door but found himself making little or no progress. He looked up and, seeing Vigée and then me, threw his hands up and grinned helplessly.

I grinned back and nodded affably, as if recognizing his difficulty. But all the time I was looking at him I was trying to gauge what kind of policeman I was going to be dealing with when, the following morning, Walter Bingel identified me as a collaborator and traitor.

34

GERMANY, 1954

We remained behind until all of the POWs had marched off to the camp and most of the local people had left the station. Vigée was, I think, impressed that I had insisted on being there until the last; and, of course, he was quite without a clue that the real reason had much more to do with my trying to keep out of sight. Before we climbed into the Citroën that would take us back to our pension in Göttingen, Moeller handed me a twenty-page list of names and ranks and serial numbers.

"All of the men who were in that train," he said redundantly.

I tucked the list into my coat pocket and glanced around the station ticket hall and beyond, onto the platform where those whose dashed hopes of seeing some long-lost loved one remained to the bitter end. A few of these people were in tears. Others just sat alone in quiet and stoic grief. I heard someone say, "Next time, Frau Kettenacher. I expect he'll come the next time. They say it might be another year before they're all home. And that the SS will be the last."

Gently, the owner of the voice—some local pastor, it looked like to me—helped an old woman to her feet, collected her missing-person sign off the ground, and guided her toward the platform exit.

We followed at a respectful distance.

"Poor soul," muttered Moeller. "I know how she feels. I have an elder brother who's still a prisoner."

"Why didn't you say something?" I said. "Suppose he'd turned up here? What would you have done?"

Moeller shrugged. "I was sort of hoping he would. That's one of the reasons I got put forward for this job. But now that I've seen that refugee camp, I'm not so sure. There must be better ways of treating our men, Herr Gunther. Don't you agree?"

I nodded.

"They don't do so bad," said Grottsch. "Every week, the camp commander at Friedland gets hundreds of letters from single women all over Germany who are looking for a new husband."

The five of us squeezed into the car and set off north for Göttingen, some fifteen kilometers away.

Sitting in the back, I switched on the courtesy light and nervously scanned the list for the names of any others from Johannesgeorgenstadt. And it didn't take long to find the name of SS General Fritz Klause, who had been the SGO at the camp. It was beginning to look as if the radiation at the camp hadn't been nearly as lethal as I had been led to believe. Then again, a man can use hate for his enemy as a blanket just warm enough to keep him alive through even a Russian winter.

"I wish someone would write and offer to marry me," said Wenger as he drove the car. "Or, at the very least, offer to take the place of the wife I already have."

"I wonder what they'll think," said Moeller. "About the new Germany."

"I imagine they'll think it's really not quite German enough," observed Grottsch. "That was my impression when I came back from a British POW camp. I kept looking for Germany. And all I found was new furniture, cars, and toys for American boys."

"Turn the car around," I said. "We have to go back."

Vigée, sitting beside Wenger in the front seat, ordered him to pull up for a moment. Then he turned in his seat to look at me. "Found something?"

"Maybe."

"Explain, please."

"As we were leaving, there was a woman back at the station seeking information about her loved one. She had written all of his details on a sign."

"Yes," said Vigée. "What was her name?"

"Kettenacher," I said. "But there was also a Kettenacher who was on the train. Who's on this list prepared by the Red Cross."

"It's not an uncommon name in this part of Germany," said Moeller.

"No," I said firmly. "But Frau Kettenacher's son was in the Panzer Corps. He was a Hauptmann. A captain, same as me. Richard Kettenacher. Fifty-sixth Panzer Corps. Last heard of in the battle for Berlin."

"He missed his mother in the crowd," said Moeller. "It happens."

"And what about all his comrades?" I asked. "Would they have missed her, too?"

"Go back," Vigée told Wenger urgently. "Go back immediately."

Wenger turned the car around.

"Let me see that list," said the Frenchman.

I handed it to him and pointed out the name.

"What do you think we should do?" he asked. "Go straight to the camp? Suppose he slips away before he gets there?"

"No," I said. "He's here because he needs to be official. He needs some papers. Otherwise, the Russian state security people could have smuggled him across the border in Berlin. He needs his discharge papers. Ration cards. An identity document. All of that in order to enter German society. To become something new. He's not going to slip away."

I thought for a moment.

"We need to speak to the real Captain Kettenacher's mother.

That old lady we saw at the railway station. We need her to give us a photograph of her son. So that when you and Moeller here go to the camp tomorrow and he tries to throw some sand in your face, you'll be able to deal with it by being able to produce a picture. You can leave asking her to me. I am, after all, a representative of the VdH."

"You said that in a way that implied you thought you wouldn't be coming to the refugee camp," said Vigée. "Why?"

"Because I think you need to keep me in reserve," I said smoothly. "Think about it, Émile. You arrest Kettenacher on suspicion of really being de Boudel. He denies it, of course. So you take him to the Pension Esebeck and show him the real Kettenacher's photograph. He still denies it: There's some mistake. An administrative error. There were two Captain Kettenachers. You let him talk himself into a corner. That's when I step out from behind the curtain and say 'Hello, Edgard. Remember me?' I'm your ace, Émile. But you mustn't play me until the end."

Vigée was nodding. "Yes. You're correct, of course. But how will we find Frau Kettenacher."

I shrugged. "I'm a detective, remember? If finding people was difficult, they wouldn't ask policemen to do it every day of the week." I smiled at Moeller. "No offense intended, Inspector."

"None taken, sir."

"So where am I driving?" muttered Wenger. "Suppose the old lady doesn't live in Friedland? Suppose she already left town?"

"That pastor seemed to know her," said Vigée.

"Yes, but there's no church in Friedland."

"There is one in Gros Schneen," said Moeller.

"Head back to the station," I said. "We'll see if anyone remembers them there. If not, we can then decide what to do."

The stationmaster, a stooping, etiolated figure, was sweeping up after the crowds. His flower bed had been trampled and, as a result, he could have been in a better mood. He shook his head when I asked him about Frau Kettenacher, but he seemed to remember the pastor all right.

"That was Pastor Overmans, from the church in Hebenshausen."

"Where's that?"

"A couple of kilometers south of here. You can't miss it. There's even less in Hebenshausen than there is here in Friedland."

Wenger drove south, and we soon found ourselves in a village that lived down to the stationmaster's description. We were just in time to see a bus leaving the village square, and the pastor and the old lady, still carrying her missing-person sign, walking away from the bus stop. Behind the bus stop was a largish half-timbered house, and behind the house was a small square church tower. The pastor and the old lady went inside the house and some lights were turned on.

Wenger stopped the car.

"Moeller," I said. "You come with me. And don't say anything. The rest of you wait here."

The pastor was surprised to see us there so late, until I explained that I was from the VdH and that we'd missed Frau Kettenacher at the station.

"I try to see all of the families in this part of Lower Saxony who have a missing loved one," I said. "But I don't think I've met the lady before."

"Ah, that's because she's from Kassel," explained Pastor Overmans. "Frau Kettenacher is from Kassel. I'm her brother-in-law. She's been staying with me in order that she could be at the railway station tonight."

"I'm very sorry that your son wasn't on the train," I told her. "In the hope of avoiding further disappointments, we've been pressing the Russians to provide more details of who they're still holding. And when these POWs might be released."

The pastor, a brick-faced man with white hair, glanced around the somberly furnished room at the sagging heap of a woman who was sitting on an inadequate-looking chair. "Well, that would be something, eh, Rosa?"

Frau Kettenacher nodded silently. She was still wearing her coat and a hat that looked like an air-raid warden's helmet. She smelled strongly of mothballs and disappointment.

I continued with my cruel deception. If I was correct and Edgard de Boudel was indeed using the name of Hauptmann Richard Kettenacher, it could only mean one thing: that the real captain was dead and had been for some considerable time. I managed to persuade myself that his cruelty and the cruelty of the Russian intelligence service that had put together this legend was crueler than mine, but only just.

"However," I said weightily, "the Soviet authorities are not known for the efficiency of their record keeping. I know—I was a prisoner myself. When our men are repatriated, it's the German Red Cross and not the Russians who establish who is actually being released. For this reason, we're in the process of compiling our own records of who is still missing. And while this may not seem like the best moment to be asking questions like this, I wonder if I might take a few details of the loved one still missing." I smiled sadly at the pastor. "Your nephew, is it?"

"Yes," he said, and repeated the missing man's name, rank, and serial number, and the details of his war service.

I noted these down conscientiously. "I won't take up too much of your time," I said. "Do you have any personal documentation? A pay book, perhaps? Not every soldier kept his pay book on him like he was supposed to. A lot left them at home for safekeeping so that their wives could claim the money. I know I did. Or perhaps a military service record book. A party card. That kind of thing."

Frau Kettenacher was already opening a brown leather bag that was the size and shape of a small coracle. "My Ricky was a good boy," she said in a strong Saxonian accent. "He wouldn't ever have disobeyed the rules about carrying his pay book." She took out a manila envelope and handed it to me. "But you'll find everything else in here. His National Socialist Party personal identity card. His SA identity card. His craftsmen's guild certificate. His ID for commercial travelers—he trained to be a metalworker, see? And then became a traveling salesman selling the things he used to make. His German state travel passport. That was for the time he went to Italy on business. His bombing victim's pass—Ricky's apartment in Kassel was bombed, you know. And his wife was killed. A lovely girl, she was. And his military service passbook."

I tried to contain my excitement. The old lady was giving me everything that could have identified the real Richard Kettenacher. Several of the documents contained not just photographs but personal signatures, blood types, details of medical examinations, his size of gas mask, helmet, cap and boots, a record of wounds and serious illnesses, and military decorations.

"The inspector here will issue you with a receipt for these documents," I said. "And he'll make sure that they're returned safely to you."

"I don't care about them," she said. "All I care about is having my Ricky returned safely to me."

"God willing, yes," I said, pocketing the missing man's life history.

As soon as Moeller had written one out, we left the pastor and the old lady alone and walked back to the car.

"Well?" asked Vigée.

I nodded. "I got everything." I brandished the old lady's envelope. "Everything. Kettenacher's double couldn't get past this lot. That's the great thing about Nazi documentation. For one thing, there was so bloody much of it. And for another, it's virtually impossible to contradict."

"Let's hope it's not the real one," said Vigée. "If he was blind, then perhaps he couldn't see his mother. And perhaps her eyes are not so good and she couldn't see him." He looked through the documents. "Let us hope you're right about this. I don't like disappointments."

35

GERMANY, 1954

The following morning, I remained at the pension in Göttingen while Vigée and some of the others went to arrest the man posing as Kettenacher. I asked if I might be allowed to go to church, but Grottsch said that Vigée had given orders that we should remain indoors and await his return. He said, "I hope it's him so that we can go back to Hannover. I really don't like Göttingen anymore."

"Why? It's a nice enough little town."

"Too many memories," said Grottsch. "I went to university here. My wife, too."

"I didn't know you were married."

"She was killed in an air raid," he said. "In October 1944."

"Sorry."

"And you? Were you married before?"

"Yes. She died, too. But much later on. In 1949. We had a small hotel in Dachau."

He nodded. "Dachau is very lovely," said Grottsch. "Well, it was, before the war."

For a moment we shared a silent memory of a Germany that was gone and probably would never be again. Not for us, anyway. And certainly not for our poor wives. Conversations in Germany were often like this: People would just stop in the middle of a sentence and remember a place that was gone or someone who was dead. There were so many dead that sometimes you could actually feel the grief on the streets, even in 1954. The feeling of sadness that afflicted the country was almost as bad as it had been during the Great Depression.

We heard a car draw up outside the pension and Grottsch went to see if they had our man. A few minutes later, he came back looking worried.

"Well," he said. "They've got someone. Yes, they've got someone, all right. But if it is Edgard de Boudel, then he speaks German better than any Franzi I ever met."

"Of course he would," I said. "He was fluent even when I knew him. His German was better than mine."

Grottsch shrugged. "Anyway, he insists he's Kettenacher. Vigée's confronting him with the real Kettenacher's documents now. Did you see Kettenacher's party ID? The man had donation stamps going back to 1934. And did you see those dueling scars on his cheek in the photographs?"

I nodded. "It's true. He was everyone's idea of what a Nazi should look like. Especially now that he's dead."

"Why do I get the feeling that you weren't a party member yourself?"

"Does it really matter now? If I was or I wasn't?" I shook my head. "As far as our new friends are concerned—the French, the Amis, the Tommies—we were all fucking Nazis. So it doesn't matter who was and who wasn't. They look at all those old Leni Riefenstahl movies, and who can blame them?"

"There was never a moment when you believed in Hitler, like the rest of us?"

"Oh yes. There was. For about a month in the summer of 1940. After we licked the French in six weeks. I believed in him then. Who didn't?"

"Yes. That was the best time for me, too."

After a while we heard raised voices, and a few minutes later, Vigée came into the room. He looked cross and out of breath, and there was blood on the back of one hand, as if he'd hit someone.

"He's not Richard Kettenacher," he said. "That much is certain. But he swears he's not Edgard de Boudel. So. It's up to you now, Gunther."

I shrugged. "All right."

I followed the Frenchman down to the wine cellar where Wenger and Moeller were guarding our prisoner. The photographs the Amis had shown me had been black-and-white, of course, and blown up after being shot from a distance so that they were a little blurred and grainy. Doubtless the real de Boudel would have gone to great lengths to disguise himself. He would have lost some weight, dyed his hair, grown a mustache perhaps. When I'd been a uniformed policeman in the twenties, I'd arrested many suspects on the basis of a photograph or a police description; but this was the first time I'd been obliged to do it in order to save my own neck.

The man was sitting in a chair. He was wearing handcuffs and his cheeks were red, as if he'd been struck several times. He looked about sixty, but he was probably younger. In fact, I was certain of it. As soon as he saw me, the man smiled.

"Bernie Gunther," he said. "I never thought I'd be pleased to see you again. Tell this French idiot I'm not the man he's looking for. This Edgar Boudel he keeps asking me about." He spat on the floor.

"Why don't you tell him yourself?" I said. "Tell him your real name and then perhaps he'll believe you."

The man frowned and said nothing.

"Do you recognize this man?" Vigée asked me.

"Yes, I recognize him."

"And is it him? Is it de Boudel?"

"Who is this Boudel fellow, anyway?" said the prisoner. "And what's he supposed to have done?"

I nodded. "Yes, that's a good idea," I told the prisoner. "Find out what this wanted man's done, and if it turns out to be rather less heinous than what you did yourself, then put your hands up for it. Why not? I can see how you could think that might work."

"I don't know what you're talking about, Gunther. I've spent the last nine years in a Russian POW camp. Whatever it is I'm supposed to have done, I reckon I've paid for it several times over."

"As if I care."

"I demand to know this man's name," said Vigée.

"How about it?" I told the prisoner. "We both know you're not Richard Kettenacher. I suppose you stole his pay book and just swapped the photograph on the inside cover—stuck it on with some egg white. Russians didn't usually pay too much attention to the corner stamps. You figured a new name and a different service would keep the dogs off your trail, because after Treblinka you knew that someone would be coming to look for you. You and Irmfried Eberl, wasn't it?"

"I don't know what you're talking about."

"Neither do I," complained Vigée. "And I'm beginning to get irritated."

"Permit me to introduce you, Émile. This is Major Paul Kestner. Formerly of the SS and deputy commander of the Treblinka death camp in Poland."

"Rubbish," said Kestner. "Rubbish. You don't know what you're talking about."

"At least he was until Himmler found out about what he was doing there. Even he was horrified by what he and the commandant had been up to. Theft, murder, torture. Isn't that right, Paul? So horrified that you and Eberl were kicked out of the SS, which is how you found yourself in the Wehrmacht, defending Berlin, trying to redeem yourself for your earlier crimes."

"Nonsense," said Kestner.

"You may not have Edgard de Boudel in custody, Émile, but

you do have one of the worst war criminals in Europe. A man who is responsible for the deaths of at least three quarters of a million Jews and Gypsies."

"Rubbish. Rubbish. And don't think I'm unaware of what this is really about, Gunther. It's about Paris, isn't it? June 1940."

Vigée frowned. "What about it?"

"He tried to have me murdered," I said.

"I knew it," said Kestner.

Vigée nodded at the door. "Outside," he told me. "I need to speak with you."

I followed him out of the wine cellar, up the stairs, and into the little walled garden by the canal. Vigée lit us each a cigarette.

"Paul Kestner, huh?"

I nodded. "I imagine the UN War Crimes Commission will be pleased to have him in custody," I said.

"You think I give a fuck about any of that?" he said angrily. "How many fucking Jews he killed. I don't care. I don't care about Treblinka, Gunther. Or the fate of some lousy Gypsies. They're dead. Too bad. It's not my problem. What I do care about is finding Edgard de Boudel. Got that? What I care about is finding the man who tortured and murdered almost three hundred Frenchmen in Indochina." He was shouting now and waving his arms in the air, but he didn't grab me by the lapels, and I sensed that while he might have been angry and disappointed, he was also wary of me now.

"So we're going back to that refugee camp at Friedland tomorrow and we're going to look at every man there and we're going to find de Boudel. Understand?"

"It's not my fault that he's not our man," I shouted back. "But it was the right call. And, assuming your information is correct and de Boudel really was on that fucking train, then it stands to reason he's in the camp."

"You'd better pray he is, or we're both in trouble. It's not only your ass, it's mine, too."

I shrugged. "Maybe I'll do that."

"What?"

"Pray. Pray to get out of this place for a while. To get away from you, Émile." I shook my head. "I need some room to breathe. To clear my head."

He seemed to control himself and then nodded. "Yes. I'm sorry. It's not your fault—you're right. Look, take a walk around town. Go to church again. I'll send someone with you."

"What about him? Kestner?"

"We'll take him back to the refugee camp. The German authorities can decide what to do with him. But me, I don't have any time for the UN and their stupid War Crimes Commission. I don't want to know about it."

Muttering in French, he walked off, probably before one of us felt obliged to try to hit the other again.

I found Grottsch, who to my surprise tried to excuse the Frenchman with the explanation that his daughter was ill. We collected our coats and went outside into the autumn sunshine. Göttingen was full of students, which served to remind me that my own daughter, Dinah, was probably in her first year of university by now. At least I hoped she was.

Walking around a bit, Grottsch and I found ourselves beside the ruins of the town's synagogue on Obere-Masch Strasse, burned to the ground in 1938, and I wondered how many of Göttingen's Jews had met their ends in Treblinka at the hands of Paul Kestner and if nine years in a Russian POW camp really was sufficient punishment for three quarters of a million people. Perhaps there was after all no earthly punishment that was equal to a crime like that. But if not here on earth, then where?

Our footsteps took us back to St. Jacobi's Church. I stopped to look in the window of a shop opposite, but when I walked away I found I was alone. I stopped and glanced around, expecting to see Grottsch coming toward me, but he was nowhere to be seen. For a moment I considered escape. The prospect of visiting the Friedland refugee camp and being seen by Bingel and Krause was no more appealing than it had been the previous day, and about the only thing that prevented me from walking straight to the railway station was a lack of money and the knowledge that my French passport was back at the Pension Esebeck. I was still debating my next course of action when I found I was closely accompanied by two men wearing neat little hats and short dark raincoats.

"If you're looking for your friend," said one of the men, "he had to sit down and rest. On account of the fact that he suddenly felt very tired."

I was still looking around for Grottsch, as if I really cared what happened to him, when I realized that there were two more men behind me.

"He's sleeping it off in the church." The man speaking had good German, but it wasn't his first language. He wore heavy-framed glasses and was smoking a metal-stemmed pipe. He puffed, and a cloud of tobacco smoke obscured his face for a moment.

"Sleeping it off?"

"A hypodermic shot. Nothing to worry about. Not for him and not for you, Gunther. So relax. We're your friends. There's a car around the corner waiting to take us on a little ride."

"Suppose I don't want to go for a ride?"

"Why suppose anything of the kind when we both know that's exactly what you want? Besides, I'd hate to have to give you a shot like your friend Grottsch. The effects of thiopental can linger unpleasantly for several days after injection." He had my arm now and his colleague had the other, and we were already turning the corner onto Weender Strasse. "A new life awaits you, my friend. Money, and a new identity, a new passport. Anything you want."

The door of a large black saloon swung open ahead of me. A man wearing a leather jacket and a matching cap was standing behind it. Another man, walking a few steps ahead of me, stopped at the car door and turned to face me. I was being kidnapped, and by people who knew exactly what they were doing.

"Who are you?" I asked.

"Surely you've been expecting us," said the man beside me. "After your note." He grinned. "You can't imagine the excitement your information has caused. Not just here in Germany, but at headquarters, too."

I bent forward to get into the car and felt someone's hand on the top of my head, just in case at the last moment I tried to resist and bumped my head on the door frame. Cops and spies all over the world were always thoughtful like that. Two men outside the car stayed on the alert, looking around nervously until everyone who was supposed to be in the car was in the car, and then the doors were closed and we were moving and it was all over, with no more fuss than if we were all going on an unexpected shopping trip to the next town.

After a few minutes, I saw that we were driving west and breathed a sigh of relief. At least now I knew who was kidnapping me and why.

"Just sit back and enjoy the journey, my friend. From here on in, you're five-star all the way. Those are my orders, Gunther, old buddy. I'm to treat you like a very important person."

"That will make a pleasant change from when I was last a guest of you Americans," I said. "Frankly, there was something about it I didn't like."

"And what was that?"

"My cell."

36

GERMANY, 1954

Two and a half hours later, we were in Frankfurt and heading across the Main into the north of the city. Our destination was an enormous curving, honey-colored marble office building with six square wings that lent the place a quasi-military aspect, as if any minute the clerks and secretaries inside might abandon their typewriters and comptometers and man some antiaircraft guns on the flat roofs. I hadn't ever been there, but I recognized it from old newsreels and picture magazines. Completed in 1930, the Poelzig Ensemble, or Poelzig Complex, had been the largest office building in Europe and the corporate headquarters of the I. G. Farben conglomerate. This former model of German business and modernity had been the center for Nazi wartime research projects relating to the creation of synthetic oil and rubber, not to mention Zyklon B, the lethal gas used in concentration camps. It was now the headquarters of the U.S. High Commissioner for Germany (the HICOG) and, it now seemed, of the Central Intelligence Agency.

The car passed through a couple of military checkpoints before we parked and entered a temple-like portico. Behind this were some bronze doors and on the other side a capacious hallway with a large American flag, several American soldiers, and two curving staircases covered with sheet aluminum. In front of the paternoster elevator I was invited to step aboard and to disembark on the ninth floor. A little nervously—for I had never before ridden one of these intimidating elevators—I complied.

The ninth floor was very different from those below. There were no windows. It was lit from skylights instead of banded glazing, which probably afforded the security-minded inhabitants yet more privacy. The ceiling was also much lower, which made me wonder if one of the qualifications to be an American spy in Europe might be a lack of height.

Certainly, the man to whom I was now introduced was not tall, although he was hardly short, either. He wasn't anything you could have described, being unremarkable in almost every way. He was, I suppose, like an American professor, albeit one who spoke fluent German. He wore a blazer, gray flannel trousers, a button-down blue shirt, and some sort of club or academic tie—maroon with little shields. The introduction was not, however, illuminating in that he appeared to have no name, just a title. He was "the Chief," and that was all I ever knew about him. I did, however, recognize the two men who were also waiting for me in that windowless meeting room. Special Agents Scheuer and Frei—were those their real names? I still had no idea—waited until the Chief had acknowledged their presence before nodding at me with silent courtesy.

"Have you been here before?" he asked. "I mean, when this building was owned by I. G. Farben."

"No, sir." I shrugged. "As a matter of fact, I'm surprised to find it's still here. Apparently undamaged. A building this size, of such importance to the Nazi war effort—I'd always assumed it was bombed to rubble, like almost everything else in this part of Germany."

"There are two schools of opinion on that, Gunther. Sit down, sit down. One school has it that the Americans forbidden to bomb it because of the building's proximity to the Allied POW camp at Grüneburgpark. The other school would have you believe that Eisenhower had this building marked out as his future European headquarters. Apparently, the building reminded him of the Pentagon, in Washington. And I suppose, if I'm honest, it does look a little similar. So maybe that's the real explanation after all."

I drew a chair out from a long, dark wood table and sat down and waited for the Chief to get to the point of my being there. But it seemed he hadn't yet finished with Eisenhower.

"The president's wife wasn't quite so enamored of this building, however. She took particular exception to a large bronze female figure—a nude that used to sit on the edge of the reflecting pool. She thought it wasn't suitable for a military installation." The Chief chuckled. "Which makes me wonder how many real soldiers she's actually met." He frowned. "I'm not sure where that statue went. The Hoechst Building, perhaps? That nude always did look like she needed some medicine, eh, Phil?"

"Yes, sir," said Scheuer.

"You must be tired after your journey, Herr Gunther," said the Chief. "So I'll try not to fatigue you any more than I have to. Would you like some coffee, sir?"

"Please."

Scheuer moved toward a sideboard where coffee things had been neatly assembled on a tray.

The Chief sat down and regarded me with a mixture of curiosity and distrust. If there had been a chessboard on the table between us, it might have made things feel a little easier for us both. All the same, a game was in progress and we both knew what it was. He waited until Scheuer—Phil—had set a cup of coffee in front of me and then began.

"Zyklon B. I assume you've heard of it."

I nodded.

"Everyone assumes it was developed by I. G. Farben. But they merely marketed the stuff. It was actually developed by another chemical company called Degesch, which came to be controlled by a third chemical company, called Degussa. In 1930, Degussa needed to raise some money and so they sold half of their controlling interest in Degesch to their main competitor, I. G. Farben. And, by the way, the stuff, the actual crystals that exterminated insects with the speed of a cyclone—thus the name—well, that was made by a fourth company, called Dessauer Werke. You with me so far?"

"Yes, sir. Although I'm beginning to wonder why."

"Patience, sir. All will be explained. So Dessauer made the stuff for Degesch, who sold the stuff to Degussa, who sold the marketing rights to two other chemical companies. I won't even bother telling you their names. It would just confuse you. So, in fact, I. G. Farben held only a twenty percent share in the gas, with the lion's share owned by another company, Goldschmidt AG of Essen.

"Why am I telling you this? Let me explain. When I moved into this building, I felt kind of uncomfortable at the idea that I might be breathing the same kind of office air as the folks who developed that poison gas. So I resolved to find out about it for myself. And I discovered that it really wasn't true that I. G. Farben had had very much to do with that gas. I also discovered that back in 1929, the U.S. Public Health Service was using Zyklon B to disinfect the clothes of Mexican immigrants and the freight trains they were traveling in. At the New Orleans Quarantine Station. Incidentally, the stuff is still being manufactured today, in Czechoslovakia, in the city of Köln. They call it Uragan D2 and they use it to disinfect the trains that German POWs have been traveling on. Back to the Homeland.

"You see, Herr Gunther, I have a passion for information. Some people call that sort of thing trivia, but I do not. I call that truth. Or knowledge. Or even, when I'm sitting in my office, intelligence.

I have an appetite for facts, sir. Facts. Whether it's facts about I. G. Farben, Zyklon B gas, Mackie Messer, or Erich Mielke."

I sipped my coffee. It was horrible. Like stewed socks. I reached for my cigarettes and remembered that I'd smoked the last of them in the car.

"Give Herr Gunther a cigarette, will you, Phil? That was what you were after, was it not?"

"Yes. Thank you."

Scheuer lit me with an armor-plated Dunhill and then lit one for himself. I noticed the shields on his bow tie were the same as the ones on the Chief's, and I assumed they shared more than just a service, but a background, too. Ivy League, probably.

"Your letter, Herr Gunther, was fascinating. Especially in the context of what Phil here has told me and what I've read in the file. But it's my job to discover how much of it is fact. Oh, I'm not for a moment suggesting that you're lying to us. But after twenty years, people can easily make mistakes. That's fair, isn't it?"

"Very fair."

He regarded my undrunk coffee with vicarious disgust. "Horrible, isn't it? The coffee. I don't know why we put up with it. Phil, get Herr Gunther something stronger. What are you drinking, sir?"

"A schnapps would be nice," I said, and glanced around as Scheuer fetched a bottle and a small glass from inside the sideboard and placed it on the desk. "Thank you."

"Coaster," snapped the Chief.

Coasters were fetched and placed under the bottle and my glass.

"This table's made of walnut," said the Chief. "Walnut marks like a damask napkin. Now, then, sir. You have your cigarette. You have your drink. All I need from you are some facts."

In his fingers he held a sheet of unfolded paper on which I recognized my own handwriting. He placed a pair of half-moon glasses on the end of his snub nose and viewed the letter with a detached curiosity. He barely read the contents before letting the note fall onto the table.

"Naturally, I've read this. Several times. But now that you're here, I'd prefer it if you told me, in person, what you have written to Agents Scheuer and Frei in this letter of yours."

"So that you can see if I deviate from what I wrote before?"

"We understand each other perfectly."

"Well, *the facts* are these," I said, suppressing a smile. "As a condition of my working with the SDECE—"

The Chief winced. "Exactly what does that mean, Phil?"

"Service de Documentation Extérieure et de Contre-Espionnage," said Scheuer.

The Chief nodded. "Go on, Herr Gunther."

"Well, I agreed to work for them if they permitted me to visit Berlin and an old friend of mine. Perhaps the only friend I have left."

"She have a name? This friend of yours?"

"Elisabeth," I said.

"Surname? Address?"

"I don't want her involved in any of this."

"Meaning you don't want to tell me."

"That's true."

"You met her how and when?"

"Nineteen thirty-one. She was a seamstress. A good one, too. She worked in the same tailor's shop as Erich Mielke's sister, which was also where Mielke's mother, Lydia Mielke, worked until her death in 1911. It was pretty hard for Erich's father, bringing up four children on his own. His elder daughter went to work and cooked the family meals, and because Elisabeth was her friend, sometimes she helped out. There were even times when Elisabeth was like a sister to Erich."

"Where did they live? Can you remember the address?"

"Stettiner Strasse. A gray tenement building in Gesundbrunnen, in northwest Berlin. Number twenty-five. It was Erich who introduced me to Elisabeth. After I'd saved his neck."

"Tell me about that."

I told him.

"And this is when you met Mielke's father."

"Yes. I went to Mielke's address to try to arrest him, and the old man took a swing at me and I had to arrest him. It was Elisabeth who had given me the address, and she wasn't very happy that I'd asked her for it. As a result, our relationship hit a rock. And it was very much later on, I suppose it must have been the autumn of 1940, before we became reacquainted, and the following year before we started our relationship again."

"You never mentioned any of this when you were interrogated at Landsberg," said the Chief. "Why not?"

I shrugged. "It hardly seemed relevant at the time. I almost forgot that Elisabeth even knew Erich. Not least because she'd always kept it a secret from him that we were friends. Erich didn't like cops much, to put it mildly. I started seeing her again in the winter of 1946, when I came back from the Russian POW camp. I lived with Elisabeth for a short while until I managed to find my wife again in Berlin. But I was always very fond of her, and she of me. And recently, when I was in Paris, I got to thinking of her again and wondering if she was okay. I suppose you might say I began to entertain romantic thoughts about her. Like I said, there's no one else in Berlin I know. So I was resolved to look her up as soon as possible and see if she and I couldn't make another go of it."

"And how did that go?"

"It went well. She's not married. She was involved with some American soldier. More than one, I think. Anyway, both men were married, and so they went back to their wives in the States, leaving her, middle-aged and scared about the future."

I poured a glass of schnapps and sipped it while the Chief watched me closely, as if weighing my story in each hand, trying to judge how much or how little he believed.

"She was at the same address as she'd been in 1946?"

"Yes."

"We can always ask the French, you know. Her address."

"Go ahead."

"They might reasonably assume that's where you've gone," he said. "They might even make life difficult for her. Have you thought of that? We could protect her. The French aren't always as romantic as they're often portrayed."

"Elisabeth lived through the battle of Berlin," I said. "She was raped by the Russians. Besides, she's not the type to give a man an injection of thiopental on the streets of Göttingen in broad daylight. When Grottsch tells his story, I imagine the French will think the Russians pinched me, don't you? After all, that's what you wanted them to think, isn't it? I wouldn't be at all surprised if your men were speaking Russian when they grabbed him. Just for appearance's sake."

"At least tell me if she lives in the East or the West."

"In the West. The French gave me a passport in the name of Sébastien Kléber. You'll be able to check me coming through Checkpoint Alpha at Helmstedt, and into Berlin at the Dreilinger Crossing. But not leaving it to enter East Berlin."

"All right. Tell me your news about Erich Mielke."

"My friend Elisabeth said she'd seen Mielke's father, Erich. That he was still alive and in good health. He was in his early seventies, she said. They went for a coffee at the Café Kranzler. He said he'd been living in the DDR but that he didn't like it. Missed the football and his old neighborhood. While Elisabeth was telling me this, it was clear she had no idea what Erich junior had been doing. Who and what he was. All she said was that Erich visits his father from time to time and gives him money. And I assumed, given who he was, that this must be in secret."

"From time to time. How often is that?"

"Regularly. Once a month."

"Why didn't you say so?"

"I might have, if you'd given me enough time."

"Did she say where Erich senior had been living? In the DDR?"

"The village of Schönwalde, northwest of Berlin. She said he told her he had a nice enough cottage there but that he was bored in Schönwalde. It's rather a boring place. Of course, she knew that Erich senior had been a staunch communist and so she asked him if living in the West meant he had left the party. And he said that he had come to the conclusion that the communists were every bit as bad as the Nazis."

"She said he said that?"

"Yes."

"You know, we checked and there's no record of an Erich Mielke living in West Berlin."

"Mielke's father isn't called Mielke. His name is Erich Stellmacher. Mielke was illegitimate. Not that the father's using the name of Stellmacher either."

"Did she tell you what his name is?"

"No."

"Give you an address?"

"Stellmacher isn't that stupid."

"But there is something. Something you'd like to trade."

"Yes. Stellmacher told Elisabeth the name of a restaurant where he regularly likes to go for lunch on Saturdays."

"And your idea is? What, exactly?"

"This is your area of expertise, not mine, Chief. I was never much of an intelligence officer. I didn't have the kind of dirty mind to be really effective in your world. I was a better detective, I think. Better at uncovering a mess than creating one."

"I see you have a low opinion of intelligence."

"Just the people who work in it."

"Us included."

"You especially."

"You prefer the French?"

"There's something honest about their hypocrisy and self-regard."

"As a former Berlin detective, what would you propose?"

"Follow Erich Stellmacher from his favorite restaurant to his apartment. And lay a trap for Erich Mielke there."

"Risky."

"Sure," I said. "But now that you've pulled me, you're going to do it all the same. You have to, now that you've partly undermined all that black propaganda I'd been giving to the French about Mielke being your agent—and before that, an agent of the Nazis. Without the cherry on the cake—me identifying de Boudel for them—maybe they won't find all those lies I told about Erich so persuasive anymore."

"It's true that we would like to get our hands on Mielke. With his father in our back pocket, we could even perhaps turn him into the spy you told the French he was. Of course, then we'd have to blacken your name to the French. To make sure they formed the correct impression about Mielke again. That he was and always had been a perfect communist bastard."

"You see, I knew you'd think of some way around these problems."

"And you. What will you want to help?"

I frowned. "I can show you where the restaurant is. Maybe even get you a table."

"We shall want more help than that. After all, you've met Erich Stellmacher. He took a swing at you. You arrested him. You must have got a good look at him that day. No, Herr Gunther, we shall want more than your help in obtaining a table at this man

Stellmacher's favorite watering hole. We shall want you to identify him."

I smiled wearily.

"Something funny about that?"

"You're not the first intelligence chief to have asked me to do this. Heydrich had the same idea."

"I've often wondered about Heydrich," said the Chief. "They said he was the cleverest Nazi of the bunch. You agree with that?"

"It's true he had an instinctive understanding of power, which made him a very effective Nazi. You like facts, sir? Then here's a fact about Reinhard Heydrich you might appreciate. His father, Richard Bruno, was a music teacher and before that a composer of sorts. Ten years before his son was born, Richard Heydrich wrote an opera entitled *Reinhard's Crime*. Oh yes, and here's another fact: Heydrich was murdered."

"You don't say."

"I was the investigating detective."

"Interesting."

"More interesting to me right now is the money that was taken from me when I was arrested in Cuba. And the boat that was impounded. That's part of the price for my help. Actually, it was the price of the deal we had in Landsberg in return for me bullshitting the French, so you're only agreeing to what your people have already agreed to. I want the boat sold and all of the money paid into a Swiss bank account, as we agreed. I also want an American passport. And, for delivering Erich Mielke, the sum of twenty-five thousand U.S. dollars."

"That's a lot."

"Given that I'm about to deliver the deputy head of the East German State Security apparatus, I'd say it was cheap at twice the price."

"Philip?"

"Yes, sir?"

"A price worth paying, would you say?"

"For Mielke? Yes, sir, I would. I've always thought that, since the beginning of this whole intelligence effort."

"Because you know I shall want you to play the ringmaster at Herr Gunther's show, don't you?"

"No, sir."

"Then I guess you know it now, eh, Philip?"

Scheuer looked uncomfortable at being put on the spot like this. "Yes, sir."

"You too, Jim."

Frei raised his eyebrows at that but nodded all the same.

I poured myself another glass of schnapps.

"Why not?" said the Chief. "I think we could all use a drink. Don't you agree, Phil?"

"Yes, sir. I think we could."

"But not schnapps, eh? Forgive me, Herr Gunther. There's a lot about your country I admire. But we're not very keen on schnapps at the CIA."

"I imagine it's rather hard to spike a glass this small."

"Don't you believe it." The Chief smiled. "Hmm. Yes, that's quite a sense of humor you have there, for a German."

Philip Scheuer produced a bottle of bourbon and three glasses.

"Sure you won't try any of this, Herr Gunther?" said the Chief. "To toast your deal with Ike."

"Why not?" I said.

"Good man. We'll make an American of you yet, sir."

But that was exactly what I was worried about.

BERLIN, 1954

M ost people go through life accumulating possessions. I seemed to have gone through mine losing them or having them taken away from me. The only thing I still had from before the war was a broken chess piece made of bone—the head of a black knight from a Selenus chess set. During the last days of the Weimar Republic this black knight had been consistently in use at the Romanisches Café, where, once or twice, I'd played the great Emanuel Lasker. He'd been a regular at the café until the Nazis obliged him and his brother to leave Germany forever in 1933. I could still picture him crouched over a board with his cigarettes and cigars and his Wild West mustache. Generous to a fault, he would give out tips or play exhibitions for anyone who was interested; and on his last day in the Romanisches Café—he went to Moscow and then to New York—Lasker presented everyone who was there to wish him good-bye with a chess piece from the café's best set. I got the black knight. The way I'd been played over the years, I sometimes think a black pawn would have been more appropriate. Then again, a knight, even a broken one, seems intrinsically more valuable than a pawn, which was probably why I tried so hard to keep it through one adversity after another. The little bone base had become detached during the Battle of Königsberg and was lost soon afterward, but somehow the horse's head had remained in my possession. I might have called it my lucky charm but for the salient fact that one way or another I'd not always had the best of luck. On the other hand, I was still in the game, and sometimes that's all the luck you need. Anything—absolutely anything—can happen so long as you stay in the game. And lately, as if to remind myself of this fact, the little black knight's head was often held tight in my fist the way a Mohammedan might have used a set of beads to utter the ninety-nine names of God and bring him closer during prayer. Only, it wasn't being closer to God I wanted but something more earthly. Freedom. Independence. Self-respect. No longer to be the pawn of others in a game I wasn't interested in. Surely that wasn't so much to ask.

The flight to Berlin from Frankfurt aboard a DC-7 took just under an hour. Traveling with me were Scheuer, Frei, and a third man—the man with the heavy-framed glasses who had kidnapped me in Göttingen; his name was Hamer. A black Mercedes was waiting for us in front of the airport building at Tempelhof. As we drove away, Scheuer pointed out the monument to the Berlin airlift of 1948 that occupied the center of Eagle Square. Made of concrete and taller than the airport building itself, the monument was supposed to represent the three air corridors that were used to fly in supplies during the Soviet blockade. It looked more like the statue of a comic-book ghost, arms raised, leaning over to scare someone. And as I glanced back at the airport, I was rather more interested in the fate of the Nazi eagle that surmounted the center wall of the airport building. There could be no doubt about it: The eagle had been Americanized. Someone had painted its head white so that now it looked more like an American bald eagle.

We drove west, through the American sector, which was clean and prosperous-looking, with lots of plate-glass shop windows and garish new movie houses showing the latest Hollywood movies: *Rear Window*, *On the Waterfront*, and *Dial M for Murder*. Ihnestrasse, close to the university and the new Henry Ford Building, looked much the same as it had before the war. Lots of chestnut trees and well-kept gardens. The American flags were new, of course. There was a large one on the flagpole in front of the American Officers' Club at Harnack House—formerly the guest quarters of the famous Kaiser Wilhelm Institute. Scheuer told me proudly that the club had a restaurant, a beauty parlor, a barbershop, and a newsstand and promised to take me there. But somehow I didn't think the Kaiser would have approved: He was never very fond of Americans.

We stayed in a villa farther down the street from the club. From my dormer window at the back you could see a small lake. The only sounds were the birds in the trees and the bicycle bells of students going to and from the Free University of Berlin like little couriers of hope for a city I was finding it hard to love again, in spite of the instant service that came with my room in the shape of an obsequious valet in a white mess jacket who offered to bring me coffee and a donut. I declined both and asked for a bottle of schnapps and some cigarettes. Worst of all was the music: hidden speakers playing some honey-voiced female singer who seemed to follow me from the dining room, through the hall, and into the library. It wasn't particularly loud or obtrusive, but it was there when it didn't need to be. I asked the valet about it. His name was George and he told me that the singer was Ella Fitzgerald, as if that made it okay.

The furniture looked like it was original to the house, so that was all right, although the water cooler in the library seemed some-how out of place, as did the periodic eructations of air that passed through the water like an enormous belch. It sounded like my own conscience.

The Am Steinplatz restaurant was at 197 Uhlandstrasse, southwest of the Tiergarten, and dated from before the war. The dilapidated exterior of the building belied a restaurant that was good enough to warrant inclusion in the U.S. Army's Berlin booklet, which meant that the place was popular with American officers and their German girlfriends. There was a bar with a dining room serving a mixture of American and Berlin favorites. The four of us—me and the three Amis—occupied a table window in the dining room. The waitress wore glasses and wore her hair shorter than seemed right, as if it had yet to grow back after some personal disaster. She was German, but she spoke English first, as if she knew that there were few Berliners who could have afforded the prices on the extensive menu. We ordered wine and lunch. The place was still more or less empty, so we knew Erich Stellmacher wasn't yet there. But it quickly filled up until there was only one table left.

"He probably won't come," said Frei. "Not this time. That's always been my experience of stakeouts. The target never comes the first time."

"Let's hope you're not wrong," said Hamer. "The food in here's so damn good I want to come back. Several times."

Rain hit the steamed-up window of the restaurant. A cork popped from a bottle of wine. The officers at the next table laughed loudly, like men who were used to laughing in wide-open spaces, possibly on horseback, but never in small Berlin restaurants. They even clinked their glasses with more panache and noise than was properly required. In the kitchen someone shouted that an order was ready. I looked at Scheuer's watch—my own was still in a paper bag back at Landsberg. It was one-thirty.

"Maybe I'll check the bar," I said.

"Good idea," said Scheuer.

"Give me some money for cigarettes," I told him. "For appearance's sake."

I went through to the bar, bought some English cigarettes from the barman, and glanced around while he found me a light. Some men were playing dominoes in a snug little alcove. A dog was lying on the floor beside them, its tail wagging periodically. An old man sat in a corner nursing a beer and reading the previous day's edition of *Die Zeit*. I took a quick schnapps with the change, lit my cigarette, and went back into the restaurant as a coffee machine howled like an arctic wind. I sat down, stubbed out the cigarette, sawed off a corner of my uneaten schnitzel, and said:

"He's in there."

"My God," said Frei. "I don't believe it."

"Are you sure?" asked Hamer.

"I never forget a man who's punched me."

"You don't think he recognized you?" said Scheuer.

"No," I said. "He's wearing reading glasses. And there's another pair in his top pocket. My guess is he's long in one eye and short in the other."

A Bavarian-looking wall clock struck the half hour. At the next table, one of the Americans pushed his chair away with the backs of his legs. On the hard wooden floor of the restaurant it sounded like a drumroll.

"So what happens now?" asked Hamer.

"We stick to the plan," said Scheuer. "Gunther will follow him and we'll follow Gunther. He knows this city better than any of us."

"I'll need more money," I said. "For the U-Bahn or a tram. And if I lose you, I might have to get a taxi back to Ihnestrasse."

"You won't lose us." Hamer smiled confidently.

"All the same," said Scheuer. "He's right." He handed me some notes and some small change.

I stood up.

"Are you going to sit in the bar?" asked Frei.

"No. Not unless I want him to recognize me later. I'm going to stand outside and wait for him there."

"In the rain?"

"That's the general idea. You'd best stay out of the bar. We wouldn't want him to feel like he was of any interest to anyone."

"Here," said Frei. "You can borrow my hat."

I tried it on. The hat was too big, so I handed it back to him. "Keep it," I said. "I'll stand in a doorway on the opposite side of the road and watch from there."

Scheuer cleaned a patch of condensation from the window. "And we'll watch you from here."

Hamer looked at my half-eaten food. "You Germans eat too much anyway," he observed.

Ignoring him, I said, "I follow him. Not you. If you think I've lost him, don't panic. Just keep your distance. And don't try to find him again for me. I know what I'm doing. Try to remember that. I used to do this kind of thing for a living. If he goes in another building, then wait outside, don't follow me in. He might have friends looking out of a window."

"Good luck," said Scheuer.

"Good luck to us all," I said, and drained the contents of my wineglass. Then I went outside.

For the first time in a while, I felt a spring in my step. Things were starting to work out nicely. I didn't mind the rain in the least. It felt good on my face. Refreshing. I took up a position in the doorway of the soot-blackened building opposite. A cold doorway. A policeman's true station, and blowing on my fingernails for want of gloves, I settled in against the inside wall. Once, a long time ago, I'd lived not fifty or sixty meters from where I was standing, in an apartment on Fasanenstrasse. The long, hot summer of 1938, when the whole of Europe breathed a collective sigh of relief because the threat of war had been averted. So we had thought, anyway. When Henry Ford had finished saying history is bunk, he also said that most of us preferred to live in the present and not to think about the past. Or words to that effect. But in Berlin the past was rather harder to avoid.

A man came down the stairs of the building and asked me for a cigarette. I gave him one and for a moment or two we talked, but all the time I kept one eye on the two doors of the Am Steinplatz. At the opposite end of Uhlandstrasse, near the eponymous square, was a hotel called the Steinplatz. The two establishments were owned by the same people; to the confusion of all Americans, they even shared the same telephone number. The confusion of all Americans was just fine by me.

It stopped raining and the sun came out, and a few minutes later so did my quarry. He paused, looked up at the clearing sky, and lit a pipe, which was my chance to get another good look at him.

He was wearing an old loden coat and a hat with a goose feather in the silk band, and you could hear the nails in his shoes from the other side of the street. He was stout and balding and wore a different pair of glasses now. There was, without a doubt, a strong resemblance to Erich Mielke. He was about the same height, too. He checked his fly as if he'd been to the lavatory and walked south toward Kant Strasse. After a decent interval, I followed with one hand on my little knight's head.

I felt even better now that I was walking alone. Well, almost alone. I glanced around and saw two of them—Frei and Hamer—about thirty meters behind me, on opposite sides of the street. I couldn't see Scheuer and decided he'd probably gone to fetch the car so that they wouldn't have to walk when, eventually, we tracked our man to his lair. Americans didn't like walking any more than they cared to miss a meal. Since I'd started to spend some time with them I had observed that the average American—supposing that these men were average Americans—eats about twice as much as the average German. Every day.

On Kant Strasse the man turned right toward Savigny Platz; then, near the S-Bahn, a train pulled into the elevated station above his head and he broke into a trot. So did I, and I only just managed to buy a ticket and board the train before the doors closed and we were on our way, northeast, toward Old Moabit. Hamer and Frei weren't so lucky, and just as the train pulled out I glimpsed them running up the stairs of Savigny Platz Station. I might have smiled at them, too, if what I was doing hadn't felt so vital to my own future and fortune.

I sat down and stared straight ahead and out of the window. All of the old police training was kicking in again: the way to follow a man without making yourself obvious. Mostly, it was about keeping your distance and learning how to tail a man who was behind you as often as he was in front of you—or, as now, in the adjoining carriage. I could see him through the connecting window, still reading his newspaper. That made it easier for me, of course. And the thought that I was well on top of it made the discomfiture that was very likely being experienced by the Amis all the more enjoyable. Scheuer I almost liked, but Hamer and Frei were a different matter. I especially disliked Hamer, if only because of his arrogance and because he seemed to have a real dislike of Germans. Well, we were used to that. But it was still annoying.

Without moving my head, I rolled my eyes to one side like a ventriloquist's dummy. We were coming into Zoo Station, and I was watching the newspaper in the next carriage to see if it got folded away, but it stayed erect and remained that way through the stations at Tiergarten and Bellevue; but at Lehrter it finally came down and the reader stood up to disembark.

He went down the steps and walked north, with Humboldt Harbor on his right. Several canal boats moored together in one large flotilla shifted gently on the steel-blue water of the British sector. On the other side of the same harbor was the Charité Hospital and the Russian sector. In the distance, East German or possibly Russian border guards manned a checkpoint on the junction of Invalidenstrasse and the Canal. But we were walking north, up Heide Strasse, until we came to the French sector, where we turned right along Fenn Strasse and onto the triangular Wedding Platz. I paused for a moment to take in the ruins of the Dankes Church, where I had married my first wife, and then caught a last glimpse of my man as finally he went to ground in a tall building on the southern Schulzendorfer Strasse, overlooking the old disused brewery.

There was little or no traffic on the square. Almost as bankrupt as the British, the French had little money to spend regenerating German business in the area, let alone for the restoration of a church that had been built in thanksgiving for the delivery of their ancient mortal enemy, Kaiser Wilhelm I, from an attempt made on his life in 1878.

I approached the building on the corner of Schulzendorfer Strasse and glanced down Chaussee Strasse. Here the border crossing point, on Liesen Strasse, was very close and probably just the other side of the brewery wall. I looked at the names on the brass bellpulls and figured that Erich Stahl was close enough to Eric Stellmacher for our clandestine operation now to proceed as planned.

BERLIN, 1954

We moved to a small and very crummy safe house on Dreyse Strasse, east of Moabit Hospital, in the British zone, which, Scheuer said, was as close to Stallmacher's apartment as we dared to get for the moment without tipping our hand to the Russians or, for that matter, the French. The British were told only that we were keeping a suspected black marketeer under surveillance.

The plan was simple: that I, being a Berliner, would contact the owner of the building on Schulzendorfer Strasse and offer to rent one of several empty apartments using my wife's maiden name. The owner, a retired lawyer from Wilmersdorf, showed me around the apartment—which he'd furnished himself—and it was much better on the inside than it looked from the outside. He explained that the building had been owned and administered by his wife, Martha, until she had been killed by a bomb the previous year while visiting her mother's grave in Oranienburg.

"They said she never knew a thing," said Herr Schurz. "A two-hundred-and-fifty-kilogram American aerial bomb had lain there for almost ten years without anyone noticing. A grave digger twenty meters away was digging, and he must have hit the thing with his pickax."

"That's too bad," I said.

"They say Oranienburg is full of unexploded ordnance. The soil is soft there, you see, with a hard layer of gravel underneath. The bombs would penetrate the earth but not the gravel." He shrugged and then shook his head. "Apparently, there were a lot of targets in Oranienburg."

I nodded. "The Heinkel factory. And a pharmaceutical plant. Not to mention a suspected atomic bomb research plant."

"Are you married, Herr Handlöser?"

"No, my wife also is dead. She got pneumonia. But she'd been ill for a while, so it wasn't as unexpected as what happened to your wife."

I went to the window and looked down onto the street.

"This is a big apartment for someone living by himself," said Schurz.

"I'm planning to take in a couple of tenants to help me with the rent," I said. "If that's all right with you. Some gentlemen from an American Bible school."

"I'm pleased to hear it," said Schurz. "That's what the whole French sector needs now. More Americans. They're the only ones with any money. Talking of which."

I counted some banknotes into his eager hand. He gave me a set of keys, and then I returned to the safe house on Dreyse Strasse.

"As far as the landlord is concerned," I said, "we can move in tomorrow."

"You said nothing to him about Stahl or Stellmacher," said Scheuer.

"I did exactly as you told me. I didn't even ask about the neighbors. So what happens now?"

"We move in and keep the place under close surveillance,"

said Scheuer. "Wait for Erich Mielke to visit his dad and then go upstairs to introduce ourselves."

Frei laughed. "Hello, we're your new neighbors. Can we interest you in defecting to the West? You and your old man."

"What happened to the idea of making him into your spy?"

"Not enough leverage. Our political masters want to know what the East German leadership is thinking now, not what they're thinking in a year's time. So we grab him and take him back to the States to debrief him."

"You're forgetting Mielke's wife, Gertrud, aren't you? And doesn't he have a son now? Frank? He won't want to leave them, surely."

"We're not forgetting them at all," said Scheuer. "But I rather think that Erich will. From everything we know about him, he's not the sentimental sort. Besides, he can always apply for them to come to the West as well. And it's not like there's a wall that's stopping them from coming."

"And if he doesn't want to defect?"

"Well, then that's too bad."

"You'll kidnap him?"

"That's not a word we use," said Scheuer. "The U.S. Constitution permits public policy exceptions to the normal legal process of extradition. But I doubt any of this is going to matter. As soon as he sees the four of us, he'll know the game is up and that he has no choice in the matter."

"And when you do take him back? What then?"

Scheuer grinned. "I don't even want to think about that until we've got him, Gunther. Mielke's the great white whale for the CIA in Germany. We land him, we get enough oil to burn in our lamps to see what we're doing in this country for years to come. The Stasi might never recover from a blow like this. It could even help us to win the Cold War."

"Damn right," said Hamer. "Mielke's the whole fucking ball game. There's very little that bastard doesn't know about communist plans in Germany. Will they invade? Will they keep to their side of the fence? How far are they prepared to go to hold on to the yardage they've already won? And just how independent of Moscow is the current East German leadership?"

Frei clapped me on the shoulder amicably. "Gunther, old buddy," he said. "You help us get this bastard, you're set for life, do you hear? By the time Ike gets through thanking you, my German friend, you'll feel more American than we do."

Hamer frowned. "Don't you think it's time Gunther should maybe get some more intel from his lady friend? Does Mielke come on a weekend? Does he come at the beginning or the end of the month? We could be in that apartment for weeks waiting for this kraut to show up."

But Scheuer was shaking his head. "No, it's best we leave things as they are. Besides, I think Gunther's already tested the limit of his friendship with this lady. If he asks her any more questions about Mielke, she's just liable to start wondering who he's more interested in. Him or her. And I wouldn't want her to become jealous. Jealous women do unpredictable things."

He went to the window of the safe house, drew back a gray-white length of net curtain, and looked out as an ambulance raced up Bendlerstrasse to the hospital, its bell ringing furiously.

"That reminds me," said Scheuer. He turned to look at Frei. "Did you get hold of that ambulance?"

"Yes."

"It's not for us." Scheuer glanced at me. "It's for the package."

"You mean Mielke."

"That's right. But from now on we never use that name. Not until he's on a private wing at the U.S. Army hospital in Lichterfelde."

"I suppose you'll give him thiopental, too," I said.

"Only if we have to."

"Ain't like it's rationed," said Frei.

Hamer laughed. "Not for us, anyway."

"By the way," I said. "Feel free to pay me any day soon."

"You'll get your lousy money," said Hamer.

"I've heard that before." I shot a sarcastic smile Hamer's way and then looked at Scheuer. "Look, all I am asking is that I see a letter from the kind of Swiss bank that treats you like just another number. And all I want is what's mine."

"And where did that come from?" said Hamer.

"None of your goddamn business. But since you ask so politely, Hamer, I won it gambling. In Havana. You can pay me the twenty-five thousand as a bonus if and when you collect the package."

"Gambling. Yeah, sure."

"When I was arrested in Cuba, I had a receipt to prove that."

"So did the SS when they robbed the Jews," said Hamer.

"If you're suggesting that's how I came by my money, you're wrong. The way you're wrong about nearly everything, Hamer."

"You'll get your money," said Scheuer. "Don't worry about it. Everything is in hand."

I nodded, not because I believed him but because I wanted him to believe that money was what motivated me now, when it wasn't. Not anymore. I squeezed the black knight in my trouser pocket and determined to imitate its action on the chessboard. To move obliquely one square to the side before jumping two squares forward. In a closed position, what else could I do?

BERLIN, 1954

The following afternoon, with our bags and suitcases packed—mine was the smallest—we prepared to leave the pension in Dreyse Strasse and move into the apartment on Schulzendorfer Strasse. None of us were sorry to be out of there. The landlady owned several cats and these were not much inclined to piss out of doors; even with the windows open, the place smelled like an old people's home. We filled a newish-looking VW transporter van with ourselves and our luggage and our equipment. Scheuer drove, with me sitting in the passenger seat and giving directions, while Hamer and Frei rolled around in the back with the bags, complaining loudly. Following at a distance was the ambulance containing what Scheuer called "security"—CIA muscle with guns and shortwave radios. According to Scheuer's plan, the ambulance would park a short distance away from Schulzendorfer Strasse, and when the time came, these men were ready to help us grab Erich Mielke.

I told Scheuer to drive north onto Perleberger Strasse intending to go across the canal on Fennbrücke, but an old building on the corner of Quitzowstrasse had collapsed across the road and we were obliged by the local police and the fire brigade to go south down Heide Strasse.

"We'd better not cross the canal on Invalidenstrasse," I told Scheuer. "For obvious reasons."

Invalidenstrasse, on the east side of the canal, was the DDR, and a new-looking transporter filled with Americans—not to mention an ambulance filled with armed men—was certain to attract unwelcome attention from the Grepos.

"Go west on Invalidenstrasse until you're on old Moabit and then right up Rathenower Strasse. We'll have to cross the canal on the Föhrer Bridge. If it's still there. It's been a while since I was up this way. Every time I come to Berlin, it looks different from the last time I was here."

Scheuer shouted at the two in the back. "That's why Gunther has the seat," he said. "So he can tell us where to go."

"I know where I'd like to tell him to go," grumbled Hamer.

Scheuer grinned at me. "He doesn't like you," he said.

"That's okay," I said. "I feel the same way about him."

On Rathenower we drove past a large, grim, star-shaped building on our left.

"What's that?" he asked.

"Moabit Prison," I said.

"And the other building?"

He meant the great, semiruined building just north of the prison, a huge fortress of an edifice that ran west along Turm Strasse for almost a hundred meters.

"That?" I smiled. "That is where this whole lousy story began. It's the Central Criminal Court. Back in May 1931, there were police cars parked the length of the street. And cops everywhere, inside and outside the building. But mostly outside, because that was where most of the Nazi storm troopers were gathered. A couple of thousand of them. Maybe more. And newspapermen crowded around the big doors of the entrance."

"An important trial was in progress, huh?"

"The Eden Dance Palace trial," I said. "Actually, it was a routine sort of case. Four Nazis had tried to murder some communists in a dance hall. Back in 1931, that was almost an everyday occurrence. No, it was the witness for the prosecution that made the case so noteworthy and why there were so many cops and Nazis on the scene. The witness was Adolf Hitler, and the prosecution lawyer wanted to show that Hitler was the malign force behind this kind of Nazi-on-communist violence. Hitler was always publicly affirming his commitment to law and order, and the prosecution hoped to expose this for a lie. So Hitler was summoned to testify."

"You were there?"

"Yes. But I was more interested in the four defendants and what they might have to say about another murder that I was investigating. But I saw him, yes. Who knew it would be the only occasion on which Hitler would have to answer for his crimes before a court of law? He arrived in court wearing a blue suit and for several minutes played the good, law-abiding citizen. But gradually, as the questioning continued, he began to contradict himself and then to lose his temper. The SA, he claimed, was forbidden to commit or to provoke any violence. Many of his answers even provoked laughter in the spectators' gallery. And finally, after giving evidence for almost four hours, Hitler lost all composure and started to rant at the lawyer questioning him. Who happened to be a Jew.

"Now, under German law, the oath is given after testimony, not before. And when Hitler swore to the truth of his evidence—that he was pursuing legal, democratic methods to gain political power—there were very few who believed him. I know I didn't. It was plain to anyone who was there that Hitler was absolutely complicit in SA violence, and I suppose you could say that this was the minute when I realized for sure that I could never be a Nazi and follow an obvious liar like Hitler."

"So what did you mean when you said that this was where the story began?"

"Mielke's story. Or rather, my Mielke story. If I hadn't been to the Central Criminal Court that day, I might not have thought it worth going to Tegel Prison a couple of weeks later to question one of the four SA defendants. And if I hadn't gone to Tegel that day, I might never have seen some SA men piling out of a bar in Charlottenburg and followed them. In which case, I'd never have seen Erich Mielke or saved his life. That's what I mean."

"Given everything that happened afterward," said Hamer, "we'd all have been a lot better off if you'd just let him get killed."

"But that would mean I'd never have had the pleasure of your acquaintance, Agent Hamer," I said.

"Less of the 'Agent,' Gunther," said Scheuer. "From now on, we're all of us just gentlemen, okay?"

"Does that include Herr Hamer?"

"Keep riding me, Gunther, you arrogant German bastard," said Hamer, "and see where it gets you. I almost hope Erich Mielke doesn't come. Just to bring you down a size or two. Not to mention the pleasure of seeing you come up short on twenty-five thousand bucks."

"He'll come," I said.

"How do you really know that?" said Hamer.

"Because he loves his father, of course. I wouldn't expect you to understand something like that, Hamer. You'd have to know who your father is to love him."

"Hamer," said Scheuer. "I'm ordering you not to answer that. And Gunther? That's enough." He pointed at the road ahead. "Where now?"

"Left on Quitzowstrasse, and then right onto Putlitzstrasse."

We drove west with the Ringbahn on our right, keeping pace with the little red and yellow train that clattered toward Putlitz-strasse Station, moving along the green verge and overgrown track like two snooker balls. The redbrick station with its tall arched window and tower was more medieval abbey than rail terminus.

Dusk was fast approaching, and under the weak, greenish gaze of the praying mantis streetlamps of the Föhrer Brücke, we drove into Wedding. With its textile works, breweries, and massive electronics factories, Wedding had been the industrial heart of Berlin and a communist stronghold. Back in 1930, forty-three percent of Wedding voters, many of them soon to be made unemployed by the Great Depression, had voted for the KPD. Once it had been one of the most overcrowded bezirks in Berlin; now, with long winter nights fast approaching and no sign of the economic revival that had come to the American sector, Wedding looked almost deserted, as if all had been taken away to the ships of the conquerors. In truth, Berlin had always gone to bed early, especially in winter, but never in the late afternoon.

Scheuer hammered the steering wheel with excitement as he turned us onto Trift Strasse. "I can't believe we're really gonna get this guy," he said. "We're gonna get Mielke."

"Fuck, yeah," said Frei, and whooped loudly.

The three of them sounded like a basketball team trying to rouse themselves for an important game.

"If only you knew, Gunther," said Scheuer, "what this guy is capable of. He likes to torture people himself. Did you know that?"

I shook my head.

"Les Bauer," continued Scheuer. "A party member since 1932, he was arrested in 1950 and Mielke beat him like a dog. The Russians sentenced Bauer to death, and the only reason he's still alive is because Stalin is dead. And Kurt Muller, head of the KPD in Lower Saxony. The Stasi lured him to East Berlin for a party meeting and then accused him of being a Trotskyite. Mielke tortured him, too. Poor Muller has spent the last four years in solitary confinement in the Stasi's own prison at Halle. The Red Ox, they call it. And you don't want to know what Mielke's done to the CIA agents they've caught. Mielke's a real Gestapo type. They say he has a bust of Felix Dzerzhinsky in his office. You know—the first Bolshevik secret police chief? Believe me, this guy Mielke makes your friend Heydrich look like an amateur. If we get Mielke, we can cripple the whole Stasi."

I'd heard it—or something like it—before and I hardly cared. This was their war, not mine. Probably the Stasi thought the CIA "fascists" were just as bad.

As we neared the end of Trift Strasse, I told Scheuer to turn right onto Müller Strasse.

"That's Wedding Platz just ahead," I said.

Approaching the apartment building on the corner of Schul zendorfer Strasse, Hamer, kneeling behind us, said, "What a dump. I can't imagine why anyone would want to swap a cottage in Schönwalde to live here."

Scheuer, who had been to the apartment himself, said, "Really, it's not so bad inside."

"Well, I don't get it."

I shrugged. "That's because you're not a Berliner, Hamer. Erich Mielke's father has lived in and around this area all his life. It's in the bone. Like the allegiance to a tribe or a gang. For an old Berlin communist like Stellmacher, this is the center of German communism. Not police headquarters in East Berlin. And I wouldn't be at all surprised if he has some old friends who live in these very streets. That's a big thing for Berliners. Community. I don't expect you get that much where you come from. You have to trust your neighbors in order to be neighborly."

Scheuer stopped the van and turned in his seat. A few meters away, the ambulance containing our security came to a halt.

"All right, listen up," said Scheuer. "This is a stakeout. And we could be here for a while until Erich junior shows up. No one mentions the Company. Once again, there's to be no Company names and no Company language. And nobody uses profanity. From now on, we're members of an American Bible school. And the first thing we take out of this van is a box of Bibles. Okay. Let's go and get this bastard."

But as we entered the building and trooped up the stone stairs, I almost hoped that Erich Mielke wouldn't come at all and that everything might stay the same as before. My heart was beating loudly now. Was it just the effort of climbing two flights of stairs with a box of Bibles in my arms, or something else? In my imagination I already saw the scene that lay ahead of us and felt a twinge of regret. I told myself that if only I'd remained in Cuba I would never have landed in the hands of the CIA and all of this might have been avoided. That even now I might have been reading a book in my apartment on Malecón, or enjoying the pleasures that were to be had in Omara's body at the Casa Marina. Was Mr. Greene still there, juggling breasts? Sometimes we just don't know when we're well off. And for the first time in a long time I wondered about poor Melba Marrero, the little *chica* rebel who'd shot the sailor on my boat. Was she in an American prison? For her sake, I hoped so. Or was she back in Havana and at the mercy of the corrupt local police, as she had feared? In which case, she might very likely be dead.

What was I doing here?

"Why did you have to suggest Bibles?" Hamer grunted loudly as he put the box he'd been carrying down on the landing outside the first-floor apartment's door. He looked at the door with obvious displeasure. "You sure about this place, Gunther? I've seen better-looking slums than this place."

"Actually," I said, "there's a very nice view of the gasworks from the sitting room window."

But in my imagination I saw only the CIA surrounding Mielke as he arrived to visit his father, and I heard only their snarling pleasure as they bundled him into the apartment, snapped some handcuffs on his wrists, hauled a canvas bag over his head, and tripped him onto the floor. Maybe they would kick and abuse him the same way I had been kicked and abused until something in me had broken, the way they had wanted it broken. And I realized that I had at last become the thing that I abhorred, that I had crossed an invisible line of decency and honor, that I was about to become the fascist I'd always detested.

"Stop complaining," said Scheuer, glancing anxiously up the stairs at the landing above, where he believed Erich Stellmacher's apartment was located.

I found the set of keys given to me by the landlord and slid one into the strong Dom lock. The key turned and I pushed at the heavy gray door. A strong smell of floor polish greeted our nostrils as we entered our apartment. I waited in the largish hallway until the last of the Amis was inside and then closed the door. Then I locked it, carefully.

What the fuck?" Agent Hamer's voice contained a tremor.

Agent Scheuer turned back to the locked door and was felled by a blow from a Makarova pistol to the back of the head.

Agent Frei was already in handcuffs. His face was pale and worried-looking.

There were six of them waiting for us in the apartment. They wore cheap gray suits and dark shirts and ties. All of them were armed with pistols—Soviet automatics with cheap plastic handles, but no less deadly for that. Their faces were impassive, as if they, too, were made of cheap Russian plastic, manufactured in quantity by some factory stolen from Germany and then reassembled on an eastern shore of the Volga. Just as cold as that river were their gray-blue eyes, and for a moment I saw myself in them: policemen doing their duty, taking no pleasure in these arrests but handling them quickly and with the efficiency of well-trained professionals.

The three Americans might have said something, but their

mouths were already stuffed with cloth and taped tight so that I only had their watery eyes to reproach me, although these were no less bitter for that.

I might have said something, too, but for the fact that the hand-cuffed men were already being marched downstairs—each between two Stasi men, as if they were being led to a firing squad. If I had spoken to them I might have adduced the months of ill-treatment I had endured at their hands, not to mention my desire to be away from their control and influence, but it hardly seemed appropriate or, for that matter, proportionate to what I'd now inflicted on them. I might even have mentioned something about the unquestioning assumption of all Americans that they had right on their side—even when they were doing wrong—and the irritation that the rest of the world felt at being judged by them; but that would have been to overstate the matter on my part. It wasn't so much that I did not care to be judged—for a German in the fifties that was, perhaps, unavoidable. It was simply that I did not care to be grateful for whatever it was the Amis were supposed to have done for us when it was abundantly clear to me and many other Germans that really they had done it for themselves. And hadn't they intended some rather similar treatment for Mielke himself?

"Where is he?" I asked one of the Stasi men.

"If you mean the comrade general," said the man, "he is waiting outside."

I followed them out of the apartment and downstairs, wondering how they were going to deal with the security men in the CIA ambulance—or had they already dealt with them? But before we reached the ground floor, we went through a door that led out of the back of the building and down a fire escape to a courtyard that was about the size of a tennis court and enclosed on all four sides by tall black tenements, most of them derelict.

We crossed the courtyard and, in fading light, went through a low wooden door in the wall of the old Schulzendorfer Brewery.

Underfoot the cobbles were loose, and in some places there were large potholes filled with water. The moon rippled in one of them like a lost silver coin. The three Americans did not resist, and to my experienced eyes, they already seemed to have acquired the compliant demeanor of POWs, with bowed heads and heavy, stumbling footsteps. A small tributary stream of the River Spree marked the edge of the narrowing courtyard. At its southern end was a building with broken, dirty windows and tall weeds growing on the roof; painted on the brickwork was a faded advertisement for "Chlorodont Toothpaste." I'd have needed a whole tube of the stuff to get rid of the nasty taste I had in my mouth. Within the word "Tooth" was a door, which one of the Stasi men opened. We went into a building that smelled of damp and probably something worse. Advancing to one of the filthy windows, the team leader looked carefully out onto a street.

He waited cautiously for almost five minutes and, having checked his watch, produced a flashlight, which he then aimed at the building opposite. Almost immediately, his signal was answered by three short flashes of a small green light and, across the street, a door opened. The three American prisoners were hustled across the street, and it was only when I put my own head out the door that I realized we were on Liesenstrasse and that the building on the opposite side of the street was in the Russian sector.

As the last of the three Americans was pushed across the road in the all-enveloping darkness and on into the building, I saw a portly figure standing in the doorway. He looked up and down the street and then waved to me.

"Come," he said. "Come quickly."

It was Erich Mielke.

40

BERLIN, 1954

He was shorter than I remembered, and stockier, too—a power-ful man who was square on his feet, with the air of a pugilist. His hair was short and thin, and so was his mouth, which made an attempt at a smile, only it came off as something sardonic, or whatever it is you call it when a man can laugh at things that other people don't find the least bit amusing.

"Come," he repeated. "It's all right. You're in no danger."

The voice was deeper and also more gravelly than I remem-bered. But the accent was much the same as it had always been: an uneducated and truculent Berliner. I didn't give much for the chance of the three Americans when they were interrogated by this man.

I looked both ways on Liesenstrasse. The CIA's security ambu-lance was nowhere to be seen, and it would probably be hours before they worked out that the team of agents they were supposed to be guarding had been kidnapped right under their noses. I had to admit, the Stasi operation had been as neat as a freshly laid egg. True, it had been my own plan, but it had been Mielke's idea to supply an actual East German border guard who looked like his own father for the CIA to follow around and lead them to the apartment on Schulzendorfer Strasse, where the Stasi kidnap team would be waiting.

The street was clear, but in the darkness I still hesitated to cross.

A little impatience edged into Mielke's voice. We Berliners could get impatient with a newborn baby. "Come on, Gunther," he said. "If you had anything to fear from me, you'd be in handcuffs like these three fascists. Or dead."

And recognizing the truth of this, I walked across the street.

Mielke wore a mid-blue suit that appeared to be of much better quality than the suits worn by his men. Certainly, his shoes were more expensive. These looked handmade. A navy knitted tie was neat against a light blue shirt. His raincoat was probably British.

He was standing in the doorway of an old florist's shop. The windows were boarded up, but on a floor strewn with broken glass there was a lantern that gave enough light to see vases filled with petrified flowers or no flowers at all. Through an open door at the back of the shop was a yard, and parked at the end of the yard was a plain gray van that, I imagined, already contained the three American agents. The shop smelled of weeds and cat piss—a bit like the pension we had vacated earlier. Mielke closed the door and put on a leather cap that added a properly proletarian touch to his appearance. Although there was a big heavy padlock, he didn't secure the door, for which I was grateful. He was younger than me and probably armed, and I wouldn't have cared to fight my way out of there.

We sat down on a couple of ancient wooden chairs that belonged in an old church hall.

"I like your office," I said.

"It's very convenient for the French Sector," he said. "The security here is almost nonexistent, and it's the perfect spot to slip back and forth between our sector and theirs without anyone knowing about it. But oddly enough, I can remember coming into this florist's shop as a kid."

"You never struck me as the romantic type."

He shook his head. "There's a cemetery along the street. One of my old man's relations is buried there. Don't ask me who. I can't remember."

He produced a packet of Roth-Händle and offered me one.

"I don't smoke myself," he said. "But I figured your nerves might be gone."

"Very thoughtful of you."

"Keep the packet."

I pulled a little bit of tobacco out of the cigarette's smoking end and pinched it tight between thumb and forefinger, the way you did when you didn't really like the taste. I didn't, but a smoke was a smoke.

"What will happen to them? The three Amis?"

"Do you really care?"

"To my surprise, yes." I shrugged. "You can call it a guilty conscience, if you like."

He shrugged. "They'll have a pretty rough time of it while we find out what they know. But eventually we'll exchange them for some of our own people. They're much too valuable to send to the guillotine, if that's what you were thinking."

"You don't still do that, surely?"

"The guillotine? Why not? It's quick." He grinned cruelly. "A bullet is a bit of a let-off for our enemies of state. But it's a lot quicker than the electric chair. Last year, it took Ethel Rosenberg twenty minutes to die. They say her head caught fire before she died. So you tell me, which is more humane? The two seconds it takes for the ax to fall? Or twenty minutes in the Sing Sing chair?" He shook his head again. "But no. Your three Americans. They won't be waiting for a delivery of bread."

Seeing my puzzled expression, he added:

"So as not to cause our citizenry undue alarm, we send our falling ax around the DDR in a bread van, from the bakery in Halle. Whole-grain bread. It's better for you."

"Same old Erich. You always did have a strange sense of humor. I remember once, on a train to Dresden, I nearly died laughing."

"I think you had the last laugh on that occasion. I was impressed with the way you handled him. He wasn't an easy man to kill, that Russian. But I was rather more impressed with the way you handled things afterward. How you gave that money to Elisabeth. To be honest, until I got your letter I had no idea that you and she had ever become that friendly. Either way, I suspect most men would have kept the money for themselves.

"And it made me think," said Mielke. "I asked myself what kind of man would do such a thing. Obviously, a man who was not the predictable fascist I had thought he was. A man of hidden qualities. A man who might even be useful to me. You wouldn't be aware of this, but three or four years ago I actually tried to get in contact with you, Gunther. To do a job for me. And I discovered you'd disappeared. I even heard you'd gone to South America like all those other Nazi bastards. So when Elisabeth turned up at my office in Hohenschönhausen with your letter, I was very pleasantly surprised. But even more surprised when I read the letter—and by the sheer audacity of your proposal. If I may say so, it was a real spymaster's stratagem and you have my compliments on pulling it off—and what's more, right under the noses of the Americans. That's almost the best part. They won't forgive you for that in a hurry."

I said nothing. There wasn't much to say, so I sucked at my cigarette and waited for the end. That part was, as yet, undecided. What would he do? Keep his side of the bargain, as he had promised in his own letter to me? Or double-cross me like before? And what else did I really deserve? Me, the man who had just betrayed three other men.

"Of course, Elisabeth's the reason I knew I could really trust you, Gunther. If you'd truly been a creature of the Americans, you would have told them where she lived and they'd have had her placed under surveillance. With the aim of burning me."

"Burning?"

"It's what we call it when you let someone—someone in intelligence circles—know that you know everything about them, and that their whole life has gone up in smoke. Burning. Or, for that matter, when you don't let them know."

"Well, then, I guess they'd already tried to burn you."

Some of what I now said I had already told him in the letter that Elisabeth had delivered: how the CIA had coached me to sell the French SDECE the idea that Mielke had been first a spy for the Nazis and then a spy for the CIA, at the same time leading them to suppose that I might be able to identify a French traitor named Edgard de Boudel who had worked for the Viet Minh in Indochina. But mostly I told him again as a way of getting the answers to a few questions of my own.

"The Amis had the idea that there's a communist spy at the heart of French intelligence, and that he might be more inclined to believe what I told them about you playing both sides by my proving reliable in identifying Edgard de Boudel as he arrived back in Friedland as a returnee from a Soviet POW camp."

"But the Amis canned that idea when you told them that you thought you had figured out a way of them getting their hands on me in person," said Mielke. "Is that right?"

I nodded. "Which probably leaves your reputation undamaged."

"Let's hope so, eh?"

"Is there a spy at the heart of French intelligence?"

"Several," admitted Mielke. "You might just as well ask if there are any communists in France. Or if Edgard de Boudel really did fight for the German SS and then the Viet Minh."

"And did he?"

"Oh yes. And it's a shame the Americans should have told the French about him now. Someone in GVL—Gehlen's new intelligence organization—must have told them. You see, we had a deal with the GVL and Chancellor Adenauer. That the German government would allow Edgard de Boudel back into Germany in return for allowing one of ours back. It's like this: De Boudel has inoperable cancer. But the poor fellow wanted to die in his native France, and this seemed to be the best way of doing it. Of sneaking him back into Germany as part of a POW repatriation and then into France without anyone objecting."

"There's not much love lost between the CIA and Gehlen's GVL," I said.

"It would seem not."

"The German son seems to have turned his back on his American father."

"Yes indeed," said Mielke. "It's odd, but you and Elisabeth are about the only two people who even know about my own father. So that was a real stroke of genius, my friend. Because, as it happens, a lot of what you imagined might be true is true. We don't really see each other much anymore."

"Does he live in the East?"

"In Potsdam. But he's always complaining. Odd how your suggestion of him coming back to live in West Berlin is so nearly true. But then, you are a Berliner. You know how these things are. 'I've got no friends in Potsdam,' he says. That's always the big complaint. 'Look, Pa,' I say, 'there's nothing to stop you from going into West Berlin and seeing your mates and coming home again.' Incidentally, the mates—his mates—they thought I was dead. That's what I told Pa to tell them, as early as 1937. I say, 'See your friends quietly in the West and live quietly in the East. It's not like there's a wall or anything.' Of course, since the inner border was closed he's started to suspect the same would happen here in Berlin. That he'll be trapped on the wrong side." Mielke sighed. "And there are other reasons. Father-and-son reasons. Is your old man still alive?"

"No."

"Did you get on with him when he was?"

"No." I smiled sadly. "We never learned how."

"Then you know what it's like. My father is a very old-fashioned kind of German communist, and believe me, they're the worst. It was the workers' strike of last year that really did it for him. Trouble-makers, most of them. Some of them counterrevolutionaries. A few of them CIA provocateurs. But Pa didn't see it that way at all."

I flicked my cigarette onto the ground and was leaving it there, but Mielke ground it under the heel of his handmade shoe as if it had been the head of a counterrevolutionary.

"Since we're being honest with each other," he said, "there's something I don't understand."

"Go ahead."

"Why you did it. Why you betrayed them. To me. You're not a communist any more than you were a Nazi. So, why?"

"You asked me a question like that before, don't you remember?"

"Oh, I remember. I didn't understand it then, either."

"You might say that after spending six months in one American prison after another I began to hate them. You might say that, but it wouldn't be true. Of course, the best lies contain some truth, so that's not entirely false. Then you might say that I don't share their worldview, and that wouldn't be entirely false. In some ways I admire them, but I also dislike the way they don't ever seem to live up to their own ideals. I think I might like the Amis a lot more if they were like everyone else. One might forgive them more. But they preach about the magnificence of their democracy and the enduring power of their constitutional freedoms, while at the same time they're trying to fuck your wife and steal your watch. When I was a cop, we gave the people of whom more was expected severer sentences when they turned out to be crooks. Lawyers, policemen, politicians, people in positions of responsibility. Americans are like them. They're the crooks who should know better.

"But you might also say I'm tired of the whole damned business. For twenty years I've been obliged to work for people I didn't like. Heydrich. The SD. The Nazis. The CIC. The Peróns. The Mafia. The Cuban secret police. The French. The CIA. All I want to do is read the newspaper and play chess."

"But how do you know I'm not going to oblige you to work for me?" Mielke chuckled. "Since you sent that letter to me, you're halfway to working for the Stasi right now."

"I won't work for you, Erich, any more than I'll work for them. If you make me, I'll find a way to betray you."

"And suppose I threaten to have you shot? Or send you to prison to await a delivery of whole-meal bread? What then?"

"I've asked myself this question. Suppose, I said, he threatens to kill you unless you work for the Stasi? Well, I decided that I'd rather die at the hands of my own countrymen than get rich in the pay of some foreigners. I don't expect you to understand that, Erich. But that's how it is. So go ahead and do your worst."

"Of course I understand." Mielke smacked himself proudly on the chest. "Before everything else, I am a German. A Berliner. Like you. Of course I understand. So, for once, I am going to keep my word to a fascist."

"You still think I'm a fascist, then."

"You don't know it yourself, but that's what you are, Gunther." He tapped his head. "In here. You may not ever have joined the Nazi Party, but in your mind you believe in centralized authority and the right and the law, and you don't believe in the left. To me, a fascist is all you'll ever be. But I have an idea that Elisabeth has some hopes of you. And because of my high regard for her. My love for her—"

"You?"

"As a sister, yes."

I smiled.

Mielke looked surprised. "Yes. Why do you smile?"

I shook my head. "Forget it."

"But I love people," he said. "I love all people. That's why I became a communist."

"I believe you."

He frowned and then tossed me a set of car keys.

"As we arranged, Elisabeth has quit her apartment and is waiting for you at the Steinplatz Hotel. So say hello from me. And make sure you look after that woman. If you don't, I'll send an assassin to kill you. Just see if I don't. Someone better than the last one. Elisabeth's the only reason I'm letting you go, Gunther. Her happiness is more important to me than my political principles."

"Thanks."

"There's a car on Grenz Strasse. Go right and then left. You'll see a gray Type One. In the glove box you'll find two passports in your new names. I'm afraid we had to use your picture from your time as a *pleni*. There are visas, money, and air tickets. My advice would be to use them. The Amis aren't stupid, Gunther. Nor are the French. They'll each come looking for you both. So get out of Berlin. Get out of Germany. Get out while the going is good."

It was good advice. I lit another cigarette and then left without another word.

I turned right out of the shop and walked around the edge of the cemetery. All of the graves were gone, and in the misty darkness, it wasn't much more than a gray-looking field. Was it just the tombs and the headstones that were gone, or had the corpses been moved, too? Nothing ever lasted the way it was supposed to last. Not anymore. Not in Berlin. Mielke was right. It was time for me to move on, too. Just like those other Berlin corpses.

The Volkswagen Beetle was where Mielke had said it would be. The glove box contained a large, thick manila envelope. On the dashboard was mounted a little vase, and in it were some small flowers. I saw it and I laughed. Maybe Mielke did like people after all. But I still checked the engine and underneath the chassis for a car bomb. I wouldn't have put it past him to send funeral flowers before I was actually dead.

As it happens, those are the only kinds of funeral flowers I've ever really liked.

AUTHOR'S NOTE

Erich Mielke (1907–2000) was minister of state security of the German Democratic Republic from 1957 to 1989. In 1993, he was convicted of the murders of police officers Paul Anlauf and Franz Lenck in 1931. He was sentenced to six years' imprisonment and paroled after less than two. Anyone interested in knowing more about Mielke could do worse than follow this YouTube link to one of the famous televised incidents in German history: http://www.youtube.com/watch?v=ACjHB9GZN18. Six days after the fall of the Berlin Wall, Mielke addressed the members of the GDR parliament. Some members objected to his calling them comrades, as he was used to doing. Mielke tried to justify this wording, declaring, "But I love . . . I love . . . all people. . . ." The assembly laughed, for this was one of the most hated and hateful men in East Germany, feared even by members of his own ministry.

Anyone who wishes to know more about the appalling conditions of the French concentration camps at Gurs and Le Vernet should read Arthur Koestler's excellent *Scum of the Earth* (1941), which has lost none of its capacity to shock. Koestler was imprisoned at Le Vernet for several months after the fall of France in 1940. *The Guardian* described it as the finest book about the collapse of France, and I can't bring myself to disagree with that assessment.

The best account of the French SS is Robert Forbes's *For Europe: The French Volunteers of the Waffen-SS* (2006). The French SS-Charlemagne were the last defenders of Hitler's Führerbunker in May 1945.

My own favorite history of French collaboration and Nazism is to be found in Marcel Ophuls's documentary *The Sorrow and the Pity* (1969).

I am especially indebted to Cécile Desprairies's illuminating book *Ville Lumière Années Noires* (2008).

There are two outstanding books on the SS-Einsatzgruppen. Both are equally shocking in their own way. Richard Rhodes's book *Masters of Death* (2002) remains the most readable and horrifying book on the subject and is highly recommended. And I am indebted to Hilary Earl's book *The Nuremberg SS-Einsatzgruppen Trial, 1945–1958* (2009) for information on the improbable fates of the twenty-four Einsatzgruppen defendants.

Of these, thirteen were sentenced to death, and four were executed on June 7, 1951. These were the last of 275 war criminals hanged within the Federal Republic of Germany.

Of the remaining twenty defendants who were not hanged in June 1951, all had been released or paroled by 1958—a fact that I continue to find incredible.

No less incredible is the fate of Martin Sandberger, who commanded Einsatzkommando 1a (part of Einsatzgruppe A). Sandberger was, until his death in a Stuttgart retirement home on March 30, 2010, at the ripe old age of ninety-eight, the highest-ranking war criminal known to be alive. A doctor of law, he presided over the murders of some 14,500 Jews and communists and was sentenced to death in 1951; this was commuted to life imprisonment, and Sandberger was paroled in February 1958.

Landsberg Prison ceased to be used by the Americans as a war crimes facility in 1958 and is now maintained by the Bavarian Ministry of Justice.

The best book on the Battle of Königsberg is Isabel Denny's *The Fall of Hitler's Fortress City* (2007).

I am indebted to a number of books about the Soviet POW camps. The best of these are Stefan Karner's *Im Archipel GUPVI* (1995) and George Schinke's *Red Cage* (1994). The best book on returning German POWs is Frank Biess's *Homecomings* (2006).

Edgard de Boudel is a fictional character based on two real French war criminals: Edgard Puaud and Georges Boudarel.

Helmut Knochen and Carl Oberg were pardoned by Charles de Gaulle and released in 1962. Oberg died in 1965, Knochen in 2003.